The Woodcutter King

Ærick Graham

The Woodcutter King is a work of fiction. Names, characters, places and incidents are the product of the author's imagination or used fictitiously. Any resemblance to actual events, locales, or persons, living or dead, is entirely coincidental. Except for the faeries. They are based on those populations residing in the Tillamook, Aokigahara and Schwarzwald forests.

InkSkald Press
818 SW 3rd Ave #1457
Portland, Oregon
www.inkskald.com

ISBN-13: 978-0998280202
ISBN-10: 09982800208

Cover Illustration: Stelladia
www.stelladiavisualstorytelling.com

To my father-for instilling in me the value of hard work,
My mother-for showing me silent strength,
My brother-for sharing his passion for reading,
My daughter and son-for the years I sat alone in a room with my head in
another world when your world was not so well.

And to mi amor… forever believing

CONTENTS

1 Fractured Suspension   1

2 Reciprocity   7

3 Songs of Spring   13

4 Duty   25

5 Faerie Traps   32

6 The Crossroads   41

7 Faerie Kings & Faerie Queens   47

8 The Alvini   65

9 Woodmares   84

10 A Murder of Crows   94

11 Aslenissia   111

12 Lhodyn of Wudelic   137

13 The Ruined Tower   163

14 A World Forgotten   192

15 The Woodland Cottage   206

16 Insignificant Nothings   243

17 The Yew Tree   265

18 Convalesce   289

19 The Brownman of Wudelic   310

20 Wudelic Woods   333

21 The Forest Spirit   346

22 Haunted Paths   361

23 The Goblyn Market   369

24 Old Gods   379

25 The Wooodcutter King   392

The
Woodcutter
King

1

FRACTURED SUSPENSION

TIME FREEZES STILL on the coldest of winter mornings.

"I dare you to touch her," Tredan's chilled whispers came to Edrick. Both their eyes never strayed from the corpse abandoned at the forest edge.

A nameless little girl.

Edrick only knew of her. She was from another village visiting family, Dregan's kin.

Seeing her distilled the cold right out of the air.

"As cold as a grave," Tredan had said when they snuck away and followed Edrick's father here. It was a kind of cold that froze the world hard, denying it of all comfort. A cold that was absent of soft snow. A dim, frozen world where timber-lions snatched children at dawn.

Tredan shook his meager purse of animal fangs and claws slung from his belt. "Six wolf teeth if you touch her."

"This is no game," Edrick warned his friend, then stepped toward the girl, slowly, respectfully.

"I think we should leave then, Edrick," Tredan called from behind him. He was nervous, Edrick could tell. "I don't want your father to catch us here. We should have waited at your home, like he told us."

Edrick did not heed Tredan's words or share his fears. This girl was alone in death and he would not leave her. Dregan's kin, her family, dared not chase after her. No villager dared braving the winter morning knowing timber-lions were hunting. Seldom do these beasts leave the shadowed forest of Wudelic. It must have been desperation that lured this starved hunter from the wilds, into the stark openness.

In past summer days of long light and playful moods, village children like this girl would wonder, "Why can't we play in the forest like the Woodcutter's children?" as they beheld the great and wild Wudelic.

"Because the ways of the forest are fickle and beguiling." The sensible parents would answer. "Those children were practically born there, like the elves and other creatures of the fey. They aren't quite the same like you or others. They are…strange."

Strange, like the woods.

Like rumors of distant seas, or tales of enormous desert mountains of amassed sun scorched sands, stained in sunset hues, as wide and wild as any ocean. Things no sensible villager truthfully knew about, but heard enough to become disinterested and dismissive.

Today, such warnings would cut into every man, woman and child like bound rope, cinched so tight, it choked them all.

But not the Woodcutters. Not his father, Edrick thought with great pride. His father gave chase when they all heard the girl's distant screams. Not one villager stirred as Edrick and his friend Tredan hurried through the village. Not a fearful peek was given from any window.

As soon as this girl stepped out of her cottage that morning, she was on her own, Edrick thought.

He approached the corpse-girl in slow reverence, stepping in his father's footprints outlined in scraped frost. Father had tracked down the timber-lion and must have chased it back into the woods. He would return, to bring the dead girl back to her family, Edrick knew. Until then, Edrick would stay. It was the right thing to do. As a Woodcutter, it was their way.

She appeared as a doll, discarded by some passing forest giant. An innocent creature cast away with disinterest. An ephemeral thing. She lay sprawled on her side, turned away from his approach, arms and legs twisted, fingers half curled. She remained in stunning stillness, but not like sleep. Instead, a fractured suspension, like the air captured by the winter dawn.

Edrick shivered. The sight chilled him from the inside, beneath his thick winter furs.

Blood saturated her woven wool skirt, deepening the bright reds, distorting the sunburst oranges and light blues of the knitted winter pattern. Her torn shirt revealed where the timber-lion feasted. Edrick had seen this carnage before with lost sheep or deer they found in the woods, but never with a person. Entrails spilled out like shredded sausage. Her stomach, liver, and kidneys, snatched away in a frenzy.

Gone.

Edrick could not take his eyes off the gaping cavity that was once her belly, soft and smooth like his own.

Unlike the death of village elders, which were somber but peaceful passings like drifting clouds against a marbled sky, this was his first glimpse of an ash stained storm swallowing the horizon. It was ugly and cruel and it forced Edrick to his knees.

He removed his winter gloves and held the girl's hand. There was no warmth, just slick, cold skin. He slid his fingers between hers. She was not stiff despite the cold. He rocked her arm gently. It moved freely as if she was just sleeping. She rolled onto her back with the movement. Her lifeless eyes gazed above.

"What are you doing?" Tredan demanded, for the fourth or fifth time. Edrick continued and would not hear him. The dead should not be touched by the living unless you have protection. Protection of an alhíelda, a faerie-guardian. Edrick was irreverent to these concerns. All he knew was that she wanted someone by her side and he would not leave her until she was buried.

She was exposed to the cold world and she should not have been. Her stomach was gone, her mouth hung open, absent of breath, and her eyes stared far into the sky. Stared beyond the blue until she saw the blackness before the stars. Saw what no child should witness in their young lives - unkind Death, and through her eyes, her soul poured out into the infinite.

Edrick wept, holding her hand, imbuing her with one final touch of life as he cradled her fingers against his cheek. His tears smoked through the air.

"You are not alone anymore," he whispered to her. "I am here with you. You won't be alone anymore."

There is a change in people when they die and Edrick saw it, though he did not know her. He wondered what her eyes saw now. Did she know he was there? Did she know his father hunted her killer?

"Bring me some straw!" Edrick ordered with urgency, remembering he was not alone. "As much as you can carry!"

"What?" Tredan replied, uncertain and afraid. Edrick shouted his request repetitively until he heard Tredan's boots gritting into the distance.

Edrick closed the girl's mouth with his fingertips. Her pale skin took the likeness of flawless snow. He leaned over until he met her eyes. "I am Edrick," he said, quiet as chill morning.

A corpse is not a person, yet the body should be respected in life and death.

Mother said people die at different speeds, some quite slow, others fast, yet it is hard to tell the moment when the soul departs. Some souls linger in this world long after the body is buried.

He hoped this girl's ghost lingered. He needed her to know she was not alone.

Time freezes still on the coldest of winter mornings. The day does not grow brighter for long hours. Time was unchanged as Edrick knelt next to the girl, holding her hand until Tredan returned with arms full of straw. He dropped it on the ground next to them, then gasped.

Edrick ignored his friend's shock and grabbed handfuls of golden stalks, stuffing her hollow abdomen.

"Stop doing that! Leave her," Tredan pleaded, tugging his shoulder.

"We can't leave her like this, empty," Edrick said in a low voice. "We have to put it back. We can't bury her empty like this."

Edrick packed the straw against her torn diaphragm, gaping with holes. The beast's maw had burrowed farther and farther toward the heart. He stuffed each space tightly, closing and sealing her. Replacing the emptiness. Warmth still clung deep inside, he thought.

Warmth. A small remnant of life remained. It gave Edrick hope the girl's spirit knew he took care of her remains with a caring touch.

When he finished, Edrick removed his winter coat and laid it over her.

"She is dead, why are you doing that?" Tredan asked.

"To show my respect!" Edrick snapped, irritated.

Winter air rushed over Edrick's bare skin, shaking his body. Punishing his body. Muscles flinched fast, faster than his racing heart.

Then Tredan leaned closer. "What if the timber-lion returns?

How are you going to run frozen stiff?"

Edrick shook his head. "I will not run. I am staying here until my father returns," he said through clattering teeth. His breath puffed like a chimney billowing white smoke. "You can go back if you want."

Tredan said nothing else. He stood motionless over the two as morning wore on. He eventually removed his own cat-skin coat and draped it over Edrick. They took turns wearing the fur and shivering as they waited for Edrick's father.

The world was terribly silent on that frigid winter morning, sluggish and harsh. The appearance of a lone figure emerged from the woods after long empty moments; Edrick's father, the Woodcutter of Athelyn.

In one hand he carried a great ax, the head of something dark in the other.

"Edrick!" Father yelled out from the distance. His voice shattered the silence like slicing icicles crashing through the trees. His father quickened his pace as he approached them. Edrick fell back, away from the girl and stood at quick attention.

All of the Woodcutter children shied from their father's wrath, but Edrick never feared him. He did his best to respect him though.

Tredan jumped. "Edrick, he killed it!" he shouted, patting Edrick in relief.

There, clutched in his father's left hand was the devilish visage of a timber-lion's severed head. It was huge. Edrick mistook it for a bear at first. This beast's eyes were not empty like the girl's, but remained menacing and fierce. Its maw still snarled. Its lips curled back revealing the jagged weapons that had stolen the girl's vital organs, swallowed her life whole.

It is a tortured spirit that remains in the body of the dead, unable to flee into the afterlife, and this thing's spirit did not yield.

Tredan stepped back as Edrick's father stood over them.

"Did I not tell you to remain with your mother?" Steam blasted forth from each word. He seemed as an animal himself, clad in shaggy, dark wintery wolf hide.

"Yes sir, you d-d-d-d-did," Edrick said, teeth clattering. The hard, cold air became an iron vice pressing into every pour of his exposed skin.

His father shook his head, then looked over what was left of the girl. Edrick had treated her remains honorably, without thought to his own exposure.

"Edrick, you are the most challenging child I have had yet. Willful. Defiant. Ignorant to what should terrify prudent children." The two held each other's eyes in the stillness. Edrick looked away first, only to look back upon the girl.

"You never waste a moment worrying your mother or I, do you?" His father asked, more kindly, with a note of resignation.

Edrick blinked. "I want t-t-t-t-to bury her." He nodded toward the girl beneath his coat, while clenching down on his jaw, willing the cold away.

Father dropped the timber-lion's head. It rolled toward Edrick. He picked it up, only to see how much it weighed. Heavier than he thought, like a wide bucket of rocks.

Edrick did not like the feel of the beast and wanted to be rid of it. But he would carry it for his father.

Father then knelt over the girl. "I will bear her to her family," he said, taking the body into his arms, gentle as if he cared to harm her no further. "I hope they find peace knowing the beast is dead." He let out a heavy breath. Edrick knew it came not from exhaustion, but from a different place.

"Follow me," Father said and turned away from them.

The two boys did their best to match the Woodcutter's long strides.

2

RECIPROCITY

WARDEN OF THE WOODS.

An ancient and proper title for the one villagers ridiculed as Woodcutter, Alaric, son of Accenan. It has been his responsibility, passed down through untold generations, to protect and serve the village Athelyn, to appease the spirits of the forest so all honest men and women could live peacefully, in the name of the king in Athéalgian.

So it was, that cold, bitter morning, Alaric rushed out of his family's home at the edge of Wudelic Woods, ax in hand, chasing after a young girl's panicked screams before the winter worn beast broke her neck. It was his responsibility to tame the wild, to ward off outside harm intruding on descent folk. Truthfully, responsibility or not, Alaric acted on impulse. Compelled by an honest heart. It was compassion that moved him, sprinting toward the unsettling cries of a young girl desperate to live.

It was his burden that he failed that morning.

Alaric could not explain to Edrick why Dregan and his kin were thankless for returning the girl. He could not explain how the sight of a dead beast frightened them more than one that lived.

"What have you done!" Dregan yelled at them. Yelled at Alaric and his son and friend. They were not welcomed inside the farmer's home. "Her death is what Lhodyn desired, or She would not have sent the beast!" The man argued, pushing Alaric away from the door, taking care not to touch the corpse. Alaric caught a glimpse of the grieving mother. The family held her inside. It took three of them to restrain her as she reached for her slain daughter. "If Lhodyn wanted the girl," Dregan continued, "then she is not ours to welcome back. Return her to the woods before She demands more of us, you dull Woodcutter."

They slammed the door on him. Left the three in the cold.

"I told you, you should not have touched her," Alaric heard Tredan whisper to his son.

Alaric turned on them. "You two should not have left the house at all!"

Tredan shrank back.

"Where will we b-b-b-b-bury her?" Edrick asked, undeterred by his father's anger or Dregan's fear. He had walked the entire distance without his winter coat, without complaint, carrying the head of the dead beast.

Alaric had led them the entire way without looking back, urgent to return the girl to her family. He now noticed with great concern how Edrick's skin lost its color.

"I will bury her. You need to go home, now. Before sickness comes over you."

"Where will you bury her?" Edrick insisted.

A burial was impossible in this cold, but Alaric spoke the answer his son wanted to hear. "In the byrgen with everyone else. Now get going. You too, Tredan. Your folks will be concerned."

"You p-p-p-p-promise?" Edrick pressed.

Alaric paused. "I promise. Now get home."

Edrick did not move immediately.

Alaric knew the child was deciding whether to follow instructions or do what he willed. Edrick finally set the beast's head on the ground. He took the girl's hand in his, trembling terribly. "Let Lhodyn p-p-p-p-protect your soul in her V-V-V-V-Vaults."

Alaric tried not to let his son see him shudder. Edrick's piercing eyes jumped from the girl to meet his own.

The boy did not realize what he said. Anyone would have said the same except the Warden of the Woods. They alone were burdened with Her secrets.

"I will see you at home, son. We will speak about your punishment when I return."

Disobedience should never be ignored, even when he did right by the girl.

The boy nodded and ran. Tredan followed.

He ran because that was the best way to warm a cold body. Alaric taught him that. Sometimes the boy listened.

His stubborn son lived without fear. He lived as the rest of them could not. But that time would end. There were few things a person could escape in life and fear could not be one of them. Even if the boy managed it for nine years, it would inevitably work its way into his heart.

There would be no mourning openly for Wylla, the girl he and his son cared for in death. Sacrificing a life to Lhodyn or any of the other gods was nothing unexpected. A young girl, an old man, a newborn. Such deaths ensured crops yielded fruit, disease passed onto the next village, that their beasts birthed calves, lambs and piglets to replace those slaughtered to feed their shrinking stomachs. There was never a sowing without a reaping. One always hoped to have balance.

But the gods mostly took without giving. That was why Alaric buried the girl. It was why he hunted that rarest of beasts, that seldom journeyed into the realm of men, to thwart their desires.

The gods that walked the earth did not acknowledge the wisdom of balance. They were like drunken kings, all of them, taking pleasure at the ruination of mortals. And all the world were their captive dinner guests. To refuse a seat at their table meant to be thrown from the hall into the inhospitable night. To suffer their company was their lot in life.

Alaric laid awake that night, thinking of the girl, the woods and all the secrets desires that seemed impossible for him. A better life for his family.

Elisial, his wife, snuggled beneath his chin, arm draped over his chest. He listened to her rhythmic breath.

"I have never known a timber-lion to leave the woods," she said. "Winter turns the most cautious creatures into brutes." He welcomed the sensation of her breath across his skin. "I would have never known timber-lions to be real unless I saw their tracks over soft ground. Have you seen them before?"

"Yes," Alaric replied. He held her close beneath mink fur blankets. She ran her fingers along his ribs and down his stomach. "They watch us always, when in the woods."

"They must be beautiful, I imagine. Like you, husband." Elisial reached to kiss his lips. He never knew how to feel when called beautiful.

"And deadly," Alaric reminded her.

Something startled the animals outside. The chickens cackled in a frenzied chorus, the sheep bleated like when they were young, separated from their mothers.

Elisial raised her head. Both she and Alaric were now intent on the sudden noise.

Living on the forest edge often attracted nightly visitors. The Woodcutters kept a few animals. A family could not live without their animals. The faerie lamps they lit every evening deterred most predators, rendering most nights peaceful. Alaric dealt with the rest.

Silence now fell across the Woodcutter household as the animals went quiet all at once.

Alaric sat up.

A great raucous clamor burst again from their small barn. The animals screeched and cried in pain, reacting to something. Then one by one, the animals fell deathly silent.

Alaric jumped from their bed and dressed swiftly. "Gather the children into our room. I'm taking Halig."

"Be careful husband," Elisial said as she crossed through the dark like a woodland spirit.

Outside, the faerie lanterns had gone out.

"What could have extinguished those flames?" Halig, his eldest son asked, readying his bow.

Lhodyn, Alaric thought. He looked to the forest. She was not done with him.

Whatever had entered the barn, still lingered. A hollow cracking of bone popped forth from inside. It fed richly, having discovered a pantry so near its forest abode.

"A timber-lion." Alaric whispered to his son. The chewing ceased. It had heard him, clearly. "His mate, I'd guess. She must be with a litter."

"She followed you from the woods?" Halig asked, surprised, afraid even.

Alaric shrugged. The reason did not matter. He killed her mate, who never returned with their morning meal. She starved in the emptied woodland. She came to feed. She came for the young ones in her belly.

But now, he would not let her keep them. He had his own kin to look after.

She screamed like a dæmon when Alaric plunged his hunter's spear into her chest. She fought wildly, fought for her cubs, as if each stab plucked another life from her.

The beast pushed Alaric into the open, fighting to escape, bending the spear shaft. She attempted to flee to where she knew it was safe. The woodland was but a few bounding leaps away.

But Alaric held her firmly as Halig pelted her with swift arrows. In only a few moments, all strength fled her powerful form. Vapor rose from the ground around them, where its blood pooled.

Alaric withdrew the spear. The timber-lion crawled away, bleeding out, mewling like a frightened cub. It would die before she entered the forest. Halig followed, bow drawn.

Lhodyn can keep her, Alaric thought with contempt. A reminder the Woodcutters came into this land before Her. Survived still and would remain.

Inside the barn, Alaric's heart sank at the sight of his dead animals. The beast seemed to kill for sport, for revenge, to burden the Woodcutters with injurious blows in an already difficult winter.

One lamb lived yet, both rear legs shredded to the bone, it would not live much longer. It lay trembling next to its mother's carcass, mute with terror. Alaric lifted the lamb in his arms and stepped back out into the night. It struggled against him.

He called for his sons. They would not sleep that night. The meat needed to be salvaged. Eadwyn, his fourth eldest, arrived first.

"Son, bring the carving knives and your brothers. We will see how well you can skin these animals."

Alaric considered the trembling lamb in his arms. He should have killed it swiftly, there, in the barn. But something urged him to remove it from its dead parents. To rescue it? he asked himself. No, he would have Elisial and Meghan prepare it for tomorrow's meals.

"What are you doing with Mathilda?" Edrick asked, once he was outside. He stood with his brothers, Eadwyn and Baldice.

"She's dying. She will make a decent meal or two. There will be plenty of meat to share with our neighbors from all our dead animals, but something tells me they will not touch it."

"No, not Mathilda!" Edrick pleaded. He ran to Alaric. "Mother can save her, I know she can!" Alaric did not expect this. This was not the first animal slaughtered for dinner.

"She won't be able to walk or graze again, Edrick. And if she does survive, she will be vulnerable to wolves and other beasts and suffer this again too easily."

"But that's Mathilda, Papa," Baldice calmly pleaded, Alaric's third child. He stepped forward. "Sunniva loves her dearly. We all do."

"Then don't mention it to her. At four years, she will remember little of the past."

"We will," Edrick stroked Mathilda's head, nuzzled her soft face, "remember."

The lamb's trembling ceased at his son's touch.

"Let Mama treat her." Edrick asked him once again. His words were tender. "If she dies, then Lhodyn claimed her already. If she lives, then Lhodyn has blessed us."

All three boys waited for a reply. There was work to be done. Alaric yielded, giving Edrick the lamb. "See what your mother can do," he finally said.

He watched as Edrick lovingly carry the lamb inside as if he held all their lives in his hands. Alaric addressed his other sons. "If it lives, you will see to her survival. You feed her and change her straw. She cannot be with the flock ever again. You children will see to her health. She lives by your hands now."

"Aye, Papa," Baldice answered. Eadwyn nodded.

Halig returned from chasing the beast. "It is dead, Father. What should we do with the carcass?"`

"Take the skin only. Leave Lhodyn Her portion."

3

SONGS OF SPRING

WINTER EVENTUALLY WITHDREW its heavy breath, receding north before the vernal equinox, allowing the sun to flow forth and scorch the bare ground, cracking the dirt faster than farmers could sow this year's crops. They all cursed the land while chipping away the parched soil like stone masons instead of securing fall's harvest. With suspicious eyes, they gazed toward the forest Wudelic, toward the Woodcutters and remembered Alaric's defiance against Lhodyn. He refused to place the child corpse in the woods. He instead selfishly buried her in their graveyard. They would not be burdened with the goddess's ire at the Woodcutter's expense. Collectively, they thought it time to pay the Woodcutters a visit.

For Edrick, winter still gripped his heart. The haunting visage of the unfortunate girl remained frozen in his thoughts. In private moments he wept for her, for her lost soul wandering an eternal winter landscape. He remembered how terribly cold he felt without his furs. Such a fate awaited any ghost denied entrance into Lhodyn's Vaults. Forever caught in a world of frost and darkness. It was a fate no child deserved.

He found escape from the melancholic mood in their family barn, where the timber-lion had feasted. Mathilda survived the frigid months, survived her injuries by Mother's medicines. Edrick took full responsibility of her care, attending her daily as part of his chores. The lamb's survival was testament to Edrick's belief that cruelty could be overcome with a determined will and caring hand, just like in the stories of heroic kings he loved and admired.

Today he had to shear Mathilda's winter fleece. The weather had not just turned warm, but miserably hot. He enthusiastically took to the task, yet remained gentle, delicately handling her rear stubs where Mother sawed off her injured legs. He was not a shepherd's son, so shearing one sheep took half a day at best.

His little sister gathered the small wooly tufts, balling it up, petting it soothingly, pretending it was baby Mathilda in her arms. She hummed quietly to herself, then finally voiced her song:

Old Browman of Wudelic Woods
Scaring off spirits and goblyns rude
With his oaken club, he gives them all chase
Have you ever seen so many monsters race?
Old Brownman of Wudelic Woods
Champion of faeries and all creatures good
With a thick brown beard and shaggy coat
You would think him a bear, or hornless goat…

"That's a baby's rhyme," Edrick interrupted. "I know a real story of Wudelic Woods. Of a king…"

"I like the song," Sunniva defended.

"A forest king and faerie queen," he added enticingly.

Sunniva sat down in a nest of fresh hay. "Faerie queen?"

"Mm-hm. Do you want to hear it?"

Sunniva nodded.

Edrick wiped his brow where an orb, the color of the sky before sunrise, sat like a jewel. It was not a large light, but a twinkling gem the size of Edrick's blue irises. They were called éardians, or ghost-lights, guardian faeries that bonded with all children three days after birth, only to fade when they became adults. But the Woodcutter's éardians never faded, to the fear and puzzlement of others. Theirs lasted until their final breath, to ensure their spirits were protected until they reached the goddess's Vaults.

Sweat continued pooling around Edrick's forehead behind the blue light, running into his eyes, stinging like fire ants.

"I bet you can't wait to shed this wool," he said to the gentle sheep, hacking off the thick fiber, rather slowly. Mathilda bleated in agreement.

"I can cool the air if you want." Sunniva said.

Her éardian was a golden mote of energy, bobbing in the air with delight. Younger children had trouble keeping their ghost-lights on their brow, which was the fashion of the Athelyn folk.

Sunniva closed her eyes and instantly her éardian halted. It spiraled down and around Edrick. He stopped shearing and fell back. The tiny light swirled around him franticly, ascending from his chest, to his head, then into the rafters. All the while the air cooled as if Ysig, the Snow Serpent, reached across winter and spring and breathed into the barn itself.

"How did you do that?" Edrick asked, mouth agape.

"I just tell it to do things and it does. Why, can't you?"

Edrick shook his head, looking at his little sister with a new found interest. "Nobody can do that. Not even mother. Not like that, so easily."

Sunniva smiled, basking in the praise. "What about the story you said?"

Edrick nodded and went back to shearing.

"Long time ago, there was a king who lived in the woods…"

"An elf king?"

"No, he was like us, just regular people, but you know, a king. He built a castle deep in the Wudelic because he wanted to protect it from evil. So well did he protect his kingdom that the faerie princess wished to become his bride."

"Did they have babies?"

"Lots of babies, the first babies to be born to a human father and faerie mother."

"What was his name, the king?"

"They called him the Woodcutter King."

Sunniva gulped. "Woodcutters, like us?"

"Yep, Woodcutters like us."

"What are you farm lovers up to?" Eadwyn asked, barging in. "Practicing to be like one of the turnip tossers?"

"Go away, Eadwyn." Edrick said. His brother, no doubt, took the trouble to find them alone. Fulfilling his role as older brother was something of an art for him.

"But it is so nice and cool in here, I think I might stay a while." He looked to Mathilda, sneering at the sight of her amputated legs. "Why Father listened to you last winter instead of making her into a meal, I will never guess."

Eadwyn made his annoyance plain. Edrick defied his father often but still managed to be given their parent's favor. His brother made it a point to speak of Mathilda's uselessness. "He should have killed it," Eadwyn said as he placed a raise foot over the lamb's neck.

"Don't!" Sunniva shrieked, squishing the wool balls in her hands.

"I should just break her neck now and throw her into the forest." His eyes darted from Edrick to Sunniva, as a fat grin spread across his impish face, as if he relished their reactions.

"No! Please, Eadwyn." Sunniva continued to plea.

The coolness in the air dissipated as Sunniva's éardian bobbed about frantically.

Edrick resumed his sheering, ignoring his brother's goading. "He is just kidding. He would not dare do it. Father would step on his neck if he did."

Eadwyn glared at Edrick. "Father told me to do it. Do it now!" He placed his toes on the lamb's neck. Mathilda innocently bleated, happy to see another Woodcutter child. She placed one hoofed leg across his foot in warm greeting.

Edrick pulled his shears back, stopping to look at his brother. "Do it then." He leaned back, relaxed, seeing through his brother's bluff.

"No!" Sunniva whimpered, turned and flopped into the surrounding straw, burying her head.

Eadwyn removed his foot, chuckling to himself, and knelt down petting the lamb. "You're such a baby," he told Sunniva.

"I will tell Mother," Edrick threatened.

"No you won't!" He threw a handful of straw at Edrick's face.

Edrick started sheering again. "And you will pick up all this wool or I will tell Mother you have been going into the woods by yourself at night."

Eadwyn's expression dropped from annoyance to surprise. He said nothing, neither admitting guilt nor refuting his brother's accusations, instead became completely cooperative. "What story were you telling?" Eadwyn asked after a moment of silence.

"The Woodcutter King."

"And the Faerie Queen," Sunniva added in a pout, rubbing her eyes. Her éardian spun around her head like a darting starling before she sent it to play in the rafters, chasing invisible faeries.

"Girl stories!" Eadwyn balked. "Sunniva, has anyone ever told you of the hidden creatures, the sneak thieves that creep nightly to the village Wall, spying on all the children?"

Sunniva shook her head. Her éardian now floated around her brow, slowly, as if guarding her from impending harm.

"Goblynsssss," Eadwyn hissed, leaning toward his little sister. Her éardian pulsed like a furious star.

"Wicked goblyns, hoping to snatch wandering children. And do you know what they do with children once they catch them!" Eadwyn lunged forward, fingers curled into claws, raking playfully at Sunniva.

"Aaa!" Sunniva jumped. Mathilda bleated in support of the startled child.

Eadwyn continued, relishing in Sunniva's fear. "They take them to the Goblyn Market, where their nasty lord, the Erlking, eats them alive!"

"Stop Eadwyn! I don't want to hear it."

Edrick set his shears down and scooted next to Sunniva, putting a protective arm around her. "Don't worry, I will teach you a charm that will protect you."

Before Edrick could continue, Eadwyn erupted with his own rhyme.

Goblyn fruit, goblyn fruit
Do not bite into the goblyn fruit
Savory, delectable, rare delights
Catches even wise children's eyes
Under dark bough and thorny briar
Into their markets of twisted desire
Little children are carted away
Goblyns whisper, In our forest, come play

"You know why village children really don't enter the woods?" he asked Sunniva, now in a nervous frenzy.

Sunniva shook her head, very slightly, as if she could not bear to know the truth, but could not possibly be denied it.

"All the children sing this song as they work the fields. I bring them apples under the heavy summer sun, when they are parched.

When they eat one or two, I tell them goblyns sold me a bushel. You should see them drop the cores from their greedy hands. It scares them white!"

Edrick giggled despite Sunniva's distress. "They are Lady Udela's apples, Sunniva. Eadwyn has never seen a goblyn, ghost or hairy..."

Eadwyn shot up, fuming. "No, but I know where to find them. Across the river! In the deep woods, in the mountains."

"Maybe, but you will never know." Edrick had finished his sheering. He then rolled Mathilda over, kissed her head and rubbed her freshly sheared rump. Seeing Sunniva clenched tight in a small ball, he let out a mirthful laugh. His smile was like the sun parting rain clouds. "When it comes to goblyns, all you have to remember is this song:

Goblyns, Mauglins, Verguls and Naughs,
Bauglirs and Thayegils- Halt and begone!
My stride be fell swift, as my arms bear long,
Release your foul souls and flee at my song!

"There is an old charm woven into these words that freezes goblyns still at the very least, or chases them away if your heart is stout."

"Mmmm. Are you sure?" Sunniva asked, eyes wide and moist.

"Wouldn't work on the Erlking. He is the master of the woods," Eadwyn interjected.

"True, but father is Warden and represents the king. The Erlking would not be a match for him."

Eadwyn snorted. "You really believe that. Father is no king's man. King's men don't live in huts, in small, stupid villages."

"Do so...."

The growing argument ceased when shouts of gathered men arose from the Lane outside. Edrick and Eadwyn both exited the barn to see a group of Athelyn villagers, led by Dregan, shouting, "Woodcutter! Out with you! Our fields are dying. Lhodyn is laying a heavy hand across our earth. You brought Her ire on us! Now answer for it!"

He stood in front of a crowd of farmers, each scowling and pointing at Edrick's home. "He snatched our niece from Lhodyn's creatures," Dregan continued, "killed it, then buried her in our byrgen! Restless spirits! Restless spirits he is stirring up. Can't protect crops from evil spirits when they lie outside the Wall! We are likely to earn three tenths less than we did a year ago, and we all know last year was far from fruitful!"

"Tell the Elders! The Woodcutters must pay us our losses. And we want more than sticks and kindling!" Many voices urged.

Edrick turned to Eadwyn, older than him by five years, expecting him to do something. His brother was spared the duty of taking a responsible course as Mother and Father emerged from their home with Halig, Meghan and Baldice following. Father stepped ahead of them all and spoke. "Shout your grievances at me and not my children, now that I am here."

Many of the men shouted all at once. Mother instinctively looked for her youngest, Edrick and Eadwyn, and now Sunniva who stood timidly behind the brothers.

The crowd shoved accusing fingers in Father's face, then at Edrick. Not him, he realized, they were pointing over him, toward Wudelic. Father lifted his arms, unable to decipher a single voice amongst the shouts.

"Take me to the Elders then, and let them judge me. Halig, to me." Edrick watched his father and brother taken by the crowd, surrounding them like angry bees when their hive is suddenly torn apart.

Mother gave her children a sympathetic look. She spoke to Meghan aside, who stepped back into the house. "Come, let's visit the woods while your father is away."

Edrick happily agreed, but Sunniva gave a whimper.

"What's wrong, honey?" Mother asked. Sunniva threw herself into Mother's wide embrace and wrapped her small arms around her neck.

"Eadwyn told her a story about goblyns and the Goblyn Market."

Edrick expected her to scold his brother. Instead, she smiled with amusement.

"Just stories, my love. You have nothing to worry. Look here."

Right then, Meghan walked toward them with four sachets suspended from a braided twine necklace. She placed each of these around the children's necks. A vibrant fragrance of mixed herbs like crushed wolfsbane, garlic teeth, mint and alraun hung heavy in each pouch.

"These will protect us from unkind spirits of all sorts. You have nothing to fear, especially goblyns. Your father and I would be the first to know if their ugly faces darkened this forest."

Mother motioned to Meghan to take Sunniva. "I need anstor for my pantry, Meghan. I will show you where to look…"

"I have seen a patch, thick with them, east of the Stones," Edrick's eldest sister replied.

"Very well then, let's go. It is has been terribly hot these days. I am going to take you children to the creek."

"Yes!" Edrick said and immediately hopped his way toward the forest.

"Mother, can I take my bow?" Eadwyn asked.

She nodded, as she took one last fleeting look down the Lane where the crowd vanished into the distance.

The woods were but a short path from the Woodcutter's home. A world of its own, deep and majestic, entering the woody shade cooled them comfortably enough. It was as if the woods commanded many things and not even the sun challenged its sovereignty. Edrick loudly sang his song of goblyn warding, alone at first, then with Sunniva. She was walking on her own now, holding Edrick's hand. Together they repelled all the goblyns and evil spirits with the magick carried in their voices.

Meghan soon left them to take another path that led to the Stones, a circle of large blocky pillars that the Woodcutter's visited often. But today a stop by the stream seemed a better destination in the squelching heat.

After a while, they met a brook and followed a path up stream until they stopped along a wide pool, not so deep, where the water was crisp and clear. Mother sat down with Sunniva on an old fir log, worked smooth to serve as a bench by Woodcutter sires long ago. Edrick stripped to his bare skin and jumped right into the water.

"Oh, it's a bit cold," he said as he popped up above surface. He continued to bounce and splash, making as much noise and mess as a nine year old boy could desire.

"Baldice, come on," Edrick shouted.

"No, I am fine," he said and sat next to Mother. Sunniva sat on her lap, head tilted forward as Mother wove wild flowers into her hair.

After Edrick's energetic moments subsided and he relaxed into an easy float, he could hear his mother and sister humming in harmony, the Brownman's rhyme.

Baldice stood, with a queer expression coming over his face. Edrick watched as he walked around the log, facing away from them. Mother eyes followed him, then she too, stood. Sunniva slid off her lap.

"Smoke." Baldice declared.

"Yes, I smell it. Eadwyn!" Their mother shouted out into the forest.

His brother had been away for some time. Edrick caught a whiff of what they were talking about, like burning sticks and dried leaves. He looked around, but could not detect any smoke. He crawled out of the pool and dressed, his curiosity suddenly piqued.

They waited for Eadwyn's reply, but when none came, Mother yelled out again. Before she could finish, they heard his startled shout.

"Eadwyn!" Mother shouted again, picking Sunniva up and ran toward his voice. Edrick and Baldice ran after her. Edrick snatched a thick stick, an improvised club, unsure of what they might encounter.

Smoke now could be seen stretched out like ribbons woven through the trees. The smell intensified, changed, becoming a putrid mix of burned hair roasting over firewood.

Up ahead, Eadwyn came crashing through the trees, bow in hand, arrow ready to fly.

"Eadwyn," Mother called to him, getting his attention. He moved toward them in a panic.

"Are you hurt?" Mother asked. She set Sunniva down. Baldice protectively took her hand. Mother pulled Eadwyn close, looking him over. He huffed and puffed hard, his face was drained of color.

"What did you see?" Edrick demanded, bursting to discover this new mystery.

"I saw, I saw…" he stammered. "Over there," he pointed back toward where he came. He then leaned in close and whispered, "a goblyn."

Mother straightened instantly. All four of them were quiet, staring intently at Eadwyn. Then Edrick suddenly burst forth with laughter, laughed at the fear written on Eadwyn's face.

"Did they sell you some fruit? Or were they on their way to the

Goblyn Market?" Edrick mocked.

"Shut up!" Eadwyn said, taking a swing at Edrick with his bow. Edrick brought his stick up just in time to block, but continued laughing, still amused at his brother's frustrations.

"Edrick, enough!" Mother hushed him, threatening grave consequences in a single look. She cupped Eadwyn's face. "What did you see? What did it look like?"

"A Goblyn!" he took a moment to describe it, his mouth working around the words, but nothing further came forth. "I mean, it scared me!" he said, nearly crying. He looked to Edrick, ashamed of displaying any weakness, but he could not help himself.

"Show me," Mother said. Her words carried strength and boldness that Edrick was not used too. "Children, stay close!" They all nodded.

Edrick's mirth deflated, overtaken by his mother's curt tone. An overwhelming curiosity still lingered as he fell in line behind them.

Soon they all found the source of the smoke and terrible smell. Eadwyn pointed to what frightened him so much. A scarecrow like figure constructed of loose branches and leaves on a wooden stake planted in the middle of the forest. In form it resembled a person with wide arms, a head and skinny torso. Yet, as Edrick stepped closer, he could see that it wore a wolf-skin cloak and a gruesome necklace around its neck. Six severed timber-lion cub heads, twine threaded through the eye sockets, hung there. Tied to one hand, a bow, the other a stone ax. Just its very presence was disturbing and unusual.

Edrick loved it.

It seemed to be smoldering from some internal fire that could not be easily seen. Edrick kept stepping closer, wanting to examine it better.

"Edrick, don't take another step!" Mother commanded.

"What is it?" Baldice asked.

"A Goblyn!" Edrick laughed. "This is what scared you?" he asked Eadwyn.

"No, it moved! It chased me and, and...talked. It spoke horrible words!" he said, almost whimpering. Edrick had never seen his brother like this, so scared. All amusement left him, but he needed to know who made such a thing and why.

"We should go back. Baldice. Go find Meghan. We will wait by the brook."

Just as he turned to go, the entire scarecrow burst into flames. Edrick stepped back as the heat rushed over him.

"Whoa!" he exclaimed, genuinely impressed, that is until the acrid smell of the burning cub flesh and wolf-skin overtook him. They all reflexively pulled their arms to their mouth and nose, except Mother. She pulled Edrick back behind her, took out a small vial of water, opened it and poured it in her hand. Then with a few esoteric words, her éardian lit up like the midnight moon. A small, gray cloud formed over the fire and drenched the scarecrow until the flames died. The remains hissed in protest, like forest snakes yanked out of their holes. The smell soon dissipated, leaving a blackened charred figure.

"Let's go back children," Mother said, turning them around. "Edrick! I said leave it! Come."

Edrick complied reluctantly. He wanted to get closer, to examine this oddity, but it would have to wait. Perhaps he could come back with Father.

Baldice was not gone long when he and Meghan met them at the pool. Her face was grave and serious.

"Mother, what happened? I heard the shouting."

"Something startled Eadwyn. It's time we returned."

"He said it was a goblyn," Edrick chided, relishing at his brother's expense one final time, knowing they were all quite safe. "Did this particular goblyn carry fruit, because I am soooo hungry." Edrick could not help himself.

"Enough, Edrick," Mother snapped.

Meghan stood next to Eadwyn, offering a slight hug. "I felt something too, in the shadows. Never had I had such a creepy feeling. The experience frightened me, I admit. I abandoned my harvest when I heard Eadwyn's shouts."

They all left the forest quickly, scuffling through the trails. They found Father and Halig talking in front of their home, no crowd to be seen. He waived off their questions about the Elders, saying all had been resolved. When he heard about Eadwyn's story, he soon left them, taking Halig and Baldice into the woods straight away. Father took Eadwyn too, despite his fear.

Edrick wondered if the villagers made the scarecrow to intimidate them. Or could it have been some offering to appease

Lhodyn? He had never known them to brave the woods outside their father's company. But it seemed clear, the scarecrow was an effigy of their father, Warden of the Woods.

That night, Mother's stories were absent of goblyns, Erlkings and magick ogres. Instead, they were of kind animals featuring talking wolves and crafty foxes. When all but his parents had fell asleep, Edrick overheard Father whispering to Mother as they lay around the hearth, "We should not allow them in the woods alone, not for a while."

4

DUTY

IN THOSE FOLLOWING seasons of summer through winter and returning spring, Alaric became more watchful when treading the forest. It seemed displeased, annoyed and irritated. "Infected," Elisial said to him under the burning summer sun as they picnicked with their children in their favorite woodland glade. Alaric wandered across his woodland boundaries, from the village to the river, north to where the forest quits and south to where it thickened, and never did he find a clue as to whom built the burning effigy.

But all the while he felt a shadow creeping from beneath every rock, spilling out from every hole and crevice. Night clung to the woods longer, even in the ample summer days. Perhaps his mounting contempt for Lhodyn showed, too openly, and She in turn revealed Her disapproval.

He said nothing of this to anyone, not even his wife.

A year passed since that winter incident before another stirring arose in Athelyn. The Elders called for a Hatanmoot, a meeting where the eldest men of Athelyn gathered in the Elder Hall for matters of great importance. And most unexpectedly, Lord Temen arrived alone, without his sons, conferring with the Elders in the fading evening hours. At sunset, the lord took to his horse, charging through the Lane until he stopped in front of the Woodcutter's cottage.

"Alaric!" he shouted from the road. "Alaric! Come out!"

Alaric emerged from his home, great wood-ax in hand,

wondering who shouted for him with such discordance that neighbors all up and down the Lane stepped out to view the commotion.

"Lord Temen," Alaric greeted in surprise. The older, noble man was saddled on a mighty horse, a beast so large and powerful, bears were said to give it a wide berth. At Alaric's approach, the two shook hands, like equals.

Lord Temen was an old warrior of the Mark. He never appeared the part of a lord with his stubbly gray beard and piercing, beady eyes. He was a man that worked the land, his pride was his horses, the mightiest draft animals in all of the North, known as Wultherons.

"I am summoning you to a Hatanmoot. Come. Bring your eldest." His words were stern and rushed out with overwhelming urgency.

"We will leave at once." Alaric said.

The lord nodded and spurred his horse. He charged back down the Lane with great haste.

Alaric turned and found Edrick standing at the door. "Fetch your brother."

Edrick nodded. "Can I go too, Father?"

"No," he said with such finality, that asking again would only be answered with his hand.

The heart of the village was the Elder Hall, an ancient building of roughhewn stones, framed with weathered timbers. It had many uses, chiefly it provided the village Elders a place to meet and discuss important issues.

Lord Temen's horse was already tied up outside when they arrived. Alaric found him speaking to the Elders in rushed words.

They quieted as soon as Alaric and Halig entered. "Alaric, come my lad," one of the Elders said. His voice was soft and quiet and did not travel well in the wide space of the Hall, but Alaric's ears were sharp still.

"Greetings, Old Caflice," Alaric said to the aged man whose back hunched forward like a broken wheat stalk. Dressed in rags of poor farmers, this man sat upon an ornately carved chair like a lord. Next to him sat two other elderly men of similar attire, crowned with thin, failing white hair revealing blotchy, flakey scalps. "I am guessing this is a matter of great importance if Lord Temen deemed it necessary to call me here himself."

"There is war!" the lord announced in a booming voice. It echoed off the high rafters and stone walls. His declaration seemed to force all the stale air out the windows and doors. All eyes fell on the man, quieting their thoughts as he took command of the conversation.

"Those filthy horse rapists have Sithric's testicles between a hammer and forge. Athéalgian is besieged!"

"The Folthnir?" Alaric asked in disbelief which quickly kindled into old anger. This could not be true. Always, the Gheldenmark men have repelled the northern raiders from their borders. Alaric himself fought in the wars of Nitherlic Vale with his friend Grindan. It was an evil time in Alaric's life where he witnessed the best and worst of men.

"This is grave news if it is true."

"It is true!" the lord shot back, as if Alaric's remark was an insubordinate challenge. "I have already sent all my sons this morning to aid the king, save the boy, of course. We Mark lords must punish these mongrel men swiftly and without restraint, break their spirits like feral stallions! It has been too long since we culled their numbers."

"But how can they have taken the king's city?" Halig asked. For his son, hearing such improbable news would be like hearing the sun turned blue and now rises in the north.

"A new king has risen among them. A monster of a man. Probably more monster than man from what I have heard. Azevral is his name. Outlandish it sounds, not Folthnir at all."

The group fell quiet, digesting every gristly word.

"We must go," Alaric finally said. All eyes fell on him. "King Sithric needs our help. The enemy is already too close, we cannot wait for them to arrive with tidings of Sithric's death. We must assemble all men and able boys from the entire vale and march west. We can reach Athéalgian in five days."

"Five days?!" Halig repeated. It seemed like an impossible task to his son, but Alaric made such marches in his youth. In war, you had to move swiftly or people died.

The Elders looked to Lord Temen. They seemed unable to issue a reply to what Alaric knew was the only true course of action. But then these old men were not warriors.

"Something must be done. What exactly, needs to be well

planned and thought out," the lord replied evenly.

Old Caflice stroked his wispy white whiskers. "Perhaps young Alaric is right." The other Elders grumbled and slapped their knees in protest. To most there, the words of the Woodcutter were always wild and uncouth. He was a child of the forest, uncivilized even to farmers.

"Leave us now to discuss this suggestion, Alaric. We summoned you to honor tradition," giving a nod to an ancient parchment hanging on the wall behind them. "You have shared your thoughts. You are, uh..." the farmer licked his cracked lips, "dismissed."

Halig opened his mouth to protest, but Alaric placed a quieting hand on his shoulder and took a step back leading his son away. Halig bit his words back and remained silent.

"I am sure whatever you decide will best serve us all." Alaric turned his son around and they both left.

He did not wait for a decision that night. There was only one thing to do. He packed for the road. He would take Halig, Baldice and Eadwyn. Halig was eager to go to war, but he could tell Eadwyn cared not to leave, though he tried hard not to show it. Elisial remained calm, reminding him, "You don't know for sure what they will say. I do not think they will walk so easily to war."

"It is no choice now. Whether they want war or not, it is coming. They must see that! Our only chance is to free King Sithric from this siege and rally all our lords against them. If we brought every man to Athéalgian, I know we can preserve our kingdom! It must be preserved!"

There was no talking Alaric out of it. He made his mind to bring all of Athelyn to the king's city. In the morning, he roused all of his neighbors, most of whom despised him, to prepare for a long march west.

"There is war!" he said to their startled faces. "Prepare yourselves for travel. Bring your eldest sons and find weapons among your shovels and scythes."

Then a message came that afternoon from the Elder Council. "They have a decision and request Alaric and his eldest at once."

Alaric returned to the Elder Hall. Before he entered, he could hear a great debate raised amongst them.

"Alaric's blood trickles from a hardy vein of honorable sires reaching far beyond all memory." Old Caflice argued. "Warden of the

Woods they are, a title bestowed upon them by ancient kings. Their family dwelled in this valley long before our Elder Hall was built, before even the Wall and lychgates were raised."

"Warden of the Wood!" another Elder scoffed. "Then does that make me farting lord of the farmers!" The other Elder chuckled in agreement, stamping his cane on the wood floor.

Old Caflice continued, "Alaric tends the woods as steward and caretaker."

"As if one could be placed in charge of mountains or the sky," another Elder rebuked. "How could anyone make such a claim or any king bestow such a duty?"

"He and his wife maintains a certain continuity with the old ways, and therefore understands the Old Gods and spirits that inhabit the land, the rivers, mountains and sky; and of course, the great forest Wudelic. And that kind of understanding is not to be mocked! For out of all our people they still have their éardians. Their ghost-lights don't fade into adulthood like ours. The Old Gods keep with them."

Alaric entered the Hall and all talk ceased. Once again Lord Temen was there, this time his youngest son stood at his side, a boy near Eadwyn's age. The village Elders sat again in front of the hearth, Lord Temen standing directly behind them. They looked put out, save Old Caflice who seemed relieved Alaric arrived in the middle of their debate.

"We have made a decision Alaric, based on your words of action."

"Glad I am to hear such wisdom," Alaric replied. "We will leave this evening if need be. I know the way. I will lead, if Lord Temen wishes it."

Lord Temen said nothing, his expression was immutable. The Elders almost seemed flustered by Alaric's quick response.

"We have decided you will go on a journey, Alaric. Alone and in great secrecy."

Alaric stared hard at each aged face for a long moment. He decided to first hear their words, hoping to find good reason in this course, before he throttled his ax haft up their boney bums.

"We need our Warden in this dire hour," Old Caflice started in a tone that did not conceal his forced flattery. "We humbly ask you to perform the duty of your title. Lord Temen has assured us that not only will King Sithric find the strength to repel the Folthnir, but his forces can withstand a siege for a full season or two. Winter will arrive and the Folthnir will have to disperse or perish in the cold. We have taken your proposal into consideration, which is sound to a degree, but we do not know where the enemy positions are, how strong their numbers, so on and so forth. It would be incredibly foolish to march blindly to a hostile force without knowing something about it.

"To that end, we request of you to find us safe passage to a place of refuge if the worse befall us and we are forced to flee. Lord Temen has messengers all along the Merchant Road and assures us we will have plenty of time to determine if and when the Folthnir approach. If you find us a safe path to peaceful lands, we will retreat as soon as word reaches us Atheálgian has fallen. Would you agree to this Alaric? Will you save us from war?"

They each grinned at him with false humility, revealing all their gaping, toothless smiles.

Alaric had not expected this. He looked into their solemn faces, there was more to their smiles than flattery. He knew fear in men's eyes when he saw them. The Elders were terrified. And if these village leaders were frightened, then what of all the other men and boys. Could these old men just wait without true action for their deaths, when the Folthnir came marching east, driving all beneath their swords. Alaric could not abide that. If they refused to fight, then he himself must flee with his family, as much as the idea tears his heart is half. His family's blood flows deep through Wudelic's soil, deeper than many tree roots.

"All right. I will go. But heed my council in this matter. In war, you must move to action when opportunity permits and your enemy remains unaware. Our opportunity is now, when Sithric's strength is lessoned but not lost. He needs all of us to rise against these invaders and match the nobility of our past sires, when they took and made these lands theirs. When they made wholesome the wild fields and woods, pushing back monsters into the hinterlands. And since that time, men of the Mark have never failed to secure these borders. A duty seen through to death, in hopes their children lived to till these fields where their bodies now lay. Farmers whose fortunes were bought with blood so future generations could spend more time wielding the pommels of farm implements that nourished and fed men, rather than the swords that destroy them.

"Do you now still hold this course, to flee, and never wonder if your hands might have lifted great evil in our dire need, when all men's hearts were united in hopes of freedom against a common enemy? Or would you rather languish in fear to wonder if our indifference sent those stout hearted men to starve, fall and inevitably crushed beneath Folthnir feet? All our lives will be unalterably changed."

Alaric awaited their reply. There was a long silence as the old men exchanged bewildered looks.

"We will await news from Athéalgian. We wait," Old Caflice repeated, stubbornly, but his voice held no conviction. No hope, no smile, just a persistent weariness, as if Alaric's words beat him down, but he would never submit to him.

"Wait then. Look for me before autumn's harvest."

"Where shall you travel?" an Elder asked.

"There is but one direction now, east. I take forest paths seldom traveled."

"It seems the least likely path for refuge."

"What better place to retreat than those paths that seems least likely?" Alaric retorted.

"May Lady Lhodyn guide you well through Her realms," Old Caflice said. The others grunted in support.

Alaric spat in disgust as soon as he left the Elder Hall. No farewells followed him as he turned toward the Wudelic.

5

FAERIE TRAPS

THE VILLAGERS FOUND themselves quite content that summer, even joyous as news spread: the Elders sent Alaric away on some fool's errand. This reprieve lasted through the summer, past winter and into spring. Alaric still had not returned, to their great satisfaction. His sons still supplied the village with firewood, trapped vermin and recovered their wandering sheep that occasionally strayed near the forest, but that was not to say all was well in the world. There were troubling rumors of war that concerned many. Northern invaders pushed relentlessly past their realm's borders. Some say that was the reason for Alaric's departure. Though the Elders kept quiet, they did appear gravely concerned. Farmers were perpetually worried about one thing or another, so was their lot in life, yet the Elder's silence on the matter of Alaric's departure raised eyebrows and was the subject of many private discussions.

Rumors arose, speaking of odd things happening in the woods once again. Only the eldest Woodcutter's children were allowed there in Alaric's absence. The forest continued to cast its spell over folk; a kind of subtle magick like beholding raw gold, or the kind that drew sailors across the seas to imagined, mystical lands. The children of the villagers refused to give in to these dark omens, for they had been taught so at birth and so stayed away.

The children of Alaric were less cautious....

"The faeries asked for help, Edrick!" Sunniva pleaded. "We have to go. Please, take me into the woods." Each word bubbled out, sweet like golden honey. She stood next to Edrick while he worked, absently curling her sun kissed locks around her finger, loop after loop.

Sunniva, child of the Sun.

Her golden éardian orbited swiftly around her small head, punctuating the urgency in her voice.

"Again with the faeries? They're just dreams," Edrick dismissed.

"No, they're not," the little girl argued back, so articulate for her age of six years. "They called me by name...and know everything about me. And Mother and Meghan said *dream* faeries are real, and that they used to visit them in their dreams too. When they were little girls."

Edrick rolled his eyes. Once his little sister had her mind on something, especially faeries, she would not stop talking about it. To everyone. Why did he even listen? She was too adorable to ignore, he reluctantly admitted to himself.

"We have to go!" she continued, pulling at his hand.

So stubborn.

"Come on, Edrick. Halig and Eadwyn are not around. I just want to go look, by the Stones, then we can come right back." In her other arm she held a soft kitten, a boldly striped, silky coat tabby. It was the same one she had cared for over these last ten days. Edrick was surprised this one had not run away like the other orphans she found.

"And what about Meghan?" he asked. "She'll notice us off."

The suggestion gave Sunniva pause. Then, "We'll take her with us."

Edrick scoffed. "Really, how?"

"Ummmm, Mother needs some berries, and anstor, and mushrooms...."

"We can't go that deep into the woods," Edrick said, easily dismissing the idea.

"But we will go?" she burst out. The kitten lazily opened one eye. Sunniva bounced up and down with excitement, but the kitten didn't stir despite the jostling. Her golden orb transitioned from a smooth orbit to what resembled a bouncing ball circling around her tiny crown.

"Only if you ask Meghan."

"Sure, let's go now."

"Sunniva, we have to check all the faerie traps, just like yesterday and the days before. This is *our* chore. And you better start paying attention so you can help me."

Mother had Edrick checking traps for faeries, baiting them with special herbs, called anstor, and atorlathe berries, every morning. Mother kept them all so busy, "to keep your minds from worrying about your father," she told them. "One day, you will look up, and there he will stand, at the forest edge, weary and proud to see his children hard at work."

Sunniva frowned, pouting her rosy little lips, the golden orb stopped abruptly and sunk to her chest. She hated chores, and this most of all.

No matter how many times he, or their brothers, or Meghan explained to her, Sunniva still refused to accept that there are good faeries like their éardians and then there are bad…troublesome…and sometimes, malicious faeries.

Faeries that spread curses like disease. Twisted spines, cauliflower warts or huge bulbous lumps beneath the skin were sure signs of faerie magick.

Nothing their mother, an alhíelda, could not remedy though.

"Did you find any yet?" Sunniva repeated at every stop as they wound their way through Athelyn.

Edrick ceased answering her after the first empty trap.

She absently stroked the kitten. "Do you hear it purring?" she asked, quiet as kitten breath.

Its snoring, Edrick thought.

"Still, no," he finally answered. "Nobody has had any trouble lately. Let's try Udela's farm. She lives near enough to the forest there is usually one or two baddies that end up trapped."

Edrick retained two sacks: one empty, for the faerie corpses, the other contained anstor and atorlathe. The aromatic anstor attracted the faeries into the traps and the atorlathe was cunning poison deliciously irresistible to the faerie's palette.

He tucked both sacks beneath his belt and walked into the Lane. Sunniva followed, floating slowly behind him, cradling the kitten with great care, her golden orb trailed like a kite taken by the wind.

Cats of all colors darted through the Lane as they passed between the cottages hugging the road. A visitor might have thought the entire town's population had been transformed into felines.

Perhaps by a witch with Sunniva's affections.

Instead, they were considered a tolerated nuisance. Best animal to deter bad faeries.

No birds dare perch near the village, for the cats stalked the roofs like royal sentinels. They strutted across the Wall surrounding the village, marking every visitor that came and went. They sprinted around pedestrian's feet and through the legs of animals pulling carts. Few villagers took care to avoid this feline swarm. Instead, people boasted of the number of cat tails captured as they traveled a circuit around Athelyn. Cart wheels lopped off cat tails like executioner blades took heads at the king's court.

It was fine sport.

With ten cats for every person, the common estimate, there was no worry about any permanent harm being done.

"So many kitties!" Sunniva chirped in delight. She said this every morning, as if noticing their presence for the first time, day after day. She skipped after them as they went down the Lane toward the village center. The cats scattered before them, wishing no harm come to their tails.

At the village center, they met Edrick's good friend Tredan.

Their meeting place was the Old Well. Tredan waited here every morning, spinning his sling around his head, taking aim at all the cats that took refuge from the Lane.

"Why do we have to always meet Tredan?" Sunniva asked, stamping her tiny feet.

She disliked Tredan because he and his family had a peculiar profession. They were furriers and hunted the abundant feline foes. Everyone regarded them as odd, approaching a reputation near equal to the Woodcutters.

So naturally, Edrick and Tredan, the son of the cat-furriers, were fast friends. They often wandered together through the village in the early morning hours. It was Tredan's task to spot and cull newly born tomcats, or feral toms that might have taken residence.

After exchanging brief greetings, the two boys set off through village, never taking the same course twice, but wandered wherever their imaginations led, until they crossed all their familiar hunting grounds.

Edrick the cunning trapper, and Tredan the fearless hunter…and Sunniva the bothersome kitten rescuer.

They eventually made their way to widow Udela's farm on the northeast side of the village without finding a single faerie or incurring the death of a single cat. Her adult sons still worked the fields, residing on Udela's land with their own families, though each had built separate homes for themselves. The widow greeted the three children at the door.

"Edrick, I have a sprig and whatnot caught in the barn. Get it out at once! It's frightening the animals and has been all night. None of my cowardly sons dare approach the trap for fear of being cursed. Now I'm afraid all my animals might have faerie pocks! Get rid of it at once!" She spoke as if it were Edrick attracting the faeries himself.

"Sure, but...you said it was alive?"

"I don't know, son. I just know the animals have been causing a ruckus, like a wolf had been trapped in there all night."

"Well, have you looked inside?" asked Tredan. "Maybe there is a wolf in there."

The old lady gave the boy a cold, disdainful glare. Like all adults, she had lost her ghost-light. Her éardian faded after childhood and her face was that much darker for it. "If there is, I'm sure the smell of cats will drive it mad with hunger. Why don't you look!"

Sunniva grabbed Edrick's hand and squeezed, unsettled by the cranky woman. Her golden orb hid behind her head. The kitten, remained oblivious to these trivial concerns.

Tredan didn't like being taunted, especially about looking, smelling or acting like a cat. He hated cats. And all the other children called him cat boy and told him he acted like one, all except Edrick.

"Well, if there aren't any toms around here I'll just leave," he announced.

"Toms?" asked Udela incredulously. "On my farm? I hate cats. Can't stand their dæmonic screeching. That's why I keep dogs, son. To keep those flea traps off my farm!"

"And that's why you always end up with faeries too," Edrick boldly replied. No cats, then you attract bad faeries.

"I'll have flowery pixies over those dæmon beasts any day...or night. Just tend to that trap and get off my farm. I'll have your mother's payment when I see a body in the bag." She turned and went back inside her cottage, grumbling. Then her head popped out of the window, "and tell your slothful brothers they owe me half a cord of wood for what your mother traded me last week."

She disappeared behind quivering curtains before anyone could respond.

Edrick, closely followed by Sunniva, approached the barn. Tredan decided to stay with them, if only to annoy the widow further it seemed. The barn was an old gray building, same as many others in the village, scaled in cracked wooden planks, with patches of green moss hiding under shaded recesses. The door was ajar. Silence clung inside. At least the animals had calmed down, if they were even upset at all. It seemed to Edrick, the widow exaggerated anything she found inconvenient or unpleasant.

A single crow sat perched on the roof ridge just above, casting its dark eye down on the children.

Athelyn cats avoided the bossy crows. Always.

"Caw! Caw!" It proclaimed, its head twisting and bobbing as if urging them inside.

Tredan loaded his sling with a rock and sent the projectile soaring. The crow dove down off the roof and circled away, only to return to the same perch.

"Caw-caw! Caw-caw!" it screeched, as if scolding the boy.

"Leave it," Edrick said, reaching to stay Tredan's arm as he loaded another stone. "Crows should not be harmed or killed. They keep company with the dead."

"Yeah, don't hurt the black bird," Sunniva echoed. "It's bad luck."

"That's the only luck I have," Tredan dropped the stone. Another black bird flew over them and landed next to the first. They chatted back and forth, "Caw-caw. Caw-caw."

Edrick flung open the barn doors allowing sunlight to rush into the sheltered space. The animals jumped at the sudden movement; mostly milk cows, though he heard some chickens fluttering in the loft above. The faerie trap hung from an iron chain bolted into the rafters just above head height, center of the barn.

"I guess there are no wolves," Sunniva peeped.

The boys snickered to themselves.

"Help me with the ladder," Edrick told Tredan, spotting it in the corner. As soon as he spoke the faerie trap shook and jangled on the chain. Sunniva shouted and ran out of the barn.

"That's strange," Edrick said.

"Shouldn't it be dead?" Tredan asked as they carried the ladder to the trap.

"That's what I mean."

"Aren't you afraid it might curse you?" Sunniva asked as she leaned over the entrance, peeking inside.

"No, it ate the atorlathe for sure or it would have escaped. Maybe they weren't ripe or something. After eating the fruit their minds get all dizzy. They can't curse because they can't think, and all they feel is, well, not good."

"Has that happened before, them not dying?" Tredan asked.

"Not to me, but it happens," Edrick replied like a learned sage.

They leaned the long ladder against the rafter and Edrick climbed up. The trap swayed and bustled about as the creature inside reacted to Edrick's approach. Edrick was not worried. He expected faeries to react like this right after they ate the berries. What seemed unusual was how Udela claimed that this faerie had been there all night. It should have been dead by now.

He unfastened the trap from the chain and handed it down to Tredan who received it confidently, holding it in one hand while keeping the ladder steady as Edrick made his way back down. Sunniva moved from behind the door frame and stood at the threshold, but still refused to venture farther inside.

Edrick looked at her and said, "This is supposed to be your job," referring to Tredan's assistance.

Sunniva gave him a complaining whimper.

Tredan smiled at Sunniva, as if assuring her that there was no danger.

Edrick rolled his eyes. Why couldn't she stay with Meghan inside the house? "All right, let's see what we have, hold up the trap."

Inside were three faeries. Their faerie-light diminished completely, as usual after consuming the berry, but they still retained their alluring beauty, two appearing as diminutive men, one, a woman, nude and thin. They were enamoring to mortal eyes, a trick of their glamor. It was a façade of these dark fey beings, a disguise to elicit sympathy from humans. One lay sprawled out, dead. Its magick long fled. It appeared grotesque, face contorted, frozen into a mask of terror and torture, jaw locked into an elongated o-gape scream. The other two were buzzing still, limbs flailing and twitching like insect wings.

"That's why," Edrick announced, "somehow three made it into

the trap before it shut. One must have eaten most the fruit and the others just partial portions. They must be suffering pretty badly."

"What?" Sunniva asked. "Why are they suffering?"

"What do we do?" asked Tredan.

"Just have them out and end it. But it will be tricky with two," Edrick replied.

"Why not just drop them in a barrel of water and drown them," Tredan suggested.

"Why do you want to drown them?" Sunniva asked. She was getting quite upset. Her golden orb flared in agitation.

Edrick thought about the suggestion for a moment, then shook his head. "Not sure if that will work, they're not cats after all. Just watch."

He had Tredan place the cage on the ground, then knelt low. With one hand he lifted the latch and pulled back the spring loaded door. He slid his hand inside to grab them both, but they darted around like fish cornered in a net, slipping through his fingers. He thrust his arm deeper, hoping to pin them against the side. But once he had a faerie in hand, the width of his arm forced the door wide enough to allow the other to escape. It flew up in a six foot arc before it crashed to the ground, flopping like a stranded fish.

Edrick snapped his arm out of the cage, grasping the struggling faerie in his fist.

Sunniva let loose a voluminous shrill, horrified at the harmed little creature. Her kitten bolted out of her arms and shot around the barn between the children.

"Grab it!" Edrick shouted in excitement.

Tredan chased after the kitten zipping to and fro, chasing the faerie around the barn floor.

The faerie thrashed about like a wounded bird struggling to fly, only to come crashing hard back to the ground, relentless in its effort to flee the ferocious kitten predator.

"Not the cat! The faerie!" Edrick yelled at Tredan and joined the chase as well. Sunniva continued screaming incessantly at them and the bizarre scene: Edrick chasing Tredan, chasing the kitten, chasing the flopping faerie.

Tredan leaped and hopped trying to stomp on the wild thing, but it was the kitten that finally caught it. She pounced on it, pinning it down and sinking her tiny fangs into its frail form.

"Good cat," Edrick praised, patting its back. He extracted the faerie from the kitten's teeth.

Sunniva ran briefly inside to rescue her.

Edrick walked shortly outside and picked up a hefty rock then turned back to the other two.

A half dozen and three crows now sat perched on the barn roof, gazing attentively down in silence.

"For live ones, when they are still squirming, it's best to end it quickly, like you would a chicken or putting down an old dog." He kneeled once again, leaning on the two figures in his left hand so just their heads were exposed. Their necks craned and turned as if they might wriggle out from beneath the child's hand, their bodies taut and rigid. Edrick raised his right hand, then slammed the rock down. Their heads exploded like two mashed snail shells. His hand sunk into their softened bodies.

"Edriiiiiick!" Sunniva screamed and ran away sobbing.

A chorus of devilish caws fell over them. Laughing, cheering, cajoling with praise.

The faeries lay very still. A purplish blood-splotch smeared the dirt by Edrick's hand where there were once angelic faces. He looked back up, the triumphant trapper, to a slack jawed and dumbfounded Tredan.

Even for a cat hunter, that seemed brutal.

6

THE CROSSROADS

THERE ARE MANY roads in the broad world, but only one place in the North known as The Crossroads.

Marking its location on the horizon from a great distance, a giant tree, a mighty mathelian rose like an archaic tower sprung from the roots of Time. Like an oak in form, its stout trunk supported a twisting wide canopy high into the sky. Smooth, white-gray bark resembled that of birch, a patchwork of thin flakey paper disrupted by deep ebony fissures. Along its surface were the God's Eyes, horizontal half-moon arches with rings just beneath it. Its meandering branches and boughs stretched wide in all directions, its canopy shading an area larger than Alaric's village. Such a thing existed nowhere else in the world, and if so, such knowledge was secret and sacred.

Campfire light now dotted the ground beneath the mathelian as Alaric viewed it from a southern approach. After nearly a year of travel, he had finally reached the boundaries of Mithledor, the last great kingdom in these lands, signifying the end of his journey.

The Crossroads marked the gateway to the North, and his home.

Despite the thick darkness, a sprawling road lay plain before Alaric's eyes, fading shortly into the horizon toward the foot of the tree. Straight and level are the southern roads. Dependable routes that made nocturnal travel easier for those desperate to reach home.

He bore no lantern, nor torchlight, as it would mark him vulnerable on the open road for any eyes that kept watch. Instead, starlight mingling with his azure éardian fastened to back of his left hand, lit his way.

Wary are travelers that took to the road at night. The wise do not depart until the sun shows its face, and even then, open roads were dangerous at best. The distant camp fires filled Alaric with the hope of a safe night's rest and possibility of warm food. Such things were sparse luxuries for weary travelers.

Alaric was not defenseless. He trekked with his long hafted wood-ax made useful as a walking stick, large enough to deter most. And over his shoulder was slung a family heirloom, a great bow named Nithledan, masterfully constructed in layers of bone, sinew and wood. Deadly accurate it was in his hands, same as his father and all his sires before. Alaric made a name for himself in his youth on the battlefields of Gheldenmark against the nefarious Folthnir raiders twenty years before.

The bow was one of two heirlooms, the other a torc, kept in constant possession. Both treasures worth more in value than his life. For they did not belong to him, he simply retained them while he lived. They belonged to his family, the Woodcutters. To the Warden of Woods of each generation.

His eldest, Halig, would receive these in due time. A time that felt all too close at hand. More so now as his first born could no longer be called a boy.

A deep darkness fell about him as he entered the penumbra of the mathelian branches. Starlight receded. His éardian glimmered like a fine sapphire jewel.

He stopped abruptly, believing he saw something moving faintly on either side of the road, yet when he stopped to scan the plains, everything was washed away in darkness. Nothing stirred again, or his eyes failed in the deepening night.

He was glad to be under the mathelian's long arms at last. To be near it filled him with a feeling of grand wonder and sincere awe, as if chasing after a fallen star to have it finally land in his hands.

The mathelian tree sheltered the actual carrefour, providing ample shelter for travelers during harsh weather. As good as any inn some proclaimed. And in its long history, someone dug a well or two, sharing the water with the huge tree, a tree that thrived in an otherwise vacant expanse.

The lone tree had no neighbors, no fellow trees in which to chat with or make remarks about men and their brusque concerns, nor little saplings to look after and watch grow through the centuries. If there was a time where other trees grew in the plains of the solitary giant, they had long retreated or been hewed down. All that was left was the lone mathelian and its transitory guests, the birds that sung about far off forests thick with exotic and unfamiliar woods and the many travelers that passed through the Crossroads.

Nocturnal insects buzzed and chirped happily from on high, charging the air with a tangible energy. A large group of merchants had settled there that night. Some two dozen people huddled around a grand fire. This was a common place traveling caravans would rest until they continued on at sunrise.

Alaric knew most of the travelers would be sleeping, but not all, not in the wilderness. They would have guards on watch at all hours. Many beasts prowled the Peliánor Plains at night, even monstrous things. But the most common dangers were bandits who made their dens close to the Crossroads.

He slung his ax over his shoulder, not wanting to appear threatening. He called out, "Hail there peaceful camp."

The guards moved with purpose, taking up torches and readying their weapons, a few archers being among them.

"Hail stranger. Stay there, where you are." They looked around in the dark for others besides Alaric, possibly for an ambush. One man strode forward in front of the others, armed with a taut bow. "Traveling alone? Or do you have companions near? No men walk the roads at night, not for long anyway."

Alaric became encouraged as they spoke Mithlian, his language, something he had not heard in a while. "I am alone. I walk in darkness out of necessity, not from desire. I knew I could find refuge at the Crossroads. I will be on my way at dawn."

"Come closer then. Let us inspect you. If all looks fair, we will gladly share our fire. The food venders are already asleep but I have never known them to complain to be awakened by a customer on these roads."

Alaric approached them cautiously. "That is glad news, my stomach has felt better days. Life on the road is wearying."

"Truer words. Especially for a traveler on foot. If you have the coin, my master has a mule or pony to spare." As Alaric drew within their torch light, their attention turned to his hand, alight with his éardian.

"Mule?" Alaric replied. "No. Nor horse or pony would I desire. I do not fare well with those beasts."

"What sort of lantern do you carry in your left hand?" the lead guard asked, readying his weapon.

"It is no lantern," Alaric explained turning his hand to allow them to inspect it. "It is my éardian. Some call it a ghost-light…"

"BACK!" the lead guard ordered, training his bow on Alaric. The others did the same.

"He's an Eldritch!" one guard shouted.

"Who else would walk the open roads at night!" another declared.

The lead guard motioned his men to fall back, to guard their masters in case deceptive violence. "Go stranger! We will not have your kind here. I care not what you are, but you shall not camp near us. Had we the men to spare, we would chase you off. But you are warned, appear again within range of our arrows, you shall be shot until you are dead. We want no part of your strange magick."

"GO ON!" another shouted. All the guards swore at him until he turned and retreated into the darkness. He left confused and dispirited. He had heard of these Eldritch before by reputation alone, but knew not why he was called one. Even in these realms of his native tongue, he was not welcomed.

At least not welcomed by the measure of men.

Alaric retreated to the western side of the mathelian tree, until he no longer viewed the harsh firelight of the merchants' camp. He found a place where a thick root broke away from the ground for a few yards before it dove back into the soil. He sat down beside it and ran his hand across the smooth surface.

He felt the grand tree stir, awakened by his touch.

"Hello, Old One," Alaric spoke into the night, in such reverence his words sounded out like moth wings. He looked off into the western horizon beyond the canopy where the stars burned and shimmered like raw jewels set in a black ribbon across the sky. He thought of building a fire, but he had no wood to burn and one certainly did not harvest mathelian wood. The night was cool but not cold.

A broad leaf slipped off a branch and floated slowly, down through the night air, landing upon Alaric's head.

"Master Mathelian," Alaric began in a strange tongue spoken to him by his parents in secret. "I had thought you were asleep."

The leaves rustled gently as if a small breeze had passed.

Alaric spoke, or rather, sung to the old tree, confessing his sorrows, his fears and his hope. Alaric told the tree of the lands he saw and the strangers within it, he told the tree everything.

"I shall be back through here in a short while, with my entire family. My wife has been waiting many winters to meet you. She has the best stories about the endless seas."

He rummaged through his pack for something. "I have something for you, Old One," he said as he pulled out a small glass vial. He opened it and smelled its contents. A briny fragrance issued forth.

"You may not be able to visit the sea, but that does not mean a portion of the sea cannot be called to pay homage to you," he said as he poured the sea water across the roots. The tree shivered, then swayed. It loved it dearly.

Alaric wrapped his cloak tightly around his body, snuggled up to the root and fell fast asleep.

Dreams beneath the mathelian tree were not common dreams, they were portals into another place, a realm where the mathelian spoke to Alaric.

He found himself beside the tree, beneath the starlight, but the mathelian was not alone. It was surrounded by his brothers and sisters of an era long past, rooted in the vast expanse of the high plains. It was the Old One's memory of a world that had ceased, but was still missed.

Alaric envisioned the mathelian tree as a pillar of deep emerald light extending into the heavens, bejeweled with an infinite number of orbs swirling about it, as if the stars had been released from the skies to wander the world. Within this light, dwelled the Old One's spirit.

As the tree spirit spoke, Alaric learned portions of his family's history, as told to the mathelian by his sires. He caught glimpses of the world in ages past: great beings of heaven at war, the breaking and renewing of the world, stars falling out of the sky and leveling mountain ranges, the coming of the eastern horsemen, the retreat of the giants into the far north, and the arrival of the Nine Immortals and their Celestial Swords…so many great events and references that Alaric seldom understood much of the subject matter. Yet, he sat patiently through the Old One's telling of a thousand lifetimes of sagacious lore.

All these things were conveyed through a wild river of memory, sweeping over him, leading from one thought then to another. He listened. Simply listened, and smiled knowing he eased the Old One's loneliness.

As the time drew on, the Old One fell silent in reflection. These were the times Alaric spoke.

"Did you enjoy your first taste of the sea?"

Yes. Such strange water. Bitter, but full of vigor. Now I know something of its nature.

"And what do you think? Of its nature?"

A wonder it is in this world, vast and deep. It holds more life than all the lands and I did not know that until now. Thank you, Alaric.

"That is hard to imagine."

I do not find much hard to imagine.

"Old One," Alaric began, changing to another subject. He ventured to voice an old concern, one that preoccupied his father. "I must learn more of my torc. You said it concealed a secret forgotten to my sires. You hinted that it could release me from Lhodyn."

Yes! Keep it safe! Do not let any outside your family possess it. Now awake Alaric! Protect it! Arise and face your enemies!

"What enemies? Lhodyn? Tell me how can I find freedom?"

Alaric, rise now! I am sorry. We will speak again. Arise and fight for your life!

Alaric opened his eyes with a knife pressed hard on his throat.

7

FAERIE KINGS & FAERIE QUEENS

"WHAT DID YOU do to that poor child?" Udela asked the boys as they returned from the barn. She thrust a basket filled with fresh vegetables to Tredan. The usual payment.

Edrick stood with a sack filled with three dead faeries in one hand and the defective faerie trap in the other.

"She's just a baby, nothing to worry about. Wants to save every creature she sees," Edrick replied. Udela's face shifted from its constant bitter visage, softening to something unfamiliar to Edrick. Pity or regret.

"She is a good child. Show more compassion," she commanded him. "These are evil times and the sensibilities of a young girl ought not to be dismissed so easily. Now, tell your lazy brothers we need half a cord of wood by the end of the month as agreed upon. Those cursed savages robbed me of most of what I had already."

"Yes ma'am, I am sure they will be delivering it by the end of the day." Both boys nodded toward Udela respectfully as she withdrew into her house. The truth was that Edrick's brothers seemed to be neglecting most of their chores lately and spent more time hunting in the woods, or at least that is what they told him. Udela was not the first to complain of their idleness.

"Are there any more traps?" Tredan asked as they left the farm.

"No, that's it. We had better find Sunniva though."

"Oh, let me find her!" Tredan nearly shouted. By that he meant he would track her. Edrick shrugged and let Tredan feign his tracking prowess as they meandered across the village 'following' Sunniva's path. Edrick suspected that she ran straight home, but he allowed Tredan his fun.

Eventually they arrived back at Edrick's home after traipsing across the inner fields of the village, those that lay within the Lane. These fields were worked by all the villagers, Commons as they were named. Even Alaric's family tended these fields, though most of them were horrible farmers, as all of Athelyn were sure to remind them. Ever did the families complain of the suffering fields farmed by the Woodcutters after rotation. But Father kept them all involved.

"It is our duty to contribute," he and Mother reminded them.

The fact was, those that did not contribute, such as Tredan's family, were deeply regarded as vagabonds, lazy beggars that did the least to get by, such as trapping cats; a useless profession, regarded as unnecessary, even though it did alleviate the town of a constant nuisance.

"Look, there she is," Tredan announced triumphantly. She sat on the Woodcutter's cottage porch, softly scratching the kitten's head still cradled in her arms, calm and unburdened.

Edrick's house was unique from other homes in the village as the back half consisted of a hollowed out giant sycamore some ten yards wide. The walls were thick and rose three stories before its height failed. A steep pitch roof was added so it appeared as a roughly hewed tower. Where the rest of the giant tree's towering upper portion remained, no one could say, though many suspected its timber was used to build their grand Elder Hall in the village center.

Jutting out from the sycamore's base was a traditional cottage forming the main living quarters for Edrick's family.

This was the home of the Woodcutters for only a few generations. There was once a time they lived in the forest, for that was their domain.

Now, they were villagers of Athelyn-un-Wudelic. Same as the others.

A wall built of stacked stone enclosed the property, very much like the Wall that surrounded the entire village. Yet at each corner were tall pillars where they hung faerie lamps, flooding the entire property with fey light at night. Edrick's yard had its own lychgates as well, one leading to the Lane and another exiting the village leading to the forest path. Such gates allowed people through the Wall, but warded against unkind spirits.

It was at the Woodcutter's lychgate where Tredan and Edrick parted. He handed Edrick the vegetable basket, sliding it over his arm. "I should get going. Father has warned me about spending my entire day with you, that I don't bring enough cats home when I do."

"I understand. I will see you later then."

"Bye." Tredan walked slowly back down the Lane, taking his sling out and loading it with a rock.

There was no sign of his brothers, just Sunniva. She turned half inside when she noticed Edrick's approach. Her expression suddenly dropped, her lips pouted. She looked across her shoulder without moving her head, as if she wanted to make sure Edrick saw how upset she was.

"There you are," he said gently, remembering Udela's words. But as he walked up, Sunniva took a look at the faerie sack, gave a small shriek and ran inside. Edrick followed.

Inside he found Meghan and Baldice busy in the hearth room.

"What did you bring me?" Meghan asked as she moved about the house minding her chores. Nearly a woman in age, she was almost a second mother with a second list of orders for Edrick.

Two mothers were worse than one.

He held out the sack and she shook it, feeling its weight, or lack thereof.

"Just three faeries," he said feebly. "And some food," raising the basket.

"Just three?" She replied and groaned. "Mother is not going to be happy. She has been stocking up on faerie oil for a while now and still she is asking for more. Three isn't nearly enough."

Edrick shrugged. "The trap is broken. It let three faeries inside."

"What? Impossible. Just set it down and Halig will repair it. Now, what happened with Sunniva? She won't talk about it."

Edrick told her the story about the barn. Baldice listened from nearby. Finding dead faeries in the trap disturbed Sunniva enough, but having to kill them was a new experience for the little one. Meghan took the sack of faeries and basket of vegetables.

"Well, she will have to get over her fear eventually. I did. Of course, you have been fearless since the day you came out of mother's womb. Never once cried a drop. We thought something was wrong with you. Then you fed like a starved piglet."

"I know, I know, I know. How many times do I have to hear

that," Edrick asked, perturbed at his own baby stories.

"She told me about her dreams." Meghan said, changing her tone. She gave him a knowing wink and leaned close. "Let's sneak into the forest for lunch. The day is so brilliant, we can have a quick little picnic. It's been soooo long."

"Nearly a year…" Edrick said. Each word stuck to his tongue like tree sap. It had been a year since father's departure. No one spoke of their father's absence much because no one wanted to voice their fears. It hurt too much.

"Baldice and I have already been preparing."

Edrick nodded, but he had not been listening, thinking of where Father might be, if Father wished he were home as much as he did. Meghan waited for a response. "Really?" Edrick replied, shaking off his thoughts. "I was thinking I would have to trick you into it. I wanted to make up for Sunniva's fright. But what about Mother?"

Meghan put her finger to his lips and winked.

"I will tell her I will be meeting Halig and Eadwyn in the woods so I can look for more anstor and atorlathe, which is true enough. And after hearing what Udela reported, I can also mention that those two boys need supervision to ensure they gather the wood they owe. What's that make, five people now who have been demanding wood? Mother will be working for free through the end of spring and summer just to repay our debts."

"It's as if they don't care anymore," Baldice added. "Like they are angry Father hasn't returned and are not working to spite him. To punish him, it seems to me."

Meghan shook her head. They all wished Father was home, wondered in secret if he would ever come home.

"Halig has to snap out of it," Meghan said under her breath. "Go get Sunniva and meet me in the yard. We will follow in a bit."

Edrick jumped at the chance to visit the forest. They loved the woods as their parents loved the woods, and like anything a person loves, being told to part with it was an unbearable request.

He found Sunniva in his mother's apothecary alcove in the back of the cottage. It was in the great chamber of the sycamore hollow, away from main living space, giving mother enough room to work without having her children disturb her, so she said. But she welcomed them if they were quiet and could sit patiently until she acknowledged them, but they were certainly not allowed in the alcove alone, except perhaps for Meghan and Baldice.

The room was a place unlike any other in the village. It was an eclectic collection of clay jars of all shapes, sizes and colors, pots and containers of all sorts that stored a plethora of ingredients. Some very valuable and rare, worth more than gold, mother told them.

"How else would you value ingredients that can save a person's life? If that's not worth more than all the jewels in the world, than I don't know what is."

"Even a mountain of gold?" Edrick once asked.

"A mountain of gold is no compensation for our family's life. I hope you come to know that, Edrick."

Even rarer, placed high above the reach of children, Mother kept her beloved books and scrolls. Mother could actually read. Edrick never met another adult who could, with the exception of Auntie Elzera.

"Reading is a type of magick that turns fools to wise men," Mother often said.

Edrick on occasions, would observe his mother at work, grinding plants into powder, mixing then weighing this and that, blending and combining liquids of all colors into potions saturating the air with exotic redolence. Potions she did not use, she traded with foreign merchants for things the village needed, like cattle, cloth or other finished goods. She alone probably had more influence over the prosperity of the village than the village Elders, Edrick came to realize.

He found Sunniva sitting on a bench just inside the room, calmly petting the kitten, kissing it lightly on the nose and whispering in its ear.

"Hello, my little cub," Mother called from her work table. Her back was to him and Edrick wondered how she could always see behind her. "What did you get me?"

"Just three."

His mother clicked her tongue. "Well, that will have to do. How was Sunniva today?"

Edrick looked to his little sister who seemed intent on ignoring him now. "I scared her and she ran off."

"Oh, how?"

Edrick told her of the three faeries.

"Give her time, Edrick. She will take over trapping in a couple years, freeing you to spend more time with your brothers."

"We haven't had a lot of faeries lately. That is good, right? That means the bad faeries are staying away?"

His mother turned to him, wiping her hands on her apron. She lifted her curly raven-black hair from her face. It had yet to reveal a speck of silver strand, which was rare for a mother who has delivered six children. Her face too, reflected her sustained youth, though her eyes spoke of a deep understanding of many things left unnoticed to most.

"No, Edrick, it is not good. Good for a while. Good for farmers as they might get an idea we are no longer needed here. But this feels like when the sea withdraws a great distance exposing the sea floor to the open air. As if fleeing from something. Instead, it only gathers its strength and disaster follows. It is a bad omen."

Edrick had no clue what she was talking about, but often she talked aloud as if her children understood everything she said. The sea was so far away. Of course, Meghan would claim she understood exactly what mother said and that all the boys were as dumb as tree stumps, save for Baldice, possibly.

Meghan read Mother's books, much and often.

"Bad? Like how?" Edrick asked.

She looked at him, then Sunniva listening quietly. "Nothing to fear, son," but she smiled her fake smile. "Then again, you haven't learned to fear anything have you?"

"What is the point?"

Meghan walked in the room with the three faeries in her hand, prepared to be mashed and turned into faerie oil, however that process occurs. Meghan quickly walked out giving Edrick a knowing wink.

"Edrick, take your sister outside. She will not want to see this."

"But I don't want to go," Sunniva blurted out.

Mother walked over to Sunniva and picked her up, patting her on the back. "Baby, mother needs to work and you might not like it."

"Are you going to hurt the faeries, Mommy?" trying to look over their mother's shoulder to where Meghan laid down the faerie corpses.

"Hurt? No. We do not hurt these helpful creatures. We need them, like chickens and cows." She kissed Sunniva's head and put her down. "Now go with your brother for a little while."

"Yeah, let's feed Mathilda," Edrick offered, holding his hand out.

Sunniva nodded, pouting as she took his hand.

The two found Mathilda in the barn, resting on her hay bed. She was always here, unless one of the children decided to take her into the open air. She started bleating when they entered, always happy to be hand fed. Edrick and Sunniva sat next to her, one on each side. The barn was one of the best places to be in the village.

Sunniva fed Mathilda straw as Edrick looked on. He petted her neck, scratched her head adoringly.

"I wish we can take her into the woods."

"I don't think she would go."

"She would go if I went." Sunniva replied.

He did not argue. "She would not be happy."

"If Papa was here, she would be happy."

Edrick nodded and kissed her cheek.

She let him. They enjoyed a few moments in silence, petting Mathilda softly, feeding her until she was content.

"Come," Edrick said, getting up. "There's Meghan and Baldice."

The four withdrew from the house secretly as not to be seen by Mother, leaving the village by climbing over the Wall, instead of through the lychgate. As they reached the forest edge, they wandered back to the path that led to their cottage, but turned toward the woods instead.

Meghan led them, walking purposefully and swiftly with a woven basket tucked in the crook of her arm. She took in a deep breath and smiled. "To be so near the forest and catch portions of its fragrance without emerging yourself every once in a while is too much to bear. Sunniva, can you smell it, the forest?"

Sunniva took a few short rapid breaths, "MMMM!" she crooned. "I can taste it!"

The others laughed, but they could all taste it as well. The forest had its own smell, its own light, its own feel; different from any other place. It was good, like cool fresh water when one was parched, or the warmth of the sun after a passing rain storm.

"It is good medicine," their mother told them, to walk in the forest often. "Good for the mind as well, if one is open to learn from it."

"I love the spring time." Meghan continued. "The air is so warm and filled with the fragrance of the woods. All the forest speaks as the sun warms their leaves; the trees call out to one another, like visiting old friends after a long absence."

Soon after they entered, the familiar knocks of axes biting into wood echoed through the forest. They found Eadwyn and Halig not idle, but busy at work.

"This is a remarkable sight. My brothers have decided to help the family out today," Meghan declared as they emerged from the path.

The boys stopped and looked at Edrick, then Sunniva, who still held the little sleepy kitten in her arms.

"What are they doing here? Does mother know?" Halig asked, leaning on his ax.

"No, she does not know and you are not going to tell. Anyway, it looks like you two have been at it all morning. Why not have lunch with us by the Stones? Sunniva was begging to come into the woods. It's been too long…" her voice trailed off. There was a silent exchange between Halig and Meghan.

Edrick was a little surprised that their sister was actually breaking the rules for them.

"All right. Should be fine," Halig conceded. "We will go with you. There were some strange tracks I wanted to investigate near the Stones anyway."

"Are you sure you want them to go with us? They need to get this work done." Edrick interjected.

Meghan stopped to consider the point.

"I don't need your opinion about my affairs, Edrick." Halig snapped back, tossing the ax down.

"Come on," she said to Halig and Eadwyn, giving her consent. "We should at least stick together. It's late spring, our neighbors are not in dire need of firewood at the moment."

Edrick's older brothers left their axes behind, taking up their hunting bows and quivers. Somehow, after all their bickering, it did not take long before they were all talking and laughing, reminiscing about the times they spent on past summer days with Father and Mother beneath the daffodil sun and chalcedony skies. The entire forest seemed as if it were theirs alone. They could not imagine a world without the Wudelic. Mother joked that she and Father found them in the woods, abandoned by the faeries. They were born of the earth, conceived by faerie magick: boys, from combining tree sap with river mud, bits of acorns and woven reeds; girls, from honey and flower petals, dewdrops and spider silks.

Born into the world after the first spring snowmelt, brought forth by the returning warmth of the sun.

It was an unending musing, that they must truly be descendants of elves, living in banishment among the human world, living as peasants in payment to some obscure offense their grandfathers had committed long ago. Each one took turns explaining this story.

"Our grandfather was the world's greatest thief," Halig claimed, "and stole a dragon's treasure along with an elf princess's heart. So out of pride, the elf king banished him to a life of a woodcutter, vexed a commoner could so easily claim such wealth for himself."

"Yeah," said Eadwyn, who always agreed with his older brother, "and his grandfather was by far a more cunning thief than he, which is why the king needed to be so harsh with his punishment. Our grandfather's grandfather was so terrible that he brought harm upon the whole world, when at a time in the past all men lived as kings and would want for naught. Our grandfather's grandfather shrewdly took all their wealth and kept it for himself, which is why there are more peasants today, than there are kings. The elfin king was provoked with such a fury, he sent the dragons to strip our grandfather's grandfather of all his wealth. And that's how dragons came to accumulate their vast treasures."

"Aye, the two of you," came Meghan's exasperated voice, "how can you two call our sires thieves! That's horrible luck. You ought not to dishonor our family, even in stories."

"We're just saying what might have happened!" Eadwyn quickly defended.

"Hmph," Meghan tossed her auburn hair. She always acted as if she was the wise and reasonable one when amongst the older brothers. Eadwyn would claim she imitated her mother, poorly. But, she was as carefree as all the rest when she was in the right mood with the right company, which never seemed to be so when around Halig and Eadwyn.

"Grandfather," she continued in her forced, mature tone, "was an old spirit, a Dominion, from when time first blossomed. Out of the moist earth he sprang, meeting the sun by first morning light on the First Day of the world.

"The brilliant rays stung his eyes until they became wet. Despite the pain, he stood in awe of the light, tears rolling down his cheeks. From that time after, morning dew appears when the sun first rises. It does this in his memory.

"He walked the world for ages until weariness took hold of his body. He settled in these woods to regain his strength for it filled his heart with love. Out of all the world, these woods were more beautiful than all others he encountered on his endless travels. Not just because of the old oaks with their mossy beards who grew up with him, or the many birds who serenaded his favorite songs, but because he had a glimpse of the most beautiful creature he had ever gazed upon, dancing here in the faerie groves by moonlight and sunlight. She was a young maiden elf, who captured his heart, whom he married at dusk, under the company of both the sun and moon. Grandfather declared their children's beauty would surpass that of any elf, present or past and..."

"What about the future?" Edrick interrupted.

"He could not speak of the future," Meghan was quick to reply, shooting Edrick an annoyed glare, then continued her reverie, "...and would bring great joy into the world for the love that would flow from their hearts. Yet the elf king, his bride's father, feared his grandchildren would usurp his throne for they would be half-gods. So the king banished grandfather from the woods, separating him from his bride. His saddened heart found no pleasure in the world outside the woods. Yet, by nature of his being he could not perish, instead he withered over time, diminished into the form of an old man.

"Time passed and he met another woman, kind and compassionate, who took care of him first out of pity, then by love. By all accounts he lived as an old man, though he would take to the woods in disguise on whimsy, but never again caught site of his lost love."

"That's so sad," said Sunniva. Her pudgy young face drooped as she walked along behind the rest, holding onto Baldice's hand. The kitten now rested across her shoulder.

"That was a great story." Edrick proclaimed, approvingly.

"That's just like our story too!" Eadwyn resentfully pointed out. He always spoke of *we*, meaning he and Halig.

"It's nothing like your story of thieves," came Meghan's retort.

"It's quite the contrary."

"You make grandfather sound like the Brownman of the Woods," Halig observed.

"Yeah, that's why I liked your story, Meghan," Edrick replied before Meghan could refute Halig's claim.

Edrick listened to all their stories with great intent. He loved stories more than most anything else. He swung a stout branch he found earlier as if it were a sword magically forged by fey smiths. Every tree he met got whacked, testing both his skill as a swordsman and the tenacity of the improvised weapon.

"Baldice, do you think our family came from the woods?" Edrick asked.

Baldice kept silent as he walked Sunniva down the path. "We were never elves," he said, his voice ever stolid and reserved. He never seemed to enjoy the woods like the rest, Edrick noticed. He was far happier at home helping their mother with the household chores. Edrick always thought he was his mother's favorite, if only because out of all the boys, he sought out her company almost exclusively. When in the woods, Baldice seemed to make it his job to look after little Sunniva, while Edrick and the rest played and carried on, without the burden of watching her. Baldice tried acting like that with Edrick too, vigilant of his every movement. But as Edrick grew older, he let everyone know he could take care of himself.

"Mother told me why she loves the woods. She grew up here, or near here," he said as he looked around, taking in his surroundings. He wanted to be precise with his words. "Her family was misplaced after the Folthnir invaded and overran their estate. They settled north of our village, near the Ruined Tower. Grandmother brought her to our village because of the trails that led into the forest. She met Father because his family once lived in the woods as well, and they married."

"Wow, great story. The mystery is solved," cried Eadwyn. He took every opportunity to voice his annoyance with his shy and quiet brother.

"Besides," Meghan put in, "we were talking of Father's side, not Mother's. What of his grandfather?"

Baldice remained passive for a moment as if waiting for the answer to reach his lips. "Father seldom speaks of his family." After a few moments, while they continued through the forest, breaking the shafts of sunlight beneath the boughs, they knew Baldice had said all he was going to say.

"What about you, Edrick?" asked an annoyed Eadwyn. "You are sure to tell five different accounts about our family's origins. Here is your opportunity to share at least one while we are all listening."

Edrick smiled then sliced the air with his sturdy branch, carving a figure eight horizontally then vertically, flourishing his armament with the fidelity only a child could portray. He already had his story in mind when the conversation first began.

"Have you guys ever heard of the Woodcutter King?" Edrick asked coyly.

"Yes, yes! I want to hear more," Sunniva blurted out.

"Of course," Meghan teased. "We are royalty, in hiding. But we should not speak openly of it, lest our enemies hear our secrets," she concluded in a whisper.

"I just asked if you guys heard of the story." Edrick said, annoyed, and then whacked a large oak branch overhanging the trail, loosening its acorns upon those behind him. Sunniva let out a girlish shriek, and Baldice ducked, covering his head. Meghan, wise in her years, stopped abruptly, letting the assault pass in front of her.

"Sithric is dead, or gone; no one really knows of his fate," Edrick continued.

"He's dead as all his men," Eadwyn pronounced with finality. He always reported who died or became hurt in the village, and with such disturbing enthusiasm.

"Who died, Baldice?" asked Sunniva suddenly concerned, working to understand the conversation.

"The king," came his succinct reply.

"Oh," said Sunniva, still confused. She looked to Meghan for further explanation, but none came. "Which king?" she peeped.

"Hey," came Halig's voice from ahead, "we are here."

The winding forest opened into a small clearing where the pines and oaks retreated, allowing small patches of wild fraxinella and yarrow to bloom beneath the open sunlight. Songbirds darted and spiraled through the open space, alarmed by the sudden intrusion of their secluded sanctuary. The children fanned out behind Halig who stood at the end of the trail, scanning the surroundings, as was his usual habit. The others remained quiet, simply listening to the forest, taking in its demeanor.

Today, the lazy wind had not stirred even to lift a dandelion seed, and the flowers overwhelmed them all with their redolence.

Near center of the field stood the remnants of granite stone monoliths arranged by some ancient hand in the order of a circle. The children called it the Stones. They stood rigid, some taller than their cottage roof, but most no higher than an adult, rough-hewn and worn through the ages by wind and rain.

Huddled within the shadows of the stone grew large toadstools with saucer size tops, forming an inner circle.

"The most critical part of its protection," according to Meghan.

For she explained to them that the elves raised the stones, as is their custom, to work the bones of the earth and call upon its power. But the faeries too, granted their power by calling upon the other benign forest spirits. She claimed that no evil could penetrate the circle, but Eadwyn and Halig never put complete faith in their sister's lore. For them, the woods seemed less of a home of the fey than the sanctuary of predators who stalked the flourishing woodland. The trees and bushes screened what would otherwise be plain and open. Here, animals found refuge and a bounty of food; and predators, their prey. Their father's lore differed from their mother's, he taught them to read the land and observe the animals as a scholar studies books.

Halig and Eadwyn moved forward, eyes sweeping the tangled grass blades for hints of animal tracks. Their hidden glade seemed undisturbed, as was how they always found it, but Halig always needed to be sure with his own senses. Their father taught them that the woods are never the same twice; it changes over time. So those who entered had to be aware.

For Edrick, his father's warning was but another story meant to scare young ones. The woods were always the same: lots of trees, lots of animals, lots of birds.

But the Stones; the stone circle was intriguing. Different from anything built in the village and that fascinated him. He wondered what other surprises lay off the familiar forest paths.

It was this clearing, with its mysterious Stones that the children claimed for themselves, away from their parents, away from the other villagers and the labor required to live.

Here they became faerie kings and faerie queens, attending their feasts of wine and elfin bread, commanding all they surveyed.

Meghan and Sunniva wove crowns of flowers for all. Edrick and Baldice were the only boys that would condone to their sisters' feminine adornment. Baldice, never complained about anything and was pleased to indulge in his sisters' fancies, while Edrick could take any object and transform it into a thing of his imagination. For him, he bore a heavy crown of gold, studded with diamonds and other gems, treasures which he had never seen but had heard from tales spun by his mother. It slumped low on his brow, not because Meghan used her head to model its size, but because no other king could display the wealth contained in his bejeweled headdress. He proudly strutted across the field, chasing the covetous bees from their flowers, while his sisters came behind and plucked their prize of petals.

Baldice sat alone, crowned in flowers, as he watched the others play out their alternate forest identities. Edrick and his sisters tried to get him to join their royal court, but Baldice never seemed to want to be more than who he was at home. Halig and Eadwyn however, thought themselves as great hunters who practiced their woodcraft away from their frivolous siblings. Halig became their protector.

After Halig walked the clearing's perimeter, he and Eadwyn disappeared into the trees, seeking out game and checking their woodland faerie traps. Edrick knew they never wandered out of shouting distance, or at least not Halig. Eadwyn was not as concerned with the others and took the opportunity to wander farther than his elder brother, hoping to capture a trophy worthy of boast. Edrick would sometimes join them, but following Halig's orders all the time severely restricted his ability to have fun. So he remained with his sisters, and with Baldice, despite their treating him like a fellow princess.

When the three had finally settled next to Baldice, who was now laying in the deep grass, they were in splendid moods and full of laughter. Baldice remained impassive, gazing into the sky, observing the lazy clouds drifting high above.

Meghan pulled out bread from her picnic basket. The four began their woodland feast of bread, creamy butter, wild berry jam and golden honey. Edrick passed around a leather flask filled with berry juice, sweetened further by his mother's secret ingredients collected from southern caravans. In that moment, the four could not have been any more content.

"How about a story Meghan?" suggested Edrick.

"Oh yes," shouted an excited Sunniva. "Kitty wants to hear about the Woodcutter King. Mother has never told us that one."

"That's because it's actually a story Father told us."

"What?" Sunniva asked in astonishment. "Papa never tells any stories."

"Well, he does, if you are out in the woods with him, at night, by the fire. He has one or two he likes to share. But around Mother he stays quiet, only because I think he enjoys her tales as much as we do. I think it relaxes him, like how Mother holds you in her arms before you fall asleep."

"Yeah," added Edrick, "he always works on his wood carvings during Mother's stories. All your toys came from Father sitting and listening to Mother speak."

"Oh, I never knew that. I will ask Papa to tell me stories too!"

Meghan began placing the jam and plates away in her basket. "Well, I really don't know it half as well as Mother, and she says she doesn't tell it half as well as Father, so it might sound quite inadequate. Father never tells us stories when we request it, only when he is in the mood." Sunniva pouted her lips, disappointed at her sister's discouraging remarks. "But," she continued, "possibly his youngest baby girl might change his mind. You seem quite able to get things from him that is far out our reach."

"Yeah," added Edrick slightly resentful, "you're their favorite. They think you're still a baby."

Baldice smiled, as if he too conspired with his parents, sharing their profuse adoration for Sunniva.

"Oh, Edrick, don't tell her that," Meghan said taking on her mother persona. "The youngest ones are always the target of affection in any family. When you grow older you don't need constant kisses from your parents, it's actually quite annoying, and embarrassing in the company of others. I'm surprised you still feel that way, at your age."

Annoyed, Edrick was quick to move on with it. "Can you just tell us the story?" No one asked for your opinions, he thought.

"All right, the Woodcutter King. Well, long ago there was a king who faced an overwhelming enemy with a vast army. The king, no longer able to find refuge in his besieged castle, fled into the forest, fearing not for his life, or acting a coward, but because he sought the aid of the elves. On his journey through the woods, he stopped by an old woodcutter's hut and asked for aid. The woodcutter quickly recognized the king and hastily took him in.

"Now the woodcutter's wife was a practical woman, to a fault and feared the hunted king would bring about their deaths as well, should they provide shelter for him. So she plotted to kill the dethroned monarch.

"She demanded a reward first in exchange for their help. The king had naught but his sole possessions: a crown, a scepter, and a ring marking his royal heritage. He gladly gave these to the woodcutter and promised to make him nobility should he help guide him to the faerie realms. Astonished, the woodcutter refused the royal gifts, but his wife scolded him for his foolishness and instead dressed her husband in the king's garb.

"She then convinced the king to dress as the woodsman, so his enemies would fail to recognize him, and thereby, succeed in his escape. The king gracefully agreed as well. Then off the two journeyed, the king and woodsman, walking toward the faerie realms.

"The woodsman brought the king to a faerie circle, quite like this," indicating the granite ruins, "and instructed the king to wait till dusk for their appearance. Then the two said farewell and the woodcutter departed.

"Unfortunately, the woodsman, dressed as the king, came upon the enemies, was slain, and then robbed of his treasures. The king fared no better, for at dusk when the faeries arrived, they laughed and mocked him, refusing to allow a peasant trample their land, and left him alone.

"Angered and feeling foolish, the king traveled back to the woodcutter's hut and along the way, he discovered the woodcutter's body assaulted and stripped bare. He realized the woodsman meant no harm, and blamed his treacherous wife.

"He took up the woodsman's ax and entered the hut once again, then chopped the evil wife's head clean off her shoulders."

Sunniva gave a gasp and looked at Edrick in shock, looking for consolation, but found only a grinning brother taking pleasure in both the story and his sister's distress.

"That's a horrible story. I don't like it," complained Sunniva. Edrick let out a laugh, taking pleasure in her childish sensibilities. "What happened to the poor king?" She asked trying to ignore

Edrick's laughter.

Meghan shrugged her shoulders. "Father's story always ended there. He said the meaning of the story is not in what happened after the end, but in what actually took place."

Sunniva though, visibly objected to that conclusion. "But..." Meghan continued, drawing out her sister's frustration, "Mother would add her own ending." She paused again, absently braiding her curly auburn hair across her left shoulder. "The king had no other choice but to live as a woodcutter, for everyone he knew had fallen by his enemies' sword, and he had no army to redress his injuries and injustice. He eventually gained the trust of the elves, who came to know him only as the simple man for which his woodcutter appearance suggested, though he possessed the bearing and manners of a noble. They taught him their wood-lore and he married a village maiden and had a family."

"Yes, that sounds better," concluded Sunniva approvingly, smiling so big it almost outshined the sun.

"I've added my own ending," Edrick interjected, hoping someone would ask him what it was, but continued anyway before soliciting any responses. "His wife was of course an elfin princess, whom he had every right to marry, but the elfin king did not see it that way. The elfin king could not see beyond the trappings of a woodcutter, a mortal commoner not fit to join his family. So he removed his kingdom from this world into the faerie realm where the woodcutter could not follow, taking the elfin princess with him. The woodcutter was alone, save for his twenty-one children."

"Twenty-one?" asked Meghan startled at the enormous amount.

"Yes, twenty-one, because all of his children made it through childbirth and eventually grew old. And the Woodcutter King made all his sons swear vengeance, not just on the men that overthrew his kingdom, but also those elves that had insulted his honor."

"Oh, Edrick, you're almost as bad as the other boys."

"I wonder if we know any of the Woodcutter King's children," Sunniva said innocently. "Do you think they live around here? I should like to meet them."

"Unfortunately, most his children and grandchildren perished, because a man such as the Woodcutter King eventually found new followers to rule and made new enemies who assassinated his children before they gained their own strength. Eventually, all the sons remained in hiding until they could claim their lost heritage."

"What is *heritage*?" Sunniva asked with her best inquisitive face.

"Your legacy; what is passed down to you from your parents. Something that is shared by the entire family. Like our knowledge of the forest. No other family knows it like we do."

"Ohhhh," Sunniva expressed in a tone that signaled her understanding, despite the confused look hanging about her face.

"Well said, beautiful child," spoke a new voice, heavy with dread, deep like mountain roots. A voice that did not belong there, in that place of peace.

Meghan jumped, spine snapped rigid like a bowstring.

And like that, the children no longer found themselves alone.

In that striking moment, they realized the woods were not what they once remembered.

8

THE ALVINI

THE GREEN PILLAR of light that was the Old One evaporated into the darkness, darkness that now clung to Alaric's wakened eyes.

Three shadowy figures surrounded him. The one wielding the knife pulled at his torc, lured by the three intertwining wires of gold, silver and copper. The man fumbled at it roughly, pulling at it hard, but it could not be removed unless Alaric willed it.

Another dark figure held Alaric's left arm. "It is no jewel!" he said, grasping at the éardian. It was like catching a cloud. "Slit his throat fast, lest he be some Eldritch or sorcerer."

A third person emptied the contents of his pack, picking through the mess scattered across the ground.

"He wears some jewelry around his neck," said the first man with the knife. His finger lifted a chain that connected the torc in front of Alaric's throat. Three triangle pieces of metal, also gold, silver and copper, hung from the chain. "It's silver and gold if it be anything. Arrowheads or something the like. But there is some trick to removing it."

Alaric remained still, unsure of what action to take. The robber with the knife noticed Alaric's shifting eyes and smiled cruelly.

"Forget this one!" said the one inspecting Alaric's hand. "I want no trouble with his kind, but I will take this," he said as he seized Alaric's bow. But as he turned to leave, the bow shook violently in his hand, startling the figure and drawing the others attention.

"It's bewitched!" said the man, dropping the weapon. "Kill

him!"

A blue crackling light erupted from the éardian, flowing over Alaric's body, taking the three bandits by surprise. Each figure became outlined in blue flame for but a flashing moment.

Alaric seized the hand holding the knife against his throat. The two began to wrestle over the ground, attempting to control it. The two were well matched in strength but Alaric knew he was at a great disadvantage and tried to keep the other two's movements in sight.

One found his great ax and stood over them.

"Kick him off and I will bury this in his chest!"

"He's holding onto me, you shit bastard," said the man Alaric wrestled.

The third man dove onto Alaric as well, throwing his arms around Alaric's neck attempting to choke him. The torc made that task difficult.

"Knife him fast! We will remove his head and take the gold!" called the one behind him.

Just then a flicker of light caught Alaric's eye in the air above them, then the one with ax cried out and spun around, slashing the air behind him. When no attacker appeared the man cried to his companions, "I've been knifed! There is someone else here!"

The two men who pinned Alaric down did not relax their hold and continued the fight.

Then the axman gave another loud shriek, releasing the weapon. "I've been knifed! I've been knifed! There is some foul magick here!" He ran off into the empty plains.

Seeing the man retreat bolstered Alaric's resolve. He kicked and pulled at the two bandits. Then there were two more flashes of light in the darkness and the man choking Alaric jumped up with a great yelp and ran after his companion without another word.

Alaric thought quickly, "Your friends have sense to run. Now you will suffer my Eldritch wrath!" With that, the man shoved Alaric off him and fled into the dark. Alaric rolled to his bow and seized it while his free hand searched the ground for arrows. All his possessions were scattered across the grass, he could not find his quiver fast enough.

"Damn!" he yelled out. His bow trembled eagerly in his hands. "Damn! DAMN!"

He sent his éardian a yard above him, willing it to burst forth with light, illuminating the ground.

But it was too late. By the time he found just one arrow, the bandits had been swallowed by the contemptuous night.

Alaric gathered his belongings quickly, finding a candle in his pack and lit it. The candle flame danced to life. Between the candle and his éardian, Alaric found the rest of his arrows and then repacked his possessions. Everything was accounted for, luckily.

He also discovered a phantom knife stuck in the ground. Once freed, he held it up and looked it over. The metal was strange, containing swirling patterns of iridescent lines over the surface. Its edge was immensely sharp. No doubt the weapon was quite valuable. Alaric wrapped it in loose linen and tucked it beneath his belt. He gathered his effects then walked to the immense trunk of mathelian. He stopped on the side facing the northern road, in sight of the merchant campfire. Despite the great ache in his feet, he stood guard against the expansive trunk as if he were a part of the tree, eyes open and wary, his ax and bow remained at hand.

He closed his eyes, but he found no rest for what remained of that night. He ran his fingers over his torc wondering, not for the last time, what secret it held. He remained alert, but rested his mind, letting it drift where it may.

A familiar voice spoke to him in esoteric words, a hidden voice. The Old One spoke of the bandits and how they hacked at him at night. They were hateful men that spilled blood on his roots for years, long before Alaric left his mother's womb. The three that assaulted Alaric were from a larger gang that has stalked the Crossroads for only a year. One bandit gang drives out another. Then the northern lords occasionally send armed men to flush out the thieves but they always returned.

"But there was someone else in the night. Someone who saw me struggle and came to my aid. Who was it?" Alaric asked.

Another traveler. They come from the far south but stay long in the North. They do not speak with me but I sense they know something of the mathelian trees. It is my belief they do not possess tree speech.

"Then in gratitude, I would teach it to him."

They are a secretive people, though I have not seen evil in them. As you saw, they are noble and do not abide hurtful violence. Even so, they are not open to others and would not be open to me either.

My guess is that they would be highly interested in the knowledge contained within me, yet would be reluctant to reciprocate.

"But Old One, who could know more than you. You are a wonder!"

But even until just a while ago, I knew not what the sea tasted like, old though I am. There is so much more for me learn. So much of the world that is beyond these heavy limbs.

Alaric wondered how much there is to know in the world, how much one could learn. How far back does knowledge stretch? When was the world worth knowing?

"Old One. Do I pray to gods that do not listen? Are the Eshenar still worth remembering?"

They hear you, same as I hear you. To most, I am just a tree. To those that listen, I am something more. Remember that and you will not lose your way.

Alaric shook his head. "My way was lost before I was born, but still I follow the path my sires laid for me. The path I ask my sons to follow."

And if you did not follow this path, what path would you take?

"The one not taken."

The mathelian laughed, a strange hollow thumping sound, reverberating like a heavy drum.

Well at least you have a path, a route your feet can travel. My fate is unalterable, beyond me to affect. Too many of my brothers and sisters have I seen taken at the end of an ax. All I could do was watch. Watch and hope. There was a time I hated those that walked on two feet or four, envied those that could attend the anguished cries of their own flesh, as mine were ripped from the ground. But such bleak thoughts must be shed if one is to find purpose outside of suffering. And there is more to this world than its suffering.

"I am sorry, I did not mean to offend..."

You have not, pupil. We all have boundaries and barriers. Crumble under them and you are just a man, same as any other. Explore them and you will be great. Surmount them and you will be enlightened.

"I do not know if you can understand. Honor is my boundary; to abandon it would be my ruin. The first of my family to betray their oaths."

I do not understand. I know honor, but I do not understand

how it burdens some men to point of ruin. Honor is a strength, if dishonor remains loathsome. Live the best way you know how, Alaric, that is honor above all else. I have seen many seasons and a thousand, thousand sunsets. Men rise and fall like leaves scattered before the autumn wind, lost to the endless horizon. Your time is now. Often, the fruit of a tree grows best in new soil estranged of their sires. Is the soil of your forbearers the best for your sons and daughters?

Alaric did not respond immediately. The head of Telanthyan, a constellation of a dragon of such immensity, its entire body could only be viewed over four seasons, its tail swallowed by it gaping maw. The stars that constituted its eye no longer burned fierce in the black sky. The sun was returning, lightening the air with another promised day to come.

I know your thoughts. You are afraid of severing your history.

"I already have plans to leave my home, but out of necessity."

Then there is your path. Sire a new line of honorable men and women, be it humble and not the prestige you desire it to be.

"We will see, Old One."

The merchant camp stirred now as dawn approached. They would be on the road soon. Alaric would best depart before they all took to the road, less they think he followed them.

"Your words have given me much to consider." Alaric replied, lifting his bow onto his shoulder. He craned his neck taking in the wondrous tree, wondering if he truly would see it again. "I will continue to search for other mathelians. I hope dearly you are not the last."

He walked out onto the road under the wary eyes of the merchant guards. The whiff of food cooking in the early morning air sent his stomach in revolt. Alaric has had nothing but acorns, dried salted meat and the occasional squirrel to quell his hunger in the last two weeks. His strength had all but abandoned him and last night's fight took what remained.

His legs went to mush before the sun was high, but he willed them to move. More and more he leaned on his ax, aging a year with every stride home. He could beg for some cart to carry him. No! That would shame his father's spirit, his grandfather's spirit. His ancestors would take their shame out on his sons and their sons.

The occasional traveler would stare hard at Alaric. Never seen a

Woodcutter from Gheldenmark, he thought proudly. Men are strong in the North, indomitable in the Mark.

"How far to Gheldenmark?" he began chanting to each traveler. Most moved away from him. They treated him like he was plagued. "How far to the Gheldenmark?" he asked another man. Alaric grabbed him by the shoulders, leaning on him as his knees buckled. "How far?" Alaric demanded.

The stranger easily shoved Alaric to the ground, where he collapsed, dropping his ax and bow. He crawled around the dirt gathering them up as people took wide berths around him.

"That light, why don't you extinguish it? It is unsettling." Someone asked. Another kicked dirt on him.

"It is my éardian, my ghost-light. It is a part of me, no different than my face or my beating heart." Alaric found his strength to stand, but he could not identify the speaker. His vision blurred under the stinging sun. Whenever he closed his eyes, his body wished for sleep.

"Then cover it up." Suggested another.

"I will not," Alaric said sharply. "It is not something I am ashamed of or requires concealment. People must take me as I am or not."

The light of the Sun seared him. Is it summer? No, no, Alaric shook his head, shook off the closing aperture of lucidity. It is still spring. But the light seemed so bright. Alaric looked toward the sky that was no longer blue, but washed out whiteness. The world was out of focus. Alaric squinted, or blinked. He thought. But the rushing blackness told him he had not the strength to open his eyes.

Alaric took a step, but it was as if the ground moved from beneath his feet and he fell. He hit the compacted dirt. The road stole his breath and sight. He laid there waiting for his strength to return. Footsteps moved hastily away, some stepped on him. Some laughed at him.

He closed his eyes. His strength finally betrayed him.

He awoke in a moving world, of rattling and gyrations. He was in a wagon filled with strange things, piled on stacked shelves, trunks, and containers of all size and build, stuffed into every nook all the way to the ceiling. Not a single empty space was spared of having something occupying it. He was in a bed, in a cabin he guessed built on a cart. Besides the busy mess that surrounded him, it was the strange smells that captured his attention. He sat up and the odor changed, acidic now, like a vinegar pine and effusion of spice and medicines. Alaric hit his head on the bed just above. He winced and rolled off his mattress into a narrow aisle. The smell on the floor was now a mix of ancient dirt and vapid flower petals. He pulled his knees to his chest, trying to steady himself in the constant rocking motion.

Something about the smell told him he is not in danger, but he still felt vulnerable not knowing where he was going and who it was that took him. He searched immediately for his bow, which was at hand, along his ax, leaning against the corner by the colorfully painted door of bright orange, leaf green and apple red.

He then groped at his neck where his torc still rested. He relaxed a little knowing he had not been robbed.

The wagon slowed to a stop. Alaric listened, placing one foot on the floor. Wait, he has seen this kind of wagon before. He scanned the cabin again. Yes, filled with an eclectic collection of tradable goods. He was in an Alvini wagon.

So either he was saved from the road or being saved for Alvini ruffians. You could never tell the intentions of these people.

A whip cracked outside and the wagon slowed to a stop. "You nasty, lazy beasts! Agh! I could tie my harness to a rock and expect more travel farther, faster!" Crack!

"Hello!" Alaric shouted. He took his great ax in hand.

"Ah, you are awake!" an old woman's voice answered back. Alaric relaxed a bit. "Well, come on out, Alaric! I'm not getting off my bench just to say 'hello.' We have a long ways to go before we get you home."

No, it can't be, Alaric thought. He opened the door and hurried out, still clinging to his weapon. The world was not what he remembered. The open and flat plains were now wild green hills crowding around him like grassy huts. Could he be closer to home, he hoped. He approached the driver, with caution, looking around to see if there was someone else other than the speaker.

"Oh, come on, Alaric. Old women don't bite, not this one anyway. But I did when I was younger!" She laughed to herself, giddily.

A woman of the same age of his mother, had she been alive, sat alone on the bench, whip in hand and smile on her face. Her silvered hair flowed like a waterfall along her shoulders in thick curls that took years off her age. She wore colorful garb marking her of another land, white blouse with geometric designs and a dark skirt. Wrapped around her shoulders was a matching colorful shawl.

"Elzera!" Alaric said to himself, breathless as his arms relaxed. He looked at the wagon. He did not notice before, but he recognized her Alvini wagon better from the exterior than the interior.

"Aye, lad it is I, the great and profitable Alvini, Elzera of Zorovia. Hey, but I don't really mention Zorovia to strangers. Bad country that is."

"How could you have found me? How did you find me?!"

"It was not difficult to find a man with a glowing orb, passed out in the middle of the most traveled road of all of Mithledor. No secret there!"

"What happened? Where are we?"

"I am sure you have many questions, but I am not going to answer them all right now!" she said, scolding him like he were an inquisitive child. "First, your family is alive and well, at least they were when I left them months ago. Hard travel it is now to get back in that country."

Alaric opened his mouth to talk, but the Alvini silenced him with a stern glare. "Elisial sent me to search for you nine months ago! Nine months have I been ignoring my business and traveling up and down these roads searching for you Alaric, or rumor of you. And right when I was losing hope, there you were, passed out like a dumb drunken peasant in the middle of the road. Gods bless me!"

"We are well on our way home, Alaric. I'm keeping my promise to Elisial, now that I found you, and I would make sure you don't die on me on our return. Here." She threw him a sack that was at her side. Alaric opened it. His eyes stretched wide at the sight of apples, bread and butter wrapped in wax paper.

"Now go back inside, eat until your stomach hurts and go back to sleep. We will be entering Gheldenmark in a couple days. Rest more. I want you to take over these damn mules after you recovered your strength. Hate these stubborn beasts." She yelled at the animals, cracking the whip several times, but the two mules seemed immune to her wrath.

"Thank you, Auntie. Are you sure my family is well?"

Elzera did not speak immediately, worry was plain in her eyes. "We will talk when you have had more rest, I promise Alaric." Her voice was now kind and subdued. "Go inside and when you awake, we will be very near."

Alaric nodded. There was little more he could do. He believed they were close to Gheldenmark. He must have been asleep for a while. The road had been rough on him. This whole journey had worn on him, but that did not matter for he would see his family sooner than he could have hoped.

He returned to the cabin and closed the door. They were quickly under way. Alaric smiled for the first time in months as he stared at fresh food and the promise he would be with family soon.

After he ate, he slept, deep and safely. If he dreamed he did not remember them, or cared, for his heart dreamed only of his family, and very soon he would know how they fared.

Elzera woke him the next evening to share dinner. Outside, a campfire was already cooking a pair of rabbits. "I think you have had enough sleep, young man. Now, I think I will have a rest after dinner, and let you drive us through the night."

"I would happily drive your cart home, but can your mules endure it?"

"Bah, since when do you care about the horse kind? Ugly mules. Stupid beasts! Not all mules, just these two. Drive them until they pass out in the road. You seem to know something about that."

They ate in silence. A decent meal was rare and Alaric savored every juicy rabbit bone, taking care to suck the marrow before he tossed them into the night. Elzera stared at him the entire time, having finished her meal much sooner.

"I see it written all over your face, Alaric, the burden of a man that takes on more than his share. A strong man tested, enduring only to be thrown in the middle of adversity again and again. Well, for now, a respite. I am glad to see you gain your strength, your appetite."

"Thank you, Auntie."

"Bah," she waived his sentimentality away. "I only fed you so I can put you to work."

Alaric laughed. Elzera chuckled too.

"Always cherished these moments, Alaric. When we can laugh. I will take my rest now." She stood to retire. "Be sure to clean up," she waggled her finger, "all this."

"Before you go, tell me what you have heard of Gheldenmark.

You said you have not been there for nine months?"

Elzera released a heavy breath that seemed decades old and sat back down.

"Athéalgian was overran after a siege that lasted many months. The Folthnir have swept through the land like a blasting arctic wind."

"Then King Sithric finally failed." Alaric's shoulders sunk, the light in his eyes darkened to match the night.

"Yes. Unfortunately, it is the news of the land," she sighed.

"Then my efforts have been for nothing." Alaric gazed into the dancing fire. He kicked the burning timbers, scattering sparks across the ground. "I spoke with the village Elders, and they urged me to find a safe route away from danger, 'If the worse befall us and we are forced to flee.' Only they are fools and would not leave until the Folthnir were in sight of the village. Then it would be too late and I fear they would suffer at their hands."

"I have heard it is too late. No merchant dare travel north into the Gheldenmark. No one has taken the far northern road for months."

Alaric said nothing more.

"Prepare yourself now. Your journey is not nearing its end, I am sorry to tell you." She left him to his thoughts. Alaric stamped the fire out until only the blue glow of his éardian remained. It burned furiously brighter than the flames ever did.

Night turned to day, then night, and more days. They passed many villages and towns as they made their way closer to Gheldenmark. Alaric drove the wagon for most of the journey, insisting that he work his way home. Elzera feigned being insulted, that even as a family friend he still must labor in order to earn her favor. But she protested very little having a very bad relationship with the two stubborn mules.

"Last mules I'll purchase. Well actually, they were given to me to repay a debt. What a fool's deal that turned out to be. The woman was probably happy to be rid of them. I need a couple of old Lord Temen's beasts. What fine horses they are."

Most of their conversation over the last few days was spent listening to Elzera vent her frustrations as Alaric quietly and politely listened, nodding at appropriate places. Catching up between the two friends took about half a day. The other days consisted of Elzera's many gripes about slow, stubborn mules, people's mistrust of magick and being accused of witchery.

"A witch!" She bristled beneath her scarf, now shading her from the sun. "As if I were one of those devious, baby-eating wenches. People might as well call donkeys, horses, if that is as much they pay attention to the world around them."

Alaric knew the subject was a sensitive issue. Most the villagers from Athelyn suspected her of witchcraft as well. His wife wasn't above rumors or suspicions either, though most would never speak such accusations near his ears.

Elzera seemed aware of Alaric's silence for the first time. "Sorry, Alaric, for running my mouth the way I have. It's just been such a long time since I had someone to share the road. And if one of us is going to play the silent gloomy part, it ought to be me. I am equally worried about your family. But just know, whatever has come to pass, if it be ill news, it was not your making. You have done more than your share for your village, be they thankful or not. You make your family proud."

"Had I not been delayed I might have been able to return home before the siege overtook King Sithric."

"Fortune has never favored the Woodcutters," she answered solemnly.

Alaric placed his hand over his torc and prayed to the Dragon Spirits, the Eshenar. "Deliver my family safely into my arms, and allow me vengeance to any that have caused them harm."

Deep in his soul, he knew it was a moot prayer, for as long as his family served Lhodyn, the Old God's abandon his prayers, though he did not abandon them. It is who he was.

On the ninth day since Alaric set out from the Crossroads, the gentle rolling hills transitioned into higher and higher bluffs and encroaching pine forests marched down into the valleys. Granite outcroppings jutted forward like rugged bastions of the wild, marking the end of Mithledor and southern border of the Mark.

One evening they found a familiar camp used by travelers along the north road, an outcropping of rock that served as natural shelter. They stopped for the night and Alaric built another fire. The two sat in silence as they ate their evening meal.

"How did you fair on your errand?" Elzera asked cautiously. Alaric never spoke of his travels once, only sharing stories of his family in better times. He knew she would get around to asking him.

"I found a fair and good kingdom. Lathiélden is my choice for my people."

Elzera nodded in agreement. "I should think Lathiélden would be easily reached through the Wudelic if the forest paths are still open to travel."

"Those were my thoughts as well, and I took to that road nine full moons ago. I had thought my journey would take but three months and I would return by the previous summer's end. We would have had arrived in Lathiélden before last year's snows settled on us, had I not been delayed."

"So what news you have?"

"The Folthnir are not the only shadows cast across our land. Something has stirred in the forest for some time and I had my suspicions as to what might be the cause. I had a dual purpose traveling through the Wudelic. One, to secure a reliable path for refugees if it came to such a desperate course. But second, to discover what source of the dark rumors I heard whispered in the trees for the past year.

"I was sure the safest and most secure route out of our lands was through Wudelic, but that now proves to be false. The forest, though wild and dangerous in its own way, is now plagued with foreign infiltrators, those of which have not been in this land for ages. I was but a week in my travel when I came upon signs of foul creatures lurking about, residing deep within the forest. I traveled farther toward the mountains, terrain men seldom travel, and encountered forest spirits filled with anguish. The feeling there in the deep woods was all twisted and deceitful, as if there were a foul secret being kept yet not willing to reveal itself. Such a feeling provoked my curiosity. It was then I fell across a band of goblyns."

"Goblyns!" Elzera cried, spitting on the ground. She made the sign of Zarya, goddess of the Morning Star in her lands, gatekeeper of dawn.

"Yes. Grim, evil folk who pursued me relentlessly through the entire length of the forest. I slept a little in the midday light and took to foot by night, or else I would not be telling you this tale today. A few times they waylaid me and I slew them, and by luck escaped. But they raged and pursued me in wrath. The forest is infested with these cruel creatures and I believe that is not the worse, though I could not say for certain what else lay hidden there."

"What of Lhodyn? How can she suffer these indignities?"

"It troubled my mind too and has weighed heavily on my heart throughout my entire journey. In those desperate times when the goblyns came on me I called to Her, begging for aid but She failed to reveal Herself.

"It was only the forest itself that led me to safety. Perhaps Aeyah, the Dragon Spirit of the woods, stirred from her slumber and heard my pleas. I spoke to the birds and they guided me correctly through winding paths. I gathered information from the deer, discovering where the goblyns camped. The trees were unhappy and cried for justice, but I found none there. For deep in the woods I discovered the most disturbing tragedy, a grove of mature mathelians hewed down, long, long ago."

"An entire grove of mathelian trees? Such a thing has not been heard of since time immemorial. How many?"

"Nine beautiful trees, growing in the most perfect circle, near a bubbling fountain at the feet of the mountains, hidden between a fold in the hills. Would I had the time, I would have spent a season searching that country for their like, but it seems bleak. No creature heard rumor of its kind growing anywhere."

"Utterly unfortunate. How could such wonders just slip off the face of the world? It is an unkind tragedy, not just to our world, but to that of our children and all future generations."

"Some things can never be undone." Alaric lamented.

"Elisial mentioned to me on my last visit, that you were placing boundaries on your children's wanderings. Keeping them close to home. She said it was taking an effect on her herbal stores, that her supply was dwindling now that the children could not venture far to gather for her."

"Last year that was so, but now I only allow my eldest sons in the woods unaccompanied by me, and only by daylight."

"That must break their heart. They love the forest dearly."

"Never would I had thought such dark times would have fallen over us."

"Each age has its period of darkness. We must prosper the best we can so our children should reach the light of better times."

"So should all parent's purpose ever be. So should any man or woman regard the future. We would suffer less darkness, in depth and duration."

Elzera's hand snapped up suddenly, signaling a need for silence. He followed her gaze to the road where she focused intently into the trees beyond. There was someone or something moving out in the wild. Alaric snatched his ax up and stood.

"Be still!" Elzera whispered sharply.

"Bandits!" he whispered back, "I have encountered them before. I will not be caught unaware again." At least this time he had a proper defensible position.

The movement happened again, three people suddenly dashed closer to the road. One lagged behind the rest as the other two helped the slower figure off the road and behind some bushes. Yet, they continued in attempt to remain unseen, but plainly one was a girl and another elderly.

"Hail there!" Alaric called out. "We are just passing travelers. I hail from Gheldenmark and am returning home. If you are my fellow countrymen, you are welcome to our fire."

There was no response at first. Whoever they were, they decided to remain hidden.

"Not bandits," Elzera said laying her hand on his.

Alaric still gripped his ax. His posture remained aggressive. He nodded and set it aside, then distanced himself away from it.

"We have food and water, or transportation if you are looking to get to a place nearby."

Timidly, a youth's head peeked from under the hedge, that of a young woman, with large sad green eyes. She gazed at the two travelers, as if resigned to what fate might be handed to her.

She remained still until Elzera called to her. "Child, it would not do to squat behind a bush like a brush rabbit. Come join us and we may share some food, and bring your friends with you. More company lifts weary spirits who have seldom seen a reasonable soul upon this road. I have already worn this poor man's ears down with my ramblings, I'm afraid he's come close to becoming a mute."

The young woman's head lowered out of sight only to reappear from behind the bush. Leaning upon her was an ancient women with knotted white hair, stained brown with dried blood. Another woman of middle age followed after, her hands clutched against her chest, fingers entwined as if she carried all three of their souls in her palms and needed to guard them from the world. She never looked up but stared far off, into another time and place, but followed faithfully wherever the younger and older woman stepped.

Alaric crossed the road and helped the old woman over the uneven ground. The young woman never left her side. "I am called Alaric, the Woodcutter," he began with a kind voice. "I hail from Athelyn-un-Wudelic. This is my friend Elzera, a healer and merchant of medicines. She can help if any of you are wounded."

The younger girl could not look Alaric in the eye and kept her gaze low whenever he looked directly at her. She trembled and appeared as if she might flee and hide if it weren't for the grandmother squeezing her hand, holding her to her side. A loud moan erupted from the woman behind them, a loud sorrowful baying, that rolled across them like distant thunder expanding across the sky. Alaric glanced back to offer help, but the woman's vacant expression still hung about her face, as if the loud cry had come from someone else.

"Their wounds are deep," Elzera quietly commented to Alaric. "Not the kind to be seen on the surface. These wounds are not easy to mend," Elzera remarked as she guided the three to sit by their fire.

"Are any of you hungry?" Alaric asked

The old woman nodded, the girl too, with desperate energy. The mother remained still. Elzera fed them and the two travelers allowed their guests to eat peacefully, not inquiring of their situation until after they had their fill. Only the young woman and grandmother ate. The mother did not respond to anyone there. She bore the melancholy face that spoke of a terrible tragedy.

"They are fleeing from the Folthnir," Elzera said to Alaric, mirroring his thoughts. "From which village are you from?" she asked gently.

"We are from fallen Athéalgian," the grandmother wailed. "There is nothing left. Nothing..." her voice trailed off.

Alaric and Elzera exchanged meaningful glances. Maybe they could say how far the Folthnir have come into the Mark.

"Are there any more of you on the road?"

"Yes....no....Just us," came the cryptic reply, tinged with reserved pain.

Alaric asked, "Where are you headed then?"

The grandmother lips remained tight and unmoving. She had no words to offer and simply stared at the empty road as if searching it for answers that never came.

"Nowhere," Elzera answered for them, "because they have never been outside their city. They are fleeing to wherever this road takes them, as long as it takes them away from what they left behind. You three will be safe with us. We will take care of you now."

They did not speak. They were as wary as a rabbit crossing a wolf's den.

"You are welcome to sleep inside my wagon. There is room enough for three. You will not be seen from the road and you have Alaric and I to watch for travelers."

"There are horsemen!" Warned the old woman. "Slavers! Hunting down those fleeing."

"I will not allow any harm come to you. You are our guests. We will protect you as family. You have my word," Alaric promised.

"And mine," Elzera added, a little more gently than the Woodcutter.

The old woman nodded. "We are thankful. But we must not linger long," her voice again trailed off as she stared into the empty road.

Alaric needed to know if Athelyn had fallen to the Folthnir as well. He sucked in the chilled air, deep, before asked his next question. "Do you know if the barbarians have moved east toward the Wudelic? That is where my village lies."

"They are everywhere!" the grandmother whispered. The girl clasped her tight, clutching at her clothes.

"You make the little one anxious," Elzera observed. "I don't think that young one can be around men."

A dark cloud settled around Alaric's face as he realized what fear a man could have placed in this young woman's heart.

"It's not just those cruel northerners we fear," came the girl's subdued voice. "There are witches, roaming the country and forests at night. That is why we have been forced take to the road, even though horsemen ride them. We thought we were safer because we could hear the approach of the northerners rather than the wiles of witches in the woods."

The old woman tensed at the mention of the witches.

"It's the witches who brought the evil men here," she whispered into the coming night, "to do their dark work and spread their terror in the daylight. Old stories are coming true, except the stories are not scary enough."

The grandmother looked at her granddaughter with sad eyes, "the worst terrors can never be described with words girl." She rested her cheek on the girl's head.

A quiet settled over the camp. The sharp snaps from the burning fire wood seemed to amplify under the thick stone shelter around them, alerting any to their presence beside the road.

"We have heard of the Hero of Athelyn," the old woman finally said, "how he served the late king. You are he?"

"I am from Athelyn, but since I have not heard your stories I cannot say to whom they speak."

"Don't be modest, hero," Elzera replied for him. "Yes it is he, the great Alaric, son of Accenen the All Hunter, son of Aldred the Hidden. He and his sires have served the king for generations because their family have always possessed extraordinary abilities and have kept knowledge of the old ways, especially the many secrets that now lay hidden in the forest they hunt."

The grandmother looked intently upon Alaric and then Elzera. "It is as the girl says, stories are coming true."

"We will stay for the night. We thank you for your hospitality. To find rest beneath a roof is too wonderful a thought. It is beyond fortune we have met two decent people such as yourselves."

"Come, I will show you the way," Elzera said. They got settled into Elzera's wagon and she closed the door to allow them rest and recover as best they could.

"If there is a safe passage from here, we can bring them to my village and care for them at our house," Alaric began.

"No, they will not want to go back up the road. They will flee if they thought we were bringing them back north. These lands are no longer safe, now that King Sithric has fallen. Misfortune has spread beyond anyone's prediction, though your village might possibly have weathered most of this without much harm. But as you can see, some carry more of the brunt of the blow than others."

Alaric paused considering Elzera's assessment. He desired more than anything to see his family, but he could not easily abandon three who needed help.

As if reading his thought, Elzera replied. "No, Alaric. You are not too far off from your home, and your family no doubt worries if they might see you again. There is great urgency in the air, all around us." She paused. "It might be because of them," she indicated their three new companions, "but you should seek your family without further delay."

"But if there is danger near, you will need me and my bow at your side."

"I can get by without the great Hero of Athelyn," she said, teasing. "I have managed for years to travel without the aid of others, including that of a man I might add. Though I have entertained the thought of taking one or two of your sons with me," she said with a wink. "Protection from ruffians I have, but having some loved-ones around lifts a heavy heart, that is what I need in my old age."

"Yes, but out of deep respect Elzera, you are just a medicine peddler, a healer, not warrior or even a warrior's wife. Elisial would never allow such an offense, to leave you like this, let alone four vulnerable women. If they are being pursued then you might need more than me around to help."

"More than you, hunter?" She repeated back to him. "I have felled more foes in my life than a lifetime of all your spent arrows and that of your father's. I know the fortune of many things, can read the stars and lines etched on the palm every person since the time of their birth. I know the spirits of this land well, better than you do. I have aid at hand when required, so worry not about me."

Alaric was taken aback by Elzera's words. She projected a sense of power that whirled around him like a rising breeze that soon passed. Instinctively he reached for his bow, Nithledan.

"I have a few things to live for yet, Alaric, and so do you. I know that good things will yet come to pass, so do not worry over much. All five of us will make it to safety."

Alaric readjusted the bow slung across his back. Its relaxed form groaned at the movement. It seemed to him as if complaining, for it had not been shot for some time. It was being kept idle for too long.

"I fear the Folthnir have reached the village. I cannot rest this night nor any other until I know my family's fate."

Elzera nodded. "It is not a thought that has not crossed my mind as well. You should go now. Do not delay! If there are enemies on the road, we shall manage somehow. Expect me at your home then. I will not abandon Elisial, even if I have to lock these three in my wagon to see her. If things are truly bleak, look for me with what survivors you find on your journey back and we will leave this country together."

The grim words struck Alaric cold, for now it was a cruel possibility that his village might no longer be as he remembered it.

"May the Eshenar mark your courageous heart and Mûl grace you with bountiful fortune." Alaric bowed respectfully.

Elzera dismissed his formality with a wave of a hand. "It is cold now. Get going. I want to sleep."

Alaric parted without another word, once again taking the blackened path home. Night grinded against him despite having an empty road to himself. He watched the miserly sun rise to his right, cursing its sluggish ascent.

He had not traveled long before a rumbling of iron shod hooves stole all precious thoughts of home.

9

WOODMARES

EDRICK SNAPPED to his feet, grasping the stick he had carried all the way through the woods and scanned the tree line for the voice's source. He thought he saw shadows creeping in the periphery of his vision, weaving through the trees, just out of sight. Dark shapes that danced quickly away, as if they anticipated his reactions and interests. Sunniva seemed curious as to who might have come to join them.

"Weeeeell…" came the strange, deep voice. It seemed to have risen beneath the children, bursting forth from of the earth. "That was a grand tale. Can't say I have heard one quite like that. Have you Master Wergedswyn?"

"Nay," answered another. "I have not heard such a tale told from the lips of mortals in my long life, but then it is a rare occasion that I deign a moment to listen their speech at all." The second speaker's voice was deep like the first, but stranger. It was a mix of aspirated consonants burbling through a thick oily voice, as if something heavy sat upon the speaker's throat, compressing every word.

Meghan reflexively pulled Sunniva to her. Her green éardian burned fiercely on her brow.

"Well, consider yourself humbled today, Master Wergedswyn, for we have had the pleasure to be audience to such charming creatures," replied the first voice.

Baldice shot up from his prone position, his face uncharacteristically distressed.

"Aye, Lord D, 'tis a fortunate day to find such delights as we have discovered here," replied the second voice, uncannily closer now.

"Who's out there?" Meghan shouted after regaining her composure. She stood, picking Sunniva up, resting her on her hip.

"Let's get into the faerie circle," Meghan whispered to the others.

"Should we call out for Halig?" Edrick asked.

Before anyone could move, Baldice spoke in hushed words, "There is someone behind us."

Two strange and large figures strode around the perimeter of the stone ring, passing through the shadows. One tall and powerfully built, the other, stocky, and grotesquely fat, waddling like a child learning his first steps. Their sudden appearance in the bright daylight alarmed the children who had always thought that menacing terrors occupied the realm of nighttime and darkness exclusively.

Each had the shape of men, in both form and movement, though they were larger than any men the children had ever known. One towering like siege craft and the other so fat it engrossed the space of at least three people.

The fat one walked on thick hocks, throwing one foot in front of the other by leaning its torso to each side so as just to make enough clearance for each step. Either his arms could not swing freely, restricted by the girth that hung off its flanks, or every effort was made to steady his movements by supporting his massive gut. His face wore the permanent expression of discontent and anger, whose eyes focused upon the young children as if they were the source of his contempt, for no other reason than the fact that they were happy and loved life greatly.

The other taller figure strode with a grace that reminded Edrick of a timber-lion, bearing heavy muscles and subdued power. He wore the tailored apparel of nobility, well cut with quality cloth, but without boots, shoes, or sandals. His feet ended with bear-like paws that clawed their way through the earth with every step. Upon its massive head, flowed a broad hat, casting a permanent shade about its form. Its skin was a wan green, like a deciduous leaf in autumn, denied its final ephemeral beauty of dusky orange or burning red, resigned simply to fade away into a darkening winter.

"Ah, and what beautiful faces to match their tender voices," declared the giant, as he paused before them, at the threshold of the stone ruins. His deep, rumbling voice contradicted the sweet content of his words, imbuing them with a ring of menace. "I do love tales and lore of all kinds, and I am impressed, admittedly, by even the simplest story, especially those spoken by children, with such endearment and wonder. How delicious these young creatures sound to two weary forest travelers such as ourselves."

"Very delicious," responded the fat one, who, Edrick was sure, made the slightest movement of his tongue across his swollen lips. He cringed at the disgusting display. Mucus smothered his upper lip and continued to issue forth from its fat, upturned nose. It looked as if the fat creature had forever disfigured its appearance by falling flat upon its face. Its nostrils stretched wide open, facing forward like a snout.

At that moment, when all the children were thinking of turning and running as fast as they had ever dared to run in their young lives, they noticed a sack slung over the giant's shoulder, easily held by one massive arm.

"Have you something for us to nibble on?" Asked the fat mannish creature, snuffling the air. A freakish smile attempted to conceal any sinister motives, but lacking the effort.

"Ah, children," came the giant's voice, as if soothing them, "you are my guests here, as this is now my clearing and it would be rude to wander off without being dismissed first." The giant threw the sack to the ground. It landed with a thud like a body hitting the earth. The fat mannish creature took two steps forward and stopped, his posture leaning forward as if losing the endless battle against his massive gut.

"If you think of leaving now, children, you will run into my pet, and he is easily startled," the giant warned in mock concern. "Little lambs, such as yourselves, that happen across his path might cause an instinctual reaction, giving him reason to give chase."

Edrick looked back, as did Baldice, who now stood with the rest. There, at the head of the trail leading home, lay a large doggish looking beast, lazily gnawing on a bone in the shade of the trees. Its hair was matted and bare in certain spots, revealing blotchy, mangy skin. It had short horns of a sheep atop its canine like head and long conical ears. It resembled a stretched wolfhound with the body that matched the girth of a pony.

"Now," continued the giant, "sit down and tell me of this

woodcutter. I am intrigued, for I have heard that such a woodcutter lives about this forest and I should like to hear more about this legend."

The fat mannish thing waddled a bit closer. Sunniva whimpered and buried her head into Meghan's shoulder and chanted "goblyns, mauglins, verguls and naughs…" The kitten shot out of her arms and ran through the clearing, lost to the tall grass.

"What should we do?" asked Meghan. Edrick was taken aback; she was asking him? He looked at her face and saw terror frozen in her eyes, pleading for an answer. Edrick looked to Baldice. He stood still, staring ahead, as if by not moving he could escape the giant's dark gaze.

The monster's face looked like stretched leather across a thick skeletal frame, jutting at the extremities of the mandible and chin. Buried deep under dark craters of the ocular pits stared lurid eyes, smiling devilishly toward the children, mirroring the yellow teeth he now flashed across his thin lipped mouth.

Edrick could not think of anything. He didn't like the look of that dog beast, nor did he expect any of them could outrun it. They would have to split up, run in different directions. He wondered where Halig and Eadwyn were. Could they be watching right now, sneaking behind these monsters with their bows drawn?

"Come!" commanded the giant, "speak while we are all together. If not, then we must get down to the business at hand!" The giant stepped over his bundled sack and sat upon a broken boulder, as if it were his woodland throne.

"But perhaps we can share a meal, eh?" came the greedy request of the fat thing, its fingers rapidly drumming its gut.

"What is in your sack?" Edrick asked bluntly, not knowing where his own words came from.

"Not in the mood for more stories then?" The giant rose to its feet, standing thrice the size of Edrick. It flashed a yellow-toothed grin again, revealing a hidden amusement. "I am but a humble peddler and in this sack are my wares." It finished by giving the contents a small kick, which in proportion to the giant, was quite significant.

"Wares not too delicate then?" retorted Edrick.

"Delicate? Why yes, they are delicate. It is a game bag where I store my prey. And these two happened to loose their arrows upon us not too far from here. I am still upset about their rude conduct. So you can understand when I heard your young charming voices laughing and carrying on with your tales that I felt relieved to have met such well-behaved children."

Meghan let out another muffled shrill, her free hand covering her mouth.

"What Meghan?" asked Sunniva, pulling her head away from her sister's shoulder.

"Halig and Eadwyn," Megahn whispered.

Baldice slumped to his knees and began nervously tearing grass out of the ground by fingertip. His éardian slipped off his brow and danced about his head like a moth around a flame.

Sunniva twisted in her sister's arm trying to look behind her. The eyes of the fat one latched on to the young girl's face, still padded with baby fat. His lips quivered. A throaty gurgle percolated from his throat. Sunniva whimpered at the grotesque display.

He continued his slow advance. After a few laborious steps, he fell to the ground, collapsing, perhaps finally succumbing to his own weight. And despite his physical distress, Edrick felt as if the corpulent creature swelled in menace. He began to crawl towards the girls, dragging his gut through the grass. Sunniva screamed and buried her face back into Meghan's shoulder.

"Go away! Go away!" Sunniva screamed, shuddering with tears.

Behind them, the doggish creature ears twitched, its head sprung up as if it had been called by name. It dropped its bone instantly and became alert, its ears scanning the clearing. A bestial scream rang out. The wailing of a slaughtered pig issued from the fat mannish creature as it crawled its way toward the children.

"Well, I'm truly disappointed that our meeting couldn't have been more pleasant. I was hoping to hear at least one more story. But, now we must take the girls with the curious lights, for they fetch higher prices at the goblyn market. As for you boys, well, I have to reward my servants for finding me game, after all."

The giant's words were lost on the frightened children who could not take their eyes off the spectacle before them. The fat mannish thing's limbs began stretching, like a sausage casing squeezed through a grinder, and its hands tensed into fists that hardened into solid hooves. Its plump face elongated into a proper snout, that of a boar, with thrusting tusks dripping with thickening drool. Unlike the previous form, this creature assumed a powerful build, thick with muscles rippling beneath its flesh colored hide. After squealing as what sounded like the death throes of a slaughtered pig, followed by a shuddering as it metamorphosed into a giant boar the size of a bull, it regained its composure. Its bestial eyes filled with a renewed hate that its previous form failed to contain and charged the children with the energy of a dæmonic beast.

Behind the children, the doggish beast was on its paws, charging at them with the lust of a crazed predator in chase of its prey.

"Run!" Meghan screamed and took off with Sunniva. Edrick followed.

The boar rolled after them.

Baldice pulled out a steel hunting knife from beneath his belt, one that Edrick had never noticed before. He held it before him with two hands clasped around the handle, as if it were a sword. Its sharpened point danced about in Baldice's shaking grasp.

Silver light flared from his éardian, cocooning him in its brilliance.

Edrick stopped as the boar closed in, allowing Megahn to continue running. He brought up his stick and prayed to Lhodyn, keeper of the Wudelic. "Dear Lady of the Wood, grant my baton the power to smite this evil."

His éardian landed on the stick's tip, radiating blue light down the wood and then along Edrick's form. It swirled him like tornado fire.

The boar lowered its head as it prepared to strike Edrick down, yet the boy who taunted many bulls in his young life, stepped to the side of the beast's flank and struck the stick over the boar's skull.

There was a great flash of light, stinging Edrick's eyes. A gash tore across the monster's snout.

The shock instantly travelled up and through Edrick's hands into his shoulders, the stinging blow felt as if he just struck a rock with all his might. The stick snapped into pieces, and the pain forced Edrick to relinquish his grip.

The light of his éardian, the brilliant blue, transferred to the beast, then faded. Never to return.

The boar, charging, received the blow and flicked its head to the side, sending Edrick's small frame flying with the swat of its massive head. Then swatted the girls down to its other side.

The beast pivoted and turned toward Baldice, who did not possess the nimble skills of his younger brother, yet remained resolved to have the beast impale itself upon his small blade. But before he could steady himself, the massive creature collided into him, seizing his frail body in its maw, dragging him across the clearing. The force of the impact crushed all the breath from his lungs.

Edrick heard the snapping of bone as the boar took his brother. Yet the next threat refocused his attention, as the doggish beast flew by him, targeting his sisters.

Sunniva screamed out as the beast seized the loose cloth of her dress and dragged her to the waiting arms of the giant. It picked her up and tucked her under its arm.

"Good," it said, "now the other. She's worth three times as much."

From the forest, a wolfish howl arrested the attention of everyone in the clearing. All the world stopped as the eerie howling echoed off the surrounding woods and granite ruins. The doggish beast's ears flickered about in rapid movement, scanning the trees. The giant scratched the beasts head behind the ear as it scanned the woods.

More wolves took up the call of the first, surrounding them.

"Get the other girl! Now!" commanded the giant. Edrick scrambled to Meghan's side, shielding her with his own body. The doggish thing threw itself forward toward the two children in desperate haste.

Then out of the woods, four blurs of smoky movement descended upon the clearing. Huge silverback wolves, the match in size of the doggish thing, charged toward them in a fury.

Startled by the appearance of the intruders, the giant boar dropped Baldice's body limply in the grass, his silver light diminished.

Two wolves raced toward the giant, one breaking off to intercept the doggish beast. Two sprinted toward the monstrous boar.

Edrick could hear faint groaning sobs from Baldice. He lived still. There was a chance they could escape this horror, he told himself. Sunniva whimpered softly under the giant's heavy arm.

"Sunniva! Baby!" Meghan screamed between bouts of wailing shrieks. Edrick wished they all would calm down, if they could only act together, they had a chance.

He could somehow get them through this.

Then his thoughts drained into blank space as the sight of the rushing devilish dog, mouth agape, exposing every spiny tooth, flooded the void of his mind. Meghan struggled to push Edrick off her, but he held her down pinning his chest over her torso. It will have to get me first, he thought.

A wolf intercepted the doggish thing's path first, colliding into it at full sprint. The two canines went tumbling in a wild churning sphere of clawing and snapping fur. The other wolf charged the giant, leaping ten yards in the air, launching itself at its exposed throat.

The giant spoke some ancient and cryptic tongue, as old as the rocks under the mountains, a speech of power. A boulder the size of Edrick sheared off the stone ruin and launched itself at the wolf, impacting it like a falling comet. The large wolf yelped and dropped to the grass, the heavy rock landing on top of it, scoring another crushing injury.

The great giant let out an amused laugh, but then his mirth quickly dissipated when a streaking silver blur slammed into his chest. The heavy giant stumbled back, tripping over the sack beneath his feet. The thick haft of a hunter's spear stuck half buried in the giant's chest.

"Father!" Edrick shouted, excited and traced back the flight of the large weapon to the trees. But it was not Father. Out ran a wild man covered in brown animal's skins, with a long gray beard that whipped around the side of his face as he charged the field.

The giant, leapt back up to his feet and shouted again in its giant tongue, then stumbled toward the stone ring, Sunniva still trapped under his arm.

The wild man gave a shout, "By Lhodyn, drop the child!" and hurled another spear.

Edrick leapt to his feet. But before he could take a step, the giant ran into the tallest stone pillar, and simply disappeared into it, along with Sunniva. The spear collided a moment after, sending granite chips and incendiary sparks flying with explosive force.

Meghan loosed a heart tearing shriek, violently wresting the grass and wild flowers from the rigid earth.

The hellish squealing of the boar erupted behind them, as the massive creature charged Edrick and his sister again, this time pursued by two vicious wolves.

Edrick grabbed Meghan's hand and heaved her up to her feet. Another wolf sprang in front of them, ready to meet the massive boar.

Instead of taking on this new threat, the boar turned, and charged toward the safety of the forest. The doggish beast ran around chaotically, distracting the wolves from the retreating boar.

Eager for a kill, the wolves maneuvered around the wild hound until one latched upon its neck while the other two grabbed a leg and tore at its vulnerable belly.

"No!" shouted Edrick. "Go after the boar!" But it was too late. The boar lowered its head, snatching Baldice's leg in its maw and dragged him screaming into the woods.

The wolves continued savaging the doggish beast, rendered quickly into torn pieces. Blood painted their coats with an oily sheen.

Edrick found himself holding Meghan. She, silent now, shuddered as if suddenly plunged into an icy river and had only now been pulled out.

The wild man was now kneeling over the injured wolf.

Edrick wanted to speak, but he found the weighted words too heavy in his mouth, his mind too weary.

The injured wolf lifted its head, breaths staggered and shallow. It let out a yelp, dropping its head back to the ground, tongue rolling out with diminishing pants. The wild man ran his hands through the wolf's coat as if soothing the poor thing.

Then a disturbing, desperate wail drifted out of the forest canopy, followed by the frenzied cawing of excited crows.

"Baldice," Edrick uttered, defeated.

The wild man stood up above the wolf and raised his spear. Without hesitation, he sunk the blade clean through the wolf's spine. The other wolves stopped their gorging and stood still as stones for a moment, acknowledging their fellow's passing.

The wild man turned toward Edrick. The man's eyes were fierce, a blazing green fire that held no sorrow.

"Tell the Woodcutter the forest is lost. The paths are closed to him and his kin."

He walked on past them, hardly acknowledging them further. The wolves looked over their fresh kill, hesitating to leave their meal, before they fell in line behind the wild man.

"The Brownman," Edrick declared in wonder. Could it be the

same figure in their stories?

"Wait!" Edrick shouted out. He found himself running after them, after the man that saved their lives. "Wait! My brothers...we need your help! Baldice..." he said pointing to the woods. Words failed him. There was just too much to do. They had to find Sunniva and Baldice. "How do we get back?"

That giant boar still was out there!

The man reached the trees and still did not stop. "The way is safe, for now. Go while you still can."

Without another word, he left them.

Alone.

10

A MURDER OF CROWS

ALARIC STOOD in the middle of the road, staring down his enemies. Three hundred yards. He could strike them down before they saw his face.

Four horsemen. Four arrows. Four deaths.

The baying of hounds sounded out in front of them. Five dogs gave chase ahead of the riders, alerted to someone on the road. They charged toward Alaric, pleased to find something that might wet their frothing maws.

This made things more difficult. Shooting a dog, even a large hound from a forward profile at two-hundred yards would be a great feat. Every arrow was precious to him. A stray one lessoned his survival significantly against nine.

He prepared himself quickly. He found a position where two great pines rose on either side of the road like woodland bastions. Protection if he needed to quickly withdraw. Better still, the eastern embankment was steep, making chase by horse difficult. He buried his ax in the pine, so if need be, he could wield it before they dismounted - if things became desperate.

A cunning, more devious man might lay hidden by the road until the riders passed by, assaulting them swiftly from their flanks, not only taking them by surprise, but adding that moment of confusion as they discerned where the archer rested.

Yet these were men, same as he, not foul goblyns or worse. Perhaps boys his own sons' age. He would not dishonor them by hiding like an assassin. They will see one man stood against four.

If it were not for the hounds, he might parlay. At least determine their purpose and send them back north alive if he could.

But these hounds did not seem open for reasonable discussions. And five dead pets would not invite a friendly reception.

Alaric raised Nithledan, taking aim at the first dog.

One hundred yards.

He willed his éardian to radiate before him, creating a blue aura, glass like, in which Alaric peered. Suddenly what was far, was made close. He picked out the heads of the hounds, and one by one, five fell within two breaths.

Nithledan, finally released from its idleness, surged with excited pride.

It did not take much time for the riders to catch up with their dogs. Two dismounted giving Alaric a chance to study them.

Folthnir, there could be no doubt. They wore no shirt or covering at all, displaying their painted skin. A paint that could never be washed off, and when applied, bled the flesh. Each man represented a tribe and their paint revealed to which they belonged. Over their chest, above their heart, they bore the branding runes of Vylkinus, their god of the Dispossessed Wilds.

Vylkinus, master of the skies and all that dwelled under it, Keeper of the Hell Fire Forge. The Folthnir were his chosen through combat and they swore to drive the entire world into his sovereignty. Gheldenmark held them in the Dispossessed Wilds like caged animals. For centuries they clawed at the kingdom's borders. War erupted every generation. Alaric was called to it in his youth. Wars that claimed his uncles.

He prayed that he would never endure those evils again, nor his sons. He prayed to the Old Gods, the Dragon Spirits. The Eshenar.

Vylkinus was the Dragon Slayer, Lord of Sky and Fire.

The four horsemen charged Alaric on great massive steeds. Alaric recognized these Wultherons from Lord Temen's stables. Their size were unmatched.

He shook off the fear rising in his heart, the thought of what these men might have done to his kin, to his neighbors, to all his country.

Fifty yards.

They rode two by two, steel drawn. Each crouched low in the saddle, hidden well behind the girth of their massive steeds. They would not rise until they rode over him, and it would be too late for a shot. Too late for any other archer save the Hero of Athelyn.

He steadied his breath.

He released the bowstring and it sung. *Shnikt! Shnikt!*

The arrows ripped through each man's skull like slivers of lightening, breaking their steel helmets and exiting clean through the other side.

They slumped off their saddles, dead. The horses kicked and reared until they were free of the bodies.

Shnikt and *shnakt* flew the third and fourth arrow. One more fell dead, but the last turned sharply into the woods. His arrow had missed its mark by an inch.

Alaric waited. Listened.

He heard the cracking of wood under iron hoof, near, but retreating. The birds scattering from the commotion. All became silent.

The rider reemerged two hundred yards down the road. He stopped.

Alaric raised his bow.

He could see the rider through his éardian light, staring back at him. Deciding whether he should take another charge, or withdraw.

Alaric decided for him.

He launched another arrow, startling the rider, thinking himself safe. He was wrong. The rider jerked but could not evade the arrow as it pierced his neck, just below his jaw, under his left ear.

The rider retreated with great haste.

"Damn," Alaric said under his breath. A survivable wound.

Alaric waited to be sure there were no others down the road. Temen's horses watched Alaric, smelled him as he stood there, then trotted toward him.

"Go! Be free," he yelled. But they did not budge.

"Had I a chariot I would make use of you. Never will you see me on your back. Go back to the southern plains whence your sires came. We true Mithlians still remember horses are strange, the mounts of our ancient enemies. Though those days are long behind and we made peace with those people, you beasts still remain strange to us."

The horses crowded around him, tall gray dappled colored beasts with long white manes and tasseled hooves. They weren't bred for riding, but hauling.

"Well, perhaps we should have a truce since we fight a common enemy," Alaric said as one horse drew up to him, lowering it head so it can be petted. It was adorned with star-like blaze. "No. I will not touch you except to push you away."

The horse stepped forward shoving Alaric back with his head. "Good, then we understand each other. Well, damn. There are probably more of them on the road and I am on foot." The lead horse whinnied as if laughing at him.

"You really want me to ride you?" Alaric asked in disgust. "I guess the need is great, I must resort to desperate measures. All right, you dumb beast. You owe me something for freeing you of foul company. Let us get on with this. The sooner I can return home, the faster you and I can part."

Two of the horses, Alaric tied up for Elzera to find. "I think I found her a gift to replace her mules," he said to them. He then unfastened the saddle and blanket of the first horse, discarding the equipment into the forest. "Woodcutters ride wild beasts, not tame." He jumped onto the large beast's back, grimacing with disgust.

Alaric slapped the horse forward and they galloped toward his home.

He rode through the day and into the night and never saw another man or horse. The vacant roads disturbed him more than encountering a legion of the enemy. It was as if all the people ceased in the world, that the land had been turned on its side and emptied. He took the straight road home until he entered the familiar hills of his vale.

By late evening the next day, as the crescent moon broke above the horizon, he saw it. The dark form of the yew tree.

Affixed at the apex of a small hill dwelled a dead and ancient yew marking the end of the Merchant Road and the beginning of The Lane, Alaric's home. The tree itself possessed the mark of decay, sitting alone on a barren and fallow hill. While most birds took care to stay clear of the melancholy yew, there was now assembled a black mass of crows clinging to branch and bough like the grip of death, taking the form of dark, sickly fruit. Their haunting caws called out to Alaric, beckoning him to join their cabal.

Alaric's mount twitched nervously, whinnying and turned to leave. He leapt off its back.

"I agree. The yew is unsettling. What has become of our land?" Something else held Alaric's eyes. In the boughs of the tree, three figures hung unnaturally from tethered ropes, one smaller than the other two, that of a child. While the other two hung from the neck, the child hung by an ankle, the other leg contorted beyond its natural range of motion.

Alaric could not take his eyes off the macabre sight as rage and grief simultaneously fought their way to his heart. His only thoughts became that of his family, how he regretted leaving them alone for so long.

"You are free," Alaric spoke to the horse, his eyes never lifted from the yew. "Seek the fields of your sires and find peace."

At his approach, the crows launched a cacophonous assault against him, a tumultuous chorus decrying his arrival. A few birds slipped off their branches and flew at Alaric, diving at his vulnerable face like devilish missiles. Some among them had the mark of Lhodyn: crows the size of eagles with talons and sharp beaks, heads bald with blood eyes and featherless wings of bats. They sat among the others like kings among the vanquished.

Alaric swatted the attacking birds but they did not relent. They brayed and scratched, whirled about him as they fought to protect their meal, their claim on death. Nithledan urged Alaric to take him up and let him put down these foul beasts.

Alaric swiftly slipped the bow from around his body, loosening arrows in all directions. The spindly razors pierced through the storm of crows, each biting into their bead black eyes. They fell like dark rain. Alaric turned upon the helpless bodies hanging from the yew tree, covered in feasting crows, bloated on flesh. *Shnikt* and *shnakt* flew the arrows freeing the bodies of the flesh thieves who stole the faces from their victims. Each skewered by Nithledan, the Night Bringer.

"You have no claim on these bodies!" Alaric shouted as he waded through the dead birds lining the ground, approaching the victims. "They are not for you but belong to the Eshenar! Leave this place you dæmons!"

The crows took up another raucous chorus, a contemptuous laughter at his protests.

Alaric looked over the victims and understood why his horse feared making the climb up the hill. What was left of old Lord Temen hung in front of him, along with his wife and youngest son.

Temen's son had a crueler fate than his parents. Scores of arrows protruded from the boy's small body revealing the sadistic sport played by the Folthnir.

Alaric thought immediately to release the bodies so he could lay their remains in the ground. Bodies so openly exposed, their spirits would not rest, doomed to wander the world of the living. He darkly wondered if he could kill enough of the crows and pile their bodies so high so as to be able to reach the ropes with less effort.

"Hunting crows bodes ill fortune for the living, Woodcutter," spoke gruff words of a familiar voice. "So they told us in war."

Down from the Lane crawled a man, weathered into his middle years, using his hands in the place of absent feet. His legs, severed from the hip long ago, lay strewn across a battlefield leagues away in the Nitherlic Vale. Hrypa crawled, partially dragged, his waist up the hill, paces away from Alaric. A look of grim satisfaction displayed across his face like a mask. Contempt shot out from his eyes.

"Hrypa," Alaric said in surprise. The village's beggar was known to avoid people, never greet them. There was nothing Alaric could imagine that would draw any person to this place of death. Yet seeing someone from the village renewed his hope that all was not misfortune.

The stunted man maneuvered his way closer to Alaric and looked upon the skeletal faces. The man shook his head after looking upon Lord Temen and his family, then crawled back toward the lychgate. "You should leave them hanging. The Folthnir hung them as a reminder to all of us. Remove them and they will come for you."

Without another word, the crippled man limped back to the lychgate marking the village proper. He leaned against the Wall, lifting a stashed wineskin and drank deeply.

"You must tell me, where is my family? How many of us have they killed?"

Hrypa said nothing. His features were stone still and his eyes filled with emptiness.

"You are alive and well," Alaric continued, "...as well as I remember you last. Tell me then how Lord Temen suffered this indignity. Where are the Folthnir now?"

"You have been gone too long. We have new neighbors now, Woodcutter," Hrypa said through a sardonic grin.

Alaric pitied the crippled man. He, Hrypa, and Grindan fought in the same wars against the Folthnir. Hrypa's legs were trampled by King Sithric's cavalry as they charged the field. Lords were rarely concerned with the fate of peasant warriors. While Alaric and Grindan returned heroes, Hrypa injuries were less glorious and much more was taken from him than his legs.

"The Folthnir?" Hrypa continued. "Our old acquaintances from once upon a time? Never imagined we would be welcoming them in our village after what they put us through, put the Mark through for centuries. Yet here they are. Our new overlords." He spat suddenly and guzzled his drink greedily. "Sithric was an imbecile."

Alaric knew Hrypa would go on speaking his mind without answering any of his concerns. To await a reply and know if his family lived or died was not worth enduring the foolish man. He would have to find out himself.

Alaric turned his back on the beggar, ignoring his rants and insults for the late Mark-lord and his army.

With three swift arcs of his ax, he freed the bodies. The crows brayed in protest but kept their distance afraid of Nithledan's sting. He broke the arrow shafts off the boy then wrapped his own cloak around him. He retrieved the blanket from his pack and draped it around the parents.

"Useless." Hrypa shouted. "It's all useless. You have legs, Woodcutter. Run away. We are all dead here! Is that what you are waiting to hear? There is nothing for you or me here except crow meal!"

He seized a loose rock from the crumbling Wall and threw it at the crows. Their braying exploded once again. Some took to their wings and attacked the crippled man savagely, as they had Alaric. There was an evil spirit in them. Hrypa swatted at them with his wineskin, but he was so overcome by their numbers, he fell to the ground and covered his face cowering.

Alaric shot the last of his arrows into the black birds. They all scattered, flying east across Athelyn. The Woodcutter helped Hrypa up, but the beggar fought his hands away and refused aid. Blood flowed from fresh cuts over his arms and forehead.

"The Hero of Athelyn saves me again!" Hrypa spat. He picked up his wineskin and shook it, determining its contents and drank it empty.

He laughed suddenly aloud. "Funny, this stupid Wall is supposed to keep out evil spirits. Yet when Death walks the land or flies in the flesh, it is allowed entry anyway. Good for throwing stones at birds though."

"What brings you here Hrypa? It is no small effort for you to climb this hill. If I remember well, there was no great love between you and Lord Temen."

Hrypa looked upon Alaric, scorning his questioning. "Blinded are those who walk all day on two feet and fail to know what lies in my heart! But no such grand revelation to me that is. How envious I am to turn my back as easily as you and find my own destiny on the road." He spat on Alaric, his breath carried the heavy stench of alcohol. "What brings me here indeed, you horse shit! To behold the esteemed Lord Temen, lord of the hoof. Witness how far his spirit soars and wonder what fate lies for one wretched, broken man with no legs.

"That is what brings me here!" throwing the wineskin across the road. "I stare not at the hanging bodies but the empty road ahead of me, cursing it! I was hoping I might have enough drink to pass out and fool the crows into thinking I died, and have them make a meal of me before I woke. But you made sure that did not happen."

"I pity you, Hrypa, not for the man I carried from the battlefield, but for the man you became in the years after."

"Is that your judgment, master Alaric?" he asked sarcastically. "Then now I have something to live for yet. To witness the great Hero of Athelyn overcome his losses and see how he endures. Return home now, Woodcutter, and see if something as precious as your own legs have been stolen from you."

"What mean you by this?!"

"I mean all is not well in your house."

Alaric could not wring another word from the vexing man. Hrypa remained still, seemingly satisfied he brought grief to another other than himself. Alaric flew past the lychgate and down the hill toward home, pursued by the laughter of crows from across the village.

The sun just sunk under the horizon when he reached his cottage, throwing his shadow out before him, watching it dissolve into the oncoming night.

From the short distance, Alaric could make out all four faerie lanterns were lit and hung from each post. Unusual, for the sunlight had not quit the land yet. Tied to the cottage's lychgate, two dogs were leashed. They began barking, alert to his approach.

Light shown from inside the cottage. Overwhelming calm settled over Alaric. The old ache of a road weary body welled up in every tissue and sinew of his being. He wanted nothing more to see his family, ensure they were safe and healthy, then collapse in bed with his wife, and not wake up for days.

Looking at the house, its familiar appearance, the history that surrounded it, built by his grandfather, settled over him. He was at home and it felt right.

The dogs that barked at him he soon recognized as his neighbor's, Oxa, who lived a house over, down the Lane. Alaric allowed them to smell him and they fell quiet, licking his palm greedily.

"What brings you boys over? Have they been having dinner parties every night in my absence," he said. Being home shifted his mood away from the dark scene of the yew tree to joyful gratitude, realizing he survived the roads. He returned to his family.

He walked past them and stopped still. Before crossing the porch, he stood staring at the door. Three black interlocking circles containing red symbols had been painted there, wards to repel evil spirits. Protection used by his wife.

Instinctively, he dropped his ax, taking up Nithledan. He had no arrow, but the bow felt better in hands than not. He paused to listen and smell the air around him, grasping for something to tell him that his family was alive and well.

"Elisial!" he shouted, opening the door. But it was held shut. It had never been barred, even when the timber-lion stalked their garden. "Elisial! Halig!"

The sound of a latch being lifted had Alaric stepping back. Oxa, a stocky fellow, swung open the door, hatchet in hand. His mouth fell slack as he laid eyes upon the Woodcutter.

"Alaric, you grisly wild man, you have returned. Elisial!" He shouted over his shoulder, "Alaric is back! Lhodyn be praised!"

Alaric relaxed at the mention of his beloved's name. He sprung up, and in a few long strides, had entered his home. Oxa, a large man rightly named, stepped aside. Inside, Alaric's fears were rekindled as he found his family distraught, whose eyes remained downcast and sullen. Not the welcome he expected.

"What is going on?" He quickly took count of his sons and daughter. "Where's my sunshine? Where's Baldice?" The red wards seared into his mind. "Elisial, what has happened? Is everyone all right?"

Elisial stood stiffly and walked toward Alaric. A profound change surfaced in her moist eyes. Not the same eyes Alaric remembered, a change he will always claim never left her. Where before they were perfect pools that captured and held the starlight, they were now fractured, like fragile glass, distorting all light unnaturally.

"Alaric..," she began, holding back tears and a sadness he had never heard cross her lips since the passing of their three infant sons. "Alaric, they are gone." That was as much as her breath allowed to escape her lips before she plunged her body into his chest and his long sought embrace.

He held her tight, not saying a word, not asking where Baldice and Sunniva were or where they have gone to. He held his words back because he needed to hold her too, hold her to prepare himself for whatever he heard next.

His children followed suit, diving into their parents in one large embrace.

He briefly looked up, and saw the downcast expressions on each and every one of them. Halig looked especially dispirited. After a few moments, Elisial began speaking into Alaric's chest, unable to say the words of woe and heartache to a face she loved so hard. The sad story of their children spilled out.

Alaric listened to each word, remaining still, squeezing his wife tighter into his arms when he learned his children had not returned from the forest.

"This is a grim tale you speak, my love. How long has it been since their return?"

"Nine weary days have fallen since then," she paused. "We thought you may never return to us too."

"I will go and search for our children. Tonight." Elisial began to protest, but part of her needed him to leave, to return with their children no matter what danger he might find in those woods.

She pulled him close and whispered into his ear, "I don't know if I can do this again." She paused to master herself, to prevent the flood of tears. "I can't lose more children, Alaric. Three were already too many…" She sobbed into his shoulder for a moment then released him. In her pregnancy before Edrick, they had lost triplet boys soon after birth. It was a wound in his wife's heart that never closed.

He hated to leave her there like this.

"Boys, outside. Meghan…" he started to speak. She clung to him as a young girl awakened by nightmares. After a moment, he began again "…look after your mother."

"Yes, father," squeezing him with her thin limbs. "Papa, you are home!" she said breathlessly. She started to say more but failed.

Alaric bent down to kiss her cheek, and then his wife, softly upon the lips. He turned and walked outside.

Alaric's sons were waiting with Oxa.

"Alaric," Oxa started, "we have looked around that stone ring. Whatever those monsters were, they are gone and…" his voice fell into a whisper, "your children too."

Alaric walked up to his friend and rested a hand on his shoulder, looking him square in the eyes. "I appreciate you walking the woods to search for my children. Elisial and I will be forever grateful."

Oxa nodded, grasping Alaric shoulder in return. "Halig led us there. We found tremendous boar tracks, the size of a bull, leading from the Stones to the deeper woods. We dared not follow. I am sorry," the large man spoke shamefully.

"Do not apologize my friend. You did me and my family a great service."

Alaric looked at Halig shaking his head. He wanted to yell at the boy for taking the children into the woods at all, and then leaving them alone as he and Eadwyn hunted. Since that winter, when the timber-lions stalked the village, Alaric seldom brought his entire family into the woods and certainly never left them alone. He realized he was partly to blame; his protection gave his children a false sense of security.

"I will fetch Grindan and Tellan," Oxa said at length. "If you want to go into the woods…" he looked over Alaric's shoulder into the darkened mass outlined against the coming night. "We will go with you, if you think that will help."

"That will be fine." Alaric responded, patting his friend's shoulder. "Eadwyn, go bring our friends here."

Eadwyn seemed put out, as if he thought Edrick should have been chosen to be the errand boy, but he quietly ran down the Lane without voicing his protests.

"I'll get you more arrows, Father." Edrick offered.

Alaric gave him a nod and off the boy went.

"Oxa, thank you for staying with my family in this dark hour. I have at least one friend I can count on."

"If it weren't for Elisial, my children would be resting in the byrgen. No matter what anyone says, I am grateful for your family."

"It is good to hear that has not changed in a year my friend."

"Alaric, what of those things in the woods, your house sits in the shadows of the forest. I am afraid they will come for us all."

Alaric smiled warmly, calming his friend's concerns. "That is why I ask you stay with Elisial tonight, with Grindan and Tellan. I will hunt the woods alone. There is no other service you could offer than that you have not already provided. And Elzera will be arriving tonight with three woman needing Elisial's healing skills and a place to sleep off the road. Look for her in my place."

"Elzera? The strange merchant?" Oxa asked, voice full of suspicion.

"Yes, her. We met on the road. I think it is good fortune she found me and travels here now."

Oxa raised an eyebrow, clearly not sharing the same optimistic sentiment

"Elzera is coming?" Elisial asked full of hope and relief, standing at the door.

"She should be here soon. I went ahead of her because she was caring for three women we found on the road."

Alaric recounted how they met the refugees and the horsemen pursuing them. He then mentioned Temen and his family upon the yew tree.

Oxa shook his head in remorse. "It is true, Alaric. Despite your best efforts, the Folthnir have descended upon us."

"They have a camp north of the village," Halig added.

Alaric's anger rose. This was exactly his fear. He felt foolish for going on the Elder's errand. He will have stern words with them if time allowed it. He should have remained, to care for his family. "It matters not where they are at. It seems the Wudelic is the greater danger at the moment".

"I will prepare a faerie lantern for you. If you are going in those woods tonight, you need my craft with you." Elisial decided, turning away toward her apothecary alcove.

Edrick reappeared with a quiver of silver fletched arrows. He gladly offered them to his father.

When Alaric was alone with his sons, he turned to Halig, striking him across the face.

"I left the whole family in your care and now your brother and sister are gone!" he said in muted rage. "You have any idea what this has done to your mother!"

Halig's éardian seared a blinding gold light. He did know, Alaric thought. But still, such boyish behavior was inexcusable.

"You are right," Halig said, holding his cheek.

"I suppose Eadwyn deserves the same treatment since he follows you blindly," Alaric shouted, "without thinking of his brothers and sisters first. How can this happen?" He asked more to himself, to the forest and all the world, than his sons standing silently next to him. There were dangers in the forest, but never these kinds of creatures. He had not heard of such things near their village. Nothing like it had roamed the woods since the time before his grand sire, Renweard.

"I don't know what to think of my eldest, the one that was to receive our family's treasures, showing such carelessness. I just want each of you to think of your brother's anguish and his cries for help, and the pain he endured at your childish play. Sunniva was just a babe!" His voice broke. He fought to keep the stronger, reckless emotions at bay. "She was just a little girl in the first moments of her life! You remember that! Their deaths will be forever on your hands. There are some debts you can never afford, and this is the first of those.

"Halig, you will stay here. You don't have your head about you to go into the woods again. This time, take care of your family with your life. You owe Baldice and Sunniva that much."

Halig bit down on his lip, stood straight and nodded.

"Good. I am glad to see your strength return. We all have fates both good and bad. We must accept what is laid before us and move forward."

The three stood in the silent darkness with Oxa, waiting for Eadwyn to return with help. After a few moments Edrick spoke up,

"Father, may I go with you, back into the woods?"

Alaric smirked, dismissing his son's questions. "If I'm not allowing my eldest to accompany me why would I allow the youngest?"

"Because I know where they took Sunniva."

An urgent tingle shot up Alaric's spine. He stepped right up to his son until he towered over the small boy. "You know where they are? Tell me boy!"

"Yes, they are where all the children go who are taken from their parents. They are being sold at the Goblyn Market."

Alaric faltered, half expecting to hear a serious answer, but anger overpowered his mood until he could not tolerate any more childish notions. He struck Edrick across the face, sending him tumbling to the ground.

Edrick did not stand, but cradled his cheek in both hands.

"Enough with your childish stories. I have walked the woods for decades. There is no such fanciful place! No goblyn markets or faeries castles or dragon treasures. This is not your mother's stories. This is life and death. There will be no happy endings when I return from the woods…"

Edrick pulled himself up, looked at Halig for help, then bolted into the house and slammed the door.

Alaric called after him, "That much I am sure!"

Halig clenched his fists, but kept his head down.

"When I return, I think it is about time we talk about you finding your own way in the world. Your mistakes must be your own, but no longer will I allow this under my house!" Alaric growled at his son.

Three figures appeared out of the night walking down The Lane with Eadwyn, two men, Tellan and Grindan, along with Grindan's large son, Bron. They looked grim and determined. Gindan, the bigger man, carried a heavy sword across his back and the other a simple sickle. The boy gripped a heavy forge hammer and a torch to light their path.

Grindan was a man of great size, one who made Wultherons appear like ponies. He was a good friend to Lord Temen and shoed all his horses as well, but his great love was in forging swords and instruments of war.

"Alaric!" Grindan greeted, leading the group. "My friend. You are home, but hardship awaited you. Tell me, has anyone marked your arrival into the village?" he asked. His face was stern and unfriendly. "Besides, Oxa here?"

Alaric thought it an odd greeting from his old friend. "I met Hrypa at the yew tree." Alaric saw that Gindan did not favor that answer.

"Alaric, the world has much changed in your absence. I suggest you leave tonight. Take your family and leave. The Folthnir roam the village during the day. You would not want to be seen."

Alaric was taken aback by his friend's warning. "I will not leave before I have discovered the fate of my children to those woods."

"We already searched the glade once, and found nothing," Grindan stated. "Take your family, my friend, and survive. We sometimes don't get a choice."

Alaric stepped closer to his friend, keeping his tone even. "I was given a choice a year ago, to leave my family and search for a safe land for our people. I have found it. Now, I will see to my family first. I will tell the Elder's my report, then Grindan, I will consider leaving if that is the best choice."

"Of course, Alaric, my old friend," the building tension evaporated with a broad smile. The large man grasped Alaric's arm and embraced him as old comrades. "Would not expect less from you my old friend. Stalwart and noble as ever you were."

Tellan offered his hand in turn, "Well met, Woodcutter." He was a thin, tall man, shaped like a sickle, spine curved from long years in the field. His grip was remarkably strong as they shook hands, only Grindan surpassed him in strength. He was as honest a man as Alaric knew, willing to help anyone without thought for himself.

"I see Bron continues to grow," Alaric said, turning back to Grindan. "I hope everything is well at home." The young man was already the size of Alaric. He worked the forge since Sunniva's age. By Edrick's age, he was already strong enough to swing a forge hammer for half a day without rest.

"Yes. We have been fortunate."

Elisial stepped out of the house with a tarnished brass lantern, housing a candle emitting a brilliant blue flame. Behind her, Meghan and Edrick followed. All sadness seemed wiped from Edrick's face and instead resembled his father, resolutely stoic.

Elisial greeted the men and kissed Alaric on the cheek as she handed him the lantern.

"I won't bother asking you not to leave, for I have already prepared myself for the tidings you will bring back. But please," she leaned into him, whispering into his ear, "on your return, take it easier on your sons. They are good boys and I wish to prevent burdening their hearts further with your wrath."

"We do not know the fates of either Baldice or Sunniva," Alaric whispered back. Her lips quivered slightly. "There is something bigger happening in these woods and I need to discover what that might be. Do not mourn yet. Whatever I discover, things will be different from now on. That I am sure."

Elisial stepped back and kept silent. She lifted her arm and Meghan slipped beneath it, laying her head on her mother's shoulder.

"Friends, I have returned after many weary miles, long months and severe trials. Alone on the road magnified such difficulties, but together, my spirits is bolstered tenfold. Grindan. Tellan. I ask you remain here and watch the woods until my return."

"No Alaric!" Grindan protested. "These woods are not what you remembered them. All mortals would find their deaths there, at night, alone, even if you were raised there. Allow us to keep you company at least."

"I move faster and quieter alone, which is a matter of safe passage through these dark woods. And where I'll be wandering will prove dangerous for others. I say that not to boast but to state that many things beneath the woods ignore my presence, where any other man would find trespass."

The others offered no argument, because they knew Alaric's claims to be true.

"Oxa," Alaric continued, "at sunset I cut Temen and his family from the old yew. I think now that it is dark, you can grab a cart and bring them to the byrgen. Get some help and bury them quickly."

"Yes, I will do this and I know more who have been wanting to do the same for a while," spoke Oxa urgently.

"Good," Alaric replied.

"Very well, Alaric," Grindan extended his hand again. "Then this is where we depart once again. I will remain the night here, if that is your wish."

Tellan nodded in agreement then said, "That is a curious lantern there, Alaric."

"It is a faerie candle and will protect me from the fey or bewitching magick."

The candle glowed like a star at birth, burning a blue flame that was brighter than any normal candlelight. Those around seeing the light for the first time could not help but smile at the delight the light instilled in them.

Alaric took up the lantern and set out behind the Woodcutter house where a path led to the Wall and the stone arch of the lychgate, marking the end of the village and the beginning of the wild: Wudelic Woods. It seemed to be guarding many secrets that he was to be master and steward. "By dawn, the next day, I shall return if only to remind my family I am well."

The group said their farewells, parting at the village threshold. They watched him depart down the woody corridor alone, appearing as a miner passing into a deep tunnel.

Alaric was not sure where to start looking, but he knew where to find the Brownman with the wolves.

He was known to Alaric as Aweirgan.

11

ASLENISSIA

THEY WERE ALONE, Edrick thought. Despite having two full-grown men next to him, Edrick felt very alone.

Without his father present, numbers did not matter. He wished he was older, like Halig. That he could follow his father into the night. That he could find his brother and sister. That he was not too small. That had a warrior's strength to protect them.

He wished he was like his father, Hero of Athelyn.

From the Wall, the other men kept watch, peering at the surrounding forest nervously, though they attempted to mask their fear. For them, standing before the darkened woods was a new experience, one that they would not soon repeat, Edrick guessed. He had walked the Wudelic at night, with his family no less, but no farther than the Stone clearing. On those occasions he, his brothers and sisters thought they had heard the distant sounds of elves feasting far off, playing mystical music and laughing at unheard tales of heroic elfish legends. His parents told them that the sounds were enchanted and that to follow them was foolish and quite dangerous. Edrick always felt his parent's teased them, but tonight, he felt that such veiled dangers were believable, for he had met the real terrors in plain daylight.

The forest remained in near silence. Accustomed shapes in the daylight lost all their familiarity in the darkness. Edrick's eyes strained to make out details of things just beyond the torchlight. The flames shed their light about in a disorganized array as strange objects in the woods shifted and strained, warped by the intrusive radiance. What he thought was a stump or bush had vacated the position he remembered them occupying, as if the forest itself fidgeted under the light.

Edrick thought he saw little creatures of child height, but thick like stone and dark like the space between stars, move about, as the shadows churned from flickering lamplight. Curious, Edrick stepped beyond the lychgate and crossed the open ground, right to the tree line. When he examined the objects closer, the shadows froze and a gnarled stump or withered bush assumed their mundane shapes.

Grindan and Tellan followed Edrick quickly, quizzical expressions on each of their faces.

Whispers of something foul could be heard between the chirping rhythm of crickets and other nightly creatures.

"The forest doesn't seem itself," Edrick casually commented.

"Come back, boy," Grindan pulled Edrick to him. "We are to wait for your father, not stare into shadows here."

"It feels like we are intruding," Edrick continued, "and I have never felt that here…before." The men remained quiet but continued to look at Edrick as if they knew not of what he spoke. "Even at night."

"What is it supposed to feel like? Your family has been gravely harmed. It feels strange to me and rightly so," Grindan replied.

"I've been here at night when I was young," Tellan said, moving a torch around from side to side, futilely fending off the darkness, burning the night away only to have it rush forth again. "It is as Edrick says, it feels different than when I remember. The difference of waking up from a good dream and that of a nightmare. I should think we'll not find sleep easily tonight."

"Come away from here," Grindan urged again and had to push Edrick gently all the way back to their garden behind lychgate and Wall.

Edrick wanted to speak further, at the seemingly persistent shadows that moved about, just out of sight, or the change in the air, which now felt damp and smelled of some decaying thing that lingered not far off the path. Thoughts of Baldice came to his mind. The odor lingered with them, as if it were stalking them.

Concern started to creep into his thoughts, that his father might be surrounded by these same shadows. And he was alone.

"I have heard many tales of Wudelic," Grindan said, never

taking his eyes off the woods, "but only one I know to be true. One that always made me to think twice when your father invited me to hunt with him in the woods." Grindan said.

Edrick and Bron hung upon every word, standing motionless under the starlight.

Grindan continued. "It is well known to many outside theses Walls that the late King Sithric had lost a son hunting near the forest, near the Ruined Tower. They say a fiend rode out of the woods, accompanied by giant disfigured owls and wolf like beasts with horns and eyes of a goat. The monsters assaulted the king's men and captured the young prince, stealing him into the woods. This thing that took the boy they called the Erlking."

"Did that really happen? I had never heard of that story," Edrick asked enthusiastically. "I hadn't heard any stories about the king or his family, except that he died," Edrick concluded in near whisper.

"Certainly it did," Grindan looked down at Edrick. "The king grieved deeply for his son. The entire kingdom did, years before you were born. The king never returned here. Some say he forbade anyone to speak of these woods."

"What is that?" Tellan asked. All their eyes snapped to the woods, expecting something dire about to burst from the trees and swallow them. Instead, the crunching grind of wagon wheels sounded off behind them, from the Lane.

Edrick nearly forgot about Elzera's arrival. He led the way back toward the cottage, running around to the front door where the warm orange glow of the hearth fire spilled out into the night.

"Auntie!" Edrick shouted in glee as he ran toward the old fortuneteller. She wasn't really his Auntie, but he never knew any of his grandparents. She has been visiting Athelyn since Mother was a little girl and taught her much of her healing arts and herbal craft. Mother said she traveled with Elzera and grandmother all over the Mark, even coming to reside in the king's court for a while. She lived in comfort for many years until the Nithric Vale wars.

"Edrick," Elzera greeted him, arms wide, "I missed you my boy! Growing tall, but not wide yet. But you still have some years, don't you?"

Halig and Eadwyn sat with Auntie around the table while Meghan was busy cutting vegetables. Mother added them to an iron cauldron above the hearth fire. They all seemed happier for Auntie's presence.

Grindan and his son Bron entered behind Edrick, nodding quietly. Tellan chose to remain outside.

"Hello Elisial..." Grindan said. They both remained at the door entrance, taking guard it would seem.

It was then Edrick noticed strange eyes peering at him from across the room.

"Who are they?" he asked, a bit perturbed at finding strangers in his home without being informed first.

Sitting huddled upon the guest's bed were three women, well one was a girl, but older than Edrick, but not quite a woman. The three appeared frightened, Edrick thought, and they all seemed to shrink back into the dark corners of the room when Grindan took notice of them. The girl looked away and her eyes landed upon Edrick. He smiled, thinking she was pretty despite her rough appearance. A dim, dull orange éardian floated above her. She didn't smile back, but gazed at him, eyes laden with grief, until he felt uncomfortable and looked to his mother for help.

It was Elzera who spoke first. "Edrick these are your guests and will be staying for a few days. Your father and I found them wandering on the road outside the village. They are in need of our care. Please make sure you show them respect and make them feel at home."

"They don't look right," Edrick replied quickly, then noticed the woman that stared across the room and into the wall behind him. He wondered if she might be blind.

"Edrick, stop staring and mind your manners!" Mother snapped at him, then smiled apologetically at their guests. "Like Elzera said, Edrick, they need help because they have been hurt, so please be kind with your words." She had finished filling five bowls with broth and laid them out around the small round table. Mother then walked to the women and helped them to their feet. Meghan followed, taking the arm of the oldest woman. Halig and Eadwyn made room at the table for their guests.

Edrick held Elzera's hand watching the three walk toward him. The old woman took small delicate steps. The blind woman followed without any aid, but Edrick was sure she could not see anything in front of her.

"This is Gaebria," Mother said, indicating the strange girl. "And her grandmother, Bresigia."

"Hello, young man," squeaked the elderly lady. Edrick nodded, but did not reply. She, alone, did not look at him strangely, but seemed rather exhausted.

"Sarghan is my mother's name," came the girl's voice as she coaxed her grandmother into her seat. The sound of her voice surprised Edrick. It sounded soft and light, like tufts of white rabbit fur. It was vastly different than her worn appearance. "She hasn't spoken for a while. Grandmother says her spirit has shattered. Then the witches stole pieces of it when we were fleeing from the men..." She stopped and quickly looked at Grindan, then backed away, standing behind her mother, a table between them.

Grindan shifted his posture, seemingly having issues with his sword scabbard, moving the strap into a new position over his shoulder.

"It's all right, dear," Elzera joined them at the table. "Grindan, maybe you should take up your guard duties outside with Tellan. We will be fine here."

"Yes. Well Elisial, we will just be outside. Elzera, good to see you again."

"But not you, you big oaf."

Grindan attempted a half smile, then turned and left, Bron following. Meghan couldn't help but smirk, which caused Gaebria to smile at the very ends of her mouth. Her smile caught Edrick's eye. Her face lifted from the darkness, for a moment. The roughness dissipated under the light beneath her smile, slight though it was. She appeared beautiful in the soft glow of the room. Edrick smiled as well.

Elzera alone fended off the melancholy that would have otherwise stained the household that night. There remained an empty chair at the table and a bowl of cold broth left untouched. The old fortune teller chatted to all in the room, even to Sarghan, who seemed deaf as well, and never responded to anything Elzera said. Edrick thought it strange, but Elzera never seemed to notice. She spoke of many things Edrick came to love, strange lands, strange people and the love of traveling and new things. "The world changes, but you wouldn't know it in this little village, which isn't a bad thing for the most part. That is why I return as much as I can. But now and again, it's not a bad idea to take a peek around and find out where the road leads and discover what awaits you on your arrival. The wind blows two ways, to bring new things in and to take old things away."

"The wind stirs but the forest remains still,' Mother whispered into the fire.

Elzera became quiet for the first time in a while. "It will stir, and it will be hard to tell if the wind moves the trees or the trees move the wind."

Edrick did not hear the wind at all and wasn't sure what they were talking about. Trees don't move the wind.

Their three guests eventually retired into his parent's bed upstairs. Edrick's brothers had made room on the floor near the hearth for their beds, blankets and furs over the straw covered ground.

"I want to wander the roads with you, Auntie. You think I will ever be able to leave?" Edrick asked.

"Well, I think your mother and father need all of you here for quite a while. But when you get older, say Halig's age and feel like you want to travel, I think I can talk your mother into lending you out for one trip."

Edrick beamed and turned to his mother, who did not look happy at all. A cloud of sadness sat upon her head, as if leaving her would bring her to tears. He tried to ignore her mood. "But you can look into the future. Can you see if I ever leave the village?"

Elzera hesitated before she spoke, and looked to Edrick's mother. "Child, I can read a great deal many things from the lines etched upon your hand, mysteries of the past and omens of the future. But such knowledge is not granted casually."

Edrick loved when she spoke like that. No one else he knew spoke in such a grandiose manner, and waved their hands about with great importance. He thrust his hand forward for Elzera to read. She took it gently, covering his palm with hers. Her hand was cool and thin, but strong with a purposeful grasp.

Her serious demeanor softened. "Edrick, I can tell your future will be well rewarded without looking upon your hand. I see it written in your eyes and your heart."

Edrick was not going to settle for that soft sentiment. He had seen her read hands of others, and always wanted his read as well. "But I have to know if we are part elfish, as people say we are, or have the blood of dead kings."

Elzera bubbled with laughter, and even Edrick's mother smiled softly.

"So, you do? Why that is important affairs indeed." Elzera said. "I can't imagine how we had not investigated this matter before."

Eadwyn gave a snicker, but Meghan elbowed him in the ribs as she walked pass. The two eyed each other with disdain, but a flash from their mother's eyes, kept them from taking things further.

"Ah, well then, let's have a look." She moved his hand toward the direction of the fire, casting a golden glow over his soft, white skin. The lines blazed red up and down his palm. He wondered what messages were written there and desired the power to read palms as well. He must remember to ask her later.

He studied her face as she studied his hand. She looked puzzled, then concerned. She reflexively looked at him, then sat back in her chair and smiled. "Oh. Well there it is. Yes. You are an elf prince, which means that you are changeling, and this is not your real family."

"What? How awful" Meghan teased in dramatic concern, "yet somehow I sensed his otherworldliness. That explains his constant defiance and disregard for our parents. Is there any way we can return him to the fey and regain their favor?"

Halig and Eadwyn enjoyed Edrick's pouting face as Meghan now took her turn to tease him. Edrick felt slightly betrayed by Elzera who smiled with amusement shared by the rest of the family. "No," he held out his hand for all to see, "she read something here. Something important."

"Oh Edrick, I was just having some fun with you. Chiromancers rarely read the hands of children because their youth disguises their future and fortunes. It is not an easy thing to do, if at all possible. Your hand tells me you are your mother's and father's son, and that you are a bold child, which unfortunately for your mother, will last until you are into your adult years."

"That is no prediction, I could have claimed that," Halig added and the children laughed again. Mother just shook her head.

"True enough, Halig. It is often easier for a family member to predict the course of their younger brother's life than it would be an old fortune teller like myself. Well, it is getting late. Seeing as there are so many crowded in your home, I will just sleep in my wagon. That's home for me anyhow. G'night children."

"Goodnight, Auntie." They all called back.

Elzera bent down and kissed Edrick on his forehead as she headed toward the door. He did not appreciate it as much as he would have, had she really read what was written on his hand. She opened the door and walked out into the night.

"Everyone, time for bed." Mother announced. She moved from her seat by the hearth and toward the door. She slid an iron latch down into a slot fixed to the wall. She had not always taken such precautions, but everyone barred their doors now with the Folthnir camping so near, even if the woods did not behave so strangely.

All Edrick could think was Father, Sunniva and Baldice were on the other side of that locked door. For that reason only, it should have remained wide open.

Their mother laid down next to the rest of her children. Edrick on one side and Meghan the other, snuggling up to her.

"How about a story," Edrick asked, hopeful.

"Yes," Meghan agreed. "Emperor Abellious and his elfin bride."

"No! No princesses!" Eadwyn sat up and looked at his mother pleadingly. "I want to hear about how the dwarves battled the giants, chopped off their fat heads and turned their skulls into cauldrons."

"I've never heard mother tell such a disgusting story." Meghan looked up into her mother's face. Elisial wore a sly smile and kept her eyes upon the ceiling above.

"Sometimes I tell stories only the boys will like and sometimes I tell stories only you girls like, and usually one is not around the other when I tell them."

"But I do have a story in mind," she continued, "one I don't think any of you have heard. Edrick's questionable heritage brought it to mind."

"Does it have princesses in it?" asked Eadwyn skeptically.

"Maybe, I have yet to find out…"

The children looked at one another as they tried to decipher the cryptic reply, but that was something they loved about their mother. She could capture their interests with but a few words that promised a story; a narrative that would divulge the mysteries of the world.

They all lay quietly listening to the fire pop and sizzle from the hearth at their feet and the steady rhythms of sleepy breaths from their guests nearby.

Their mother began, "Long ago, this forest was not as it seems today. It was the home of good things like the noble elves, who tended the forest and saw to the growth of all the plants and trees. They planted every wild berry bush, and with help of the faeries, coloring the woods with numerous flowers.

"Faeries are the sometimes seen servants of the elves, who usually cloak themselves in magick to prevent mortals, like ourselves, from catching them at their work. They are divine beings of a lesser order than the elves, who all serve the Forest Spirit."

Elisial paused, seemingly reflecting on her words. Edrick felt as if all the cottage emptied suddenly with the interruption of her cadence, then he realized why the room felt so strange. Sunniva often asked questions, like who the Forest Spirit was, but instead, the room remained voiceless.

"We villagers often think ourselves alone out here next to this great forest, but we only think in terms to others like us, other mortals. But there is another kind of people who are our close neighbors, but hidden. In the days when the Wall around the village was first raised, the elves labored with village men in its construction, in order to keep out the beasties and nasties and unkind spirits of the wild. And from time to time, they honored us with a visit, and we would have feasts in our old Elder Hall, which is where the village chieftain made his home."

"Our Elder Hall?" Edrick asked, never having heard his mother speak of the village origins before.

Elisial gave a warm smile, looking delighted to have been asked the question. "Yes, that old, crumbling hall, where we now celebrated our festive days and auction our beasts, was once the hall of warriors and minor kings."

Eadwyn perked up a bit, interested that, so far, there was not a single mention of a princess.

"What happened to all these warriors and kings?" Edrick asked.

"Well for the most part, their blood remains in all of us. There just aren't as many kings anymore."

"Killed by those that conquered them," Eadwyn put in.

Elisial continued. "After many long years measured by our count, the elves forgot about us and ceased their visits. Like Eadwyn said, our kings fell to outside kings, who fell to others, which brought in a different people and habits and the old ways were forgotten by most."

"But you know the old ways, Mother, and Father too," Meghan said.

"We do, but that seems little comfort to me now."

Her words struck Edrick cold, who like his brothers and sister, didn't quite know how to take their mother's feelings. Both their parents always told them they were special because they remembered the ways of the world most people had forgotten. They lived under the grace of the Dragon Spirits, the Eshenar.

"But then many generations ago, a little girl wandered near our little cottage. A beautiful creature with hair like silky strands poured down from the nocturnal sky, saturated with motes of starlight. Possessed of jeweled eyes of deep amber, it was as if looking down a well and into the earth's heart. She was elfish and spoke strangely. She called herself a name that sounded like a song from her lips, but was difficult for any man to repeat, though young girls could sing it like a melody. So they called her Aslenissia, or *Image of Beauty*. She appeared young, of Edrick's age some eleven winters, yet that did not prevent most men to find her beauty ensnaring, and for the women, daunting.

"She left us gifts of rich honey and warm elfish bread that always kept moist. She spoke to our hunters and revealed places within the forest where they might capture the best sport. She came alone to the Stone circle accompanied by strange lions of a deep brown like rich earth, dappled by black spots, ones we have never seen before nor have known signs of their tracks in the forest. They were her guardians and stepped in silence.

"The villagers didn't understand her generosity because she asked nothing of them, and spoke little or not at all, though she was quick to laugh and was always merry. They in turn offered what best gifts they could, which she accepted graciously and seemed pleased. I think it pleased her just to be in their company, though I'm not sure what it was that drew her interest. After a while, she taught some of the girls her knowledge of the forest, secrets of plants and animals. But then, mysteriously, she stopped her visits and that was the last anyone could remember seeing the elves, and that was long ago. They called her Princess Aslenissia whether she was royalty or not, because she had a noble bearing, was wise for her age, and had knowledge of the world that must have come from formal studies, or so they thought."

"We had never heard of this elfin princess, Mother." Meghan said. "Do any of the other villagers know this story?"

"They might know it or a tale that speaks of an elfin princess I described, but completely unattached from any relationship to this village. For them, elves are not to be trusted, like witches and talking animals and many strange and rarely experienced things. They only know tales that cast such things in a dark light, never celebrated. That is why they fear things outside the Wall."

. The dreams that followed his mother's nighttime stories were always vivid and colorful, and this night seemed to last days, as Edrick inhabited the conjured images of his mother's tales. "Storytelling is a subtle magick," Mother once said, "one that plants little seeds into young minds. And as the child grows, so do these seeds, into flowering vines that wrap around the heart and soul until the adult finds themselves completely changed. They find the world not so scary, nor so mysterious, and they are prepared for the sadness that lies in the shadows and are delighted by the wonders they encounter, but are not surprised, because they have heard about them all their lives."

"And yet there are some things stories never prepare you for," was their father's grim, stubborn reply.

Edrick had always believed dreams prepared him for what was to come. They explored the parts of the story that remained unspoken, that could only be reached by him, because he knew where to look, where to explore. He knew when asking questions was not enough, and he had to see with his own eyes what lay hidden behind the silence of the words.

The forest, the faerie circle, at night beneath the stars, where the young Princess Aslenissia met the villagers was now before him, and he stood in the location where he saw his sister taken, and his brother dragged into the woods. He should have been with his father that night. Led him to the stone circle. He wanted to join him on his quest. But he realized he needed to hear this story and learn of Princess Aslenissia.

The air had a coolness that accompanied spring time nights. Despite the darkness and stillness, he could somehow see the woodland clearing well enough in the purple and blue hues, lit by waking stars and dark moons. He noticed a small figure standing in the center of the stone circle, a girl outlined in starlight. She faced him though he could not make out her fine features.

"Sunniva!" Edrick shouted, hopeful, and he ran toward her.

An explosion of movement erupted from the tree line, as shadows pulsated around him. Edrick halted, alert. What was that, in the woods? He had seen such moving shadows before in the forest, that very night, he remembered. However, the night did not look like this, as if he was seeing the world from underwater and the sunlight was diffused by the weight of an immense ocean above. There were things of shadows in the forest that pursued him, but did not wish to be seen.

"Move into the circle," sung a musical voice drifting across the clearing. She did not shout despite the distance. The starlight carried her voice. "Hurry, Edrick."

"Sunniva?" Edrick walked cautiously again toward the circle. He had heard that before, to step into the circle. It was Meghan who spoke then, but they found their way blocked by two foul monsters. He crossed the grass and expected something to grab him, block him from seeing Sunniva…

But as he entered the circle the veil of darkness lifted off the small girl. She was not his sister, as she appeared strange and beautiful. Edrick knew she was more than a girl. Her eyes glowed gold, chatoyant under the starlight, like brilliant amber gems, and her hair sparkled like silk spun from the very essence of night. Her skin was dark, like the raw earth. She seemed the fairest creature in all the world.

Edrick knew her from his mother's words, knew the name given to her by his people. "Aslenissia," he declared and wonder floated upon that name.

A smile warmed her face and a delicate light danced around the color of her eyes. "I have not heard that name in a while. It is a beautiful name, one I will always welcome to hear."

"Why are you here, now? My mother said you stopped visiting the village? Why did you stop?"

"I never stopped. I have watched your people for many years. I have cried many times seeing old friends pass into the mists of oblivion, and their children pass, then their children. I have watched you and your brothers hunt. I have seen your sisters dance in this circle which warmed my heart. I have always been here, because this is my home, and we are neighbors, and some time back, we were friends."

"Us?" Edrick asked with excitement.

The young elf burst in laughter. "No, not you, Edrick. I mean elves and men."

"Oh…" Edrick said, embarrassed. She was stunningly beautiful, like nothing Edrick had encountered before. He became increasingly uncomfortable in his simple clothes, torn and patched many times. She, decorated in a lavender dress that looked to him as if she wore a large flower, petals flowing down her waist, appearing as noble as his mother described. She continued to smile at him, which gave him a feeling that she could see him behind his clothes, that nothing stayed hidden in her presence. "Are you really a princess?"

"That is a rude question," and she laughed again, easily, amused at his simple inquiries, he thought. Her lips too, resembled petals of a pink rose, its texture as delicate.

"Are you the son of a woodcutter?" she replied with whimsy.

"Yes, and an alhíelda."

"And a storyteller," she added.

"Yes, my mother…she spoke of you. I know you now. I see you."

"And how are you? Is your family getting on?"

"We are still in grief, but I know they are still out there." Edrick pointed to the forest and the deep shadows. Her eyes followed his finger. The shadows retreated from her gaze, and a sadness came over her.

"Sunniva must be found." She replied, sullen.

"My father seeks her now. He will not fail."

"He will fail. He will be stopped. And they will keep him out."

"Who? Who will keep him out, the monsters? My father knows these woods. He has a title, passed on for generations, a title people have forgotten, but we have not; and he continues to serve. He is the Warden of the Woods. He will find my sister, and my brother."

She sighed, her breath rolled out in a pillowy mist. She stepped close to him, taking his hand, the same hand Elzera read that night. Her skin was soft and smooth like an infant. She had a fragrance that wrapped around him and pulled him closer until he felt uncomfortably close, but knew not why he felt so. She drew the hand up then pressed his hand between both of hers, cradling it against her chest.

"You must come find me. I am lost Edrick. Together we can find your sister. Your father will fail, but you will not. Remember the old ways, Edrick. Learn as much as you can from your mother." She spoke with grave urgency, pressing his hand tightly against her body. He felt her heart beneath her breast, throbbing with wild life.

The shadows rolled out of the woods like thick smoke, the light in the clearing diminished, as if the starlight were candles snuffed out of existence. He found this world shrinking into darkness.

"Promise me this. Seek me out," she pleaded with soft words.

"But if my father fails, how can I? I'm just a boy, and I couldn't even protect Sunniva, or Baldice. I can't do anything but cause harm..."

The shadows writhed as it rolled toward them, a dark tide washing the land, erasing the world. It would overtake him and Aslenissia in a moment. He tried pulling his hand away from hers. This time he was going to run, but she held on to him.

"Promise!" she commanded.

"Yes, I will!" he said with urgency. He tugged hard to free his hand from her unnatural strength. "I promise! Let me go!" he yelled as the darkness washed over them.

His hand was free, but he did not know if she released him or if she was no longer there. There was nothing but darkness the rest of the night.

When the morning began, Edrick could not rightly remember. He was outside in the sunshine and its rays were hot against his skin. It wasn't until he felt the sun burning, did he realize he had woken and left the night far behind. It was a strange sensation, as if he had stepped into another world. He knew he had dreamed. He knew it was important, but his mind was blank. He shut his eyes, and thought hard, but it was only darkness that came to him, until he opened his eyes again.

"Edrick," Elzera called to him from the house. "Come here boy and say goodbye."

He hurried across the yard, confused as to what he had been doing or when he woke or left the house. Elzera stood next to her wagon with his family, saying farewell to them as she prepared to leave.

"You are leaving? But I haven't had time to ask you questions, about the Goblyn Market, Princess Aslenissia, or what would keep my father out of the woods."

His brothers stepped to the side to allow Edrick to pass. Elzera waited, arms out wide.

"What's all this about goblyns and princesses?" Edrick squeezed her as hard as he dared, not wanting to hurt the old woman. "And your father keeps others out of *his* woods, not the other way around."

She didn't understand. He needed to talk to her. She was the one adult that listened to him seriously when he needed to speak his mind, and he didn't have to worry about what she thought of him.

"I want to ride with you." His mind raced for a way to speak to her. "Just until you pass under the yew."

"No, no, no. You are not going there," his mother swiftly corrected. "None of you children are to venture to that side of the village without your father or me."

"Ah, well how about I drop him off at Grindan's shop. I'll have him send Bron back with Edrick."

Edrick was hopeful, and pleaded for his mother to agree.

"Well you did finish many of your chores early this morning..."

He did? He didn't remember that.

"Fine, but no farther than Grindan's shop. And you are to come right back."

"Yes, Mother."

Edrick helped Elzera into the wagon. She often accepted his help where she would berate strangers for thinking her so frail or needy. Edrick was about to follow her onto the bench when a voice stopped him.

"Wait," called out a girl's voice.

"I would like to accompany you," spoke Gaebria timidly stepping into the sunlight from inside the cottage. "I would like to see your village in the daylight."

Elzera smiled and looked toward Edrick, and gave a wink. "Sure child, there is room for one more on my bench. Edrick, slide over and allow room for our guest."

Edrick scooted next to Elzera. From the bench he could see his mother and sister smiling, the same sly smile Elzera gave him a moment ago. As Gaebria climbed up the side of the wagon, Edrick extended a hand to help her into her seat. Her hand yielded like dough in his grasp. She gave him a quick smile before she settled next to him.

"Thank you," she shyly spoke. She appeared different in the morning light, her rough and dirty appearance washed away, her hair brushed, decorated with delicate braids running across her cheeks, her ghost-light rested atop the crown of her head. She wore a dress borrowed from his sister. He suddenly felt awkward sitting next to the strange and beautiful girl.

Elzera snapped the reins getting the horses moving. She began chatting right off as they pulled into the Lane, recounting the time she had these two awful mules that caused her such a headache. Father found her two of Lord Temen's horses, which she was proud to have saved from a life at the hands of the Folthnir. Edrick noticed she didn't mention anything about what happened to Lord Temen or his family.

"We know about the lord. And I know why mother wants us to stay near the house. We saw the crows pass over us. They roost in the forest, then take to the fields usually, to eat the grain. But a few days back, they flew to the Merchant Road, where crops don't grow."

Elzera looked at him, studying his demeanor. Edrick felt sad despite not knowing Lord Temen or his family well at all.

"The crows, they never flew back," he added.

They passed Oxa's house, where he and his sons were working the fields since early dawn. He stopped to wave at Elzera, Edrick and Gaebria. Edrick stood and waved back.

"So what did you want to ask me, that you think I might have the answer to?"

It was the dream. He couldn't remember it until it burst out of him when he needed to remember. "I had a dream last night, it seemed important but I can't remember it all. But then I asked about what would keep my father out of the woods. That was from my dream. That's all I remember."

Elzera sat in silent debate, Edrick guessed. She was a shrewd woman, but her forceful personality gave her away when she became quiet. Carefully chosen words were soon to follow.

"There is a long history here in your village, one that I don't have the time to share, though I would love to, and I know you would love to hear. So I say, listen to your mother's stories, not all of them are nonsense like your father believes, some of them are history, and some of them are secrets, masquerading as nonsense."

"Like the Goblyn Market?"

"Yes, such things are true."

"I know they are. And the elfin girl, she's real too."

"Elves are real too, of course."

"Then what were those monsters we encountered?"

She sighed. "Signs of the world growing darker than it ought to be. Your family's loss is testament to that."

"But what are they called? Surely Meghan described them to you."

"Yes, in great detail. The tall green one, sounded to me to be an ogre, which as you know, are fond of eating children. The other is a dæmon passing as a man, one that has the power to change his shape to an animal. Such things have not been encountered in this forest for ages, if ever. And this is why I must leave you so suddenly, Edrick, or I would stay and overturn every rock in that forest until we found Sunniva and Baldice. That I would promise. But I have to leave your father to that task alone. There are just too many pressing problems that an old lady like myself must go search for answers."

"And how do you do that, search for your answers?"

"Oh, well that is a trade secret, Edrick. It would take years of apprenticeship before I would even considering answering that question."

"I have always wanted to learn to read hands as you do. Do you think you can teach me someday?"

"I do. But I don't believe there will be time."

That's what he admired, she never said no and always left things as possibilities. That is how all people should approach life.

"What did you really see in my hand?"

"Oh, *now* you are asking the tough questions. I wasn't ready for that, but I should have been." She chuckled lightly. "Yes, your hand. So you don't think you're a changeling."

"Not likely, but it could be possible."

"Well *you* think highly of yourself. It is as I said, it is difficult to discern the destiny of a child. But…"

She lingered, fidgeting and tossing the reins a few times. More secrets. She would tell him, he knew. He needed to remain patient.

"You have interesting lines. I wonder if your brothers or sisters have such lines, but I would not want to gawk at their palms like a nosey old woman."

Edrick held up his palm. Pink lines crisscrossed his skin like plow marks in a field. He then remembered holding the soft palm of a girl, from his dream.

"It is all speculation Edrick, I cannot say for sure, so I won't say anything and fill your head with wild claims," she said with finality.

"No, its fine, I want to know."

She considered him for a moment. "Then I will tell you."

Edrick beamed. He was ready to hear this, waited to hear this all his life.

"When you are older and I can be sure."

"What! You can't say that!"

"Sometimes we are told things that we don't want to hear, so learn to move past it! The faster you do that, that faster you will be on your way to becoming a man."

She was trying to trick him now, so he would stop asking her.

"All right. Fine."

Edrick turned his head away from Elzera in frustration, only to be face to face with Gaebria, whose smile was now radiantly, and annoyingly, wide.

"What?" Edrick snapped at her. But she didn't seem offended at his rudeness, and contrarily, giggled at his reaction.

"You are so boyish, it's cute."

Elzera cackled aloud. "That he is. Charming isn't he?"

I'm not charming, Edrick yelled out, in his quiet thoughts. I'm tough and intimidating, and indifferent to girls and all their silliness. But as Gaebria's smile hung on her face, Edrick, found his anger diffusing. They soon arrived at the village center where the craftsmen worked, like Grindan. Elzera stopped the wagon in front of the Elder Hall.

"Edrick, I want you to swear to me, to obey both your parents, and mind Halig and Meghan. Your mother especially needs you, so behave yourself, and treat her kindly."

"I will, Auntie."

"And those troubling feelings you carry with you in your heart, concerning Sunniva and Baldice…" she paused to look into his eyes. Edrick looked back knowing he could not hide his heart from her. "Do not push those feelings away. Embrace them as they come, then leave the grief behind you. That is the only way to heal."

So she knew? She knew his sister and brother were not coming back, and this was her way of saying it. He wanted to cry, and would have, but remembered Gaebria sitting next to him. So he did exactly what Elzera told him not to do, he pushed those feelings away.

"Well, at least when you are alone, heed my words. Anyway, Gaebria, you are a lovely child, and you can take that same advice. Trust in Elisial and Alaric, they are good people. I have a feeling your mother will be cured in time, under Elisial's care. See to your grandmother. I will be around again sooner than later, as is my custom."

Gaebria cast her eyes down and did not look up, but nodded instead, acknowledging Elzera's words.

The two watched her off, standing beside one another. They remained until Elzera made her way up the inclined path that led to the Merchant Road beneath the yew tree. A moment later there was an uproar of corvine wailing as scores of crows shot up into the sky in a sudden panic. They scattered in all directions fleeing the village and the yew tree in great haste.

"I guess Auntie frightens them," commented Edrick, not the least surprised.

"That is a good sign," Gaebria said then turned to Edrick, quietly waiting.

Edrick stared back at her, not knowing what to say, or do. He had never been alone with a girl before, especially a pretty and unfamiliar one.

"You shouldn't stare at me like that," she said after uncomfortable moments.

"Uh...Oh sorry," Edrick turned and stepped away feeling slightly awkward.

Gaebria stepped toward him and pulled his hand, gently, to turn him back around. "Not that I don't like you..." she corrected.

Edrick could see she was upset, but he realized it was not with him.

"It's just I wouldn't want you to grow up like that. As one of those men that leer. I mean, you weren't, but...I just don't want you to grow up to be someone like that."

Edrick wasn't sure what she was talking about, but gave an obeisant nod.

Pleased, she looked over his shoulder to the building behind. "What is that?"

"That's our Elder Hall. Mother said it was once a palace to kings. Come on, I will show you." He took her hand and the two ran inside. Edrick thought it would be great to show Gaebria his knowledge of the village. He had hoarded stories to tell and he finally had a captive audience to share.

As soon as they entered, the smell of animal stench struck Gaebria. She threw up her hand across her face. Cats filled the hall as if this were a feline palace. Each one froze as the two entered, then quickly bolted out of sight. Cats alone could not explain the entire stench, which was also littered with piles of excrement.

"It smells like a barn. Why do you call it an Elder Hall?"

"Because important business is conducted here."

Gaebria carefully made her way to the center of the building, tip toeing around piles of animal waste. "Since when are animal droppings important business?"

"No, not that. It will be all cleaned out by Summer Solstice, and again on Harvest Festival. In spring, no one meets here that often because they are busy in the fields. But during the winter this place is kept clean. Unless it freezes, then we might have some animals back in here."

"In Athéalgian, we keep our animals in stables and barns."

"Where do families meet then?"

"We meet in each other's homes if we want to talk."

"Yeah, but what about weddings and funerals or feasting to honor the gods?"

"In the city squares, or guild halls, if your family is guild. Father was a tailor to the lords," she said with pride.

"Oh. That is strange." She was starting to use unfamiliar words, Edrick thought.

"No, *this* is strange," pointing to the clay pots and wooden crates stacked toward the roof, wagon wheels and broken ploughs. It seemed anything that was not wanted anymore by the villagers ended up here. And all about were the cats, scurrying in and out of shadows, dancing through their many hiding nooks and concealed crevices. They kept silent, tolerating the intruders, though watchful and alert.

"Why does your village have so many cats? I didn't notice them last night, but they are everywhere. Did you have rat problems?"

Edrick stared at her in disbelief. "Doesn't your village have cats too?" he answered, as if the very presence of these cats should be self-explanatory.

"I lived in a city," she corrected him. "A few, but not everywhere. We have dogs too, which probably keep the cats away. Why so many?"

"Because of the faeries," Edrick said, thinking that should explain everything.

Gaebria stopped and stared at him, frustration building on her face. She seemed to be waiting for some elaboration.

Edrick thought this girl was dense and he was beginning to think the city was full of strange and backward people, just as Elzera once warned him.

"Because cats can see the Fey. So, they warn us when there are bad faeries in the village, so we know where to place our traps."

"Traps?"

Really? She doesn't know about faerie traps?

"Yes, we have to trap the bad ones to get rid of them, or the whole village would be overrun with them, causing all sorts of problems."

"And you don't have that issue with cats?"

Edrick didn't understand. He just explained why they had cats.

"Never mind," she said. "So do cats ever catch the faeries?"

Edrick shrugged. "I guess they might. They probably eat them like they eat birds, but I have never had any dead faeries at my doorstep. How do you guys get rid of faeries?"

"I guess we don't. We have a wall around our city, like a hundred times larger than yours. I think it keeps things like that out. But they seem to be around out in the pastures and fields that lie outside the city, so I hear. But no one ever seemed concerned with them, I mean really concerned with them. In fact, I can't remember anyone except children speak about them."

Edrick didn't like her tone. She was acting as if he were speaking about childish things and was making it all up. He thought he should go check the traps and see if he caught a rogue faerie. That would keep her mouth shut.

"What's that?" she asked pointing to a framed parchment hanging on the wall. It was decorated with words, as Edrick liked to say. The curvy lines and dots and uniform rows seemed beautiful to him.

"That is one of our village secrets," he said quickly forgetting his frustrations as he was given another opportunity to show off his knowledge.

"A secret in plain sight?"

There she goes again.

"Yes," he said sharply. "I will show you."

He wasn't supposed to touch it. The Elders had forbidden all but Elder Council from handling it. But as his father held a titled position, Edrick would someday be afforded the right to hold it. Father told him that there was a map behind the words, one that showed the secret paths of the forest and the different villages in the surrounding areas. His father claimed, since no one ever touched the parchment, no one ever knew what was on the other side.

Edrick stacked up a few crates so he could reach it. He climbed up and delicately lifted the frame off its mountings and brought it down.

He flipped it over and there on the other side, was a map with brilliant colors; painted green forests; ribbons of silvery blue ink for the streams and lakes. In black ink were more words scattered across the surface and markings for towns and things of importance. Some of the words penned in large red lettering. Edrick never knew what any of it meant, but after years of sneaking into the hall and studying the cartography, he inferred the location of his village.

"We are here," he said with authority that could leave no doubt in her mind.

She looked at him impressed. "You can read?"

Edrick considered lying in hopes to impress her further, but decided that the truth was more impressive. "No, but I know we live next to the forest, and this is the old Ruined Tower. So this circle just south of it must be our village. Look, here is the Elder Hall. And just west of the village are the Stone Circle marked here...." His voice trailed off, "where we met those monsters."

Gaebria placed a hand on his back and patted him, then spoke softly, "I lost loved ones too. I'm sorry, truly sorry for them. But your father might be able to find them, right? We know of the Hero of Athelyn in Athéalgian. Your family is old and reputable. They served the king in times pasts. I would have never guessed he was just a village woodcutter."

Edrick was astonished. In his own village, most people thought of his family as oddities. To hear that other places held his father in esteem was a grand revelation. Perhaps she was not as ignorant as he first thought. It then occurred to him, how it seemed the villagers had forgotten such important things and why they were important.

"I didn't know my father was so well known. It makes me happy to hear that."

"Well, Edrick, son of Alaric, Warden of the Woods, it is my honor to be the bearer of good news." She spoke teasingly, but truly sincere. "That must make you a boy of importance. The future Warden of the Woods."

Edrick smiled, thoroughly flattered. It was her turn to smile at him, as she looked into his eyes until he blushed and looked away, back to the map.

"What are these lines, in the forest?" She asked him. "And the dots?"

"I'm not sure. That is one secret I have yet to discover. There have been times I've wanted to ask my father, but then he would know I peeked at the map." It just occurred to him one of these might lead to the Goblyn Market, to Sunniva and Baldice!

Gaebria parted her lips to ask another question, when shouting erupted from outside the hall. Edrick jumped. He rushed back up the crates to place the frame back on its mounting.

Gaebria turned toward the door, hustling across the floor. "Hurry," she whispered back.

Edrick moved the crates away from beneath the parchment, then kicked the torn clothes around floor, covering the drag marks left behind.

Gaebria let out a muffled shriek and ran back across the hall to the opposite door that led behind the building. Her face was full of terror as she glanced at Edrick. "It's them!" she whispered harshly, "they're here for me. I have to go."

"Wait!" Edrick yelled as softly as she. He ran, scattering the cats, as they dashed out of his way. They reached the door, but hesitated, listening for movement. Edrick reached to open it, but Gaebria stopped him. She was absolutely terrified and silently pleaded to him to not touch the door.

"What if they are out there?" She said, shrinking back against the wall.

He opened the door slightly and looked through the crack of

light. The yard behind was empty of people. Edrick turned back and rushed over to Gaebria.

"There is no one. Come. Grindan's shop is not too far. We can be safe there."

The mention of the large man did not reassure the frightened girl. "His wife will keep us well hidden," he added. "Just trust me."

He reached out to her. She turned away, reflexively. There was more shouting, things falling and pottery breaking from across the hall, outside. Then the far door burst open and a Folthnir youth stormed in. Gaebria jumped and seized Edrick's hand. The two rushed out the back door, not looking back.

Running, they crossed the yard to the nearest building. Grindan's shop was not far off. Smoke from his forge left a dark smudge in the sky, an aerial trail they could follow.

Edrick led the way toward safety. There was no cover as they raced over the open ground. Edrick saw a group of Folthnir warriors to his right, standing near the area where Elzera dropped them off. A few of the villagers were sitting, some lying in the dirt at their feet. The men's heads turned as they caught the movement of Edrick and Gaebria flying from them. They shouted and gave chase.

"We're almost there," he assured Gaebria. Her grip was tight. She trembled with fear, sending vibrations up his arm.

He steered her left, cutting sharply along the shop's outer wall. They were about to turn the corner when Grindan stepped out. They crashed into him. He snatched them up in each of his muscular arms.

Gaebria instantly screamed and started thrashing, tugging at the large man's hold. Edrick rushed to speak, "Grindan, you have to hide us. They are after her."

Yet instead of releasing them, the blacksmith picked them up, one under each arm and carried them away from the shop, away from safety, back toward danger.

"What are you doing?!" Edrick yelled. He now fought against the man's giant strength. He swung his leg and kicked the man's thick shin. His bones were like iron, sending pain up Edrick's leg as his toes buckled beneath his own force.

The three Folthnir arrived and slowed as Grindan approached. They were not men but youth, around Eadwyn's age. Each wore wolf hides across their shoulders, and a mask of wolfish visage. Black paint stained their skin, swirling in strange patterns around their necks, across their chest and around their right arm.

One boy drew a short sword and led the way, while another two drew arrows on short bows.

Grindan threw Gaebria to the ground first, then Edrick, as if they were sacks of coal.

"Who are they?" asked the youth swordsman in broken Mithlian.

"This is the son of the Woodcutter. The girl is not from this village."

"I am Edrick," he answered for himself. Grindan and the others simply ignored him.

"The Woodcutter? They are saying he returned and cut down the bodies from the yew."

"Yes, he was here but he fled back into the forest last night."

The youth scoffed. "He is afraid of us then?"

"No. He lost two children to the dæmons in the woods." Grindan's voice was flat, unemotional, devoid of the person he seemed last night.

Edrick saw the Folthnir tense at the mention of dæmons.

Grindan was different, cold and distant. Why was he talking to their enemies?

"What dæmons?"

"I'm not sure. Dæmons that ate this boy's brother and sister."

Gaebria lay still upon the ground. Tears pooled in her eyes, though she did not make a sound. Edrick had enough of this chatter and stood up. The youth with the sword pummeled Edrick in the stomach, blasting the breath out of his lungs. Edrick doubled over and vomited, falling into his pool of acidic fluid.

"Take them." The youth ordered. Edrick and Gaebria were hoisted over the shoulder of each Folthnir.

"How many more sons does this Woodcutter have?"

"Two. The eldest is close to a man's age."

"Good."

They turned and walked toward the Lane where two more Folthnir in wolf mantles guarded a handful of prone villagers.

The youth spoke to the other two in the Lane. Edrick then saw four more Folthnir holding the reigns of nine horses down the road. One tall warrior with a bandage around his neck stood behind the rest, holding the leashes of five hounds. He commanded all there with just a look.

"Where is this Woodcutter's hovel?" the youth demanded from the submissive villagers lying in the dirt road.

They all pointed back down the Lane.

12

LHODYN OF WUDELIC

ALARIC FOUND THE STONES bathed in silver, crescent moonlight, imbuing them with a haunting glow. Like barren bones they rose, erupting out from the earth, skeletal remnants of a people that long slept. No soothing sight were these ruins, powerless they remained, same as their makers in this age.

In the Wudelic, the elves remained as ghosts.

The brilliant blue candle light revealed signs of the horrific scene that unraveled over a week before. Alaric read the tracks written in the disturbed earth as he walked through Edrick's account in his head. He found the spot his children stood, one taken into the woods, one taken toward the stone circle. Sunniva would be difficult to find if Edrick's account of the scene was accurate.

The Stones too, told a story. The taller ones had been recently cast down and broken in two. Unfamiliar runes were carved on the ones that remained standing, newly etched. Sunniva could have been taken anywhere. He had nothing to follow.

Grasping his torc, he prayed to Mûl, Spirit of Fortune. "Through your wisdom, guide me down the path that leads me to Sunniva and Baldice."

To Telanthyan, Spirit of Light he prayed. "Stay with my children until I have them back in my arms."

He was left with only two options, find Aweirgan, the man he believed saved his children, or wait for Lhodyn to summon him.

He prayed to see Aweirgan's face first.

He discovered blood, dried, clumping the grass together, leading to a forest path. The great boar tore up the earth as it crashed through the trees. Alaric followed the tracks and those of a man with wolves pursuing it.

Owls cooed from hidden recesses, an inquisition for the one that entered their nocturnal domain. Across the woods they sounded out. Always they seemed near and ever vigilant.

The boar took a path well known to Alaric. It would lead him into the deeper woods beyond the river, the boundary he held his children to.

He was only twenty paces into the woods before great fluttering moths swarmed around him. Their wings spanned a foot and colored like ash. They circled his head, obscuring his sight, attracted by the faerie light. Alaric swatted at them, flinging the lantern around, but there were too many. Plumes of sooty dust burst from their delicate wings. Alaric squeezed his eyes shut and rushed away from them in his blindness.

A soft caress of wind touched his face when suddenly the lantern tore out of his grasp. A great white owl, with tines of a woodland doe, snatched the light away, flying into a distant tree where it perched.

The light diminished into darkness.

"Ooooo, ooo, ooooooo!" it called to him, then clacked its beak in a rapid, tight succession, like the sound of two bones being knocked together, popping and smacking in hollow notes. The moths scattered in the owls wake. Alaric could only see its large disc eyes reflecting back to him.

The owl did not cease with its bone clashing noise as he hiked through the forest. Other owls joined it, until all the forest was filled with the racket.

Tracks left by heavy boots continued down the trail. There was a pause in the chase. Here, there was a confrontation between the boar and Aweirgan. Alaric searched around the trail and found a group of animals gathered around something, feasting on something. Alaric chased them off and came to where they ate. He found the arm of a person, chewed and already smelling foul.

Alaric dropped to his knees, sure the arm was that of his son, Baldice. This was no way for his gentle son to die. This was no way the kin to the Warden of the Woods should be treated.

He cursed Lhodyn.

As if in response, a furry crawler bolted out from the brush and seized the arm, carrying it off into the night.

She will answer for this! He swore in silence.

Alaric ran through the woods, chasing after Aweirgan's tracks. He must find him. Alaric trusted his words, trusted that he could make sense of this darkness that now lay over these woods. But the trail shifted, taking him in a different direction than where the tracks led. He stopped and back tracked, but the trail shifted again, leading him farther away from the trail he had been first following.

He cut across the woods, where there were no paths, even as the vines and branches seem to lay hold of his feet and legs, impeding his chase, until another trail suddenly appeared before him. He stopped and changed direction, not willing to follow these false trails.

Lhodyn was working against him, delaying his search for Aweirgan.

He yelled into the night. "Why does Lady Lhodyn act against me, the Warden here, without provocation! My family and I have been gravely harmed. I hold any that impede me unjust and my enemy."

The forest stopped again, the vines that ensnared his feet went slack. The owls ceased their chattering clicks, their eyes widened upon him, focusing their scrutiny.

Then a tide of brambles snaked around his legs, around his torso, wrapping around his wrists and neck. He quickly drew his knife. He fought back, slashing at the plants, severing the limbs before they found purchase over him. Slowly, the vines overpowered him, pulling him against an ash tree where it bound him securely, the thorns painfully piercing through his linen and leathers.

A haunting laughter rolled through the gray trees, a mad delight of an old crone echoed toward him from some remote distance. It was not the voice of Lhodyn, who always projected an image of power, youth and beauty. The sound gave Alaric cold shivers, despite himself. He looked around for the emergence of the goddess or something sent in her service. The wide, moon shaped eyes of the owl creatures stared back at him, never blinking.

Despite being bound to the tree, Alaric grasped his knife still, working against the vines with miniscule slices. He was rendered vulnerable to whatever dark beasts or creatures that now stalked these woods. He must now fight to keep himself alive if only to return to his family.

The owls began their clicking and popping once again, but with excited intensity. Something then stirred in the woods, snapping dead twigs beneath its steps. Slowly, strange wolf like creatures, with eyes and horns of goats, silver beards and bristling quivers along the ridge of their backs, prowled toward Alaric. Something of a dozen, at least, crept out of the shadows. They did not move toward him directly, but instead circled him ominously.

Alaric then realized what approached. He waited for the Lady's prime servant.

The Nithyng.

A low growl, deep and resonating as a landslide, silenced the owls and their incessant clacking. Faint yellow eyes appeared in front of Alaric in the darkness. Large eyes. Bigger than the strange owls, and they did not appear above him, but opposite his own.

Out stalked a huge wolfish beast as tall as a Wultheron stallion, but it too had the blended features of goat and deadly quills bristling upon its back. It was thick in body, wolverine like, dæmonic in disposition as it bared its teeth, snorting threateningly. Riding upon its back, a figure sat astride regally, possessing the form of a man, yet bestial in countenance.

On this rider's head rose a rack of antlers, twisting tines that formed a wicked crown. Its ears were long and doe like, its eyes milky white, bearing the gaze of the dead. Its face was masculine with delicate features that seemed once handsome, but now ancient and decayed. It now resembled a hardened feral mask, wild and uncompassionate. The rider approached Alaric on his monstrous stead until the beast's sizzling breath roasted the Woodcutter's face.

The rider swayed slightly, his head pivoting slowly like one of the perched owls, from left to right. It inhaled the cool woodland air and released chilled breaths of white smoke.

It spoke slowly. "Alaric…son of Accenen, son of Aldred, son of Eldred, son of…." it breathed in again, this time leaning closer, "son of Childric, son of Hererinc, son of Vselwulf, son of Hilderinc…."

He paused again as he slid off the beast's back like an engorged tree snake. Then with a touch to the neck, he dismissed his mount. It joined the others encircling the tree.

"…many, many, are the sons of Renweard, first of Wardens. But their blood thins like a stream poured out into desert lands. It is no wonder our Lady no longer tolerates your filth traipsing around her abode. The smell of your kind soils the purity of this land."

Alaric freed his arm and continued to sever the vines from his chest. The creature of Lhodyn appeared unconcerned, leaning closer until its white spheres floated at the tip of Alaric's nose. It peered through eyes lacking pupils, unnatural orbs of blank white space. It held Alaric's gaze, if its action could be called such, without the proper portals to take in light.

As soon as he was free of the foliage Alaric snapped his knife to the things throat and rested it there. Through the rigid coal forged steel, Alaric felt the faint signs of life flowing underneath its skin as he desperately pressed against its hoary throat.

"What eyes mortals possess," it rasped, "like starlight housed in a vessel of frailty. It is valor alone that keeps the flames of some from diminishing into utter darkness, valor to meet out forces greater than thee in the face of impending and unalterable destruction."

"And has the fire within you been plucked and sealed away without hope, Nithyng?"

"Such a question warrants no answer," the creature snatched Alaric's wrist and twisted it over until his bones painfully locked at the terminus of their natural motion. His knife plummeted toward the ground.

"The Lady hungers for the fires burning in mortal bellies and her beasts are want for their flesh." He threw Alaric to the ground. Deftly he sprang to his feet, Nithledan in hand, arrow seated on the string.

"Ah, the Lady's bow. She will be glad you have returned it."

"It is my family's bow."

"No longer."

"I came for an audience."

"So here I am," it tilted its head forward, slightly, "Her servant to receive you."

"No!" Alaric bellowed. "I have a need to see Her and no substitute."

"Your son is dead. He belongs to Her now, in Her underground Vaults he awaits the Hunt. Your daughter, given away to those loyal to our Lady-Might."

The creature crooked his head, as a wolf might express interest in an unwary mouse that suddenly caught its attention.

Alaric said nothing. He held his arrow ready. Nithledan quivered at his fingertips, eager to impale the body of this ancient creature.

"Our Lady has had a change in heart recently. She has not been pleased by your long absence, your neglect of duties, your disregard for oaths. You are treacherous, Woodcutter, and as you have discovered, your kin risks much by stepping into Her realm."

Alaric's anger swelled throughout his body, blood surged through his eyes. *It* was accusing him of treachery! It was Lhodyn that betrayed him, and everything his family did for that ungrateful and loathsome goddess.

Shnikt came the whisper of Nithledan's voice, lashing out like a viper's venomous fangs. The arrow plunged into the thing's chest, but not its eyes! Behind Alaric, a bestial chorus of growls threatened to tear him asunder. He spun around, another arrow in his fingertips. Large yellow-green eyes bore down on him from all around. Mad wolves, with strange eyes stalked toward him.

Another arrow flew from his fingertips, but a shadowed blur of a horned owl ripped it out of the air as it flew past. Then another missile, and another, rushing toward those disturbing goat eyes.

Then the Nithyng commanded from the darkness two words, "Biwawan onweg."

Before the arrows could cross the space between Alaric and the beasts, motes of purple light, like sparks spilt at a fey forge, erupted out of the air, surrounding the shafts. A burst of wind followed the light, deflecting the arrows harmlessly around the creatures.

Alaric expected to be mauled under the heavy claws of the wolfish beasts, but they instead halted and abruptly turned away.

The Nithyng cast the arrow that impaled its chest at Alaric's feet. Alaric turned to face it, not at all deterred from sending more barbed tips through its flesh.

It appeared unharmed and composed as when they first met.

"Your rage is wonderfully pleasing. I have lost mine long ago," it said with hint of longing.

"Do you feel anything at all?"

"Yes," it answered simply. "Hate."

For the first time, Alaric pitied the creature. To be enslaved to Lhodyn for so long and carry out her biddings, her cruelty, and realize freedom was unattainable. He picked up his arrow, looking at the barbed tip, the clean tip that bore no blood back to him. No possibility of death.

"Have you forgotten who crafted this weapon?" It wondered.

"No."

"It hates as well." The Nithyng extended a hand toward Alaric's bow.

Nithledan quivered with malice. Alaric did not desire to relinquish it, but the Nithyng was its master. He felt compelled to hand it over.

"I can feel it," it said as his ash colored skin stroked the polished wood, as if a merchant appraising a rare object. "It still retains its spirit from the time we hewed the tree down. How very powerful that wood is." The creature handed the bow back, then absently rubbed it hands against one another.

"But not enough power to slay you," Alaric challenged.

The thing smiled, like a decrepit old man. "Is that your wish Alaric, to see me dead? I had nothing to do with the death of your children." It began to walk away, as if their business was concluded.

Alaric followed. "I know what you desire Daenuarion. I can release you from Her."

It halted.

Alaric guessed at what it truly hated.

"I will go to Lhodyn and speak for my son and daughter. But I don't consider this matter concluded, even if I could walk out of these woods with them in hand and unharmed. My forefather Renweard made an Oath to Lhodyn to uphold the woods, to see it flourish. But this is darkness!" He extended his hand, sweeping the woods around. "Not what he swore to endure. He swore in allegiance to an idea, to serve in honor of the true spirit of the woods as it was then, not to serve as a blind slave and have her alter and blight the land with evil."

"But that is where you are wrong Woodcutter. Upon swearing, Renweard was told to cut down a very significant tree, a mathelian tree. And out of its corpse I was tasked with crafting the Lady's new servant a mighty bow, and I named it Nithledan. Such a tree was the last of its kind for leagues around, if such things still inhabit the world. You see, Renweard betrayed one master to follow another."

"Liar!" Mathelian trees were on par with the gods, trees that held immortal spirits. Within Alaric's own family, they were greatly revered and even worshipped. "She lies to you and you spread her taint like a disease. It was not always this way, prince. Think back, to your youth. Remember the beauty of Wudelic."

"Mortals have no memories of the past, just stories. Sweet, tasty lies. Truths are often bitter fare." It continued walking away. Out of the shadows lumbered the Nithyng's large steed. It fell into pace beside the Nithyng, ignoring Alaric entirely.

The horned owls followed their master, flying silently through the air, like woodland ghosts. One flew over, dropping Alaric's arrows at his feet, then another, as if all the woods were telling him he was utterly powerless.

"I'll make you an offer, Nithyng," Alaric yelled out. "To rid this land of Her, together!"

"If such a thing were possible I might consider an alliance, but I have lived many years and seen many Woodcutters buried beneath the roots of numerous unknown and forgotten trees. As they say in your foolish village, your family's blood runs through this forest. Goodbye Woodcutter." The creature swiftly climbed upon the large beast's back and stormed off into the darkness of the night.

"And what of Aweirgan?" Alaric called after it.

The other beasts had withdrawn as well, for Alaric saw no further sign of them, not even a distant howl indicating they were not far off. Alaric collected his knife and arrows. There was but one choice now. He must confront his Lady-Might.

Lhodyn, he had been told through family lore, was a goddess that wandered the world and found the beauty and power of Wudelic enrapturing. Many gods walked the land in those distant ages, for there was a powerful enemy that pursued them, one that remained unknown to him or anyone he questioned about such knowledge. She was at first generous and benevolent, having found a respect from the suspicious elves that were already masters of the Wudelic. But slowly she asserted her power, controlling the hearts of the beasts and the spirits of the faeries that inhabited the land. The elves contested her, but fled for fear of harm to those that were once friends, forest creatures that came under the influence of the goddess, those they loved.

But men had no such understanding or bonds to the woods, not even Alaric's sires, who struggled as any person would to survive in past, harsh climes. To enter into a pact with such a goddess guaranteed advantages over the service to any king, or alliance with the elves. Alaric wondered, was it desperation that made his forefather choose his path, or as legend speaks, his self-possessed nobility, recognized and rewarded by Emperor Abellious. If it was as the Nithyng revealed, it was regrettably the former.

These were the old ways, he bitterly thought.

There was a location his ancestors retreated to when in need of audience with the Lady. A pool of pristine spring water laid hidden deep within the forest, where no paths or trails led. It was marked only in the minds of the Woodcutters, who imparted their knowledge from father to son. Alaric made his way there and found his path unobstructed.

The pool never flowed anywhere, even during the heaviest rains and yet it remained clear and clean, free of mud or any other kinds of pollutant marring other stagnant pools. As Alaric approached it now, he noticed it appeared not like the disk of silver he had known from past visits, but had darkened into a glass of lightless obsidian.

The grove stood quiet and still.

He spoke a small prayer to Telanthyan. "Shine your light on me. Lend me your strength."

Alaric took a moment to master his rage and remember courtesy.

"Lady and Mistress of the trees, of all those within its bounds, and those that dare tread under Her leaves, or burrow beneath the ground," he began declaring her prestige and eminence. "I, Alaric the Woodcutter, son of Accenen the All-Hunter, son Aldred the Hidden, implore an audience with the Green Lady. I have an urgent matter that needs discussion, one of great importance." His voice faded into the open space, sinking into the black surface of the glassy pool, lost into the depths of the surrounding trees.

Nothing stirred at first.

Lights blinked into life high above him, floating down from the tree canopy, tiny motes of heavy blues and deep purples. The lights were soft and did nothing to expel the thick darkness of the night. They floated down as stardust, descending slowly, rotating deasil around the black pool, and gathering near the surface. Alaric watched the procession of faerie light, wondering at the distinct change of color from what was once familiar to him, colors that were once shades of sunlight, oranges and yellows, gold, or emerald greens of the forest. This appalling contrast reaffirmed Alaric's impression that Lhodyn and all the woods has metamorphosed into something unfamiliar.

The faeries continued to gather around the pool, floating silently out of the forest like ghost-lights beckoned back to the grave. They infused the water, passing through the surface as starlight through glass. Some broke away and floated around Alaric, churning in front and behind him. He felt a charge of energy expanding through the air. Whispered voices moved near him, slipping into his ear like gently murmurs of a forest breeze.

"Alaric the Woodcutter has finally come to seek audience with the Lady, even as the time of his summons has expired," whispered a small voice.

"Many moons have turned since our Lady last met with the Woodcutter, Alaric. She is not pleased to have you visit now," whispered another.

"Yet there is an unfinished matter She wishes to speak to you about, Alaric, son of Accenen, last of the Oathholders. Show her respect!" it demanded. Then in a harsh, hurried whisper, "She comes now!"

Last of the Oathholders. What vitriolic accusations!

The faerie lights had finally settled into the pool where they grouped so closely together that their tiny individual lights now became one brilliant sphere, illuminating the entire watery mass. Alaric felt something emerge from the forest and enter the grove, something powerful and full of wrathful energy. He neither saw nor heard Her passing, but knew She arrived. This feeling surrounded him, filling the grove. The air began to buzz and hum, taking on the scent of the ancient, like the delved earth recovered from a deep mine.

"Oathbreaker!" A loud accusing voice thundered. The water depressed and rippled as if something heavy crashed into it. The pool lights burned fiercely then exploded above the water surface, taking the form of a giant woman filled with faerie light.

Alaric controlled his emotions.

"My Lady, Mistress of the Forest. What have I done that has deemed me unfavorable?" he demanded.

"Summoned you were three times to an audience. You failed, and not even a reply!"

"But Lady, I was forced to leave my home. I made my intentions and reasons clear. Our lands are at war, and all our families are in peril."

"We care not for your homes or your priorities! It is Our priorities that should be your concern. Many generations your family has been in Our service to our mutual benefit. Now such service has been terminated due to your neglect. Never has a time come such as this where enemies have arrived in Our lands and camped on Our doorstep like thieves. We now seek only those that have unflinching loyalty."

New enemies? Was she referring to the Folthnir? A threat to her?

"Lady and Mistress of Trees that is exactly the nature of my audience. Our enemies are the same, as they have been when my father served you loyally, as all of my kin. These men must be expelled..."

"Don't contradict Us!" the voice boomed.

Water lunged out pool like an amorphous limb, slamming into Alaric, lifting him clear off his feet.

"We have declared those who are Our enemies and those who have failed Us. Your service ends now and all your privileges are forthwith revoked. Your status is as any other mortal. We will have you surrender Nithledan," she exclaimed.

Alaric stood defiant, indignant of her claims.

"This bow I care little compared to the lives and deaths of my family. You, too, swore to protect my family and all in my household. You failed this oath. What is fealty without honor?" He threw the bow down violently. "There has been a travesty committed under your house against my son and daughter. How have you allowed this?! I care not for my life and will submit before you, but I demand you release my son's spirit trapped in your purgatory Vaults and deliver me my daughter!"

There was a reproachful hush across the forest, shocked at the Woodcutter's open and vulgar outrage.

"Yes, Baldice remains with Us." Her voice was calm, yet remained menacing. "A fair price for not slaying you as soon as you trespassed into Our forest. You desire to flee Our realms, then flee coward, and be gone! You have dishonored Us and your sires, tonight."

"No!" Alaric shouted back.

"Mortal, Our patience is not retained for the foolish!"

She paused. Her voice started again so sweet, "Daenuarion so desires to spill your blood. Has so, for so long. Shall We grant him this one selfish desire?" she asked playfully.

A haunting chorus of laughter rose around the glade, the sound of cackling delight of women, young and old. Alaric then noticed the Nithyng standing across the pool, hidden within the trees, barely visible in the darkness, save his glowing white eyes.

"Let me take up this bow and hunt down the monsters that murdered my children. Allow me to recover my son's and daughter's bones and place them in sacred earth so they will pass through the Splendid Gates to the Hallowed Halls. Allow me this, I beseech."

He dropped to his knee and bent his head.

"You want to hunt, Woodcutter? Bring Us each and every one of those northmen's heads. Only then might We consider a reprieve on this doom."

Alaric did not expect this. It was impossible even if he desired it himself. Even then, he would lose Sunniva if she remained alive, and all his family would be in grave danger unless they fled with Elzera south.

"These northmen must be made to recognize who is goddess of this land. They have already placed alters and made sacrifices to their far-off gods, who have no ears in Our realm. Yes. They must be taught to fear and respect Us! What say you, Woodcutter? Do this and you might find Our favor again."

"What of my daughter Sunniva? Deliver her." He willed himself to speak the next word that tasted of vile dung. "Please, my Lady-Might."

She laughed at him. The other haunting voices joined in. The Nithyng stepped forward out of the trees into the glade.

"No." She said simply. "And if you have lost the heart for bloodshed then just lead them to the forest edge so my children might dispatch them. Shoot any that flee. Is that not what you did in the human wars?"

Alaric stared into the black pool, his wrath overflowing. This is not how he will be treated! This is not what his father or grandfather endured! They were not the lapdogs of these things. There is no way they could have suffered this.

He snatched Nithledan from the dirt. It trembled with hate, taut with utter fury. It felt Alaric's thoughts, which in action, was delayed by the space between a heartbeat. Silver streaks lashed forth from the bow and its master, flying freely into the dark, into the hidden laughter of the night. Arrows flew with purpose from the tips of the Woodcutter's fingers and the soul of the slain spirit trapped in the ancient wood.

Screams tore through the glade as the hidden women fell from the trees into the black pool. Alaric ran hard before even one corpse crashed through the water. Screeching voices called out after the Woodcutter, a doom proclaiming treachery. Alaric had no hope to escape the forest. There was but one refuge that lay very close. Not but a hundred yards away there was a portal, a gateway to the Faerie Realms.

Large, smooth faced boulders formed a threshold the size of a cottage, leading into the ground. Dolmens they were called, built by ancient elves to protect their world.

He ran to it and disappeared.

A new world filled in around Alaric, replacing the darkness with an eternal glow. A night sky shimmered like a fragile shell of translucent pearl, studded with infinite jewels of scintillating stars. A myriad of rainbow hues sparkled in those celestial facets, as if Maey the Sky Dragon herself spun the stars for no other reason than behold such enchanting delights. This was the world of the Fey, the Realm of Faerie, where darkness had no hold in places or people. It was a land where Alaric came to know as hallowed. He rarely ventured through the portals, at first in fear, then in reverence to a land that he wished not to defile.

Alaric took a moment to rest and compose his senses. He looked back at the portal, the bare rock dolmen appeared as it was in the forest. To his understanding, those creatures could not follow. Everything else in this world was altered in some way, different and wonderful or empty and strange. Like the sky, that had no sun, nor moon, but would illuminate during the days in cycle with the sun of the mortal realm. It seemed to Alaric as an azure silk screen enshrouding the world. And upon the other side was the sun of his world, projecting its light upon the exterior, diffusing its rays through the delicate fiber.

The trees, flowers, and animals were as different as the colors that painted the vista. When he first experienced it as a child, he was afraid. He thought he had died and he was in a land where there was no return. He then learned there was no evil here, or if there was, it was afraid to emerge. The beauty in this world had been crafted to appease the hearts and spirits of the fey, and it was good. It was a world that held no portal to evil, unlike his, which suffered evil and brought darkness to his doorstep. And this is why mortals were not welcomed unless they were under the power of the fey. Those who passed without leave were trespassing.

Alaric set out west, as best as he could determine it, walking at first, and then jogging. He was in danger here despite the good nature of the realm. He passed through the ancient trees of gnarled golden bark adorned with purple and red leaves, etched with silver veins. Flowers petals glowed like embers in the distance, yellow and silvers scattered through the groves like a reflecting pool capturing the hidden stars beneath the forest canopy. Strange insects hummed and chirped in sing song voices from up high and beneath the brush. Many years ago, he had stolen time in these woods. He brought flowers to his wife when they were young and told her they were gifts from angels. The magnificence of it all was deceiving, for the guardians of such beauty protected their lands with vain jealousy.

There were beasts that roamed the woods vigilant and watchful. As he now passed under the boughs of strange and delectable fruits infusing the air with redolent temptation, those beasts must now have their maws pointed skyward, catching the faint traces of his foreign presence in the air. He made for the first portal that came to his mind, the stone ring of the children's glade.

The ruins of shattered and broken stones.

Damn. He needed another exit.

It had been too many years and Time in the fey lands clouded his thoughts. It held captive his memories until he returned to familiar lands. All thoughts slowed. He felt the grasp of his purpose and urgencies slipping from his mind. The fey forests were enchanting, intoxicating. Each breath of the air was like sipping wine. What a wonderful thing it would be, to rest beneath the vibrant trees, to taste the lush fruit upon his lips while he waited for morning and the bedazzling brilliance of daylight.

No! He scolded himself. He fought off the ensnaring effects.

He noticed his pace slowed and now he was walking. No, he was drifting over the ground.

Keep running, he told himself. It is just the power of this land at work. If he surrendered to it, he might never return. They would find him and make him their captive. Better than death; but no different for his family.

Elisial.

Her love for him. Their love. The children that meant more to him than his life, than all life.

Yes, that was it.

He had forgotten. That was how he was able to come and return. Love was real, was the only charm that took hold of the heart, and kept the lure of the world from taking over.

A violaceous flower with carnelian specks adoring the petals. Elisial's favorite. He plucked it.

Elisial. His love.

He found himself running again, to the west. He found another dolmen half buried in the ground, the entrance gaping wide like a bear den.

"What is the hurry, Woodcutter?" came a gruff voice, when Alaric approached the gateway.

Upon a stone pedestal, an old man sat near the dolmen's entrance, smoking a thin wood pipe, breathing out smoke through stained teeth. Strange was his appearance, his hair was thick and bushy, long silvery tufts like fox tails crowned his head. Long pointed ears poked out from his silvery mane, twitching forward at Alaric's approach. His face was mostly covered by his hoary beard as if he wore a mask of leather across his eyes. But most strange of all was the bushy silver tail flickering in the air behind him.

Alaric eyed him warily. A heórdraeden, guardian of the faerie gates.

"Do not pass without acknowledging your elder, younger man," he warned.

"Are you a man, or elf, or something else?"

The old man chuckled. Billowing smoke wafted on his breath rising into a crown like ring that sat upon his brow.

"An elf with a beard? No, I am a man, same as you."

"Same as me?" Alaric repeated quietly to himself, doubtful. "Then let me pass. I only fled into this land out of desperation. I had no intention to trespass."

"Hmph," the old man replied, exhaling smoke. "But here you

are anyway and trespassing is what you are doing, is it not? Not that it is my concern entirely. But, I will have to report your travel when I'm asked. But your kind, I mean a Woodcutter, haven't much entered the woods often or lately, though Time spins differently here than there, so I recall. I wonder how old that makes me?" He puffed on his pipe a few more times lost in his own thoughts.

"You are quite old," Alaric answered with certainty.

"You know me?"

"Yes, you are the Gatekeeper."

"Ah, yes. That is good. You entered, now I need a payment for my masters."

"I have nothing."

"Then you shall not pass," he said with finality.

"What if I do something for your masters?"

"Something?" he scoffed.

"Perform a service, one they desired for centuries?"

"And what would that be precisely, younger man?"

"I will purge the forest of the Lhodyn."

The old man choked and hacked up smoke, rocking on his high seat. He put an arm down to steady himself, leaned over and looked back at Alaric. "Don't sell me lies, younger man," pipe stem pointing at him in accusatory threats. "I'll keep you and sell you to the elves. Have you scrub their garderobes. Whooh yeah, that'll be the place for ya."

Alaric stepped forward toward that dolmen, irritated at the delay. "This is no jest. Let me pass. If you are a man as I, then you have a family as I do, and they need their father and husband. And my village needs their Warden."

"Well younger Warden, just *halt!*" Alaric froze like a fly crashing through a concealed web. His whole body froze still, unable to move even a finger.

"I can't say I believe your hoopla and braggin' but you Woodcutters have some merit left from the old days...those times of my youth. You may pass, but let me warn ya."

Alaric found himself relinquished of the hold, enabling him to turn and look up at the old man. His eyes must have been once blue, and despite the weak light, they now appeared a dull gray.

"Messin' with Lady Lhodyn is serious business. Incurring her wrath will be the ruin of you and those you care about. I may not walk the earth anymore, but from one man to another, there are some things on this world you must submit to and know they are your better, fair or not. I will let you pass, but if you ever cross this way again, leaving won't be so easy. They seem not to care too much about the goings on of the mortal world, but we know. We know evil has been brought in. We know and maybe they might want to know why. And I'm thinking you have some notion of it, so I will let you pass to see to your affairs and look over your kin as best you can. But you will be looked for."

Alaric said nothing. He considered the old man and thought about what it must be like to be trapped in this place of delights and richness, but having to serve out an eternity as a slave and never knowing the familiar pleasures of home.

"I do not think I will be back. But your masters know where to find me."

Alaric passed under the dolmen. The passage was short. Air rushed around like a storm until he was released back into the thick darkness shrouding the Wudelic. He was far north of the village and would have to trek back some miles south. The forest edge was within a hundred yards. He made for it, then turned south. He looked for the midnight star, which now had circled toward the western horizon. Dawn was upon him and the sun would be up before he reached the village. This night was over.

As he journeyed back, his body succumbed to exhaustion. Sleep, absent for nearly two days. He put distance between him and the forest as he crossed the fields north of Athelyn, the pastures beyond the village crops where Lord Temen once grazed his horses. There was a stable near, a shelter placed in the middle of the fields where the horses could find comfort when caught in bad weather. Alaric found it vacant. Straw still lined the ground. He made himself a bed and slept. He did not allow himself to sleep long before he set out again. The sun had not even reached a quarter of the sky.

The fields were vibrant green with wild clover flowers. Elwyn's hives were scattered throughout. Sitting upon a raised platform suspended upon staddle stones were groups of cone shaped bee skeps woven from golden straw shining like imperial palaces in the warm daylight. Bees lazily drifted in and out of the apiaries, oblivious to their impending destruction, for Elwyn would plunder their hordes of golden honey when it was time to harvest.

This is what mortals were to Lhodyn, to all the gods, maybe. All their toil and struggles were at the expense of creatures that plundered and scoured the bounties of their lives to feed their gluttonous appetites.

He would not allow his children any further harm. They must flee.

He hoped Elzera arrived and still remained. They would leave that day if they could manage it. He would take the three Athéalgian women with them. They would make a new life, in new lands, under new gods.

Tredan greeted Alaric on the Lane in front of their home. The boy stood, gawking at him, slack jawed. "I didn't believe them when I heard you came back. We thought you died in the forest somewhere."

"Happy to disappoint everyone," he shot back.

He did not mean to be so cross, not to Edrick's friend.

"I was sent to give you a message," the cat furrier said, his voice now subdued.

Alaric paused, inviting elaboration.

"Uh, well, Grindan said to come see him right away and uh, the Elders need to speak with you. They convened in the Elder Hall. I think it is important."

"Thank you, Tredan." He turned into his yard.

"Uh, Master, have you seen Edrick?"

Alaric stopped. Don't tell me the boy has run off again!

Tredan must have seen the anger rising in his face because he backed away. "Just tell him to stay away from the village center. The wolf men are there."

Tredan turned and ran down the Lane.

The Folthnir were in his village! Alaric's mind raced.

"Father!" Meghan cried out, running out the door, hugging him fiercely. She wept quietly in his arms.

Elisial followed. She said nothing but it was written on her brow. He shook his head slowly.

"Something has, indeed, occurred in the woods. I think…," he stopped himself. He let Meghan finish her hug then told her gently. "I need to speak to your mother."

Meghan nodded and went inside. Elisial seized his hands and

kissed him.

"You spoke to Lhodyn," she guessed. She always knew. Elisial always said he had this drained look about his face, as if he just ran fifty miles.

"I have angered her," he snorted at the understated fact. "Our family is in danger here. Everyone is. We must leave at once." Elisial made to speak but Alaric touched her lips. "I know it will be hard. It is the lesser of evils."

Elisial said nothing, then, "Sunniva? Baldice?" She could only mouth their names.

Alaric did not know what to tell her. He could lie and spare her a broken heart. But he could not.

He would not.

"I came across Baldice's body. He has passed." She trembled. Alaric held her tight. "She told me Sunniva lives. But She would not aid me at all. She cast me from her court, released me from my oaths."

Elisial was so quiet. She wept for their son, but her strength did not give way. After a while Alaric spoke again.

"I have disgraced my family." He finally said.

"No," she said. "You have never. There is no other man in this world as true as you."

She slowly stepped back. "Do not take all these burdens on yourself my love. Even iron shatters with enough force. A tall pine bends to the wind where a stone tower topples."

Alaric looked into his wife's face. He searched her eyes for the slightest sign of disappointment, shame. He found none there.

He never would. "It is time to bend to the wind."

"I will have the children pack in secret. I wish Elzera had remained."

"She will be back," he said. "We will be ready when she returns."

"How much time do we have?"

"We never had time, it belongs to the gods."

Elisial cast her eyes down. "Alaric, I am afraid. The boys were summoned to the Elder Council, I was not allowed to accompany them. Edrick too, has not returned home."

Alaric gently lifted her head. "Why did you not mention this sooner." But he already knew better. She didn't have to give him an answer.

"Tredan said Grindan wished to talk to me, as well as the Council."

"Then, you better go. Bring home our boys. We will start preparing for the journey."

She released him. He could see it wounded her deeply, having been gone for so long, only to see him dashing off into the woods on his return, and now to attend the Elder Council. He reached beneath his shirt and produced the flower, pick from the Faerie Realms.

He held it before her.

She nearly melted. She took in both hands, smiled, then cried.

"A departing gift. A promise of my return and hope for the future."

He turned and ran down the Lane. He should have retrieved more arrows, then he realized Grindan could provide all he needed.

Ringing hammer strikes carried into an unusually vacant Lane. No cats, nor people occupied the road. He rounded the shop where Grindan labored with his son Bron, both bathed in the glow of forge fire. Grindan's oily hair hung around his face, shivering with every forceful blow. He shouted orders to his son above the din who held a heated metal rod with tongs. The two usually worked well together, but Grindan grew frustrated with his fidgeting son.

"Dammit. Go fire it up again."

Bron shot Alaric a quick glance before he turned around and doused the iron back in the forge. He pumped the bellows furiously feeding the appetite of the glowing coals.

Grindan must have caught the look and turned around. His frustration remained on his face a moment longer than Alaric expected until it became the familiar face of his friend.

"Alaric, you made it out of those woods. Good. Good. What signs did you find in there? Anything of your children?" He shifted his hammer into his left hand and dropped the free hand onto Alaric's shoulder. The big man's weight poured into his body like molten iron.

"Something of them, yes." His son's severed arm flashed across his thoughts. He took a quick look around the shop. There were newly forged swords and spear tips in tall wicker baskets.

"I hope you can put these arms to good use. If the Folthinr are near, your craft and labor will bear fruit."

"Yes, and that's why you have been summoned to the Council.

Come," he said jovially, "let us go together. Bron, keep to your work," he said sternly. He threw off his apron and set his hammer down. The two walked to a crowded village meeting. Alaric was sure the entire village was in attendance, even the cats gathered on the rooftops to see what was to be made of the grand commotion.

Such meetings were convened to settle small disputes between neighbors or husband and wife. The Elders also ruled on village policies that were not officially under the king's law, but were upheld as more of custom.

It was customary in times of distress that the Elder Council met often, in good times they met seldom.

Alaric gave much thought as what he might say to the Elders on his long return trip home. Yet, things were now far beyond what he expected. The entire village needed to leave at once and trust in him to guide them to lands they have never seen.

Grindan led as they entered the Elder Hall. The stench was nearly unbearable. They had not prepared for a council, evident by the strong smell of cat urine and scat. Throngs of people already crowded inside, sitting upon crates and barrels, talking quietly of the Woodcutter's appearance from months of absence. Three elder men sat mid–hall, in front of the hearth, on chairs Alaric fashioned for them years ago in homage, decorated with scenes of village life. Their mood was subdued and quiet. They stared into the vacant space in front of them, ignoring his entrance where the others stopped and took notice. Alaric nodded to his neighbors as he walked passed and read on their faces a familiar expression. They were all afraid.

Yet there was one man that displayed smug delight as Alaric entered. The stunted form of Hrypa sat on the floor next to the three Elders. Never had they suffered this man's presence in the Hall, but now he remained at their side, feeding their council.

Alaric stood in front of them and waited to be addressed.

"Alaric." Old Caflice croaked in acknowledgement. "What news do you bring of your over long journey?"

"Two of my children are dead because I have been away on your errand. What news do you bring me? What despair has befallen my home that have welcomed murderers openly into our village."

The people murmured in hushed speech around him. Alaric was being openly disrespectful.

"Do not take your personal misfortunes out on us, Alaric!"

Hrypa answered for them. "It is the habit of your family to venture into wild areas of the land, where people of good sense avoid."

"We lament your loss," answered one of the Elders timidly. "To lose two young ones is a great tragedy."

"You have known the perils of the forest all your life," spoke another Elder, "and have allowed your family to venture into those perils knowingly. It is only so long that you can throw rocks at a wolf before it returns to take your hand."

"Yes, the perils of the forest," Alaric fumed. "How you people think danger can be avoided so easily and yet you invite a pack of wolves to feed in your home and expect no harm to come of it. My family is my concern, as your families should be yours. Now that you let them in there is no way they will wish to leave. Then why send me away for naught?"

"It was not for nothing," replied Old Caflice. "It was wise to know where we could flee before such a thing became necessary, instead of fleeing into the face of some other danger. But they caught up with us in your over long absence. We agreed you should be gone three months, returning well before the fall harvest. Now winter came and went, here you finally are. We have had new considerations in your absence."

All three nodded.

So it is all my fault! Alaric grasped Nithledan tight in both hands, squeezing it, for if he did not, his hands would seek their necks.

Hrypa's face lit up with dire satisfaction. "There are rumors that have arisen, saying there is a group of the king's men hidden in the woods, that they sought the Brownman who is rumored to be some sort of agent of the king. Some think that you may be aiding these men, placing the entire village in great danger, to our new allies, the Folthnir."

"Is this what you think, that I have some ulterior reason to leave my family the moment I arrive home? When we all should be departing these lands without delay!" He looked around to the villagers in attendance. They averted their eyes and would not look at him directly.

"There are no Mark men in the woods or anywhere!" He fumed. "There is no king and we have none but ourselves for protection." Alaric looked around the room, at the men and women, some of them with their children. Had they no idea the threat the Folthnir brought them? He calmed his voice before he spoke again. "I have found a land of refuge. There is a mighty kingdom to the south and east that is open to refugees that pledge their men and sons to the king's armies. It is a long journey and the more difficult with so many, but we can make it. The southern lands are fair and don't suffer these intrusions. The lands are fertile and rich and the king, just..."

A great dissent erupted as some, hearing hope for the first time, the idea life could return to normal. Most argued that such plans were foolish, that leaving their lands, their ancestors, would anger Lady Lhodyn and they will be cursed.

The three old men still did not lift their eyes from Alaric and shook their heads instead, in silence. "We will not go," was all the explanation given.

Alaric thought quickly, for another argument to convince them to flee. Now and not later.

"As Hrypa said, I just returned from the woods and I have found the remains of my son, Baldice."

There was a gasp from the people around. Someone asked about his girl, little Sunniva.

"Something evil has settled in Wudelic and it is attacking us."

"No. They attacked those foolish enough to enter," argued Hrypa.

Alaric ignored him and faced the crowd. "I am removing my family far from here. If there are any that wish to join me, brave men and women, stand next to me. I have planned out a route. It will take some fifty days to reach this safety."

"Alarming these people needlessly is foolish, Alaric." Old Caflice reproached. "They have enough daily worries than to scare them with wild tales."

"What is this? When have I been called a fool so many times in one day? You placed in me the responsibility to save our village from impeding death." He looked toward Hrypa, the one man who looked entirely pleased. Moments of silence passed. Alaric wanted to grab each one and shake them; compel them to speak. That is what he resented in these villagers; they acted as sheep, easily herded by the dog with the loudest bark.

"No other man could have delivered upon what I set out to do. You all have trusted me to take you into the woods in times of famine, to hunt and allow your pigs to graze in the mid-winter and not one animal was lost because of my vigilance, when none was asked of me. And now my children have died, and because of you I have been separated from them for months where I should have protected them, and you all turn your backs to me and call me foolish!"

He was shaming them under his fury. He hated to herd them like sheep, but he would play that game if he had to.

"It is only a fool that heeds the advice of fools! And that I shall no longer endure."

"Enough!" yelled out a booming voice. A large Folthnir warrior pushed his way through the throng, shoving men and women to the ground, followed by a handful of swordsmen draped in wolfskins. This leader, though, wore armored mail of beast scale, bright red as if painted in blood. A fresh bandage dressed a wound on his neck. Alaric instantly recognized him as the rider on the Merchant Road.

Grindan moved to the warrior's side. "Alaric, you are no friend to any of us any longer," his comrade announced.

"What accusation must I now endure?"

One of the Folthnir in wolfskin, stepped forward, hand on his sword. Alaric strung an arrow in one fluid movement. Then all the swords sprang forward in reaction.

Old Caflice raised his hand and stepped to Alaric, pushing his bow aside. "This is what we feared, Alaric!" he shouted, on the verge of tears. "We knew you would fight them if they came. We knew as long as you remained among us, you would have us all die fighting them. I wanted to spare you the truth because you helped so many times."

Alaric hands went slack, his arrow dropped to the floor.

They lied to him.

"You were dangerous, so we sent you away. We had no intention to leave the village. Ever."

"You deceived me?" This entire time, it was all a lie.

"I am sorry, Alaric. We deemed it a wise decision considering the doom we faced."

"My children died while you sent me away, for cowardice!" Anger rose in Alaric's throat from his churning guts. This was more than treachery. He had been betrayed!

A Folthnir youth moved quickly to snatch the fallen arrow

dropped by Alaric.

The bandaged Folthnir held up a similar arrow. The silver fletching was notched seven times, Alaric's mark.

"These are nefarious arrows among my people, Woodcutter." The leader said. "Mark Assassin is what we named you from the wars. And here you are in this backward place still killing our people. Vylkinus has finally delivered you."

The Folthnir roared in unison, "Hyuk-ra!"

Alaric looked to his neighbors and the Elders. Regret and cowardice was written across all their faces. So this is the doom they have passed on me. "I would have died for all of you as I would my family." He said to Old Caflice. "Had I stayed we would be free."

"So you say."

The Folthnir leader walked passed Alaric, up to Elders. "Bahahahah," he bleated in staccato like a goat, pulling at their beards until they bowed their heads. "Why you people listen to old goats in this barn? And what's this?" the Folthnir asked seeing Hrypa at the Elder's feet.

"Lord, it is I that told you of the Woodcutter's coming," Hrypa beamed like a superb sycophant.

"This thing with no leg speaks!" the Folthnir mocked. The others laughed in derision.

"What strange things you keep in this village. Old talking goats, herds of cats and useless beggars." He raised his sword above Hrypa. Alaric drew another arrow and pointed it to the Folthnir's temple.

"I think from this distance, I will not miss," he growled. "Kill him, and I will take all your lives."

"Alaric," Grindan spoke evenly. "They have your boys outside. His death would be their death."

Alaric faltered, looking to his friend. Seeing there for the first time, his betrayal. "Papa!" he heard Edrick yell from beyond the door.

He dropped Nithledan. He was defeated.

The Folthnir warrior plunged his sword into Hrypa's chest, over and over again until blood washed over the floor. Women screamed and children cried out. The Elders flinched and cowered.

"Old warriors should die in the field, not live as half-men."

Two Folthnir wolf skins rushed toward Alaric, colliding into him, slamming their fists into his face. Lights exploded across his sight, then he was pummeled under fists and boots.

The blood of Hrypa washed over his face.

They dragged him out into the sunlight. His eyes stung. He was thrown on to the dirt Lane, while the Folthnir mounted their horses. One warrior bound Alaric's hands to a rope, the other end secured to the rider's saddle. There was a large company of warriors.

One handled a large pack of barking, snarling hounds. His sons' necks had been tethered together, held in front of their snapping maws.

Alaric looked around for his bow. Tredan stood in the Elder Hall doorway, expressionless.

"Boy, find my bow and bring it to my wife. Let her know what has happened." The boy nodded and ran into the building.

The riders were all mounted. The wounded Folthnir, the leader people called the Huntsman, shouted to all those that were hiding in the huts around them. "The Theign will be pleased that you have shown your loyalty and aided us in capturing this murderer. Such obedience is favorable. Look at this man. This is how our enemies suffer!"

He spurred his horse. The rope snapped, cinching into Alaric's wrist as he jerked forward, dragging him down the Lane.

The anguished cries of his sons chased after him.

13

THE RUINED TOWER

IT WAS A PLACE of rumor and a source of stories, an ancient monument Edrick always desired to explore. Standing alone on the valley plain, a few miles north of the village, a strange relic that had no history, just invented tales. The tower was of another time, outside memory. It belonged to the old ways. A testament to a history of men who built the village Wall and the Elder Hall, a time that existed just beyond the tangible.

Spirits were said to reside there as well as elfin kings and ogre tyrants. Yet now, smoke rose from its roots and foreign men made camp upon its fields. In the distance, as Edrick and his brothers approached, captives of the Folthnir, it stood crippled, leaning slightly, like an infirmed stone giant obdurate and scorning the power of the earth. Its bones were strong and stubborn, built by skilled hands, mighty hands, but mortal hands. It was a remnant of earlier days approaching its end.

Battle-horns blasted out from behind crenulated walls surrounding the old keep, announcing the arriving captives. These walls fared far worse than those encompassing the village, revealing sunken lines and gaping holes in great spans. Roughhewn timbers had been constructed recently to fill the wall's breaches. The gatehouse must have fallen long ago. Perhaps the stones were pilfered by villagers to assimilate into their homes. In its place, a wooden structure was constructed, complete with a crooked wooden portcullis resembling bent wheat stalks.

The morning Elzera departed, they came for them, Edrick and

his brothers.

The villagers lied to Mother, "The Elders are summoning Alaric and his sons." It was a trap to lure Father. The wolfmen bound them all, threatened them with the hounds.

They promised them they would all die, said Father was a murderer, a killer. They spoke of his conduct in the war, how he slayed wounded Folthnir while hiding in a blind, too scared to face real warriors. It was all lies, Edrick knew. After they captured Father, Edrick and his brothers were forced into a caged wagon.

Eadwyn sat, knees drawn to his head, face hidden between his legs, never looking up. Halig though, looked around, wanting to see where they were going, though he avoided looking at the men directly. Edrick remained fearless in his anger. He looked into every man's face. He wondered how people could be like this, like monsters, uncaring of others. Some looked backed at them with an evil disdain. Others avoided his gaze. In their eyes he saw many things; cruelty, indifference, pity, and regret. Not one man was the same, but the cruel ones outnumbered the others, and these others were as terrified of the cruel ones.

An all-consuming anger stormed in Edrick's heart. The ragged faces of the three women in his home came to his thoughts, especially that of Gaebria and Sarghan, wiped clean of joy, stoking his wrath. Mother's silent tears and his sister's cries greeted them as they passed by their cottage, bound for the tower.

"Father will set things right," Mother said as they passed, running after them. "Edrick! Don't do anything reckless."

Edrick wondered how anyone could set things right. Wild and dangerous men had their will with anyone, took what they wanted, and killed who they wanted. No one challenged them except in fearful whispers

A great fire burned in his chest, incinerating all other emotions.

The rickety portcullis ascended as they neared. Watchful guards glared down over them as they entered the tower grounds. Edrick felt like he and his brothers were being assessed like fresh pigs brought to butcher. Halig looked to Edrick, then to Eadwyn. He was afraid, but did not turn away like Eadwyn.

Inside the gates, a horrid sight unfolded. People packed into wood lashed cages. Each person, frail with emaciated bodies. Some were naked. They crowded against one another, all standing like gathered timber bundled tight. Men, women and children were separate, each grouped in their own pens. They watched Edrick and his brothers pass by with vacant eyes. Their faces were blank, devoid of humanity. Sarghan possessed the same demeanor, of one not present; dead on the inside. The reek of feces and urine overcame Edrick as they were drawn pass. The captives were kept worse than any animal Edrick had known in the village.

What struck Edrick was their silence, their complete acceptance to their condition, their resigned submission. They did not cry out or lift a pleading limb. Edrick stared at them and searched their faces for something familiar, not really knowing what he wanted to see. He wanted to cry because it was missing, in all of them, cry if they could not. But he refused to shed any tears there in that place.

The wagon lurched, then stopped abruptly in front of the tower. The base of the structure retained its strength from ages past, seemingly hardened over time unlike its failing extremities. A single iron bound gate was set in the middle of the tower wall, the only visible entrance that Edrick could tell. Eadwyn chanced to look up. He trembled, shuddering like a new born calf. Edrick never saw anyone so terrified.

Two men in beast scale hauberks, armed with swords, followed the wagon from the front gate and stood near. The driver called out to another, speaking their horrid language. The wolfskin youth who caught Edrick, followed them here. He dismounted and came running over, taking hold of the horses as the driver climbed down. The driver yelled at Edrick and his brothers, then drew his sword and pointed to the rear of the wagon.

The youth translated, "Out, sheep!"

Halig stood up and helped Eadwyn to his feet. Edrick stood and followed the two out, then off the wagon. Immediately, the driver rushed toward Halig and bashed his head with a mailed fist, sending him sprawling to the ground. Eadwyn fell back. He threw his hands up defensively. "Sorry, sorry" he stammered.

The youth laughed, relishing their fear.

Halig eyes rolled in different directions for a moment then blinked back to focus. The driver looked back to Edrick, daring him to help his brother to his feet. Edrick didn't care if he was struck down too, but he heeded his mother's words, and controlled his rash urges to fight back. The driver shouted at them again. The other two guards shoved Edrick and his brothers against the tower wall, pressing their backs hard against stone. They looked out over the grounds. It was filled with many things that failed to capture their attention; for their eyes lingered still, upon the slave pens directly across them.

The driver left them and crossed the courtyard. The wolfskin youth taunted them. "We are going to hack off your limbs one by one, like wet timber. How does that sound Woodcutters?"

The driver quickly returned with a pack of Folthnir warriors. Edrick turned to look, but the guard seized him by the jaw and twisted his head to face forward. He shouted at him and his brothers, then forced them to their knees, making sure they remained still. Two men walked in front of them while the others crowded behind, each man bearing militant postures. They bore swords on their waists except for one tall man that seemed out of place, dressed in strange garb unlike Edrick had ever known. His face and features were different than the rest. Where the Folthnir skin were fair, this man skin was tan, his hair dark. But it was the man that stood at the center of them all that commanded the attention those around, a warrior older than their father bearing a full gray beard.

This was the Theign, warlord of the Folthnir. Fully clad in mail of scarlet dragon scale, bright and supple. Under his arm he carried his horned helm gilded in gold trim. On his hip was a jeweled sword with teeth of some mighty beast forming the cross guard. He was the type of savage warrior Edrick had always imagined from stories he heard of the northern wars, terrible and menacing.

He spoke without addressing anyone in particular but the driver answered him directly. The wolfskin youth came to the Theign's side, assuming a smug look of power. The Theign and dark man inspected their captives closely, then the dark man spoke.

"You are the sons of the Woodcutter, Alaric?" He spoke with an accent, sounding as foreign as his appearance.

"Yes," Halig replied.

"Good," the dark man said. He spoke to the others then continued. "Your father has been away for many months. Why?"

"He….the Elders sent him to find a land where we could escape this war," Halig answered.

"There is no escape from the Folthnir," the foreign man taunted. "Your father seeks alliances then. To what country did he flee? Who is his commander?"

Halig seemed confused. The last question did not make sense to Edrick either. "He fled to the Lathiélden. The Elders commanded him to go."

The foreigner seemed unconvinced with Halig's answers. When conveyed to the Folthnir, they scoffed and shook their heads, some shouted at the boys. Edrick saw death in their eyes. Others spoke with reservation. At last the foreigner spoke again.

"And why did he flee into the forest after being gone for so long? What does he conceal there?"

"Conceal? We lost our brother and sister to monsters..."

"Your brother and sister are in the woods?" he scoffed.

Halig was about to answer, paused and looked to Edrick quickly.

"Don't look to anyone but me!" shouted the robed man.

"They were in the woods. We think they are dead," Halig answered quickly.

"Then why is your father searching for dead children?"

"We were hoping they are alive."

"If they are not, then they will be. My friends will see to that. Tell me, how well do you know these woods?"

"I know them well, as much as my father." Halig said with pride. That was an exaggeration Edrick thought, perhaps he was trying to protect Father.

The dark man spoke to the Theign. The warrior replied and departed into the tower followed by the others. The dark man remained behind.

"You see those creatures in the pens? Those are our guests, as you now are our guests."

"Where's our father!" Edrick burst aloud. The guard struck Edrick, his head spun into the wall. He stumbled against the force but refused to fall down.

The robed man continued. "On his way. We will keep you around to ensure he remains talkative...and if he decides three sons are not worth his life, then you and the other sheep will be taking a long trip south to the lands of my lords. You will be kept alive, if any of you have the heart to live," he eyed Eadwyn doubtfully, "but the lords of my land may value your youth in passionate ways."

Halig spat on the foreign man. The guard moved to strike Halig, but the dark man stayed him with a look. "I see obstinacy is a trait of the Woodcutter and his sons." The foreigner pulled out a pocket cloth and held it out. The guard hesitated, then took it and wiped the spit from his clothes. The dark man caressed Halig's face, feeling his young skin with his fingers. "Such a delicate young man might fetch high prices in the right circles. Such a handsome boy. I myself would find the experience of breaking your spirit quite pleasurable." He forced his finger in Halig's mouth.

Halig turned his head away from the man's strange touch.

The tall, thin man just smiled then turned from them, speaking orders to the guards. The three were led away from the tower and past the slave pens. Four wooden posts, the size of tree trunks, were driven into the ground, each were roughly equal spaced from the other. Edrick knew evil business took place at these posts, for they were stained titian with dried blood, long streaks fell down toward the earth. They were each bound to a post, arms pulled behind their body, wrapping around the wood.

They were left alone. Left to wonder their fate.

Edrick and his brothers dared not speak. Empty moments passed as sun fell farther out from the sky. The captives in the slave pens always watched Edrick and his brothers, frozen in their masks of indifference, staring perpetually, as if awaiting the inevitable. A commotion on the wall above the gate broke the monotony. The portcullis raised and warriors rushed out. When they returned they escorted their mother into the grounds. She was alone and bearing a woven basket in one arm.

"Mother!" Edrick shouted. He wanted to tell her to run, flee before they imprisoned her too.

"Shut up!" Eadwyn yelled back, alarmed. "We should not speak," he whispered.

But then Halig called out to her too. The dark man emerged from the tower and met her. They spoke for a while.

The sound of Edrick's pounding heart drowned out all other noise as he watched his mother. What were they saying? The robed man then looked at her with suspicion as she handed her basket to a warrior. The guard inspected it and then the foreigner, before giving it back to her. Their encounter concluded and the foreign man retreated back into the tower. Mother nodded submissively, never raising her eyes from the ground. She was allowed to approach her sons.

"Mother why have you come? This is no place for women," Halig gushed out. "They won't allow you to leave. Flee and forget about us."

"No, don't!" Eadwyn cried desperately.

"I'm here because my sons are here," she stated as if that were an obvious reason, "and I agree, this is no place for a woman, my sons, or anyone else. I came to make sure you were not harmed and if you were I was going to make sure you lived. Have they hurt you?"

"No," Edrick assured her, cutting Eadwyn off before he could speak. His mother turned to her youngest son. He saw tears forming in her green eyes. He looked away afraid the sentiment became infectious. "Edrick. Please hold your tongue and think of your brothers first before yourself...and your mother." She added tenderly. "We will get through this. We will."

She kissed them each, just once. Her face was unreadable, a frozen statuesque beauty of hardened skin, holding back an avalanche of emotions. "I will remain here as long as I can," she promised.

"No, Mother you must leave," Halig implored, "there is nothing you can do here. You have to look after Meghan and yourself now."

"How can Father make this right?" Edrick demanded, remembering her last words as they were carted off. Mother looked to Halig then Edrick.

"You're right," she ran her fingers through Edrick's sweat soaked hair, then cradled the back of his head. She looked into his eyes. "Some things can't always be amended even by your father. But we are a family and whatever comes will be endured by all of us together, not alone. Meghan is safe enough. I won't leave my boys." Edrick saw more than stubbornness in her, a challenge to any to cross her will.

"And what of Father?" Eadwyn asked.

She hesitated. Edrick could see she debated whether to speak of it or not. But she answered, "They have been making a sport of him, dragging him behind a horse like a criminal. I believe it is their intention not to kill him yet or they would have."

"Bastards!" Edrick yelled at the tower. Halig and Eadwyn looked at their little brother in astonishment.

"Edrick, HOLD-YOUR-TONGUE!" Their mother growled.

He did, reluctantly.

The heat of the sun extracted tears and sweat from the boys

forced to stand against the posts. Their faces swelled from where the guards struck them. True to her word, their mother never left them, remaining near. She rubbed plant salve on their bruises and a mashed paste that protected their skin from the sun. The barbarians never seemed to mind her presence. When she talked with the dark man earlier, there was some understanding reached, but their mother never spoke of it. She didn't speak at all except to ask how they felt. She gave them water by soaking a loose rag in a horse trough and then wrung it in their parched mouths. They waited there with their mother wondering if their father would arrive, or maybe he was dead already.

Edrick's world fell out beneath him ten days ago and it continued its freefall into what felt like an abysmal chasm.

There was a blaring of horns in the late afternoon. The portcullis raised its decrepit maw, welcoming its grand prize.

A handful of Folthnir riding horseback passed through the gatehouse, including the Huntsman and his hounds, dragging their father's body across the dirt. Grindan followed them driving a cart loaded with swords and metal craft. His mother gasped and grabbed hold of Halig to steady herself. Halig pulled against the rope restraints. "Father!" he shouted.

The tower door flung open and out marched the Folthnir warlord along with his retinue of warriors including the foreigner following obediently behind. The Huntsman dismounted, bowing his head to his Theign, the other riders followed his lead. They then lifted their father's body out of the dirt. His head lolled down. His clothes were tattered and soaked in blood. It was a gruesome sight, one Edrick would never forget.

"He's not..." Edrick began, unable to speak it. It was not possible. But then his father's head rose stubbornly to meet the warlord, eye to eye. The Theign gave his father an appraising look then approached Edrick and his brothers. Their father was dragged behind him.

The guards dropped their father's body at their feet. Mother dove down and pulled their father onto her lap, embracing him gently.

"Elisial?" he asked, his voice weakened far beyond anything Edrick knew.

"Is anything broken?" she asked, gazing into his blood stained eyes.

"Heal him. If he dies, you and your sons will follow," the foreigner threatened.

The Folthnir chained their father around the neck to one of the posts, then left them, ignoring them entirely the rest of the day. Mother attended father's wounds immediately, laying him down with a gentle hand.

From her basket she produced a linen cloth that had been steamed clean, along with medicines and salves. She opened a glass bottle filled with a golden liquor and had father sip from the vessel until it was near empty. She offered the last portion to Edrick and his brothers. It was their mother's best medicine, something she called faerie wine. It was her most valuable and most potent curative, one that she spent months formulating. It imparted strength into the imbiber that was supernatural. The flavor of piquant honey greeted Edrick's tongue and burned his throat, yet once he had the flavor coating his mouth he desired more.

"He will be fine, boys," she finally announced as the sun set. A slave boy Edrick's age brought them food, inedible waste fed to the pigs, but mother made them eat it after inspecting its contents.

"They want us alive or they would not send food. I want you to live, so eat." She fed each of them, their father first.

Day faded into night. The pale sickle moon sliced across the sky, bleeding the Ruined Tower in wan gray light. Enough to see the captives in their pens fidget restlessly as they slept standing. Edrick and his brothers could not sit either, but at least they were not crowded together.

Night dragged on longer than Edrick ever experienced. He did not realize late spring nights could be so long, so agonizing as if it held captive the morning light. Sleep came in stubborn increments. In one waking moment, he watched his mother and father whisper softly to each other. Father touched his neck and handed something to mother. She then quietly came to Edrick and knelt down. In her hands was father's torc, the one thing Edrick remembered his father never being without.

She placed it around his neck. It was large on him and could be seen above his shirt. She tore a ribbon of cloth from the hem of her skirt and wrapped that too around his neck to conceal it. "Your father and I think you should hold on to this for a while. Just until we leave this place."

"It should go to Halig," Edrick responded properly, though he felt privileged at having received this precious heirloom. "He is the oldest."

"Listen, Edrick." She cradled his head and whispered into his ear. Her voice was burdened with sorrow. Hot tears dropped onto his cheeks. "If there is a way for you to leave, even if it's without us, you must go. Find Meghan at Oxa's house and hide with her. Wait for Elzera to return. She will take care of you."

Edrick couldn't accept what she was telling him. He must have been shaking his head because she replied to his thoughts.

"Do this one thing for us, Edrick, without being so stubborn. You are my bravest child, I know you are not afraid of them, I know, or any danger. Yet I know your deepest fear, for it is mine as well. But you must face it. We all do. It is better some of us live than none at all..." she wept a little more, quietly, clutching him tightly, kissing his head. He waited patiently, wishing he could hold her back.

He too, cried.

"And if Halig is able to go with you, when all is safe, give the torc to him. And if not him, then Eadwyn. Do you understand Edrick?"

"Yes," but I won't do it, he answered in his thoughts, I won't leave you or Father.

"Good. How are you feeling?"

"I am fine. Father?"

"He is a strong man." She took a deep breathe. "He will recover."

She kissed him one final time and went to his brothers.

Many more hours passed until daylight finally crept out from the other side of the world. Edrick was awake and slept little. He was surprised by the coming daylight for there were no birds singing, just silence.

Crows gathered on the tower walls, looking down at the men and women as if they discovered a tasty feast so conveniently gathered in cages. There was no morning meal for Edrick and his family, just water delivered by mother.

As day wore on, horns blared out and the portcullis raised once again. A train of wagons with wooden enclosures pulled into the tower grounds. The foreigner met the wagon drivers, shaking their hands in greeting. Folthnir warriors opened the women's pen and loaded them on to the wagons. Edrick became tense as he feared they might seize their mother and throw her in with the rest, but they did not come.

The silent captives now voiced their despair, hands of the children and men reached into the open space toward the women forced into the wagons. People cried bitterly. Some women had to be dragged and thrown into their new cages. Mother wept as they watched on. It was outrageous to Edrick, to see families torn from one another.

The wagons now weighted with their human wares, departed slowly, slipping into the world beyond the walls and disappearing to all those present.

The foreigner watched them depart until the portcullis fell shut.

The crows laughed cruelly at the men and children left behind.

Edrick stared into the now empty pens where the women were. He wondered how often this occurred. Were his neighbors next to fill the vacancies?

As if hearing Edrick's thoughts, the foreigner made his way to the Woodcutters. He looked at them as if inspecting them, determining a value.

"Remarkable," he said looking at Father, "he seems to be recovering quickly."

Nobody spoke or moved. Edrick wanted to spit, kick dirt and yell at the filthy man, but he kept his eyes on his parents, daring not to upset them.

The man then looked to Edrick and his brothers, studying them equally.

After a long silence, the foreigner asked, "Why does this one have no light," speaking of Edrick.

"He lost it in the forest when our brother died," Halig said.

The foreigner freed Edrick from his bonds and seized him by the roots of his hair. "What is this light? Why don't others have it in your land?"

Halig shrugged.

"It's our éardian," Mother whispered.

"What is the meaning?"

"It is a bonded faerie, one that guards our spirit until death, accompanying it to the spirit world." She said.

"And if you don't have one, like this boy?"

"We have one, even if you don't see it. Sometimes we face some danger, our éardians will expend their power to protect us. They depart, having spent their strength, but will return on our deaths to guide our souls through the land of the dead. Without it, we become wandering ghosts."

"It is a bewitching light. Better to not have it."

Mother shrugged. The foreigner looked on them still clutching Edrick's hair. "Still, it is beautiful I admit," he said after a moment. "We have heard of you, People of Light."

He turned away from them, pulling Edrick along with him. Edrick grabbed the man's thin arm but followed without resisting. The foreigner threw Edrick into the vacant slave pen. He landed on his chest. Urine soaked feces flew up into Edrick's face, clinging to his hair. The foreigner smirked and left him. Edrick wiped the feces from his eyes and nostrils. A shovel was thrown at him, hitting his head. A cruel voice from behind chuckled and said, "clean," in a Folthnir accent. These barbarians can talk after all, Edrick thought.

Edrick shoveled out the cage for hours, cleaning it for whomever was to occupy it next. A slave boy, the one that gave him yesterday's evening meal, removed the muck in a wheelbarrow to somewhere out of sight. He noticed the boy's right ear was cut clean off. On his left cheek, a festering wound puffed out from a branding iron. Edrick tried to speak to him but the boy shook his head wildly, holding his finger to his lips. I guess talking is not allowed, Edrick thought to himself. Just across the pens, the portcullis remained shut but he believed he could fit through one of the openings. He could flee into the forest before anyone noticed.

As he thought about how easy he could escape, considering mother's desperate words, the Theign reemerged from the tower with his militant entourage.

One Folthnir opened the door to the men's slave enclosure and pulled out the nearest wretch. He led this slave to the empty post where Edrick stood. The man was bound in the same fashion as Edrick, arms bent around the post. The warriors savagely tore off his shirt and trousers, revealing his shaking naked body. Edrick looked away in shame as he suddenly urinated himself like a beaten dog. More wolfskins gathered around his family. Edrick found himself unable to continue his work and stood anxiously watching.

Then there came a sharp clang from an iron door shutting. Edrick whipped his head to see the slave boy locking him inside.

"Hey!" Edrick rushed toward the boy, but the slave took off in a full sprint and disappeared around the tower. He shook the bars and inspected the lock. There was no escape.

A stool was set for the Theign to sit. The wolfskin youth, stood by the warlord's side. The youth produced an exotic whip of scarlet scales, long and slender. The tail of a young dragon it was, lined with spiny bone. He snapped it repeatedly, provoking the tied man to flinch and gasp.

The foreigner spoke. "I told the lord what remarkable healing the Woodcutter has shown. Our lord desired to see for himself."

The Folthnir lord spoke. "My son, Ator, is young. He must learn to put fear in the minds of men. Pain is fear. Those who deal the pain are the ones who control men."

Ator stepped forward, cruel whip in hand. He looked on Edrick's family with haughty malice.

The captive man was then immediately whipped. The wolfskin youth took pleasure at every pain laden scream. The captive's skin tore open, flying off his chest. He wailed in agony. The crows cried back to him, mocking him, bouncing up and down as if asking for more, goading the men in their brutality.

"These wounds, can you heal them?" the foreigner asked harshly after the first lashing.

Mother nodded.

Ator whipped the man again. Bone and scale tore into the muscle. The man screamed out with every cruel lash.

"And these wounds?"

Mother nodded. Her hands covered her mouth, holding in her cries of horror.

The man was lashed again and again until mother conceded. "Stop!" she begged them. "I cannot heal him, he will die. Please, this is evil work!"

The blood rained over Edrick's family, tiny red droplets fouled their faces. The man's flesh had been torn through his muscles, exposing bare rib bone. His head too, was not spared the cruel whip. He bled relentlessly. Pools gathered below, mixing with the parched dirt. Pieces of his face were missing. His eyes were swollen, covered in red.

Everything in red.

The Theign barked out more commands. Out from the tower another man was brought, blindfolded and gagged.

The whipped slave was released from the post. He slumped into the pool of blood. Edrick watched as the dying man was then dragged to the Huntsman. His dogs whined, begging to feed as the scent of blood filled the air. The whipped man moaned, oblivious to the danger. The Huntsman nodded and they threw him to the frenzied dogs. He was devoured within moments.

The crows worked up a fervor, some daring to fly into the mass of hounds to snatch a morsel.

Edrick said a prayer for the man, whose soul would wander the world disturbed and wrathful.

They then tied the new captive to the post. His clothes were torn off same as the slave. Lastly, they removed his blindfold and gag.

"Please!" the man whimpered. He spoke Mithlian, though his cadence was strange, noble maybe. "I have told you the truth. I have not held anything back. Ask him!" the man cried out, desperate. He motioned to their father.

"Woodcutter, you know who this man is?" The warlord asked in a thick accent. "He evidently knows you."

"I have never seen him before. What crime is against him?"

"He is a traitor to your people," the Folthnir lord replied. "He led us here, to you, and this forest. He says the Mark king fled here."

Alaric shook his head. "I would not know. I have been away a long time."

"So you say, so everyone says. But you are some kind of little lord, huh? Some kind of fallen noble or something. I know you Woodcutter, we all do in the north. Your infamy lives as a curse in our land. You assassinated hundreds of our warriors in the long years of war between our two people. Silver feathers with seven notches is the mark of many widows and orphans in my land. I would never have thought to find this great assassin in a backwards village on the edge of the Mark. I assumed to have found such a great warrior in Sithric's court. My King Azevral was looking forward to finding your body amongst the dead there.

"So when my men discovered the dead bodies of three of my outriders struck down by nothing more than a single silver fletched arrow into the eyes, I was suddenly reminded of your legendary reputation. And not only did we find you, but your whole litter." The Folthnir chuckled.

Alaric said nothing. He looked into mother's face, something unspoken passed between them.

"Yes! Yes!" the prisoner blurted out. "He, his family are titled, some kind of Steward of the Forest. It used to be the emperor's forest, when this land was named Mithlian. King Sithric fled here! Ask him! Ask him!"

"You see," the Folthnir lord said, hand extending to the groveling man.

"If such a thing is true," Alaric spat, "I know nothing. If he did flee, he was foolish to do so. I am sure he is dead. Tearing the skin from my flesh will not change my answer."

"So you say. Well then, I will take a different approach."

The Folthnir lord gave a nod. From the shadows of the tower emerged Grindan with his iron smithing hammer. His face was grim, a piece of cold steel and hard eyes.

The Folthnir lord spoke something to him in their language. Without a word to his father or his mother, Grindan assaulted the prisoner savagely. His bones snapped under the heavy blows. The blacksmith struck the man's joints, breaking first, his feet, then his arms and elbows. Last, he swung at the man's knees, battering his legs against the wooden post. The man screamed out, chipping his teeth as he bit down against the agony. Edrick had never seen such cruel, barbarous acts. He couldn't believe what he witnessed was real. But it was hearing the screams that jolted his heart. Never had he heard a person cry out in such pain.

After the brutal beating, a warrior drew a dagger and severed his hamstrings. The man's feet slid forward, crashing down on his knees. His shins stuck out before him at an unnatural angle.

He wailed in convulsions. He spoke words that were unintelligible, mashed sounds that were mostly moans and sobs, but Edrick knew what he wanted. "Kill me," he said.

"We have." The Folthnir lord said. He stood, leaning over the prisoner. "I think Death will meet you in the darkest hour of night. Traitors deserve slow deaths." He turned to Alaric. "You have until sunrise to think of answers I want to hear. And if you have nothing useful to say, then the first to be broken is your eldest, then this one," pointing to Eadwyn, "then," he looked over his shoulder to Edrick standing dumbfounded in his pen, "the runt. And last, your wife who will endure the worst. That I will see to." He grinned, his followers laughed in prurient glee. They were proud of their evil work. Took joy in the pain.

Edrick watched the Folthnir lord depart in confidence, assured he would get his answers. He looked across the grounds to Edrick, and Edrick back with hate filled eyes. He clenched the shovel in both hands, imagining he was bashing the man's face, breaking his nose like an egg. The man halted, the others stopped behind him, taking notice of Edrick's silent defiance.

"Father," Ator said, "let me remove his skin and replace it with fear and respect for my Theign."

With a nod, the Theign's swordsman marched toward Edrick, drawing his weapon.

A sound, a low hum rolled across the grounds. An energy spun into the air. The crows danced now on the walls, where more were gathering. They bobbed and hopped along the stone like a mad cabal. Some took to their wings and flew widdershins around the tower forming a black halo.

The swordsman closed in, Edrick held his shovel tight, ready to take on the armed Folthnir. He would have to open the cage if he wanted to kill me, Edrick told himself. As the swordsman raised his hand to plunge into Edrick, his beard hair launched off his face like scattered grass blades flung in the wind. The large warrior startled, cried out, dropping his sword and clutching his bleeding skin. Edrick was sure he heard laughter, like children, but cruel and remorseless.

Then there was a clamor all around. Something was happening and Edrick guessed easily enough. Faeries had come, and they were not the good kind.

There were others whose hair, beard or otherwise were suddenly plucked from their flesh until tiny pin pricks of blood erupted from their pores. Some men's skin turned orange and then clenched over onto their knees vomiting violently. Others stripped out of their clothes as lesions of boils, warts and rashes crawled over their flesh. The entire camp disintegrated into a chaotic display.

On the walls, the battle horns sounded out.

Deep, brutal, blaring horns sounded out across the camp. A low drone that quelled the energy Edrick first felt. Edrick found himself laying down, covering his head under the weight of the strange notes.

Then everything became still and silent as the horns paused. No one moved. They then sounded again, accompanied by the heavy percussions of drums rumbling from inside the tower.

A chanting rose up like a coming storm rolling off the mountains. Out from the tower rushed the Folthnir battle priests, singing deep baritones, followed by sluggish bass notes carrying a strange enchantment. These men wore long linen robes of black with scarlet hems. Runes, etched upon the cloth in gold, seemed to almost catch fire in the light of the sun. Under their robes were scarlet mail scales, same as the Theign, and they wielded shields and warhammers. They sung on, continuously accompanied by the drums and horns until the crows scattered and the warriors recovered.

Suddenly their voices ceased, and it felt to Edrick as if a heavy blanket had just been pulled off him. He looked around, warriors had poured into the tower grounds, armed and ready for battle. The faeries had left and they had no further disturbance that day.

One of the priests shouted to the skies triumphantly then all the warriors shouted in unison. The lord then greeted the battle priests and the group retreated inside the tower. The morbid calm returned.

Mother was talking to the tortured noble man hanging off the post. She slipped something into his mouth. He became relaxed and slumped forward. Edrick guessed he had received poison. His soul would pass into the land of shadows.

The sun set and a cold crept over the ground. Edrick shivered, leaning against the cage wall. He stared at his family from across the grounds until his eyes became heavy and he fell asleep.

He was shaken awake almost immediately, so it seemed at first. But the moon had already climbed high. A small hand was on his shoulder, reaching from behind him. Another hand slipped across his mouth to muffle a shout. Edrick relaxed and the hand withdrew. It was the slave boy. Edrick stared at him, skin covered in mud and feces. It was as if he wore the night air on his flesh.

"Do not talk," he whispered, no louder than a mouse twitching its nose.

Edrick nodded.

The boy just stared at Edrick. Seeing him as if he were a ghost, looking pass him to something beyond.

"I know a way out. We can escape," he said finally.

Edrick sat up straight. "Yes!" he whispered back, growing

excited.

"You know your way outside the wall? You live here, yes?"

"Yes."

"Ok, we leave now. But NOT into that forest!" He whispered as loud as he dared. "We run the other way."

Edrick looked back to his family. "I must take them with me."

"No," the boy said. "No-no-no." He had a key in his hand and inserted it into lock. "Just you and me. They are already dead, same as the rest."

"No," Edrick countered and sat back down. "I will not go without them." His mother's voice echoed in his head. "Leave! Flee," her voice urged him. But he could not. He would not.

The slave boy looked up from the lock suddenly. He appeared defeated. His hands dropped from the door before he unlocked it. It was as if he did not expect that answer. As if he expected Edrick to be as reasonable and as terrified as he was. As any of them were.

"You must come," he begged. Tears wet his eyes. "I do not want to die…" He sniffled, wiping his nose. "I am afraid of the woods. The dæmon Erlking lives there. He will snatch us up if we don't find our way out quickly."

"You can go!" Edrick urged him. "Just go west, away from the woods. There is a road. Follow it south. You will be all right," he promised.

The boy continued crying, as quietly as he could. He pleaded with Edrick again to go with him, but Edrick would not go without his family. The boy held out his hand to Edrick. Edrick looked at it, wondering what he meant, but took it in his. It was cool and rough. The boy ran his thumb over the back of Edrick's hand, gentle and consoling.

"I understand," the boy said. He then ran off into the darkness, but not toward the portcullis. Edrick sat in thought and wondered if he made a mistake. It was as if it was not enough to escape, but the boy needed someone to escape with.

Edrick stared into the black night where the boy ran off, looking for him to return. He did not.

Before the daylight crept back out of the eastern earth, Edrick heard them in the air. The crows were returning, sneaking back in near silence, humbled possibly by yesterday's event. When the first gray streaks of light cracked into the cold black sky, Edrick saw them, their dark silhouettes against the fuliginous horizon, huddling together on the walls like hooded monks of a black god.

They stirred the air. Again they flew around the tower, greater were their numbers this time. Faster was their speed. Churning and winding like an unblinking eye in a storm.

Then a bright light threw out a long shadow beneath Edrick. A light growing in the west. Mother lit a candle, a faerie candle and it burned a brilliant blue. It parted the dark around his family, like a raised shield parting a rain of arrows. She looked to him. He did not know how to read her face. As if she pleaded for him to run far away and to come to her all at once. He smiled to let her know he was all right. Her eyes teared up instead.

I love you little one, she said without a sound.

I love you too, he replied in silence.

Moments passed in heavy heart beats as they peered at one another through the gray dawn.

Horns blasted the chilled air in deep, droning wails. Folthnir warriors rushed onto the tower grounds in full battle attire, armed and falling in formations. Their attention turned to the sky and the amassed crows above them.

Another blast from the horns signaled impending battle. War drums pounded within the heart of the tower once again. Edrick looked around, wondering what it was that aroused their fury. Something beyond the walls? They were all climbing the ladders and spreading across the parapets. Arrows were loosed into the outer fields. Others attacked the crows who barked at them as they slipped off the walls easily escaping injury, taking to their wings and landing again out of the men's reach. Taunting them with the corvine laughter.

Mother lit more candles, placing them at his brother's feet. From her basket she removed a glass vial and clay jar. She tipped the jar and poured ash into her hand, then marked a circle, a large outer one around Edrick's family and three interlocking rings inside, followed by a sprinkling of water from the vial in the air, while speaking words of an alhíelda.

Phantom whispers with strange tongues landed on Edrick's ear accompanied by ghostly laughter, childlike, making his hair stand on end. Ghostly little people manifested themselves for moments then faded, hundreds of them surrounding the area like swarming insects.

Dark faeries! Never had Edrick seen so many or could have possibly imagined that many existed.

Out of the tower burst the Folthnir Theign and a contingent of fearsome warriors, among them the battle priests and the foreigner who held a tall staff with a crystal prism mounted on the end.

The Huntsman shouted orders then climbed the ladder up the walls. His hounds were set off their leashes and they charged the gatehouse jumping on the wooden beams, barking furiously, begging to be let loose into the fields beyond.

The slaves in the pens cowered, huddled down as far as they could, closing their eyes. Edrick felt sorry for them, to feel trapped and uncertain. He grabbed his shovel and began to dig beneath the pen wall, determined to escape and reunite with his family.

The Folthnir lord shouted to his men in two languages, first in Folthnir then in Mithlian. "These things in the woods, whatever they are, have heard the voice of Vylkinus! He has put fear in their hearts and they are compelled to seek their deaths on our swords. This land has new gods now, gods of battle and blood, of the limitless sky and deafening thunder. We will burn the earth with the light of Vylkinus's Hellforge and all creatures will cower beneath our war drums. We will tear this sky with lighting and suffocate the land with thunder. My father and grandfather have encountered many gods of conquered lands of the past, only to see them fall beneath the hammer of Vylkinus, thrown into his forge and split over his anvil. Ulfserkers, it is time to earn a place among your Blooded brothers!"

Edrick had never heard of other gods or knew foreign people worshipped gods other than his. This Vylkinus sounded terrible and strong. The wolfskins became invigorated, yelling out cheers and bursting into song, much like Edrick heard yesterday. Challenging the gods was inviting curses and disaster. Were these men so brash and proud that they would defile Lhodyn? He did not want be present to see how Lhodyn answered these fools.

Edrick made quick progress with his digging when screaming disrupted his attention. Bodies of dead men began to fall from the walls. Edrick told himself to ignore the commotion, to focus on escape but his curiosity overcame him.

A large three faced owl with horns like an elk glided over the grounds and landed upon the tower. Eyes unblinking, it gazed down at the humans. Its head bobbed around, its orbed eyes of black pitch locked on something of interest among the men. Baying howls rumbled beyond the walls, not like wolves but deep and sorrowful as hounds from the underworld. A pack of beasts, wolf-like with sharp quills along their back but stout like wolverines, appeared now along the parapets, attacking the warriors, catching them in their huge maws and tossing them to their deaths upon the ground.

Upon one huge wolf-like beast rode a figure bearing a leathery mask. Antlers grew out of its head, a nine point splendor. It seemed man like, but its limbs were elongated; its fingers shaped liked long talons, and its legs misshaped into that of an elk hind. About its body hung mossy coverings either growing from skin hidden beneath or it was thick fur taking the appearance of moss. Draped about its form, hung a heavy cloak of black which stirred not as it rode, nor moved at the slightest lift of the wind.

Edrick's mouth dropped.

The slave children screamed in terror from their enclosure, for they knew this thing that rode upon these strange beasts, as every child who lived near the forest. The Erlking was the creature of darkness that snatched children at night, sucked the breath from babies, and mere presence imparted nightmares to children. The Erlking was a childhood terror, who murders parents and steals away children.

It crept to the edge of the wall, then the mount began to walk vertically down the side, as if it were a spider, clinging effortlessly. The rider, nor its cloak and draping moss, leaned forward toward the ground, instead seemed as if he were still on the ground and everything fell toward their feet.

The Theign barked orders to his men and they struggled to regroup into a defined formation. The dark man began chanting, the air distorted around the crystal like heat emitting off fire. From it, a shower of light flashed across the barbarians. Edrick thought he made a mistake and burned his companions to ash, but the light bounced off them harmlessly. Instead hundreds of tiny screams poured out of the air, and the tiny bodies flickered into existence for a second before being forever silenced. The crystal shifted from clear glass into a sinister puce.

The dæmon wolves rushed toward the warriors crashing into their ranks, crashing down the wall like an avalanche. More and more came from beyond the wall. Most men were thrown to the ground.

The warriors regained control, hacking and slashing at the snapping maws of the vicious creatures. The dark foreigner stood next to the Folthnir Lord acting as his body guard, repelling any beast that came near. The veteran warrior kept a cold, hard face and shouted orders and gave directions to the fighting men. There were so many of these beasts that they were quickly surrounded, trapped between the wall and tower.

The Huntsman's hounds rushed at the wolfish beasts, but they were no match in strength or ferocity and seemed more like cats chasing wolves. Yet these hounds were fearless and attacked until they were torn asunder. Edrick noticed father's bow in the Huntsman's hands. He attempted to fire it but he could not draw the string back at all. He could not master the weapon and so retreated, leaving his hounds to die without their handler.

The Erlking leapt off his beast, landing on the children's pen. He tore open the ceiling and reached inside with its long limbs. It grabbed a child, a girl, and flung her into the air. A horned owl plucked her from the sky and flew over the walls and out of sight with the child wrapped in its talons.

It continued to snatch children from the enclosure, flinging them into the air where more horned owls flew off with them until it came under assault from the Folthnir Lord. He stood amongst his greatest warriors, hurling spears at the creature. The Erlking dove and dodged the first volley then leaped toward them, landing on one warrior breaking his bones despite his hauberk.

As soon as it landed, the Erlking took on all nine men in battle, clawing at them with its limbs, lifting men into the air, hurling them against the tower. It fought with a wild ferociousness. The battle priests mostly hid behind their shield as the dæmon pummeled them, beating them away from the captive slaves.

Edrick dug desperately trying to escape but it seemed like too much. He looked all around, frantic that some creature would notice his vulnerability. Battle raged everywhere. His family were luckily out of harm for the moment. The light of the candles not only seemed to keep the beasts at bay, but repelled them. Father stood now, holding Mother, guarding Halig and Eadwyn, unafraid it seemed to Edrick. If only Father had a bow, he could at least defend their family. That's when Edrick noticed in the growing morning light, the key the slave boy had been fiddling with was still lodged in the door. Whether on purpose of left in despair, the boy left Edrick a means to escape.

He unlocked the door and flung it wide. The quick movement caught the attention of the beasts all around him.

From the shadows beneath the wall walked three figures dressed in gowns of ash and earth tones. Youthful women they appeared, one holding a branch of a pine, one an elder and one an ash. Leaves still growing forth. The first witch, in a shimmering blur, moved through the chaotic battle with amazing speed and leaped on the pen containing the children. She took the place of the Erlking, continuing to steal children, she tossed them to the monstrous birds who carried them off into the direction of the forest.

Another trained her attention on Edrick, screaming at him with a shrill voice. His vision blurred, his strength momentarily left him as he fell to his knees. The woman snatched him by the neck, nearly breaking it, Edrick thought. An iciness radiated across his skin from her touch. A cold that made his soul shiver. As his sight returned, he saw his mother standing near them. Before he knew what was happening, she threw a faerie candle at the witch and spoke a single word. The witch screamed, leaping into the air, dropping Edrick. Mother scooped him up and rushed back toward his family. Edrick looked back over his mother's shoulder as the witch was enveloped in white smoke, clinging to her like a strangulating shroud. She ascended to the height of the walls and when the smoke cleared, the witch was nowhere to be found.

"Are you hurt, Edrick?" Mother asked, her voiced trembled in a way that concerned Edrick, for he had always known Mother to be calm.

"No. We have to find a way out of here!"

"There is no way out. Not right now."

They were back with his father and brothers. Mother set Edrick down and handed Father a Folthnir bow and quarrel of arrows she must have snatched from the battlefield. Edrick looked on his mother with a new sense of awe. Not only had she rescued him, she brought father weapons. His brothers seemed to have barely taken notice of him as they seemed transfixed on the battle beyond.

"Edrick," Father said with a relieved smile. He squeezed Edrick's shoulder then took the weapons. Edrick looked up to his father. His strength had returned and there was a grim determination on his face.

All was not going well for the Folthnir. They were now gathered together with their backs to the tower, savagely fending off the dæmon wolf horde. They had long spears which worked well to keep the beasts at bay, but they could not defeat them and their deaths seemed inevitable. Their slave children were being taken from them without challenge.

"It seems the Folthnir god is not so strong in our land," Father said. Yet just as he spoke, war horns took up once again, and there followed a response from within the tower. Three strident responses bellowed forth from its interior. The iron tower doors burst open and out of the darkness five massive figures squeezed from the tower threshold. Giants, the height of four men, waded into the battle. They were clad in iron plate from head to foot, wielding massive hammers, axes and towering shields that seemed like portable walls. Upon their armor were runes marked in red, as if painted in blood.

The enemy was taken by surprise and the giant warriors pressed the dæmon beasts away from their Folthnir allies. Within moments the Folthnir had the advantage as they fell in behind their giant companions. The beasts fell back, but did not retreat. The Erlking, though, seemed not so brash. He gave a mighty leap and landed on the walls above the gatehouse. The Folthnir swarmed across the tower grounds, securing their slave pens which were now mostly empty of children. The pens holding the men had been ripped apart, though the enemy seemed not as interested in preserving their lives as the men had died with nowhere to retreat.

The two remaining witches came to the Erlking's side, and they stood looking down upon the men and giants, smug and indignant. They were out of their reach for a moment, as the giants could not climb up after them. The Folthnir were fetching new ladders to take the battle to the walls.

"This has been but a warning from the Lady of the Woods, Mistress Lhodyn," the Erlking shouted. "Renounce your god, your weakling deity of bearded boys. What strength do you have without these giants? Your singing birds scare us not. We have paid you a visit, so please come into the woods and witness a real power! But beware, the unrepentant shall be dragged into milady's Vaults."

The Erlking cast a lingering eye over Edrick's father, inducing involuntary trembles over Edrick and his brothers. Then his mount returned and the Erlking took to it. Both leapt over the wall and were gone. The witches lingered a little longer, seemingly frustrated at the sudden end of battle.

The first of the men that reached the walls, charged the witches. They laughed playfully, then glided off the parapets, remaining suspended in the air. In their place, a dark shadow remained, spreading out like smoke, swallowing the warriors until they were lost from sight. The witches were gone, gliding into the forest heights, before the smoke dissipated revealing nothing but the warrior's effects. Armor and weapons crashed down to the walls. There was no accounting for the men for which the items belonged.

The battle was over.

The Theign sheathed his weapon first, then the others warily followed. The dark foreigner remained at the lord's side. The Folthnir secured the walls, and reports went around counting the casualties and those who succumbed to death.

The Folthnir lord made his way to Edrick and his family, the only ones who escaped harm. "What was that dæmon?" he demanded.

"Lhodyn's servant, chief guardian of the woods," Alaric replied. "You should leave, now, for they have not revealed their true strength. They have underestimated you today, but be sure they will tear your men apart when they return."

The lord said nothing. He surveyed the grounds, his fallen men, his mighty giants that saved them from death. "And how is it the Woodcutters survived unscathed when many of my valiant warriors died like sheep among wolves."

"We have our own magick, and I know their weaknesses," Mother said.

"You, too, are a witch!" A Folthnir priest accused, thrusting his war hammer forward.

"No, I am not a witch. I am a healer, an alhíelda, and know how to counter the ways of witchcraft. They have not revealed their strength at all, and neither have we. Lord, I know a way to hinder Lhodyn. There is an old ritual that will inhibit those beasts and spirits as a wall would hold back men, like the circle I drew around my family. It will not bind them, but will be an obstacle they will find difficult to remove. I can place one around this tower, but I ask you release my family."

The warlord looked to the foreigner for council. The dark man studied the woman then nodded. "I have heard such professions here in the North. They claim to be different from witches because their study is of faeries, primarily, and derive their power from that knowledge. Any person of magical study knows that witches and faeries do not collaborate, and are instead at cross purposes."

"But weren't some of these creatures faeries?" asked the Huntsman.

"Yes, but under the power of Lhodyn I would guess. All this land has fallen to some curse and now we understand the source. I have heard of such things, it is a grave concern."

The warlord considered the council in silence then spoke, "I judge what the Woodcutter has confessed was truthful. The woods are evil and beyond his influence and if Sithric did indeed flee here, it was not to his benefit. I will spare your lives for as long as you serve me. But you will swear to me as your lord, and my word is law. I will then consider this ritual and spare your life. It seems you Woodcutters have uses beyond killing my men."

Their bonds were released. Father made his brothers kneel before the warlord without explanation. Mother even dropped to a knee, but Edrick remained standing looking toward his father, asking him why. His father pushed Edrick to his knees then turned and did the same.

"I swear my life and that of my family, to hold your authority above all others and declare your enemies are my enemies. My word is my life."

"We will uphold the oaths of our father," Edrick and his brothers replied.

"Swear to High Lord Vylkinus," one of the priests demanded. "Lord of Gods, Shaper of the World, Keeper of the Light! And curse Lhodyn's name. She is a witch that shall be thrown on the Hellforge, this land will be purged of her darkness."

To this, the Woodcutters remained quiet. They looked to their father, who kept his head bowed. "I swear to Vylkinus," he stated through a clenched jaw. "I curse Lhodyn's name and pray she be broken on the Hellforge."

"We will uphold the oaths of our father," Edrick and his brothers replied.

"We accept your oaths and hold your lives as payment for service. What protection does your wife speak of?"

"The forest goddess is vengeful of proud men and has wiped out ancient kings that made their abodes near these woods long ago, just look to this tower to see the truth. If you plan to remain here and keep this land as yours, you must prepare. We know our lives are forfeit but you will need our knowledge to overcome this enemy. You must fell the trees and burn the bodies of theses beasts and dead faeries. Then scatter the ashes around your tower. This must be done now while her pride stays her hand."

The battle priests spoke to the Folthnir lord in confidence. Edrick could tell they were not receptive to the idea. They did not trust mother's skills and regarded her as a witch, just like the other villagers.

"They will do as you suggest," the Theign answered with finality.

Through Mother's instruction, they performed a binding ceremony along the tower's perimeter. For ten days they hacked down trees and burned them in mighty bonfires then gathered the dead corpses, throwing them on the pyres. The trees became angry and swayed and shivered furiously.

Though they spared Father's life, they did not withhold from making further sport of him. They worked him with little food and water or sleep, forcing heavy loads on him, whipping him forward until his strength gave out. He faltered after three days, stumbling while burdened under a load of thick tree limbs. He fell sideways, falling beneath a hundred pounds of wood.

Edrick heard something snap and was afraid it was his father's bones.

"Elisal," Father called out. His voice was parched, a whisper of his mighty self. He reached to Edrick.

"Father, I will bring her," Edrick said. He wove through the Folthnir and laborers until he found Mother.

"Come, Father," was all he had to say, pulling at her arm.

"No one leaves until the task is complete. No one." The Theign threatened.

"Fetch your sister and bring her straight here," Mother urged Edrick.

He ran off and found Meghan waiting for news at Oxa's cottage. Together they returned to Mother's side, out of breath. Mother recited both instructions and ingredients to Meghan and sent them both to fetch the appropriate medicines from their home. They ran the entire distance, returning quickly to their father. Meghan started a fire to brew the necessary medicine.

"I will help," Edrick offered.

"That will be good," she replied and had him stir while she added ingredients into a portable cauldron.

Mother was away, giving directions to the villagers who carried ashes from the burn piles and marked lines around the tower's perimeter. She took baskets filled with ash and thrust them into the hands of the warriors.

"This must be tossed at every site where blood was spilled by your men," she stated as the last of the fires smoldered into coals. "I expect your tower to be assaulted soon, maybe all the village," she warned. "Lhodyn despises your foreign gods. She craves your souls."

The men looked to their Theign for permission to ignore the impertinent alhíelda. He instead gave a nod of compliance and turned away indignantly.

When the medicine was ready, Meghan ladled a small amount into a cup and brought it to Mother.

"It's ready, I think" Meghan asked, offering the cup to Mother for her approval.

With her weary, ash stained hands, Mother affectionately embraced Meghan's chin, tilting her head up. "You are doing well Meghan, you will be a wonderful alhíelda soon." She tasted the medicine. "Yes, feed it to him in small spoonfuls. Edrick, you are helping?"

He nodded eagerly.

"Good. Support your father while Meghan feeds him the medicine. After this, prepare a sleeping draught. He needs a long sleep. If he awakes, he will not allow himself to rest and recover."

Mother had Halig and Eadwyn build a small shelter for their father to sleep in, a secret place near the apiaries of the northern fields. Despite the Theigns threats, Mother had somehow kept their attention off Father. The two brothers carried him to the shelter. He was already taken by the sleeping medicine.

Megahn remained by Father's side, tending to him day and night.

Edrick assumed the role of the messenger between his family. He helped as best he could but spent most his time searching for the slave boy who wanted to escape with him. He never found him again.

Edrick stared often into the woods. Despite the sun and cloudless sky, it remained dark as if night still clung to branch and trunk. The trees lined up like soldiers in formation, winding endlessly into the horizon.

Somewhere, his sister waited for him. Perhaps the slave boy and other children waited with her.

14

A WORLD FORGOTTEN

PAIN SUNDERED ALARIC'S strength. It tore into him no matter how much he fought it, trapping his life, his dreams, his desires.

The battle was done. His wife's medicines coursed through him, but the pain became intolerable. Pain he concealed from his family.

Thoughts turned to death, the ultimate curative. Like sleep, an eternal rest. No more running, no more fighting, no more enduring the accumulating burdens.

This became his secret wish. His selfish desire.

But not that of his family's. Elisial was his life. He was their children's life. He had to stay for them. Everything for them.

He held those darks thoughts down, deep within him. He had to. As long as his strength remained, he fought for his family's lives.

He had only one thought now. Escape. Leave the village and forest behind. Take his family south to Lathiélden where war was only rumor and haunted forests a thing of legends.

On the first few days after the battle, he led his boys and the village men in felling the trees, until a sharp pain in his ribs forced him to set aside his ax. The Folthnir closely watched him and would not let him rest. They forced the largest loads of timber on him, whipped his legs when he stumbled. They were relentless in their torture, denying him food and water. Edrick would steal food for him when the Folthnir's attention were diverted. Yet, the scraps he obtained were little relief from the pain in his body and soul.

After the fires around the tower quelled and the smoke fluttered far above the trees, Alaric succumbed to the darkness.

He remembered falling, but never hitting the ground.

Love filled his heart when the world went dark...

Not darkness, but just away, and nothing replaced it immediately. His wife's words were the last sounds that played on his ears, but it was her love that stayed with him, from the time he was a young man smitten by her green eyes, to this place where he found himself, alone and adrift.

There was no ground beneath him, but it was not as if he floated in the sky. The forest was near, the tower was near; there were people around, though they remained silent. He could feel them, many souls, all around him. Love was lost among them and they awaited its return.

How long he dwelled in that gray space, he could not tell. It neither hurt nor provided any sort of comfort, save in the absence of the pain left behind. Love kept him warm in an otherwise cold space where the sun could not be seen or felt, despite the absence of darkness. It was just a gray existence.

A humming din arose, surrounding him in the obscure distance. It occupied the grayness for a while, moving about him, drawing toward him, then retreating; approaching closer, settling, then falling back again, like the eternal play of ocean waves. It was an insect's buzz, thrumming and congealing. Alaric guessed it was the sound of a bee hive, not the swarm of flies preying on carcasses. It drew closer after a while, until it wrapped around him. The sound was now intense and vibrant. His chest reverberated back into consciousness. Where he had no body a moment before, one materialized to confront the disturbance in the grayness. The swarm swirled around like a whipping desert wind spinning across the barren sands of mythic lands. The bees agitated the air with every wing beat, awakening his body, radiating from his heart and moving through his limbs. He could smell the heaviness of the pollen, a mix of eclectic flowers gathered together, fanning life back into his lungs. On his tongue, the ambrosial promise of honey.

At last, his eyes opened.

He stood in the exact place he remembered collapsing, near the tower at the edge of the forest. The light was strange, familiar to another world he frequented on some occasions, the world of the faerie. Though this was not the fey land, for the sun burned vigorously in the sky, blanketing his body in warmth as he awoke from the grayness, distilling the love he felt into his veins where it would be delivered back into his heart. The field was vivid green and the sky a thick, smalt blue. The humming of the bees fell away but remained in his thoughts.

"The Lady awaits us, Renweard," came a gentle voice clothed in strength.

Alaric turned to see the speaker. Behind him were men gathered into a train of followers, and standing by his side, a familiar figure. It could not be true! The Nithyng! Appearing elegant and tall, strangely elfish in a certain regard, though elk horns grew out of its brow. It did not appear as the dead thing Alaric was familiar with, but was a strong vibrant figure.

"We must arrive before the gloaming or She will be cross," the closest man urged. He was a young man with an honest face.

"We?" Alaric stammered, to imagine he and that thing had any common destination. "You are speaking of Lhodyn?"

A gasp flushed out over the gathered men. The Nithyng's face fell serious. "Lady-Lord Lhodyn," he corrected sternly.

The men here were all dressed in woodsman attire, each one possessing a huntsman's bow across their shoulder. A few of them hauled small hand carts of bee hives, twenty in total Alaric would guess. Also, they carried grains gathered from farmer's fields, freshly harvested.

"All of us are going to confront Her?" His questioning sent concerned looks across the men's faces followed by hushed comments.

"Confront Her?" asked the man that spoke once before. He pulled Alaric aside, away from the Nithyng and spoke softly into his ear. "Have you lost your resolve after committing this far? It would be bad for everyone if one of us did not swear oaths to Her. If you have had a change of heart, brother, I will take your place. I will be the Lord Consort, if this position seems too much for you now." A flash of greed crossed the man's eyes where honesty held fast.

Alaric's thoughts spun in confusion. His brothers had been long dead and this man did not resemble any of them. How did he come to find himself here? He tried to reach for thoughts of a time before the grayness, but could force no recollections into his mind that granted him any perspective. He studied the man before him, a man of humble means, warn leather boots, linen shirt and pants mended with patches many times over. Silver feathers of his family's make stuck boldly above the man's shoulder, secured in a quiver slung around his torso. Most of the men were all of similar manner in appearance, men of the woods, not farmers or workers from the apiaries. Every single one of them possessed their ghost-lights upon their brow. Their éardians had not fled them. He glossed over his own form and found unfamiliar trappings, possessions he was sure were not his own. He reached for his bow where he found it hanging in the same familiar position across his shoulder, but it was not Nithledan, but much lighter.

And on his neck, his torc clasped securely as it once did, before he passed it off to Edrick. His fingers touched each of the three arrow heads, felt the sharpness of their point. A silent reassurance flowed through his touch and into his body, as if he were connected to the one who crafted the heirloom.

Then came a whisper.

Follow them.

Alaric looked around for the speaker, a voice of some youthful girl that matched the tenderness of the two words, but there were none but men there and a few cream colored butterflies dancing in the sunrays. Without further questioning he stepped away from his *brother* and up to the impatient and still haughty Nithyng. Its face was young and still kissed by the light of the sun. Its skin, like stained walnut grain and not the familiar bone white. What place had he found himself where things are so familiar yet so strange?

"Lead us then to your mistress, o woodland prince," Alaric breathed out the quiet words that only the Nithyng could hear. The venom of his tone bled out plainly despite his discrete manner. The Nithyng wrinkled his face, its eyes searched for clarity among Alaric's visage. Frustration built as it could find none.

"You will find the Lady-Lord well pleased with your fidelity," it replied as it walked away, leading the band across the open green fields. "She is looking forward to this new relationship between men and woodland creatures. To be frank, She searches for a kind of people who appreciate her compassion, wisdom and vision of the world."

"So it is true," Alaric's brother interjected, "that the elves have lost her favor?"

The Nithyng laughed gleefully and patted the young man's back. "What joy She will find in such company, to be so bold and naïve all at once. Just be careful as to when you address Her directly, such a demeanor might not always be interpreted so generously as I, who understand your folk better than She."

Alaric studied the tall creature intently. He could not believe the thing's flattering self-description, nor the friendliness in which it was delivered. Yet Alaric admitted, it genuinely seemed convivial in contrast to the creature of darkness he remembered.

The procession moved slowly, solemnly through the field, following a trail Alaric walked many times, a trail that connected the village to the Ruined Tower by circumventing the woods, yet as they proceeded, the sight of the tower never took shape. Alaric knew the land well enough that he marked where the tower should have been, even if he could not see it, as was the case now.

"It's not here," he said with astonished breath. He began to understand. Heedless to any of the others who now all paused in their march. Alaric waded across the open ground to where the tower should have stood. The ground had never been disturbed, never felt the gnawing slices of industrious shovels.

"Brother," Alaric began as he turned back around to see the mixture of annoyance and confusion in the reaction of the men there. "I would like you to speak the title the Lady-Lord will pronounce on me this day."

His brother straightened his back, eyes shifting in confused suspicion. "Aye. You will be hence forth known as Renweard the First, Lord Consort to the Woodland Court, Chief among Men." The pronouncement half stunned Alaric who expected the name, but not the title. Warden of the Woods was the familiar title he had known all his life.

"Now, my soon-to-be Lord, we must away before the gloaming. I would not want tardiness to be our first impression as nobility, at our own ceremony," his brother urged, leading him back to the group.

"I apologize for my strange mood, there will be no further delays. Let us receive this distinctive title."

"Now that is the answer of a Lord Consort," the Nithyng replied, showing his friendliest smile Alaric had ever encountered on the ancient creature.

From here, they turned toward a path leading them into the Wudelic. Once inside, Alaric remained quiet, struck by the emerging beauty surrounding him. He gazed all about as they made their way over the winding forest paths. This forest was not the familiar realm he knew; it was so fresh and light. Sunlight did not just pour in from the forest canopy but coursed down through the limbs of every tree and spilled out over the wild flowers, filling every dark hole. Not a grander scene had Alaric ever known. His heart raced, same as the time when he laid eyes upon his wife in her youth. So alluring and vibrant, full of life and secrets, flirtatious to the pleasures promised. This is the forest he wanted his children to know. This is the world his ancestors guarded. Every man here, some of them well aged so that their hair was a seasoned white, all retained the light of the fey from the times they were but three days old. It was remarkable. Alaric walked amongst legends somehow. He now wandered through a world forgotten.

They marched deep in the woods for hours, resting only when necessary. The men rotated the burden of hauling the carts amongst themselves. When Alaric offered a hand, he was politely refused the menial task. Then when the gloaming was upon them, as the final light of the sun was at their backs, they entered a grand clearing of the Woodland Queen. The towering trees parted before them revealing a hidden grove nestled in a small vale. Center to the scene was a waterfall spilling over a rock cliff into a pool of a purity, consisting of the alchemic qualities possessed in quicksilver. The water did not crash down upon the waters in a wild fall, but graciously poured freely from the higher height, anointing the world below. There, directly forward of the falls, sat the Lady-Lord enthroned upon a tiny island in the center of the pool. This was Her court and She held an audience of varying creatures, all gathered and intent upon their guests. Shafts of sunlight formed ethereal pillars throughout the scene. Dainty butterflies bounced around the Lady-Lord's head in an aerial ballet. Then from the court below, horns sounded welcoming the guests. The Nithyng urged them to their correct positions before the Queen.

The men separated themselves from Alaric, his brother and the Nithyng, taking their offerings of honey and grains to the Lady-Lord's servants. The Nithyng led the two brothers around the pool making toward one of the small bridges that crossed onto the island.

A full audience of creatures gathered about the shore, chief among them were the radiant elves, tall and regal in form, wise and powerful in countenance; they wore gowns of elegant fabric. And despite their masterful presence, their eyes held no arrogance or the haughtiness of mighty lords, but sadness and vulnerability. Each one met Alaric's inquisitive gaze. Eyes that asked him to not go through with his committed course.

Yes, we are sorrowful, came the same soft whispering in reply to his thoughts. *You must know. This is what transpired.*

Alaric made to speak, but he knew not whom to reply. No one stirred.

Alaric, his brother and the Nithyng crossed the bridge and approached Lhodyn waiting for them upon her throne. All three bowed, lowering themselves to a knee. Alaric instinctively kneeled submissively as the power of the being before them resonated clearly, as clear as the sun stood in the sky. Lhodyn, too, appeared transformed, younger and quite alluring, her form not the strange features of various woodland creatures he was familiar with, but instead She assumed an elfish figure, more faerie-like than the elves were. She wore a crown of living flowers, white of petal with golden centers. Her clothes were similar, long vines that curled around Her seductive body, though she mostly appeared nude. The scent of this divine creature roused the blood in the Alaric's loins. Intoxicating, like a barrel of mead coursing through his veins. Suddenly who he was or where he was became of little importance, he just knew he loved this creature, loved Her and desired to serve Her, to please Her greatly.

To the Lady-Lord's right were six figures, all elves, a man and woman with children of varying ages. As Alaric glanced over them, his eyes landed upon the smallest, a girl with deep amber eyes and molten jet hair. She held his eyes, against his wishes, for he wanted to return to the sight of his beloved and cherished queen. But this little one would not allow it, she held him without effort.

You see now, she spoke, without moving her lips. He was released to look back upon the queen who regarded him with amusement.

"We greet the Wonder of these Woods with open hearts," he found himself saying, addressing the angelic creature enthroned before him. "We come bearing gifts of honey laden hives, companions to the flowers that adorn your court and have captured your affections."

The Lady-Lord nodded regally, a thin smile gracing Her face.

The Nithyng took his place to Her left side, then beckoned someone from the audience to approach them. They awaited a servant bearing an ornately carved box, slender in width and the length of a man. The servant offered it to the Nithyng who in turn dropped to his knee and offered it to his Lady-Lord after opening the lid. She reached inside to retrieve a long staff of an unstrung bow. There, in Her delicate hands, was Nithledan, newly wrought.

"Renweard, chief of men of these lands," the Nithyng began, standing upright, handing the casing back to his servant. "You have been summoned by the Queen of the Forest to become the first mortal lord appointed to her illustrious court. In receiving this title, her Highness grants you this symbol of her trust, to execute Her will with highest fidelity, regard Her holdings with tenacious spirit, and uphold Her law and judgment in unquestionable faith. Your mortal life will no longer be at threat to maligned spirits that plague the land, will no longer be subject to the predatory creatures that hunt your kind, from this point onward, you and your kin and all those under your protection shall in turn earn the protection of your Lady-Lord."

"I humbly accept Her grace and swear an oath, that I and my kin, shall hold no other in higher regard than the Lady of the Trees, for it is Her forest that has sustained our blood for generations, in time immemorial." The words again were not Alaric's, but he spoke them just the same. "There is no better cause than my Lady-Lord's will in all things."

"As I swear, and bear witness to Renweard's oath," his brother added enthusiastically.

The queen laughed like a youthful girl, carefree, well pleased with the offering. She held the bow staff to Her face, absently nuzzling the polished wood against her cheek. "Rise and face your queen, sons of the earth."

The two stood and turned, meeting the gaze of the court.

"You are my servant Renweard and I name you Lord Consort to the Woodland Court." With the pronouncement, applause erupted, accompanied with trumpet fanfare, the loudest cheering coming from Alaric's fellow woodsmen.

When the cheering settled, the queen continued. "Nine days before, in your first act of service, I commanded you to fell the ancient tree hidden deep in the woods, for which you have executed well."

At this pause, Alaric noticed the immense sorrow that washed over the elfish family next to him. They looked upon him accusingly, as if he acted a great harm upon them. "And from this wood, the rarest of all woods in this world, I give back to you a gift that will aid you further in my service. Behold Nithledan, the Night Bringer!" Her voice changed from a soft delicate lilt, into a commanding queen. "Fashioned by the diligent efforts of my chief servant, Daenuarion, Prince of the Elves, Protector of the Forest, this gift shall endure and be passed to every generation to signify your station and oath sworn to me this day."

"It is an honor greater than any simple woodcutter deserves. Your words alone have filled my life with riches that cannot be measured."

"We would be hard pressed to find another man, of noble birth or not, that spoke as eloquently as you, humble woodcutter." Daenuarion remarked. "Continue to speak thusly and Emperor Abellious might abdicate his thrown in light of man nobler than he, one such as you who keeps the company of gods!"

Another rousing cheer went around, hailing the Lord Consort, greatest amongst men, sons of the earth!

Alaric reached forward with both hands stretched out, palms up, averting his eyes from Lhodyn. The mighty goddess passed the bow into his possession. He shuddered and fought to look up into the eyes of the mighty, ruthless queen as pains of energy and bitter emotions coursed through him. Evil memories of the vile act exploded into his mind: a grand and ancient mathelian tree, as old as the forest itself, wickedly chopped down by Renweard. The ancient, wizened spirit crying out, pleading to this mortal who desired to be more than a peasant, to be a king at the feet of a god.

Renweard betrayed his ancestors! Alaric realized. Alaric knew his thoughts in that moment. He knew that Renweard committed a vile act, that his people worshipped the tree and learned much of their woodcraft from the teachings of the mathelian. And contained in this bow was a part of the slayed spirit, imprisoned, helpless, remade into an instrument of death. It was a great evil. A secret he shared with none of his followers.

The queen released Her grasp of the bow and Alaric pulled it into his chest. The fragrance of the queen's scent lingered to his ecstasy. His brother laid a hand over his shoulder, sharing his pride and appreciation for this moment.

"Rise again Lord-Consort, for there are two immediate tasks ahead of you that need your attention."

The audience fell silent.

The queen continued. "First, as you have noticed, the bow is left unstrung. Daenuarion assures me there is only one proper animal that will serve as the string of that bow," She paused dramatically allowing Her audience to guess before her pronouncement. "A dragon!"

The court gasped. A dragon was no ordinary beast. Only legendary men faced such terrors, risking great calamity. Symbols of both death and destruction. Life and renewal. The embodiment of power on par to a god. Ancient and tied to the land, air and oceans. They were the sovereign voices of the world, the chief spirits of the elements. Dragons were the reason the rains fell and seasons took shape. To declare the slaying of a dragon was telling the world that Lhodyn was declaring Her power.

"You will find one of these vile creatures has taken hold in the high mountains of *my* forest. Immediately remove its head with your woodcutter ax! With its sinews you shall fashion the bow string. Such a prize brings me to the other task."

The audience now hummed in whispered excitement. The sense of anticipation of the next task was palpable.

"You shall then deliver the head of this base creature to the mortal king who holds the lands of Mithlian west and north of my forest. A gift from my court to theirs!"

Applause erupted accompanied by cheers expounding the might and virtues of the glorious queen.

"Brother!" Alaric's brother breathed in shock. He was wide eyed. Jaw, slack. Alaric's tasks were near impossible, equating to death for him and any other that accompanied him.

"I have no choice but to accept my queen's least desire as if it were my life's work. I shall not fail you!"

"See that you do not, for there is more to my wishes once these initial tasks have been completed, on which I will divulge to you upon your completion. Now let's feast in your honor for I imagine it shall be some time before your return, victorious, to my court!"

Her smile was wicked and serpentine. Truly, She asked too

much, but there was no question, She expected Her will to be done.

Daenuarion led the two men away from the lithe goddess. Smirks of grim satisfaction replaced the sullen glowering eyes on each and every one of the elfish faces. They desired his death, it was plain. The crowd slowly followed the Lord Consort and the Woodland Protector to a festively decorated field, forward of the pool in the queen's court. A long table was set out before them filled with many desirable foods a man would want: breads, cakes, meats, wine, mead, fruits and aromatic soups. Daenuarion led Alaric to the center of the table and held a chair for him to sit. Renweard's brother and his men were invited to sit on Alaric's left, the elf prince taking the right. The noble elves that stood next to Lhodyn approached the table along with their elfin entourage.

Daenuarion stood. "Allow me to introduce my family, King Onethyron and Queen Ænoriah."

Alaric and all his men rose and bowed. "An honor your majesties, we are in your service."

The two said nothing and took chairs directly across from Alaric.

"And my siblings Prince Anathelon, Princess Quelian, Prince Firas and least, but most lovely, Princess Nefahvæd." Each one of them took seats to the right and left of their parents, Princess Nefahvæd never took her eyes off Alaric.

"We have many tales of the elfish people, every child desires to meet the fey folk. It is a dream come to life for me and all of our men," his brother imparted diplomatically.

The king lifted a single eyebrow in acknowledgement. The queen sipped from her crystalline chalice, gazing far off as if there were some concern on her mind.

Daenuarion returned to his seat, noticing the reactions between the men and the dismissive nature of the noble elves. He spoke again, "Do not be so discouraged by their silence my dear fellows," he said addressing the men, "they are taught from the time they are young that men are beneath them and wayward in the ways of the world. So now that the Lady-Lord desires to make you lords, my parents have become, let's say, distraught." He laughed boyishly, as if he spoke some private jest, whose meaning was aimed at his family.

There was a silence accompanied by suspicious glares exchanged across the table.

Daenuarion continued after filling up on some fine fare, "you see there is a long standing insult amongst these people, and I say these people for I no longer count myself among them ever since my father gave me away as tithe to our High Queen," he paused as if inviting his father to add any superfluous comments to his recounting of the conditions under which he found himself in Lhodyn's court, "that men, even good men of quality like yourselves, ought not be elevated in the same regard as them. The High Queen has always argued the virtue of men, their fierceness to loyalty of those they love. She has always held the position that the sons of earth be represented in Her court, and my family have been sulking ever since. But they fail to understand the depth of Her wisdom, the expanse of Her world vision. A united world of all peoples, under one monarch. An example of this," he bowed his head touching his antlers, "believing elves to be limited in form, She granted me a new likeness, a crown that can never be removed, eh father?"

"We too have similar traditions amongst our lords," Alaric explained in the voice of Renweard. "It is a custom to exchange princes amongst two lords in an act of peace. Each is reared in the other's court to maintain an alliance."

"Exactly, Lord Consort! So pleased I am to know you clearly understand courtly politics," he raised his chalice up in salute, Alaric and his men raised theirs in response. "You see, father, how gracious these people are, not crass simpletons as once believed."

The king finally showed signs of acknowledgment and turned his slight attention toward his son. The queen swiftly draped her hand over his arm, which drew attention to his clenched fist. "Do you not see what is being done to your people?"

"My people, father?"

"She mocks all of us and She seeks to injure us further."

Daenuarion leaned forward across the table, a terrible storm rising in his words. "I would watch how you speak in the court of the High Queen, father. If not, I will be compelled to act on Her behalf. You are coming dangerously close to defaming our High Queen, your majesty," he ended in a heavy tone.

The two locked eyes for untold moments. Tension spread down the table to all present. Everyone's attention was upon the king and prince, knowing if one provoked the other, violence would be swift. Alaric, as Renweard, was placed in an awkward position. He had to back Daenuarion and the High Queen, but he did not want to battle the elves for whom his people regarded as near gods in his own people's legends. He felt compelled to alleviate this feud for the moment.

He lifted his cup and spoke. "I enjoy this meal, in my honor, with Fine Folks, thanks to the benevolence of my High-Queen. I for one will always honor both courts. I am humbled today by Her and the company She keeps."

The King leaned back into his chair. He regarded Alaric again. Anger fled his eyes as he looked Alaric over. "That is a mighty gift adorning your neck, humble woodcutter. I wonder how long Lhodyn will tolerate it."

"It is a family heirloom. Sacred to my family."

The king's eyes settled on Nithledan. His head shook slightly. Alaric knew Renweard hewed the tree in defiance to the elves wishes. It was a perverse tragedy the elves may never forgive.

"Sacred? Yes, I know what you mean. But prepare yourself for the day when your High-Queen instructs you to remove that sacred trinket, or remove your head. Such difficult choices are imposed on all those who keep Her company."

Alaric could not determine if that was a threat or dire warning. His brother shifted in his seat, as he too found the tension uncomfortable.

"Let me tell you a story, Lord-Consort," the king continued, "as it might illuminate you as to the value such a gift the Lady-Lord bestowed upon you today. And to you, son, for there shall be a price for bringing that...that thing, into the world," he said, pointing a rigid finger at Nithledan.

"We, elves, were once the gardeners and stonemasons, architects and dreamers of this world. We followed Ilpha's plans, adding our own artistic nuances upon the grand house built for none other than the sons of earth. And when the time had come to depart as we finished our labors, some of us fell so in love with our own creation's, we begged our Lady to allow us to stay and tend to the house as it aged, act as stewards, to occupy the house until Her Children arrived. After much pleading, She deigned it so, and appeased our childish impulses."

"But it came with a high cost," the Queen replied somberly. "We took the form of mortals, complete with its inherent weaknesses and base desires."

"How were we to know?" came another elf lord, staring into his cup of wine as if peering into a deep well and fathoming the bottom.

"We knew little of what we asked, but we should have minded Her stern warning," said an lady elf.

"And so here we sit, mighty lords, beings of heaven, dining and cajoling with woodcutter lords, would-be slayers of dragons." There was more written upon elf king's face, but it passed in silence.

Renweard's brother was getting visibly upset at such talk, "Men are not as robust or knowledgeable as those creatures who have walked the world from the Beginning, but we measure greatness by facing the unknown and the uncertain with steely resolve and a stout heart. Renweard is such a man who willingly faces dragons when called to. For that is our task and we meet it out because it is asked of us! Because our honor compels us!"

"I am unsure of the meaning of your words, but I will reflect on them for some while," the king replied dismissively.

The festive mood was long stolen from the guests that night. The elves excused themselves soon after and retreated into the darkness of the woods beyond the glade. To where specifically, they never declared. Daenuarion congratulated Alaric on standing up to the king and his antiquated ways, and not shying like a peasant in the face of a grim lord. "You will have to adjust to many such encounters, for the High-Queen does not allow them to stray off for long, or far. She takes a certain pleasure in their subservience," he chortled callously. Alaric knew better to laugh at the expense of family. He did not approve this irreverent behavior.

His men were led to a place where they would spend the night, upon beds of straw and furs, beneath the open skies. "We have no dwellings out here in the wild, so please accept these humble accommodations. We prefer to be close to the earth and not shun the wild with walls or roofs. Perhaps you shall build your own hall here if you wish to remain with us at court." He chuckled again to himself. "I wonder how She would react to that. Goodnight sirs, sons of the earth. Tomorrow, you have dragons to seek!"

They all slept and darkness returned to Alaric.

15

THE WOODLAND COTTAGE

EDRICK FELT USELESS as his mother's concerns were focused on safe guarding the tower. She spoke guarding words and scrawled symbols into the dirt, intent on leading the ritual. Meghan tended to Father, which was nothing more than watching him sleep and ensuring no further harm came over him. So Edrick decided to check the faerie traps around Athelyn. Mother could always use more faeries for her medicines, which he now suspected were running low in supply after the ordeal they all endured.

It was nice to be back in the village, but strange too. Empty of people. Each doing their part at the Ruined Tower. The familiar pings of the blacksmith forge told Edrick not all people helped, Grindan was as industrious as ever working at his forge. He met up with Tredan who seemed to be wandering a little more aimlessly than usual. When he spotted Edrick, he seemed relieved and ran up to him.

His friend looked Edrick over then hugged him. They never hugged. Edrick pushed Tredan back confused and annoyed. "Hey, what are you up to?"

"I'm just so glad to see you," he said holding back tears. He had been crying. His cheeks and eyes were red, and nose, snotty. Edrick didn't know quite what to do with his friend. "It's just that they took my father and, and…"

"Who, the wolfmen?"

Tredan nodded and sunk to the ground. He did not look up.

"We were sleeping in the Elder Hall when a group of them came in the middle of the night. They set their dogs on all the cats, on us. It was horrible. Papa and Mama jumped up and made to run, but they grabbed them and just beat them for sport. I hid, and then ran when I could. Papa didn't say anything to them. Mama screamed. They rutted over her like tomcats, Edrick. I ran when they fell asleep."

"Where did you go? Why didn't you run to my house?"

"I would have but I was afraid of them. That they would chase me with their dogs. I ran into Udela's fields and slept in one of the barns with the animals. I need to find out what happened to Mama and Papa, but I'm afraid. That they still might be there."

"I will go find out for you. How about you meet me by my house?"

Tredan nodded. "How's your father?"

"He's just sleeping...from the medicine. Mother hasn't said anything but we can all read her face. She's worried about him."

Tredan wiped away his tears. "He will be fine, Edrick," he whispered. "He's the toughest, bravest person I know." Tears began to fall again, slowly this time. Edrick felt guilty. He always felt that Tredan secretly envied him and his family, though they were outcasts as much as them. Yet, others would reluctantly admit a small amount of admiration for his father, a man who knew the wilds, that lived with dangers that others ran from. And the Elders had this inherited respect for the Warden of the Woods, until Grindan turned them against him. Fear is a taint on people's hearts, it spreads and infects all others unless it is removed, or countered by a stout heart. A heart like Father's.

"Father always said people desire a life without courage, because it means they have yet to face that which really scares them. That they do not have to make the hard choices, the choices they don't ever want to make."

Tredan blinked, blankly, clearing his tears.

"He told me no one escapes this world without knowing fear. Fear is what drives our choices one way or another. Fear is what makes us mortal, and the gods, gods, for they fear nothing. Your father is brave for he protected you with his silence, right? You were not hurt and he did what he could to make sure you fled without their notice."

"I guess, but it's not the same."

"It is the same."

Tredan looked around. He was still terrified. "I will meet you at your house by dusk. I just don't want to be out in the open during daylight."

"Ok. Then be careful."

He and Tredan parted, going separate ways. Edrick made his way carefully through Athelyn until he arrived in the village center. The Elder Hall doors were flung wide open as if it were the summer faire. Edrick expected to see armed warriors, axes and spears in hand, instead there were a half dozen boys his brothers' age. Ator, the Theign's son, was among them, shouting orders to some of the village children to clear and clean the Hall of all its contents.

"What is going on?" he asked those few villagers standing around outside, but no one knew their intentions. All their stockpiled wares that would have been sold at summer market were broken and thrown onto heaps of debris. It would take all of the day to finish cleaning the entire building. Edrick left, not seeing signs or word of Tredan's parents and continued checking the rest of his traps. They were all empty and no one had any problems or encounters with faeries for weeks. That in itself was unusual.

The village was not as it was. Many were forced into helping the Folthnir. Those left behind murmured about what their actions portended. The regular cycles of village life had been halted. There was no sign of Tredan's parents anywhere. He returned home at sunset to share what he found out.

"Did you find them?" Tredan asked hopefully. He waited near their small barn.

"No." Edrick wished he would have had a better answer, but honestly he was afraid to find out what really became of his parents, and he certainly didn't want to be the one to tell Tredan.

"Oh. Mind if I stay in your barn with Mathilda here?"

"What are you talking about? You can stay inside with us. Mother would insist."

"Really, it's fine. I'm more comfortable with animals then I am with people. It's just what I'm used to. I feel safer. I can't explain. And don't tell your mother I am here just yet. I think that it's better that way."

Edrick led Tredan inside the small barn and helped him clear an area with fresh hay to rest for the night. "Are there any mice around here? I like to talk to them before I sleep."

"No. No mice come around here. There have never been mice."

"There are where we used to sleep. No cats to kill them. Not rats. I hate rats, but little field mice." Tredan laid down and tucked his knees up to his chest. "I'm going to sleep now."

"I think I will stay with you tonight."

Tredan just smiled as he closed his eyes. Mathilda looked on the new visitor suspiciously as to why a boy lay in her barn. Edrick shrugged. He cleared another spot next to his friend and laid down beside him. He simply lay next to Tredan, listening to his relaxed breathing, absently petting Mathilda. Sunlight faded into darkness.

Night came and then sleep. Black, empty sleep.

It was good.

The next day Edrick left Tredan sleeping next to Mathilda and checked in with Mother at the tower.

"We have done as much as we can. Have you been to the house? How's are our guests?" she asked.

"They are fine," Edrick lied. Well, he did check on them a couple of days earlier when he and Meghan gathered the ingredients for Father's medicine, he just had not been there recently.

"Tell them we will return today. Have you been to the village? I heard those brutes have occupied the Elder Hall."

"They are tossing out everything. No one knows what their plans are. Can't be good."

"No," mother agreed, her voice drifted off as she looked back toward the direction of the village. "It can't be good."

"It's too bad your wards don't work against them, huh mother?"

She smiled, a weary troubling smile, then hugged him, laying his head to her chest. Edrick could hear her heart beat, strong and full of life, resonating like compressed thunder. "Yes, that would be nice. A ward to guard against the evil in men's hearts. The world would be a much better place."

"I will let the women know you will be returning. I should go and change the bait on all the traps. There hasn't been any signs of the bad faeries."

"I wouldn't expect too much trouble for a while, you might have to work with your brothers instead. You should take Gaebria with you. I'm sure she is restless being confined in our house."

Edrick did not care for that suggestion, but nodded anyway, as if he would consider it. He came home and found Tredan talking to Mathilda.

"Hey!" the boy greeted him warmly. "I love your lamb! She's so gentle and strong. I can't imagine having my arms ripped off by a timber-lion."

"Yeah, I saved her life. Father was going to kill her but I begged him not to." Edrick thought of Sunniva, who loved Mathilda with gentle innocence. "Anyway, I'm going about town. You want to come?"

Tredan shrank away from the suggestion, but before he could refuse, Edrick offered, "The wolfskins don't seem to be looking for you. I'm sure they did not notice you at all. Come on, we can see if anyone has seen your folks."

The boy scratched Mathilda's head, whispered his secrets to her. "Ok, but if I sense anything weird I'm taking off."

"Sure, sure. Don't worry, nothing will happen," Edrick said confidently.

The two left the small barn and entered the cottage where they found their guests. Gaebria was curiously scrutinizing mother's alcove with all its cornucopia of ingredients. Bresigia was cooking over the hearth and humming to herself. Sarghan sat at the table facing the doorway, staring blankly at them as the two boys entered, blinking as sunlight drained into the dark interior.

Gaebria skipped up to Edrick when she noticed his entrance. "How is your father? I would feel awful if things did not go well for him and he ended up like Papa." She took his hand into hers before he could react.

Edrick smiled awkwardly. That was a strange manner of wording, he thought. Today, her hair was braided into a single plait, resting across her left shoulder. Her éardian's light was no longer orange, but more hawks-beard yellow.

"She means well, son," came Bresigia's chipper voice. "Of course he will recover dear, he is a stout man of the wild country. No doubt he will be back on his feet and strong as a bear as he ever was."

"Yes, he has survived quite a few illnesses thanks to my mother's medicines. Her healing is known in all the villages along the Merchant Road. People request her skills in desperate circumstances, or at least they used to."

Gaebria nodded in slow agreement, as if she would not believe what the future held until it came to pass.

"Well, I, uh," Edrick slowly withdrew his hand from the girl's soft fingers, "I was just checking on you ladies and to pass on my mother's message, that they are on their way back with my father."

"Marvelous!" Bresigia said. "Lunch is ready for them. I'm looking forward to helping with your father and get your mother off her feet."

"I am just leaving. Have to go do my chores."

"Oh, Edrick I have something to tell you," Gaebria blurted out. Edrick walked passed her, not the least curious as to what she might say and gathered the anstor and atorlathe needed for the traps. The girl followed him around the wide alcove, shadowing his every movement.

"What is it then, Gaebria? I have to get going," he finally asked, a bit irritated when she obviously was not forthcoming with her words.

She stole some furtive glances at her mother and grandmother, then whispered, leaning close to his ear, "I cannot tell you in front of them." The warmth of her breath caressing his ears caused goose bumps to break out all the way from his neck to his navel. Why does she have to be so strange, he wondered.

"Well, that's everything I need, so I will see you all later," he said nervously and swiftly retreated toward the door. Tredan waved farewell and left with him.

Gaebria followed.

"Wait, Edrick," she called after him, shuffling to keep up, "I had this dream..."

Edrick was not in the mood to chat, at least not with her. He hoped he might find some trapped faeries, maybe he could scare her away by pulling their heads off in front of her.

She caught up to the two boys, and continued her conversation. "It was a strange dream. It seemed so vivid. I have had dreams where I think it's real when I'm in them, but then wake up and know it was a dream. But this one was different..."

"What dream?" Tredan quietly ventured. She did not look at him, but continued to stare at Edrick as if Tredan said nothing at all.

Edrick wondered if he should take off in a sprint. He took a sideward glance at her; she was taller, with longer legs. Would it even possible to outrun her?

"It was like I was awake in the dream, that I actually left the cottage…"

He could at least lose her in the village with a head start, he knew the best hiding places.

"…and wandered in the forest. Is there large stones, arranged in a circle there?" she asked.

"What?" She finally said something that grabbed his attention.

"Yeah, great big rocks, like pillars, except most were broken, or cast down. They formed a ring. And there were these old houses, large old houses and great ruined walls hidden behind curtains of ivy…"

Tredan looked to Edrick, knowing full well what Stones she described.

"What houses? What are you talking about?" Edrick demanded.

"The forest, the dream I had, only it was more real."

Images of Sunniva surfaced. Her terror laden cries echoed in his ears. "Tell me everything you saw," Edrick urged.

"Well, I woke up in the night, at least I thought I woke up. I'm still not sure if I did wake up or if in the dream I woke up, because the details were very clear, like a memory, not like a dream at all. I don't know how else to explain it, I mean how it felt."

"Gaebria!" Edrick shouted. He was getting impatient. The thought of his sister's words to him that morning, words that led to her disappearance and Baldice's death, echoed through this girl's voice. He wondered, had he stopped to allow Sunniva to tell him everything about her dream, would he have discovered something suspicious and devious that would have prevented the tragedy.

"Just tell me what happened in the dream," Edrick demanded impatiently.

Gaebria looked confused, then hurt.

"I'm sorry, it's just I think what you have to say is important and I just want to hear all about your dream," Edrick added, amending his tone.

"Well, I was getting to that before you had your fit. I wouldn't have even mentioned it at all but they mentioned your sister's name."

"Sunniva! Who told you about her?"

"The faeries, in the dream."

Edrick took her by the hand and led her off the Lane. He felt too exposed on the road. He sat down and pulled her down with him. She gave out a cry as she almost tumbled down.

Tredan wasn't sure if he should follow, but did anyway.

"Did you see her?"

"No, but she's with the faeries."

"How do you know?"

"Because the faeries told me she's there, she's safe and they asked me to go there. Actually, they said all the children need protection. We should all go. They said they will speak to all the children, but one of us needs to lead them. Assure the other children that they will be safer in the Faerie Realm."

"Did you see them? When they spoke?'

"Yes, tiny beautiful people, with wings of dragon-flies, some butterflies. When I looked upon them, I get that feeling that I have when I see a baby, that kind of adoration, something like love."

"That's their glamor. It's how they trick you into doing what they want."

The girl looked at him suspiciously, as if he were speaking of a baby possessed of evil intent. "What would they want to trick me for?"

"You don't know this," Edrick paused. He realized he did not say anything to anyone about Sunniva's dream. She talked about it before, it was just one of those things she talked about that wasn't important. But now it seemed quite important. So much about Sunniva seemed more important now that she was gone. "I haven't said this to anyone…"

"What is it, Edrick? It has to do with my dream? I knew it was real!"

"We won't say anything, Edrick, promise," Tredan added.

"Sunniva had a similar dream that morning, saying the faeries told her to meet them in the woods. Only there were no faeries in the woods. Those monsters were waiting! It was like they lured us there through deceit or magick."

Gaebria slowly shook her head. "No, she is still alive Edrick. They protected her from those monsters. Our éardians will protect us, it protected her and she needs our help!"

"But Edrick lost his light," Tredan added, hoping to be helpful.

She looked into the woods, eyes lingering, then back at Edrick. "I was afraid of the woods when I first arrived. In the city, we hear terrible stories of ghosts and witches in wild places, but we also hear stories of men that still have their éardians. To us, those are just stories, but your family still has theirs. This place makes me believe in things that I once thought were false. I have hope, for the first time since Papa was murdered."

Hope. Edrick struggled with saving that one precious gift that seemed to have fled all others in the world. He believed Sunniva was alive, he knew it in his heart. He wanted to bring her home. Then a memory awoke in him, he had his own dreams of the elfish girl, Aslenissia. She too whispered that Sunniva was alive and urged him to search for her. That together, they could save Sunniva.

"I had my own dream too, actually," he finally admitted.

A powerful smile lit up Gaebria's face.

"The night you guys first arrived. It wasn't a faerie but a beautiful elf girl, like the one Mother told in stories."

"Did she speak to you?" Gaebria must have seen some sort of answer on his face. "She did! She told you to search for Sunniva, didn't she?"

"Did she, Edrick?" Tredan inquired, equally intrigued.

"Sort of, she said my father would try to find her that night he went into the woods but would fail, and that I must find her instead.....she would help me find Sunniva."

"She was right. Your father couldn't find her," Tredan added with a measure of meekness, not desiring to imply his father was anything but a great man.

"The forest speaks to us, Edrick. I can't stand the thought of your sister being trapped, surrounded by all those terrible things a moment more."

Her sentiments moved Edrick. He longed to hear someone speak those exact words, to voice the outrage of an innocent soul like Sunniva abandoned to a terrible fate. He wanted to hear his parents say those exact words.

And they never did.

He was conflicted. He thought perhaps there was something reaching out to him, that only he could save his sister, yet the raw memories of the monsters he found in the forest the day his sister claimed faeries spoke to her still stung his heart.

"What were these forest houses you mentioned?"

"I don't know, it's terribly hard to remember now. Like stone mansions I used to see in the city. They were deep in the forest. And I had the feeling that was where Sunniva was, at least it felt that's where they wanted me to go."

Edrick thought of the map hanging in the Hall. It marked the village and the tower; and in the forest, it displayed a mystery that remained in his thoughts: another village within the forest. Words adorned the map, though he could not read them. It must have meant something.

"I think there is a hidden village in the woods."

"Has your father been there?" Tredan asked in excitement.

"I don't know but I have seen it on the map in the Elder Hall."

"What map?" Tredan asked. He lived around that hall all his life, he should have noticed.

"It's a secret. On the reverse side of the king's paper there is a map."

"Yes, Edrick showed it to me," Gaebria added.

Tredan looked hurt. "How come I don't know about the map?"

"It was a family secret and I should not have shown her. I was not supposed to show anyone. But I will show it to you now." Edrick wondered why he did show Gaebria at all. Just wanted to impress the city girl, he supposed.

"What of the Folthnir? They are everywhere," Gaebria asked.

"I don't know. Let's just look. I might be able to sneak by."

"I don't think I want to go. I'm staying." Tredan said.

"No, you have to come," Gaebria insisted. "We are all in this now, this secret. We must go after Sunniva."

Tredan looked to Edrick and Gaebria. He clearly preferred to remain behind. "Ok, let me tell Mathilda goodbye."

Gaebria and Edrick looked at one another and then back at Tredan.

He turned and ran into the small barn and came running back with his favorite sling in hand.

"Ok, I'm ready."

"We will see how it is down there. If anyone of us gets in any kind of trouble, we will leave and meet back by Udela's barn."

"I don't know where that is," Gaebria quickly added.

"It's fine. I won't let you out of my sight."

Edrick thought for a moment she blushed, but hoped it was some trick of the light.

The three did not take the Lane into the village center, instead they walked across the Common fields, where there were buildings and shrubs, places they could hide or obstacles that they could run behind. The only ones left working the fields were children and the women, all the men had been pressed into serving the Folthnir.

As they cut through one of the fields, a boy ran up to them. "Hey Edrick! Stay off our plots," yelled the boy Rodor, Dregan's son. "If my father was here, he would toss all of you into the Lane and beat you with his mule rod!" He was near Baldice's age and as tall, but of an opposite temperament. Where Baldice was gentle and understanding, Rodor was rough and intolerant. The image of his father.

"Only because his father is sick, or else he would beat you and your father for making such threats," Tredan shouted back.

The tall boy rushed over to them and shoved Tredan with open malice, causing him to stumble and fall. His sister, little Rinan, laughed from a distance. She was of the same age as Edrick and every bit as spiteful as her brother. Her hair was a messy dirt brown, unkempt because she fought everyone, especially boys. She skipped her way over and stood next to her brother.

"I thought catboys were supposed to land on their feet," she taunted.

Edrick immediately stood in front of his friends, throwing the faerie trap onto the ground, as Gaebria moved to help Tredan up. Rodor ignored him, looking past, to get a better view.

"So, this is the beggar girl your father brought home, is it? Getting a nice collection of strays, are you Edrick?"

Edrick shoved the boy back. Rinan screamed obnoxiously as if he had just pulled Rodor's heart out. She only wanted to draw her mother's attention and try to get their mother to help deal with Edrick and his friends.

Rodor picked up a rock out of the soft dirt, raising it over his shoulder ready to throw, then suddenly backed off. A familiar hum of Tredan's sling buzzed energetically in the air behind Edrick. Everyone knew how deadly accurate the cat hunter is with his sling.

"Just leave, get out of here. Your family has caused all of us enough harm," Rodor ordered the two boys.

"Drop the rock and we will go," Edrick demanded.

The older boy hesitated. He did not want to seem like the

weaker one there, so he threw the rock at Edrick's trap, busting the wood. Tredan kept his sling humming.

"I heard your father got the piss beat out of him by those pigs. Is he dead?" Rodor spat in defiance.

"Edrick, let's go. Think about Sunniva," Gaebria reminded him with a gentle voice. She motioned for Tredan to lower his arm and put the sling away.

Edrick was close to launching himself at the taller boy, if it weren't for Gaebria's disarming words. She was right. They had a plan and he was wasting time with these two.

"What's that about your sister, she's dead isn't she?" Rinan asked with contempt. She always despised Sunniva if for nothing more than possessing beautiful golden locks in a village filled with dark heads.

"No, she's not!" Gaebria insisted. She locked arms with the two boys in hers and pulled them away, toward the village center.

"We're going after her!" Tredan called back, as if such idea challenged everything the two defied.

"What do you mean?" Rodor shouted after them. He began following them, his sister too.

Tredan took it as a threat and bent to get another rock to load in his sling. Gaebria held his arm so he couldn't raise it as the two farmer children approached them again.

"Sunniva is dead," Rinan concluded, as if she challenged the three to contradict her.

"Yeah, well we will see about that," Edrick said.

"How?" Rodor replied as if he wanted evidence presented right there and then.

"You wouldn't care. Anyway, you guys would be too afraid. We're going into the woods," Tredan said.

"Tredan!" Edrick felt betrayed. If they had any chance of leaving, they had to go secretly.

"Liar!" Rodor shot back.

The three friends said nothing further and turned around, heading toward the Elder Hall. The two farmer children followed.

"Why don't they go back home?" Gaebria asked.

"Who cares? Let them follow us. They will lose interest soon enough," Edrick concluded.

So the five children wound their way through the small fields in the middle of Athelyn until they arrived at the village center. Edrick could hear a commotion coming from the Elder Hall. He looked at Tredan, gauging how he might react at the sight of the wolfskins. He held his sling in his hands, fidgeting with it nervously.

"I think you should put that away, we shouldn't draw any attention to ourselves. I will walk around the Hall to get a measure of the situation. They are still there, looting our things."

Edrick could see the fear in both their eyes. They were probably using all their strength just to stand within sight of the men. Rodor and Rinan caught up with them.

"What? Is your sister here? I don't see her," Rodor teased.

Edrick ignored his comment. "What are they doing?" he asked the two.

Rodor looked down at him as if he just asked a rude question. "It's not my business what those pigs do. We stay away from them. That's how we survive this war."

"Fine, I will find out myself." Rodor's mouth dropped as Edrick stomped away from the pompous farmer boy. This will shut him up, he thought.

Instead of being shown up, Rodor and his sister continued to follow. Edrick rounded the Elder Hall. There were carts stacked with barrels of the village's stored grain, along with father's woodwork, jars of Elwyn's fine honey, and all the village's superfluous goods needed to be sold at summer market, gathered up or tossed into the road. Worse yet, a pile of feline carcasses were stacked to Edrick's head, flies swarming greedily. Inside, Ator and the other wolfskins stood overseeing a few village boys sweeping and scrubbing the floors.

Grindan was in the middle of them, the only adult there. A freshly brick laid furnace had been built in the center of the Hall. He was preparing it for a firing, filling it with coal. Next to him was a cart filled with iron chains. Suddenly the memory of the enslaved people at the tower overcame his thoughts.

"No." Edrick said in quiet defiance.

"What?" Rodor asked. Edrick turned and saw the two standing directly behind him.

It infuriated Edrick. "Why don't you go ask the 'pigs' what? If not, go hide behind your mother's skirts and stop bothering me and my family!" His outburst was powerful and raw. Rodor stepped back expecting a punch. His outburst caught the attention of the wolfskins, who easily recognized him.

Suddenly, Rodor and his sister were nowhere to be seen.

"The Assassin's son, look," one of the Folthnir youth shouted to Ator. The village boys stopped their work and looked as well.

"Come here boy!" Ator called across the hall. "We have work for you."

Edrick crossed his arms. The Hall was filled with them, how was he to get the map? Three wolfskins swiftly ran up to him.

This was the heart of their village, Edrick raged, and not a single villager made a stand against them. Occupying the tower was one thing, a crumbling ruin no one visited, but claiming the Elder Hall was outrageous!

"Grindan! How can you let them defile our home? YOU are the traitor to us! Not my father!" Edrick exploded. He could not help it. This was sacrilegious. Their Elder Hall, their one structure where all the village would come together to share in weddings, funerals, and holiday feasts, had been gutted by these invaders. Where were the Elders? They must know about this!

The boys seized Edrick and dragged him inside, pulling him in front of Ator. The young man's face was full of pride. "My father might have let your father live, but I'm without mercy. You are my slave now, boy. And you will have a pathetic miserable life. My horses will lead better lives than you."

With one look from Ator, the boys threw Edrick to the ground. Heavy boots trampled him with wild enthusiasm. "My hounds will have a better lives than you." They lifted him back up, before Edrick could blink or spit in this boy's face, Ator pummeled him across the jaw and another into his gut. Edrick became woozy, he shook away the blackness behind his eyes.

"The flies licking my shit will have better lives than you."

Grindan looked on from the furnace, expressionless and unmoving.

Edrick made to talk, but Ator slammed his fist against his mouth. "You have no voice anymore slave, it is now my voice and I will tell you when to talk." He hit him again, striking his ribs. "You have no body now, it is my body and I will tell you when to move."

Unwanted tears welled up in Edrick's eyes, he pulled his arms away from the two boys on each side, to wipe away any sign of weakness, but they held him firm. "Ha! I made the little girl cry."

They others laughed. The boys holding Edrick shook him. "Cry little girl. Your father isn't here to save you, is he?"

"Get me some rope," Ator commanded. "I won't have one of my slaves cry in front of my father," Ator lunged into Edrick again with his rock hard fist, eliciting a whimper. Ator stood up satisfied. "You represent me now, slave. Today, all the tears will leave you and you will be more than a peasant's son. You will be a Folthnirmæder, slave to a prince."

Grindan stood behind the boys, shaking his head slightly. Bron walked into the Hall from the other entrance pushing a small cart of blacksmith supplies from their shop. Bron nearly dropped the load at the sight of Edrick being hoisted by his feet into the rafters. The Folthnir pushed Edrick around, swinging his body through the dusty air.

Edrick caught Bron's voice behind the Folthnir laughter. "Father, please talk to them! He's just a boy." The large blacksmith simply walked away pulling his son with him, out of the Hall into the open air where the gathering eyes of the villagers gawked at the scene unfolding.

Gaebria and Tredan then appeared bravely at the doorway. They were holding hands, standing stiff and terrified, but resolved to help their friend. Run! Edrick thought but the words were stuck in his throat; locked behind his eyes. Blood filled his head and pounded against his skull. They shook him violently again, like woodland game caught in a snare, and laughed as he cried out.

"Stop," Gaebria muttered. Or did she? The wolfskins did not react.

Tredan's sling was in his hand. Bron grabbed his arm, ripping the weapon out of his grasp. Edrick wasn't sure if he was helping his friends, or harming them. Grindan pulled his son away, chastising his son for getting involved.

That's when the wolfskins noticed them, staring, terrified and wordless.

"Look here, a cat boy and a little kitten. Come looking for your mum, boy? Where did she run off too?" The boys laughed.

They should have ran, left him there, Edrick thought. They had a plan. Meet at Udela's if they were in trouble.

"Run," he mumbled out, sounding more like another moaning sound.

A Folthnir boy grabbed Gaebria and lifted her off her feet. His gaze roved over her developing body. "Look at this. Near ripe enough, young kitten." He pulled her close, smelling her hair. Gaebria cringed. "Nice kitten aren't you?" She head butted him, blood spilt out of an opened gash.

"Dammit!" he yelled. He threw an arm across her throat and choked her until she fell limp.

Tredan fought against his captor, wriggling around like a caught chicken in the hands of a butcher. "Hang this one up too, behind the other. I have a game in mind." Ator commanded. "This is the son of the famed assassin, is it not? So let's see which life he will save, his or theirs."

The boy holding Gaebria continued choking her with one arm. Her faced drained white. His other arm moved about her body, groping her, his face filled with a sick excitement Edrick had never encountered.

"Ator, you have to let me have her. She hit me, I have a claim to her," the boy said in exited words. Ator's demeanor seemed angered by the request. "I mean after you have her first."

"No," Ator said. "Tie her by her hair. Put her behind the cat boy."

The boy holding Gaebria didn't move immediately. He was busy lifting her skirt with his free hand. Ator stormed up to him and threw rope in his face. "Hoist her up!"

He and another boy dragged her in front of Tredan and tied the rope to her braided hair. They threw the other end over the rafters and together they hoisted her as high as Edrick and Tredan, a foot off the floor.

Gaebria cried out over and over, kicking wildly, swinging in circles. Ator pushed her legs aside and punch her twice in the ribs. She stopped moving. Her face brightened red as the weight of her body pulled against her scalp.

"I have a game. Whoever wins, fucks her first." Ator announced. The boys stopped, stunned. "Whoever loses must rut on the cat boy!"

"No way!" one boy spouted out.

"Don't lose then. Get a bow and a handful of arrows."

One of them left to fetch the items. The others looked at Ator in confusion as he walked to the far side of the room, and urinated on the wall. "We have worked too much these past days. I want to have fun now," he said over his shoulder.

He finished and strode up to Edrick, looking down at the inverted prisoner.

"Now, I have three little slaves. But I will give you one chance to save the little princess there. If not, she will hate you all her life for what we will do to her, little assassin."

The boy returned with the bow and quarrel of arrows.

Ator started swinging Edrick, Tredan and Gaebria like pendulums, motioning for the other boys to help. "Start a line at the front of the hall. Each of you gets one arrow. Fire at my piss stain. The closest arrow to hit highest point of the stain, wins."

The boys fell in line fast. "Shoot between them?" one of them asked doubtfully, watching the motion of the swinging children.

"Yes!" Ator shouted. "And if you hit any of my slaves I will make sure my father sends you to shovel horse shit for a month!"

They didn't ask what would happen if they hit the girl.

The first one fired high, the arrow lodged into the far wall near the rafters.

Ator shook his head. "Get over here! Take over. You obviously lost your chance." The boy surrendered the bow to the next in line and then took over swinging Edrick and Tredan.

Another Folthnir boy shot, taking time to aim, observing the timing of the swinging bodies. His arrow hit just right of the stain.

"You pathetic fucks are sure making me feel good," Ator said at the back of the line. Three others shot, one arrow went too high, one hit the stain but low, near the floor. One grazed Edrick's shirt, deflecting its path just enough that it flew wide.

The boys laughed at the shooter, who so far, had the worst results.

Edrick then had a thought. He'd rather take an arrow then allow them their game. He began bending his torso around interrupting the smooth motion of his swinging.

"Eh! Keep him swinging! He's blocking the shot." Ator called.

"He's doin' it himself," the boy called back. Edrick suddenly stopped after a swift punch to his kidneys. His body became taught as the pain radiated out. "Hah, now he's a lump sack of shit." The Folthnir shoved Edrick again, getting him swinging.

"If you do that one more time, I will shoot you!" Ator

threatened Edrick. "And that won't count as my shot," he amended, addressing the others. They of course would not disagree.

The brawny young man drew the string back to his cheek, steadied his breath and fired. The arrow split directly between Edrick's, Tredan's and Gaebria's moving bodies and hit the top of the stain. "Damn," a couple of the boys muttered in defeat.

"There is still one more to shoot," Ator said. "Spin him around," pointing to the young Woodcutter.

They began spinning Edrick. All the contents in his belt spilled out from his pouches, the atorlathe and petals of anstor. The boys knelt to the ground and investigated. The fragrance would be new to them, seductive. They licked the berries then ate them. Each smiled as they gathered more berries spilt over the ground and gobbled them up.

"Enough! Cut him down," Ator said at last. The boys didn't understand. "Just do it!"

Edrick crashed onto the floor boards. He wanted to lay there forever. The world continued to spin.

"Come here slave. Show me if you have any of your old man's skill. Prove to all of us how much better you are than us. If you score a better mark than me, I will let her go. If you hit her, I will kill you. If you hit your friend, I will kill your friend. If you want to go home, then just leave them and run like a little coward!"

Edrick got up slowly. Blood drained away from his head. He fell with his first step. The boys laughed. It felt like all the world was sliding down hill. He fell back to his arms.

"Give me the bow!" Edrick shouted, defiant.

"Drag him over here," Ator commanded.

They dragged him to where Ator stood. He put the bow in one hand and the arrow in the other, then stepped back. "Keep pushing them," he said to the boys standing by Tredan and Gaebria. The boys finished eating all the atorlathe, and stood licking his fingers. "Those were the best berries I ever ate," one said.

Edrick opened his legs into a wide stance to keep from toppling over. He could not even see the wet stain on the other side of the hall.

"Shoot!" Ator yelled.

Edrick shook his head, he was fighting to keep from vomiting.

"Shoot slave! What you want does not matter! SHOOT NOW!"

Edrick shot blindly. The arrow went high and into the ceiling.

The boys laughed. "Looks like she's yours Ator."

"No. Shoot that way!" Ator leveled the bow, aiming at Tredan and Gaebria, putting another arrow in Edrick's hand. What a fool, Edrick thought. The spinning slowed. He could see Gaebria's eyes shut tight as she fought against the pain and fear.

Ator stooped low, inches from Edrick's ear. "SHOOT SLAVE! SHOOT!"

Edrick stepped back and pulled the arrow to his cheek, pointing it right in Ator's face. The sudden movement caused Edrick to stumble and he fell sideways, as if a giant had just lifted one end of the hall, but he kept the arrow pointed right between Ator's eyes.

Ator panicked, realizing his mistake. He looked to the other boys for help, but they were just as off their guard as he.

Edrick shot.

Ator crunched down. The arrow grazed his cheek as it streaked past.

Edrick fell to the floor, the bow dropped from his hand.

Then a Folthnir boy fell hard to the floor.

The swift acting atorlathe was already having its effect. The second Folthnir swayed as if he were inebriated, stumbling toward Gaebria, crashing into her before hitting the floor.

"What's going on?" Ator bellowed. The other three Folthnir rushed to the aid of their companions.

"My head, it's not right!" One of the boys on the ground shouted, clutching his temples.

In the confusion, Tredan pulled out a secretly stowed knife, a claw of a timber-lion fashioned into a weapon. He cut his tether and fell unnoticed. He landed with the grace of a cat. He was up quick, passing the knife to Edrick.

"The walls are moving! Breathing! I'm bewitched." The Folthnir pointed, accusingly. "She cursed me! Slit her throat."

Confused, the Folthnir drew their daggers, but their minds must have quickly put events into focus. "It was those berries," they realized. Murderous eyes stared at Edrick and Tredan.

Then Grindan walked quickly pass, carrying two buckets of water. "Drink!" he commanded, "then puke and drink again. You might yet live, you fools."

It was their chance to flee, but Gaebria and the map, each

needed rescuing. The map seemed like the one thing left untouched, overlooked in the Hall. All he had to do was bolt across the floor, remove it and run off.

"I have to get out of here," one poisoned Folthnir boy cried, pushing Grindan aside and spilling a bucket. Water spread across the floor. He ran out into the crowd, crashing into the stunned onlookers who did not react fast enough to get out of the crazed boy's way.

Grindan left the one bucket and picked the empty one up to refill it. "Make sure he drinks every drop. You. See to that one outside."

As the two Folthnir walked past, another figure dashed in. Bron ran down the length of the Hall to Gaebria's aid. He lifted her in one arm and cut the rope. She fell across his shoulder.

"Drop her! That's our property!" Ator yelled.

The other poisoned boy began thrashing about, foaming at the mouth. Ator returned his attention back on his sick companion, trying to get water in his mouth. "You are dead, peasant. All of you! Fruit on the crow's tree, I swear to Vylkinus!"

Bron didn't hesitate or heed the Folthnir's threats. "Come on!" he yelled at Edrick and Tredan. Bron made for the back door that Edrick and Gaebria escaped through a week ago. Tredan followed. Edrick made a dash toward the map, lifted the frame parchment from its hook and then sprinted out the Hall.

"Thief!" The villagers cried. "He's stealing the village Writ!" *Thief*, it was an ugly word, as close to being a murderer in small community like his village, where sharing was a way of life. Known thieves are banished.

The four made it out the door, but they had to move fast. Bron seemed to have no destination in mind as they ran past buildings. "What are you doing with that," he asked frantically. He was panicking, there was no possible safe place that they could hide.

They all paused for a moment after rushing through the village, heading back toward Edrick's house, in the direction of the woods. Bron gently lowered Gaebria onto the ground. "Can you run? How are you?" She could not reply at first, her head hung down. Bron lifted a finger to her chin. As soon as he touched her, she screamed out. She flailed her arms at him, scratching and hitting.

"Gaebria!" Edrick jumped in front of a stunned Bron. "We are your friends! It is me Edrick."

He raised an arm out protectively, but the taller girl slapped his hand out of the way and struck him across his face. She cried out, pulling her hand close to her chest, cradling it with her other arm. She sat down and wept.

Edrick shook off the sudden pain and they all stared at Gaebria, not knowing what to do. She began digging her fingernails into her forearm until she drew blood, still weeping.

"We have to get going," Bron urged, taking a few steps away from them.

"Gaebria…" Edrick said as gentle as he could.

Gaebria stood up and wiped her tears, smudging blood across her cheek. "OK, let's go." She looked at Bron. "Thank you for helping us," she said with quiet words. "You got the map." She said to Edrick. "So, our plan worked." She forced a smile.

Edrick nodded, breaking off the frame and rolling the parchment up. He did not know how to address what just happened with her. "Bron is right, we must keeping running."

"Where?" Bron asked

"In the woods."

Bron quickly turned south, leading them to the village byrgen, to the burial mounds.

They passed the southern lychgate marking the end of the village, and the beginning of the wild. The southern land past the Wall was not worked like the northern fields. It was pasture land, where they sent their cows and sheep to graze. The path leading out of the southern lychgate led to only one location, the village's byrgen. This path was not straight but zig-zagged across the fields so restless spirits would not be able to find their way back toward the living, to bother and haunt their relatives, or take vengeance upon those who transgressed against them in life. The Wall itself was a barrier against evil spirits, so Edrick supposed this path and the byrgen predated the Wall's construction.

The byrgen itself had no Wall, it was just an area of the southern fields where stones erupted up out of the earth, shaped deliberately at one time, but now resembled rotted troll teeth, abandoned and unwanted. The children gathered there to rest.

"Why did we come here?" Tredan asked as he stooped over, recovering his breath.

"This was all I can think of where no one would be at, though there might be shepherds out in the field. They most likely are not near," Bron replied. He wheezed, gasping for air.

"What is wrong" Gaebria asked?

"Asthma, I just have asthma when I run."

"I never knew that. Mother could treat it," Edrick offered.

"I…I don't let many know, I mean, actually, only my mother knows. My father would see it as another weakness, and I have far too many in his mind."

"You must be one of the strongest fellows in the village. You risked your life for me," Gaebria said quietly. Bron's cheeks flushed a bit. "I mean all of us," she added.

From the village, two figures came running toward them. Bron stepped in front of Gaebria. "It's not Folthnir…" Bron announced. They saw soon enough that Rodor and Rinan had followed them.

"What do they want? They probably led the Folthnir, we should keeping running!" Tredan blurted out, shaking, he was ready to run even if no one else did.

"No," Edrick replied, holding his arm. "I think they are alone. I don't think they will follow us much longer. Let's see what they want."

"You think they should know where we are going?" Bron whispered.

"It doesn't matter."

The two ran up. They looked outwardly skittish and upset. Edrick readied himself for more taunting and ridicule.

"You guys ran fast!" Rodor said, greeting them.

"You would too if you had Folthnir at your heels," Edrick replied.

"Maybe. They would have caught up to us, I think."

Wait, was that a compliment? Was he admitting that he wasn't better than them?

"What do you want? Why follow us?" Edrick asked.

"We just couldn't believe the way you talked to them! They were going to kill you and all of you just stood up to them." There was obvious mix of admiration and astonishment in the way they looked at the group of four.

"That was completely mad," Rinan added. She stared at Edrick with a new kind of interest. It made him very uncomfortable to hold their attention in this new way.

"Yes, I agree, mad," Bron added, as if he couldn't believe his own actions.

"No, not crazy," Edrick corrected. "Only to those that can't see plainly what is right, or are too afraid to act on what they know is wrong."

Everyone remained quiet, as if they wanted to disagree or comment, but thought it best to remain silent as to not reduce the significance of Edrick's boldness, despite what he believed.

"So what are you guys going to do now? You can't go back, they will kill you for sure."

"We are not going back, we are going in there," Edrick pointed east, toward Wudelic.

Rinan and Rodor mouths dropped open, in unison. Their suspicions were confirmed, the group of four were mad, and were going to die very soon.

There was an uncomfortable silence shared among them, as reality caught up with the children, there in the byrgen.

"Let us go with you," Rodor asked in a small voice. Rinan whipped her head around to face her brother, as if the madness were spreading, infectious and deadly.

"What?" Rinan, Tredan and Bron all asked simultaneously.

"Look, we're not stupid. We know the Folthnir are planning something horrible. They are all scared. Father. Mother. All of them except you Woodcutters, and Bron, I guess. If we are all doomed then I would rather face my doom in those woods. We feared it all our lives but have lived peacefully enough all these years. Better that, than die under the boots of strangers that treat us like animals, leading us to an indignant slaughter."

"Sheep can never become wolves, is what mama says," Rinan added, "and sheep no matter what their number cannot kill a pack of wolves."

Edrick shook his head. "We are people. The Folthnir, farmers, Woodcutters. We are not sheep or wolves. We choose to act as one or the other, animals do not. Come with us then. We are not sure where we are going, but we will find the Goblyn Market, where my sister was taken."

"Goblyn Market? Is there such a place?" Bron aksed.

"Of course!" Edrick said harshly. He was frustrated at the constant disbelief in the world. "And the Erlking! And ogres and witches and faeries! Everything you hear about from your mother since you were a babe, it's all real outside this stupid village wall if you sheep ever had the courage to wander away from the fold. Those things are real, so the Goblyn Market, too, is a real place. The ogre mentioned it when they took Sunniva. I have this map that shows secret places in the woods. I don't not know what the words say, but these woods used to be home of elves…and men too dwelled here. Men that built the tower, the Wall, and the Elder Hall. Things sheep forget about."

"I never knew there was a map behind the writ. I thought it was just words." Bron said.

"No one knows except my father and the village Elders. For the Elders, it's a meaningless fact. Incidental. To my family, it's a reminder of the way the world once was. Its history."

"Ok, so where are we going. Let's see the map," Bron offered.

Edrick spread the parchment, unfurling it against a tombstone. The children gathered around, looking at it for the first time with wonder. Not one of them had ever seen a map before or knew quite how to read it.

"How can you use this? You can't read. This is as meaningless to Woodcutters as it is to farmers. You went through all that for nothing!" Rodor declared.

Rodor seemed to be slipping back into his old self. Edrick quickly grew angry. "This is the village," Edrick pointed at the picture depicting the Elder Hall and a line surrounding it, the Wall. "And this is the byrgen, we are here. East is the standing stones and across the river are buildings. A secret village. And there are these other places that we could check."

"Who made the map, Edrick?" Bron asked.

Edrick shrugged, rolling up the parchment. "The village founders, the ones who built Athelyn."

"Then why would they put a Goblyn Market on it? That would not make sense?" Rinan piped in.

"Because it would be a place to avoid, a place to search for children when the Erlking came and snatched them up. You think kings leave the lands of their enemies off their maps?"

The group became sullen, reluctant to challenge the Woodcutter boy any further.

"So then, Edrick, where's our first stop?" Bron asked. They all looked to Edrick. They were asking him what to do. They were asking him to lead.

"We are going to the Stones, then we will follow the trail where Baldice ran off."

"Shouldn't we arm ourselves first, or something?" Rodor asked.

"You want to go back and get your turnip knives? Have you a sword hidden beneath your bed? We go on faith Lhodyn will keep us safe. It will have to be enough. If we do face the evil things in there, we have no strength to best them, so if any want to return home, then go now."

"We will be safe," Gaebria added, "the faeries will protect us. They told me in a dream."

No one seemed to know what to make of that. Rinan pulled at Rodor's arm. "Let's go Rodor. It's one thing to face the Folthnir, but to walk the woods is mad. We need to get back."

Rodor stood, looking at his sister. He was conflicted. "No," he finally said. "I will go with Edrick. We are sheep and I want learn the old ways, when men were masters of the woods."

"From Edrick?" Rinan scoffed. "He's just a boy."

"A boy who stared down the Folthnir and almost took an arrow to save this stranger," indicating Gaebria. "He would do that for her, he would act no less for us. No, I need to do this."

Rinan became fearful, "I don't want you to die, in there."

"Go home, Rinan. Tell mother and father whatever you want, but I'm going into the woods. I want to see what wonders are there. And maybe we will meet Death there too, but at least we will not be the sheep of Folthnir."

The group departed the burial grounds, following Edrick east toward the trees. Rinan stood watching them, hands on her hips. "Wait, don't leave me behind, I will come. This is so stupid! You are all so stupid!"

The six children crossed doggedly into the forlorn forest; only Edrick did not look back as they passed the threshold.

He led them through the shadows as the sun descended toward the western horizon. They stayed close to one another; only Edrick and Bron had walked these woods, ever. Edrick would have assured them that there was nothing to be afraid of; such a sentiment was true a few weeks ago, but not that day. Maybe not for many days, or many months to come. But as they traveled, the woods seemed subdued. Not like his last visit, at night, where the air was energized and teemed with watchful eyes. It seemed to be asleep, or indifferent with the children's trespassing. Maybe it was the sunlight that tamed the woods and things would change as darkness seeped into the air. Edrick did not like that thought, being stuck in the woods at night. Not since he saw those shifting shapes, those shadows that stalked them. He had never heard of anything of its like.

Gaebria moved up next to him, and slid her fingers between his, as was her habit of late. Her hold was nervous.

"It is a beautiful place, I can see why your family loves it."

"It's hard to think that anything treacherous might walk these woods," added Bron.

"Shhhh, don't speak of evil things, lest it finds you," Rinan warned. Bron only shook his head.

"Baaaah," bleated Tredan. Though his nerves were not any less steady.

"It feels safe enough," Edrick assured them.

They continued through the woods, each one quiet and watchful. Edrick thought the best place to start would be the stone circle, but he found himself giving in to Gaebria's lead. She whispered to him as they went, how some areas seemed familiar, that she must have encountered the path in her dreams.

"I know they are guiding me Edrick, I feel them leading us."

To where, Edrick wanted to know. They were going deep, and would eventually meet the river, the boundary that his father told all his children to never cross, for the forest became truly wild and unpredictable. But the river was wide enough that the children never contemplated a means to cross it. They were all satisfied to remain in this patch of forest. It was their corner of the forest. The Woodcutter's forest.

Gaebria stumbled upon a path and seemed pleased with herself, as if she found what she had been searching for. She smiled to all the children, assuring them that all was good in the world.

"It should be soon, I think."

The sun was kissing the western horizon now. Edrick had misgivings about lingering in the forest after nightfall. "Perhaps I should look at the map, I might discover where this path leads."

Gaebria shrugged her shoulders indifferently, as if it was a moot gesture, but cared not to dissuade him. Edrick knelt down and flattened the map on the ground. He could not tell if such a small path would be indicated on the map which seemed to reveal only important locations. But he studied it anyway, wanting the rest of the group to think that they were not, indeed, lost.

"Look, there are lights floating in the twilight path not too far off," Rinan said.

Edrick looked up. He saw golden lights floating slowly in the air then blink out of sight, only to reappear near where it disappeared.

"Glow bugs," Edrick dismissed.

"No, Edrick," Gaebria replied in building excitement. "I think those are faeries. They want us to follow. Come on."

Before he could reply, she dashed off down the path, Rodor and Rinan following. Bron shrugged helplessly and jogged after the three. Tredan stood next to his friend, understanding Edrick's growing frustration.

Gaebria eventually led them, again holding Edrick's hand. She was following what she experienced in her dream. They never visited the standing stones, which Edrick didn't really want to see anyway because the memories still pained him. They stayed on the west side of the river, but traveled north into a very wild area where Halig and Eadwyn hunted. There was no Goblyn Market here, that Edrick was certain. How long would he allow them to be led until they stop and turn east to find the Goblyn Market? It must lie somewhere east of the river, where Lhodyn walked the woods, where the map would be needed. But he thought Gaebria needed to at least explore her dream before they could move on; once she realized it meant nothing, then she would either turn back, which was probably best or they could begin the real search for his sister.

The lights continued to flicker like candles on a window sill, yet as they pursued them, the lights would extinguish and appear farther into the forest, off the path. Edrick didn't think this was a good idea to follow these lights, whatever their source might be. He had never seen these kinds of lights, behaving like this. But the children ran on, excited and hopeful until they came across an abandoned cottage.

They all halted, surprised to see the solitary house, lost in the wilds. Their heads collectively turned to Edrick, the expert here. He stared back in silence, offering no answers. He was not familiar with this place, and his brothers never mentioned it, nor his father. It looked similar to the cottages in the village, save someone took the time to build it from stone. The roof was not thatched straw but made of wood shingles overgrown with thick moss. It was entirely surrounded by a wall of stack rock, just like their Wall around the village with a single lychgate. And around a corner were headstones of a small byrgen.

"This is it," she whispered to him. The glow bugs floated in the air around the cottage. The light of day slowly drained from the world and darkness was in full on the east.

"It's not on the map. I'm not sure where we are."

Then, before he could say another word, light abruptly flamed to life through the tiny windows, smoke rose from the chimney. They detected warm and delicious food spreading seductively through the night air. Edrick blinked, for it seemed the fading sunlight distorted his sight. The cottage still seemed old, but not the skeleton of a building it once seemed moments before. It was as if a curtain had been lifted revealing a long lost secret. Something or someone lived there, and in the darkening forest, the cottage even looked inviting.

The aroma of roasting meat over a fire, mixed with fresh bread drifted through the cooling dusk air. It was as if the scents sought them out. Edrick's stomach grumbled, as did Bron and Tredan.

"Do you smell that? I have never smelled anything that good, ever. Who lives here?" Tredan asked.

"The elves," Gaebria answered in a hushed tone. "The faeries brought us here to meet the elves."

Edrick furrowed his brow. Elves would not live in an old cottage. "Let's go find out. It's dark and there is nowhere for us to spend the night and I am sure we ought to find shelter if we are to remain in the woods."

The children easily capitulated under the lure of a warm fire and what promised to be a savory meal. They walked up to the door, gathering behind Edrick. He knocked, ready to address whomever might be inside.

"Good evening. We are Athelyn children that have found ourselves out in the woods too long and let darkness take us before we could return home," Edrick spoke to the door.

Heavy footfalls stamped against the wooden floors, shuffling around the cottage, then the person neared. There was a pause.

A heavy stern voice answered back.

"Who is this at my door? Goblyns!" the voice of a man called back. "Goblyns at my door? I warn you, if you are goblyns I shall hew you through with my ax."

Gaebria gasped and stumbled back.

Edrick prepared himself for facing something horrible, something monstrous. "No, we are just children from the village, I assure you sir."

A metal latch turned, a sharp click snapped, then the sound of a wooden brace lifted and moved aside. The door cracked open and light landed over the children.

Aromas of all kinds of foods overwhelmed them as a strange man in a full beard greeted them, looking upon all of them with a stern face that conveyed alert strength. The man possessed a weathered look, like wood left out in the sun, a long wiry beard that fell to the middle of his chest and wore an old cap. In one hand he held a double bladed woodcutter ax, in the other, a lantern.

"Children?" the man addressed them with suspicion. He seemed to be speaking to himself rather than Edrick. "Six of them at that, all on my doorstep."

He continued to stare at them, and they, back, for about a hundred heartbeats Edrick thought, before someone spoke.

"Sir," Bron addressed, "sorry to disturb your meal, but we seemed to have lingered in woods longer than we ought to and now would ask for lodging rather than cross the woods at night."

The man looked at Bron, seemingly taking in his appearance. He then looked upon Gaebria, and his expression lightened. "You girl, seem so familiar, which is odd, for I haven't had any visitors here since I was a younger man."

"Sir, I was told to find you, I mean this house, by the….by the faeries."

"Faeries? Them? They told you." He paused and looked away in thought as if he were trying to remember something vital. "Well, they wouldn't go speaking to goblyns. But this could be a goblyn trick. Goblyns love to trick you, change their appearance and such, to lure you into dropping your guard before they murder you, or some other wicked business."

Tredan leaned over Edrick's shoulder and whispered, "Or appear as a crazy old man in a cottage no one's encountered before." Edrick smirked, but he had a point.

"How do we know you are not a goblyn?" Edrick riposted.

The man was taken aback, clearly offended. "Hey, it ain't me beating on your door, begging like sad whelps." He grabbed the door, ready to slam it shut when Gaebria stepped forward.

"Sir, we are no more goblyns than you, I assure you. Let us prove it. Edrick's mother is what they call an alhíelda, a faerie guardian. And his father a well-known Woodcutter, by the name of Alaric, perhaps you have heard of him?"

"Alaric? Yes, of course I have heard of him. Very well, come inside before your child-flesh starts attracting the goblyns out of their wretched holes."

The children rushed in, drawn by overpowering scents of the exotic foods. Inside, a long table was set for seven, adorned with fare of all kinds, bread, roasted meat, pies and cakes, and fruit no one could call by name. The cottage was richly decorated, a stark contrast from the drab exterior. Heads of various animals were mounted around the walls of the room: wolves, timber-lions, deer and elks antlers thrusting out like woodland dignitaries, bears whose visage bore frozen snarls, and there were boars and even a massive eagle's head, the size of a timber wolf. It was an impressive collection.

The cottage itself was simple, a single long room that reminded Edrick of the Hall back in the village. The hearth was located toward the back of the room. It was large and constructed of sturdy river stone. Over the mantle hung a shield. Painted there, a coat of arms depicting a rearing stag, its head lowered as if ready to clash with an enemy. The antlers were like bolts of lightning. And curiously, the stag bore a rider, an archer armed with a bow, drawn back, ready to fire. Perched on the archer's shoulder was a small dragon, its tail coiled around the archers arm. Behind them, a diamond formation of twelve stars hung in the heavens. Among all the things in the room that seemed new, the shield seemed out of place as it looked old, the paint faded and neglected. Above the shield there seemed to be a place where something else hung, but long vacant.

In the stone arch of the fireplace were twelve animal carvings, reliefs, similar to those animals mounted on the walls. On the keystone was a stag head with crossed arrows in the field. Three stars surrounded the stag forming the points of a triangle. Then radiating out, were two different kinds of wolves, a bear, an owl, an eagle, a timber lion, a fish, and a tree; each one also had a single star above the image, for a total of twelve stars, likening to the image on the shield.

"Sit then, children. You are my guests." The old man said from the front of the hall. He had finished securing the door, latching it and throwing the timbered bar back across it. The ax now leaned in a corner and the lantern hung by the door.

Gaebria was the first to take a seat, then Tredan. Rinan and Rodor sat together, at the far end of the long table, leaving an open seat closest to the chair at the head of the table, where presumably the old man sat. How strange all this food was laid out for one man. Edrick took in his surroundings carefully. His curiosity kept him from sitting. He and the woodsman were the last standing.

None of the children moved to eat, though everyone of them eyed the cuisine with intense desire. They were awaiting permission.

The old man walked around the table and stood next to the chair at the head of the table, directly in front of the hearth. "Come join your friends, young man. You are my guests for tonight. Tell me what brings you into my woods?"

My woods? These were anything but his woods, a stranger that he had never seen nor heard of in any tale before. The old man seemed to notice Edrick's reaction and his gaze lingered over him.

"It's quite marvelous," Gaebria started. "I dreamed of this cottage and this fine meal last night. There were voices that spoke to me, gentle, loving voices of the faeries. They said, 'seek out the cottage, it will set you on the path to Sunniva. We will guard all the children against the evil men.'"

Edrick sat down. He felt that they shouldn't be speaking so plainly about seeking out his sister, until they knew this stranger could be trusted.

"It sounds as if you have a tale to tell. Well, I do too. I love swapping tales. Haven't had the opportunity to do that in a long while. Please eat, children."

Before he could utter another word, the children dove into the fine fare, all that is except Edrick, who was intent on understanding this woodsman, and the cottage.

"Hungry, are you?" addressing the group generally. "I will admit, the faeries took to whispering in my ear this morning about having guests tonight, that I ought to have a fine meal ready to welcome you. Didn't half expect it to be true, but then again I'm not foolish enough to be ignoring the whispers of the Fair Folk."

The old man noticed Edrick not eating. The man leaned over the table and cut off a leg from a game bird, and set it on Edrick's plate. "There you go, son. So, have you a question? You haven't taken your eyes off me since I opened that door."

"Exactly who are you? You are not from the village. What is this place?"

"Edrick! Don't be rude," Gaebria chided.

Edrick looked at her and the other children. "Have you all lost your sense of danger? We're in the woods, not in some noble's castle. My sister was lured out here by dreams, the same kind Gaebria has, and we were ambushed by monsters. Now we have conveniently stumbled onto a cottage I have never heard of and find a meal for six guests conveniently laid out for us. It all looks like bewitchment to me."

The children stopped abruptly. Tredan's mouth was stuffed like a winter starved chipmunk. He looked around to the other faces, searching for their reactions. Gaebria stubbornly resumed eating.

The old man leaned back in his chair and let out a roaring laugh. It was an infectious gleeful laugh that had the children smiling in relief. All, that is, except Edrick. He crossed his arms, sitting as tall as he could.

"How well you would do here in these woods, young man. So I am a witch am I?" He laughed even more. It was a mocking laugh. Edrick's face burned with frustration. The children didn't seem to mind, and even giggled as they continued eating. "Ha! Look around boy, my family have lived in these woods for generations, before the men rode into these lands on their horses, when my people, men of the forest rode the horned beasts. These are my woods, these are my ancestral lands, do you not realize who I am?"

Edrick stood up, he couldn't take it anymore. His chair flew back, his fist pounded on the table. "These are my woods, my father's woods and I have never heard of you!" He roared. This liar, this imposter made the same claims that were told to him and all his brothers and sisters from their father's lips. "Bron, we need to go. This was a mistake. We need to go."

He looked at all their faces. There was a mixed look of surprise, embarrassment, disappointment and anger. Edrick realized their fattened bellies gave them a sense of gratitude, a feeling that Edrick just betrayed. Bron looked at Edrick and back to the old man, then back to Edrick. He then relaxed and started eating again.

"I know who you are," he said between bites. He was calm, annoyingly at ease. "I am surprised Edrick hasn't guessed yet. You see, Edrick knows all the stories of the woods and maybe one of the few children that believes in everything he hears as truth. We all thought of him as naïve, as is usually what you find in boys his age. Edrick plays games in the woods, acts out his stories like no other child. His mother is the village's finest storyteller."

Edrick sat back down again. It was obvious no one cared to leave, or bothered to even release the slightest scrap or morsel from their greasy fingers. He gave in and tore into the drumstick.

It was delicious

"I had always thought most of those stories were, just that, stories, until Sunniva disappeared, and witches and dæmons walked out of the woods, in plain daylight, for all to see. Edrick has already seen one legend, the Erlking. So looking at you and where we are at, I would have to guess you are the Brownman, at least that's what we call him."

The children all nodded in simple agreement. The mystery was solved.

Edrick dropped his drumstick of meat, shaking his head furiously, his mouth full. He erupted like a volcano, "Dat's not him," meat sprayed over the dinner table. "I saw the Brownman, he rescued us from the ogre and that dæmon pig. He chased them away with wolves. This imposter is not him."

"Edrick," Bron started, "you and your brothers went through a lot. It happened so fast, it doesn't surprise me you didn't recognize him. You even said, he came out of nowhere, then left just as quickly."

"Ask him then," Edrick challenged, and didn't wait for a response. "Who are you?"

"A friend of the woods that goes by many names, but you may call me Brownman if you like."

Bron looked at Edrick, his expressions saying, I told you so.

It was ridiculous. This wasn't the same man. They both were tall, scraggily and, well.... wild. Yet there was something about the real Brownman that this man did not possess. A sort of melancholy, a sense of defeat, but stubbornly defiant. This man acted like he were the king of the woods.

King of the woods?

Edrick's mind raced. There was another story, that of the Woodcutter King, the one who spoke to the elves and such. Could he be different than the Brownman, or were they the same?

"Realized something did you?" The woodsman asked. He had already joined the meal with the rest of the children, eating very slowly, picking and choosing his food carefully.

"I may be mistaken about you," Edrick admitted. If this was the long lost king, he had just made the worst, most foolish impression that he could have possibly had made. The woodsman watched him, making Edrick feel very childish and rude. So he busied himself by diving into the food laid before him.

The food was exotic and all of it incredibly delicious, of a quality that more than a woodcutter could provide. Edrick and the others had never eaten food so fine, so flavorful. They never knew food could be this enjoyable, even fun. At the end of the meal they sat chatting excitedly to one another as the woodcutter sat at the head of the table smiling, satisfied to have hosted a grand dinner.

Edrick reflected on what the woodcutter said when he greeted them at the door. "Master," Edrick began, "do you know of a Goblyn Market? Is there one in these woods?"

The woodcutter raised an eyebrow. "I have heard rumor of such a thing, or course," he did not seemed pleased at the question.

Edrick continued cautiously. "My sister was taken by monsters. I must locate the Goblyn Market. If you don't know where it is exactly, could you tell me the direction?"

"I would never think to send you children to such a place by yourselves." He stood up, pushing his chair back. Suddenly he seemed quite menacing. "Do you know what you are asking? Or what manner of creatures visit such a market…no." He looked at all of their faces sternly. His face softened when he looked on Gaebria. "Nevermind. This is not a topic suitable for this company. Look, you are upsetting your friends." Indeed they were startled at the grim discussion.

"Now children, you must spend the night. The forest is not a place that should be traveled in darkness with wolves, bears and other beasts lurking about," he paused then added, "or the monsters of Edrick's past, especially with bellies as stuffed as yours. Lie down by the fire and I will tell you a tale."

The children agreed all too easily and found that there had been blankets and pillows laid out on the floor, where they were sure was a bare wood before. "But you have to promise me, children. You must come back and visit me, soon. I will tell you something that the other adults might not reveal to you and it is a sad knowledge. But those strange men in the village want to take you all away." Some of the children gasped. The man's words were strong though his face held concern. "And I would hate for that to happen. You see, I am all alone and I escaped the detection of those bad men. I think it would be a good idea if all you children came to live with me. I will build a new home, just for you children and you will be safe and well fed….you did like the food didn't you?" There was a loud chorus of enthusiastic approval. "And I do enjoy to hear the laughter of children again."

"What about our parents? They should come too," Edrick put in. The other children nodded, but seemed shy about imposing on the man's hospitality.

"Oh, well children, I will be honest. Hosting all your parents would make things difficult. I could hide you children, but parents, well they just cause all sorts of trouble. You can see that. All they manage to rouse is harm and lies. The faeries disdain that kind of behavior, which is why they sometimes cause mischief around your village. They only do it to teach grown-ups lessons, and look how they repay them. By trapping them like vermin and smashing their little bodies up into paste and oils to make useful things out of them. That is not a proper way to treat the Gentle Folk."

The children all turned to Edrick and what little suspicion they held over Edrick and his family, shifted to horror and disgust.

"His mother catches faeries and does exactly what you said," accused Rinan, seemingly on the verge of tears. Edrick turned red, and shifted uncomfortably. The man did make it sound like a backwards practice, and for the first time, felt a little ashamed of his family and who they were.

"Yeah and he traps them in cages," accused Rodor.

Tredan gave an apologetic look, embarrassed for his friend.

"Well, young master woodcutter, you would do better to practice your woodcraft. Faeries, I hope you will learn, are friendly and are especially fond of children. They will never do you harm."

"Can we see them? The faeries I mean," blurted out Gaebria.

"Oh, that you will, for sure. In due time. They are around us as we speak, but they will only make themselves known when they have deemed you trustworthy."

"That's not true," Edrick whispered. The man turned to Edrick.

"What was that young Woodcutter?"

"Faeries *can* cause you harm, but only if you invite harm to be done to you. They are something like fire, useful, but if mishandled, you find yourself burned and disfigured." The man simply shook his head slowly, as if apologizing for Edrick's contempt.

"They will never hurt children," he replied confidently.

"Evil faeries will."

"There are no evil faeries, just those that seek justice on adults who did them harm."

"To children too. My mother said so."

"Have you ever been harmed by faeries?" asked the man gently.

"Well, no, but I have been trained to handle them with care…"

"And adults?"

"Well, of course…"

The man said not a word further, but let the silence speak for him. Edrick's brows furrowed in frustration. He was trying to trick him, but why? Why was he treating him like this, humiliating him while the other children were treated like royalty? Edrick flopped back onto his bed, crossing his arms over his chest.

"Tell us your story," Tredan requested. Edrick shot his best friend a glare, for the betrayal of not sharing in his anger. But he understood. Tredan was just glad he was not the focus of the woodcutter's scrutiny.

The woodcutter spoke of wonderful tales that sent them all to a dreamless sleep. When they awoke, food was already laid before them as the previous night, yet it smelled far more seductive, the table being laden with sweet breads and exotic fruits the children had never encountered. They ate until they were stuffed. The breakfast was even better than the supper. At the end of the meal the man told them, "All right children, now is the time to choose. All but one of you may stay if you wish. At least one must return home to fetch the others."

There was a little bit of an outcry as they expressed how they would miss their parents. The man quieted them and said, "Once everyone is here, I have decided to lead you all to the Faerie Realm straight away. It is secret and guarded, and only children, those of pure hearts, may enter. When we are there, your sorrows and worries will be washed away."

"I'll go," Edrick said without hesitation. He just wanted to leave, to get away from the strange man.

Gaebria also jumped up and shouted, "I will do it. I will go. I will bring as many as I can. It will hurt my mother and nana but I will tell them where I will be. I will tell all your families."

"No, children!" the woodcutter cut in, with the first hints of harshness the children had heard. "Your parents must not know. For which parent would willingly depart with their children and not accompany them? No, they cannot know. Gather the brave children. Tell them that they need my protection and they will see their parents again very soon after I drive out those Folthnir from our lands. That's what needs to happen before it is safe for you children to return. A war is upon us and you children must find shelter and not let your parents worry about your well-being. Once you are safe, I will share news with your parents. They will be relieved and they will be thankful."

The children thanked him and continued eating a second round. Edrick waited for Tredan, but he was still stuffing his face with sweet rolls. Finally, Edrick and Gaebria walked out the cottage and found the path that led them back to the village. It seemed to have moved from the day before, taking a different direction, Edrick was sure. But before too long, they heard a voice that shouted for them to wait. Tredan came running after them.

"I didn't want to leave you, Edrick," he said, apologizing. "When the woodcutter told me the faeries would never accept you because of your violence against them, I couldn't think of going to the Faerie Land without you."

Edrick stomped away from the cottage, filled with resentment.

16

INSIGNIFICANT NOTHINGS

ALARIC LEFT THAT PLACE, that body, behind. For immeasurable moments he dwelled there, beyond the grayness.

He wondered where he went and what it meant. Had he been a spirit walking the world as a ghost, intersecting his ancestors on the paths of the dead, learning their history, discovering their tarnished legacy? Secrets whispered throughout generations, but never openly spoken. It was a far harsher injury than anything inflicted upon his body.

It was a wound that bled into every generation. It wore them down into insignificant nothings, despised Woodcutters. If it were not for Elisial, his family would be total outcasts.

Pain wracked sleep overtook him. Elisial burned faerie oil and foreign incense. The pungent scent filled the small home for days, clinging to their clothes and hair. She and Meghan then took turns applying other exotic medicines over his wounds. He was in a daze for a while as he drifted in and out of dreamless sleep. Voices spoke to him, yet he could not remember the words or the speakers. It was not until two days passed that he pulled himself out of bed. He felt remarkably better, yet not fully healed. The wounds across his back and chest, from being dragged behind a horse for miles, were healing well. A bitter taste coated his mouth, evidence of potent medicine Elisial fed him daily.

But the better medicine was feeling her lips on his, having her hand over his heart as they lay together, anticipating every breath warming his skin.

"You have done well, my love," he said to her, as he rose from bed. "I need to get back on my feet. My hardened body does not like the soft comfort of bed."

Meghan and Eadwyn came over to help him up, each bracing an arm. He allowed them to help, though he did not need it. He thanked them with a grateful nod. Halig watched from the shadows of the far corner. Edrick and the young girl, Gaebria, were plainly absent. Bresigia greeted him cheerfully. She clasped her blind daughter's hand, as if the sight of his recovery meant something significant for them.

"I can use something to eat," he said, rubbing his thinned stomach. "It's as if you have been starving me this whole time."

"Aye," Elisial answered back, "one less mouth to feed was a benefit for the rest of us."

Alaric smiled, she was as enduring as ever.

"Yes, Papa. Sit and we will feed you," Meghan said sweetly. They ate together as a family, mostly in silence. Bresigia led Sarghan to the table, joining with them in meal. Afterwards, Alaric felt the urge to wander outside, feel the spring sun on his skin.

"I will see what has become of the village after my absence. It seems ill things take root when I am away." He was hoping to see some sign of Elzera. He needed her help, her strength, her wiles.

"I will accompany you husband," Elisial said, flustered. It was clear by her tone she did not want him to leave the cottage yet, but refrained from arguing. Perhaps she did not want to waste the energy on something he set his mind on doing anyway.

Alaric welcomed her company though he knew that she wanted to keep him there, in bed, that she would wait over him for weeks, as if he were a young child. Possibly longer. But he would not have that. There was too much to do. Escape. He needed to take them all away.

"I would walk alone, but I suppose there is sense in having someone keep me out of trouble."

"You are in the care of an alhíelda, there is no escape from our kind."

"Don't I know, and in the twenty some years after I found myself in your care, nine children have been begotten…"

A silence filled the cottage. He rarely mentioned the boys that had passed away. Their triplets. Only three children were present with him now.

"Where is Edrick and Gaebria?" Alaric finally asked, thinking they should have returned now for meal.

Elisial turned away, tightening the shawl wrapped around her shoulders and began to attend to her apothecary alcove, straightening bottles and jars, making sure the labels of all the ingredients where perfectly facing forward.

Her burst of movement ceased when her fingers settled on the fey flower Alaric had brought her. She lifted it off the shelf and caressed the petals along her cheek. "He and the girl have been away for a while. They were last seen in the Elder Hall, being tortured by Folthnir boys before they escaped with Bron's help. No one has seen or heard of them for two days…"

Her voice failed her. Alaric sensed there was more.

So Grindan's son defied his father. That boy was showing some deep strength to go against his old whilom friend.

Halig stepped forward, "Father, they said he stole the village Writ. They are speaking of handing him to the Folthnir, and ridding the village of him." There was a sense of urgency in his words, a challenge to set the world right. To stop being the shunned outcasts of Athelyn.

Alaric turned to his wife, "Is this true?" It could not be. The document was the sacred property of the village. To many, the presence of the Writ signified the importance of their small village to the king and his court. Even if Athéalgian fell, Athelyn remained. A part of the kingdom was kept alive.

She nodded, but could not look at him directly.

He shook his head in protest. He cursed his weak body. It seems his jest were true, trouble rises out from of his footsteps. "How long have I been asleep?"

"A week papa," Meghan whispered. "I thought you might not wake up," her voice trailed off.

A rage took him. He wanted to yell at them all, curse himself for being so weak. He was always the one to rectify people's mistakes. And now another child of his, missing and accused of thievery. A thief under his roof!

"I will discover the truth behind this. Where's my bow?"

Elisial turned around, eyes hardened with resolve. "They took it Alaric…I could not stop them." He remembered seeing Nithledan in the hands of the Huntsman. "I had your bow, but they came for it when they took the boys to the tower."

Her face said it all, regret, shame, apologetic and sorrowful. He walked over and wrapped his arms around her waist, kissing her hair, which smelled of wild flowers, the same as when they first laid together beneath the oak tree in their youth. "It seems you need a long rest at my expense. You should get off your feet."

She stepped back and wrapped her hand over his and nodded slightly. Her finger slid over his skin, feeling the raised veins and stray hairs she knew so well. "I'm sorry, Alaric," she whispered, restraining a mountain of feelings. "I can't do this without you. I prayed for you to come back to me. We need you."

"You have done more than I can expect, for all these years." He wiped away a couple of rogue tears and kissed her forehead. "You are not to blame, indeed it is you who deserves much praise. I owe you my life, manifold. We will find Edrick," he kissed her again. "We will see what can be done about my bow, but most important, we will leave this place. We must. It is cursed. It is a doom sown by my forefathers and I have sustained that crop which has poisoned us. We shall leave it here to rot and find a new home elsewhere."

Elisial laid her head on his shoulder. "As you wish," she answered, then added, "it will be hard. So hard."

He turned to face his family, Halig, Meghan and Eadwyn. His three eldest, three of nine. The six younger ones gone, passed out of the world or on their way out it seems. Children were supposed to be boons, not accumulating burdens. "We will find him," he assured the three. "If Edrick did or did not do what they accuse him of, it does not matter. We will leave this place. Bresigia and Sarghan, you are welcomed to travel with us. Gaebria, I'm sure, is safe with my son and he will guard her with his life. That I know of him.

"I know Edrick wishes he could have taken Sunniva's place in those woods. That she came home, perhaps instead of him. He blames me and I deserve some of it, I admit. Leaving my home was against my heart when I departed last summer, even as I knew the woods grew dark, and my loyalty in a goddess that cared nothing for mortals, formed not of faith, but in obedience to tradition that I have come to realized was misplaced, for generations."

"Father how can you say that?" Halig interrupted. "This is our sire's land. You taught us our blood sprang from these woods, we are the last of the First People. We are the Wardens of the Woods! What do you mean the Writ means nothing? You told me, it proves we are freemen, that Emperor Abellious imbued our family with title, charged us as stewards to these woods and these lands. And you spoke of more, that we keep the secrets of the woods…"

"Enough, Halig! What I said in the past was in error. We are nothing more than Woodcutters."

Alaric ceased. That name!

"Always have been, always will be."

It was vile. A label for their crimes against the Old Gods.

"We are not nobles, our heritage was not stolen from us. We live as we were meant to, and we will not die living out foolish fantasies, entertaining false notions."

Halig shook his head, looked to his brother and sister, then finally to his mother for help.

"Certainly we can all talk of this later," Elisial said soothingly. "All that needs to happen now is your father regaining his strength and finding Edrick and Gaebria."

"Maybe the Folthnir did take him," Eadwyn meekly suggested.

"Then we shall have him back," his father added fiercely, "along with my bow!"

"Is even what you said about Nithledan true, Father?" Halig taunted, "or is it just a simple woodcutter's bow? Why not let them keep it?"

His mother took Alaric by the hand and pulled him out the door before his anger erupted into action. He and his son locked glares.

Elisial led Alaric down the Lane until he calmed. The Lane was entirely empty and all the fields were missing their farmers as well.

"He is not all right, Alaric, none of them are. Halig is unusually defiant and quick to anger. Eadwyn unusually helpful. And all Meghan does is worry about everything. It seems only Edrick has kept his head about him."

"How dare he speak to me in such a way! I'm his father!"

"I know, I know, Alaric. Just let me talk to him first. Then you may have your words. He has stepped up while you were resting."

"As you wish," Alaric let out a deep breath. "Have your say with him first." All Halig seemed to care about was their family's title, an empty position of a past era. A situation Halig believed Alaric had the ability to reassert, to impose on others, to demand a castle from a dead king or some other preposterous notion. Anything but deliver wood to people who thought of them as strange, treated then with suspicion and contempt.

They continued to walk toward the village center. He stopped and stared down the vacant Lane.

He did not want to look at the faces of any whom had turned him over to the Folthnir. He did not want to show his contempt, though they deserved it. It was not for them to see. So he left the Lane, turning north, past the farm fields into the open expanse that once held grazing Wultherons. Not even the beehives remained, each skep was toppled over, its golden contents stolen. The fields were silent.

His feet took him back to the forest. Alaric gazed into the woods, eyes seemingly like that of a stranger. What was this place that was once his home? He felt now, in some ways, what the villagers must have felt beholding the woods; confused, afraid, paranoid about its ambivalence. He walked along Wudelic's edge still desiring to return, wondering if such a thing would ever be possible.

Something then caught his eye, an animal with silvered fur, the size and build of a small dog, illuminated with a faint glow, creeping and darting through the brush. It moved with stealth at first, then crossed open ground as if to draw his eye, asking him to follow, but he would not. Alaric knew what this creature was, a forest spirit in the shape of a fox.

"What is that?" Elisial asked. She noticed it too, as they walked along.

"A ghost," he replied. "And nothing more."

It went by several names, but he called it a Greyorn. It was a curious thing, one among many of the mysteries of the forest. Great animal spirits were known to wander the woods, but most were never seen by those outside Wudelic. But this one, thrived on causing men harm or at the very least mischief and misfortune.

Alaric turned from the woods, not wanting to be bothered further. They had ranged some distance south of the village, stumbling on to the burial grounds. He found the rocks marking the graves of their triplet sons, dead naught but three days after birth. Etched in each tombstone were three marks, one mark for the year of their death, one their age, and one the symbol of their family, the Woodcutters: a stag head with two arrows crossing behind it, three stars upon its crown. They were never named. They did not live long enough for that.

Elisial stared at the three graves, her breath nearly still. She was a stranger to this place.

"We should have come here more often," she confessed after moments of silence and reflection.

"I always thought you desired to avoid this place."

"I did. You should have brought me here anyway."

Alaric kissed her head and pulled her close, tight.

It was a difficult birth, one Elisial could not recover until weeks later. He had almost lost her too. An alhíelda from another village stayed with them, but she did not know her craft half as well as Elisial. Most of what she practiced was superstition.

In Athelyn, three days after a baby is born, the faeries of the woods visit each newborn, bestowing gifts, blessings that stayed with them all their lives. An alhíelda's duty saw to the correct preparations that ensured a generous visit. Offend them, and the faeries will curse the infant, or worse, continue to visit the child throughout their life and plague them with misfortune.

The births did not go well at all and their triplets were taken by the faeries. Given to Lhodyn. The alhíelda was mad, claiming that the three boys were ill omens, birthed on the Blood Moon and destined for evil. Rumor of their birth spread through the village, that three boys were born, cursed. Elisial bled for days. She could not protect her boys from the inept alhíelda.

Alaric placed their bodies in the village burial grounds, knowing that their souls were already claimed by Lhodyn. He accused the alhíelda of being a witch, something he would have never had done, knowing this would cast suspicion on his own wife. But the woman let his three sons die. The villagers chased her into the woods. Alaric followed later once he buried his sons, but he lost all signs of her. Perhaps she was a witch. He always had his doubts.

From then on, the villagers whispered how Death made its mark on the Woodcutters, adding to their suspicious reputation.

Whilst in reflection, three orbs, spectral lanterns of silver, gold and copper light rose from the ground beneath him. They floated aloft like soft dandelion seeds, drifting across the grounds of the dead. Blurred faces hid within the lights. Alaric seemed to be peering through a portal into another world. He reached out to them, but they swayed away from his hand. Slowly they drew away from him, as if drawn into the forest. Then the ghostly silver fox leapt out from the trees and chased the lights away, batting at them like a playful pup. Alaric instinctively reached behind his back for his bow, that which was not there.

The ephemeral lights became lost to the forest. The ghostly fox did not chase after them but instead trotted toward Alaric and sat on their children's grave, facing Alaric and Elisial, laughing. Laughed like a creature filled with cunning delight.

"Woe is the Woodcutter," it began mockingly, "woe to the village of Man. The forest laments the tears shed by the mothers of children it will lose to the Lady."

"What is this ghost?" Elisial asked, stepping behind her husband cautiously.

Alaric kicked at the little fox. It jumped easily though, with a sort of lazy grace, around the man's boots, landing with the softness of a cat.

"An insolent little dæmon!" Alaric replied.

"I know what's on your mind Woodcutter. But you still have a problem, do you not? After you collected your family, where to go? How to escape with enemies in all directions?"

Alaric said nothing and looked into the sky. Smoke rose thick in the air trailing away from the village. Something burned black.

"I can take you and your family safely through the forest. I know all the faerie gates to get you swiftly through and out of the woods and into new lands. She will not be able to track your path, and those stupid northerners certainly would not. It's your only solution. But I must have a single payment. Your torc."

Alaric shook his head, reflexively placing his hand on his bare neck, where the torc once rested since he was Halig's age.

"I have passed it on to my sons. It is theirs now."

"Too soon, wouldn't you say…you couldn't have possibly told them what it is?"

He was not entirely sure what it was. "They know enough to keep it safe."

"That is too, too bad Woodcutter. For a payment of this rarity I would have even fetched one of your lost pups and saw them back into your arms."

Elisial stepped forward, "What do you know of Edrick and Sunniva? Tell us ghost!" She trembled. Alaric had never seen her tremble, in fear or rage.

The fox regarded her for the first time, as if she suddenly appeared. "I know many a great deal of things, alhíelda," it answered sinisterly. It then laughed once again. "Tell me alhíelda, for I have wondered many times about your ridiculous name. You call yourselves *faerie guardians*, then go about trapping them like rats and smashing them up into pastes and oils, jams or jellies or whatever you witches do…"

"She's not a witch," Alaric growled.

"It's fine Alaric. I can see it is as you say, an insolent dæmon aiming to find vulnerability among us. I'm sure you do know many things, including the answer to your own question. Your true aim no doubt is to understand this alhíelda. We are as we say. We guard against faeries, and guard those faeries that take up the cause of men. Faeries are spirits, similar in essence to you, but they have no will of their own. They are the water that falls from the skies, the wind that blows through the trees, the fires that feed on wood. They are these things, elements that can either harm or heal."

"You have much to learn."

"I do not disagree," she said, dismissive. Then quickly asked, "So what of our children? Sunniva is alive? Edrick? Where are they?" Elisial demanded again, taking another step forward.

"The woods are its own domain. Those that cross these paths become Lhodyn's subjects. Alaric knows this. It is her will to allow those to pass to and fro. He is here."

"Where?"

"It looks like we both desire something. You two, your children. Me, the torc. You desire escape. I desire escape. Oh, I forgot to mention my masters' desires," his voice then dripped with venom, "they demand a toll for your trespass, younger man. One of your children will not be returning to the mortal realms. So choose which."

Alaric realized what this Greyorn was. He wore a different form in the Faerie Realms.

"NO!" Alaric roared. "You will never touch my kin, dæmon! Crawl back to your masters and leave the mortal world to mortals."

The fox jumped back, laughing despite himself. It twirled, wriggling around in delight and snapping at its own tail. "Well, I suppose that will be your answer for now. But my offer still stands.

Escape this place, Alaric. You are a better man than to be kept like this. They deserve better." With that, the silver spirit darted away, returning to the woods.

The byrgen became much colder.

Silence hung between the couple.

"It speaks like a devil, in riddles."

"The devils of the world seem to be converging here all at once. What hope have we, Elisial?" Alaric sighed.

She did not answer, but wrapped her arms around him. For the first time, it held no comfort for him.

"What do you suppose is burning?" Elisial finally asked, looking into the sky. Her voice was without any alarm or distress, just stoic resignation.

"Our lives," Alaric sighed, "if they were candle wicks. And the wind blows again, buffeting our flames. When our fires go out, it is our children that must carry our light."

"Yes, our children," she bent down and kissed their sons' gravestone. She held the smooth granite between her hands. "And we must protect their flames until they have children of their own."

"This is how it should be. Come, my love, let's find what new disaster claims our village today."

Elisial told him of what she had heard of Edrick's boldness, his confrontation and threatening of the Folthnir boys with a bow. It brought a smirk to Alaric's face despite himself. Edrick was bold, but still a child, with all impetuous impulses of youth, yet had more courage than most men he knew. Alaric witnessed such youthful boldness on the battlefield. Those fools parted from the rest of them on the first day of fighting.

"Why would he have taken the Writ? It was something of little value for an illiterate village, just an old relic, something part of the Elder Hall as much as the timbers and floorboards," Elisial wondered.

"There is a map on the back of it. I have shown him and Halig. Besides myself, they are the only two that have seen the map. I doubt even the village Elders remember there is a map."

"A map? Of what?"

"This village, and the surrounding countryside, showing the extant of my stewardship or those of any other future Warden, including the Ruined Tower, the villages of Alnefirthe, Sacrisnax,

Ethelas, Wuldenor and of course the forest and all its ruins."

"Ruins? Where? You have never said any of this to me? Can you read what it says? How do you know?"

They stopped, Elisial clasping his arm, wanting his full attention.

"I know because that is what my father said to me and my brothers, it is what my grandfather said to my father."

"Oh, Alaric, I didn't mean…"

"It is fine my love. I do not take your questioning as doubts. You are the only person in the world that knows my heart, my burdens, and does her best to share in them. To soothe my wounds, both body and soul. Without you, I am nothing. The only true steward I am is of House Rhitterheort, the house my sons will assume when we are no more."

Elisial embraced him, holding him tight. "Baldice would have never followed your ways."

"I know. I knew my son well enough to understand he would have made a far better alhíeld than a woodsman. I would have been proud of him for that."

"I know, I just wanted to hear you say it."

Three of his other sons would have become Wardens, and now that he decided to desert his position, he wondered if his sons would follow him to an unknown fate.

When they reached the Lane, people were swiftly moving along, toward the village center. Families, together, wordlessly walked toward the smoke.

"Father," Halig called to them. He, Meghan and Eadwyn rushed to their parents. Halig and Eadwyn wore bolts of arrows around their backs. He carried an extra set, handing them to Alaric.

"The Elders have called a Hatanmoot. I think it is because we were attacked at the tower. Some are saying they will kill people if they don't go. Bresigia and Sarghan refused to come."

Alaric looked to Elisial. "We should go too."

Halig's spirit fell. "No! It is some kind of trick to force us into those cages we saw at the tower. Now is an opportunity to fight. We can hide somewhere in the wild and pick them off one by one. We can do this, pa!" He was so sincere and excited with the thought he could escape, that they could do something to change their situation.

"Fight? The three of us against them. Did you not see how they repelled Lhodyn's host. You think we have a better chance, boy?"

Alaric slapped the bow out of Halig's hand.

Halig stepped back, quickly picking it up, hurt and betrayal burning across his face.

"I thought he was mad too," Eadwyn said dropping his bow, "but he was sure you would go for it."

Alaric shook his head. "This is no game. The wild is no place for us now. What of the women you left behind? Who will take care of them? Edrick is not even with us and you just want to leave?"

"Well, we have to do something! We have to make them pay for what they did to you."

"Are you that proud?" Alaric asked. Did he raise his son to be like this? He wondered if he himself acted this proud.

Halig said nothing, looking to his mother.

"Leave your bows, boys," Alaric continued. "Our people do need our help. We won't hide. We will stand with them."

"No!" Halig yelled. "I will not stand next to those that sold you to our enemies. They almost killed you!" He screamed at the families walking down the Lane.

"Calm down," Elisial said, raising her hands in attempt to pacify their son. Halig backed away. His knuckles whitened as he clutched his bow.

"They are afraid, Halig, same as you," Alaric said. It was as if those words sliced his son by sword blade. Halig was livid, dropping his bow, he threw the bolt across the fields.

"The blood of our family is on you, old man," he stormed down the Lane ahead of them.

Alaric's blood boiled as his son scolded him like a child. Deeply pained that his son was oblivious to see that it was his concerns for his family that were wearing him into a shadow.

They reached the Elder Hall where a crowd of villagers were gathered. Wolfskins lurked around the perimeter, watching with cagy eyes. A few were mounted, including Ator and the one they called the Huntsman, surveying the throng next to an empty caged wagon. One similar to that which hauled the women slaves from the tower.

The rising panic was palpable. "This is it, they are taking us away," whispers floated through the village.

All eyes fell over Alaric as he approached. They withdrew from him like sheep in the presence of a beast. "The Woodcutter brought this on us," they accused. "It's his family that should be brought before them. Not us!"

Halig glared at his father and no one else.

The Elders were lined up at the head of the crowd. Before them a fire burned over the collected remains of the village treasures, things stored in the hall for generations. Alaric stepped out of the crowd to look at all their faces, a mix of fear and anger.

"The Assassin is here!" one Folthnir cried out.

"Here! Woodcutter," Ator commanded, kicking his horse forward. "Where is your son? He has much to answer for."

Alaric stood tall, "I will answer for my son."

"Alaric," Elisial said from behind, pulling him back, but he did not yield.

"You will, Assassin, for all dishonorable deaths you have taken on the battlefield. Vylkinus hand-feeds the souls of our enemies to Baeloth's open maw. It especially hungers for the souls of assassins. Bring your children before me, especially that runt."

"What you want of them, I will provide."

The Folthnir laughed, along with his warriors. "As you wish, master Woodcutter."

Elisial pulled Alaric back. "Alaric, this isn't good, they are gathering the entire village. Look at the Hall, look what they have done."

The Elder Hall as Alaric knew it was no more. Severed heads removed from the quilled wolfish beasts were set on posts, each bearing a crown of flies. Red runes had been painted across the interior walls, similar to what Alaric saw on the priests' robes. Inside, a Folthnir battle priest heated something on a hastily constructed forge, and Grindan stood proudly next to him, watching on. This was no longer their Elder Hall. This was now a temple to their foreign god.

Grindan noticed Alaric's gawking. He left the forge and walked up to Alaric. "Finally, Woodcutter, you have seen the old Hall restored back to its true form, a place for warriors, for great men who are the conquerors of the world, not whiny craven peasants that find it fit to store their grains, garbage and goats. This temple will assure our survival. It signifies that we bow before the Lords of the North."

"Just now, you stood where they killed Hrypa. Why have you turned your back on us?"

The large man snorted as he approached Alaric. "On you, you mean. Just speak plainly Alaric. I saved this village from slaughter. You and I know the cruelty at their hands. Sithric lost the war. Now we must move on and accept our fates."

"Look at their faces, Grindan. It is not over for them. You think only for yourself."

The blacksmith shoved Alaric to the side and stood in front of the crowd. "Those that swear to our Theign and our new gods," he shouted to those gathered, "shall receive the protection of the Folthnir, a grip that extends from Mithledor to the Haunted Realms. Embrace this protection, I urge all of you!"

"You think it is so easy to accept murderers as kings?" Alaric asked.

"They care not for the dead king, for what lord gives a damn about beasts of labor that fills his stomach with grains sown by their hands, lines his pocket with the riches gained by our harvested lands? Our Theign will set us free. He is granting us this valley as ours, to make of it as we wish."

"You believe his lies, a people who steal not only our food, but steal our people away and send them to unknown lands as slaves."

"We are all slaves Alaric! And beggars and cripples! We have never been our own masters. There are many more things in this world that bests us, beats us, that takes from us with utter cruelty. So now they have a choice, the master before them or the master they will meet in chains, in foreign lands, leagues away from their family and friends. You think of me as a pathetic fool! I pity YOU Woodcutter, for being a willing servant to a goddess that turns on you. Whose neighbors despise and mock you. Whose disobedient sons insult your house?"

"Then why did you look for my children in the woods if you hold me in such contempt? Why help if you already betrayed me before I even left?"

"I repaid you for what friendship we had, honest enough it was. I did not ask for these things Alaric, no more than you. But now, you, they, must decide how you want to live, from this moment. That choice itself is not always granted. When one king dies and another takes his place, does this change any of our lot? You either welcome it, or you cut the kings head off and take his place."

"Fear is a madness that settles over the craven heart, that sees order and calm where there is none," Elisial interjected. "Grindan, there is more fear in you than all the village."

Grindan laughed. "The same madness could be said about your pride and indignant righteousness. Simple folk don't desire war. They run and rightly so. I knew you would stand against the Folthnir, I had the wisdom to separate you from the village before you led them all to their deaths. You think you can save them still, Alaric? Only in death do we find the freedom we desire. But sometimes, it's the death of another that guarantees our lives.

"There are no heroes to put the world aright, are there, Alaric? No heroes, no gods, old or new. Just men who have the strength to impose their will. Just men who have the wisdom to recognize their place and act accordingly."

Grindan circled back to Alaric and leaned close so only he would hear his words. "So assassin, Hero of Athelyn. Are you going to free these people or honor your vows to your new Theign? "

"If death, as you claim, is there only freedom, it seems you have already brought it to them."

The two locked eyes. A myriad of thoughts and feelings rushed Alaric's mind, chiefly he wondered if the blacksmith had not the Folthnir to back him, could he defeat his old friend. Could he kill him if he had to?

Grindan turned and entered the temple. He held his hand out to the battle priest who handed him a glowing brand. His eyes never left Alaric. It was a glare that was hard and bitter.

Grindan yelled out. "Step into the temple of Vylkinus and receive the Light of the Forge. Here is the Theign's brand, and only that which belongs to the Theign shall remain here. The Elders have extended their welcome to the Folthnir, and for their wisdom, they shall be the first to bear his mark."

Old Caflice shuffled forward, requiring the assistance of a young man, named Beran, to cross the ground. The old man walked up to Grindan and grasped the blacksmith's free hand with both of his in greetings, as a sign of respect. After a silent moment, Old Caflice turned to the crowd and spoke. All became quiet, for the old man's voice was weak and did not travel.

"My neighbors, all of us are farmers, simple people of the soil. We know our animals and the earth here in this valley as well as the eagle knows the sky and fish know the rivers. Remove the fish from the rivers and they will die. Deny the eagle the sky and it will perish."

"Great men come and go. Claims to the land never cease, but we shall always remain. The fish live in the rivers same as they always do. But when lords are hungry, they must fish, and they protect their rivers from others, from the bears and eagles, from other fishermen. So take these brands as an emblem of your protector, of the men that will die to let us live in this valley and allow peace to return to our lives. This is the right thing to do."

No one stirred, no one made a sound or reaction to what the Elder said. But Alaric could feel it. Could feel the uncertainty, their fear, their desire to escape to an imaginary haven, one they falsely sent Alaric to discover a year ago. Now they all quietly accepted their fate.

The Elder turned back around and faced the temple. Beran retreated into the crowd with a cold look from Grindan. One of the battle priests wielded a long pole with an iron wrought collar fashioned to end, thrusting it into the old man's neck. It gripped him tight like a bear trap, squeezing him, choking him. Grindan quickly lunged forward with the red hot brand, searing the old man's left cheek, his free hand grasping behind his trapped head.

Old Caflice yelled, a weak mewing yelp, then collapsed while Grindan firmly held his head, trapped between his grip and the brand. Once Grindan was satisfied, he was released from his grip and the collar. The old man's body dropped to the ground. He moaned as a helpless calf pushed from a heifer's womb, unable to stand, weakened and overwhelmed from the world. Beran swiftly came to his side and dragged the first Elder away as the next stood in his place.

"Come. All of you! Anyone who runs now will be caught. Here is where you receive our mercy. If your kin are not here now, then it is too late," Grindan said.

Alaric looked to his family.

Halig's eyes were filled with such bitterness. He could see his son blamed him for what was to come. At least Edrick and Gaebria were not there. There were so many children gathered. They began to cry, the fearful cries rose into a chorus. Families embraced each other, stumbling forward in groups as the Folthnir warriors surrounded the crowd, herding them closer to the temple.

"Vylkinus is your new god. Swear to him now!" A priest

shouted.

A subdued murmur mumbled a praise to Vylkinus.

"You weak mewlings. Vylkinus does not protect the weak, but the strong, the fearless! As the Theign's property, his protection extends to you."

"You must get behind the others," Alaric instructed Elisial. "There is no other alternative. I will step in front, behind the Elders."

Halig shook his head but said nothing. He looked at his mother, as if hoping she might defy their father's orders, see their father's weakness as he did. See through all this madness. She, too, shook her head, but it was not in defiance but in sorrow, in knowing that this was the beginning of worse things to come. "All right."

As Alaric turned, a man was thrown to the ground, his family shoved forward, following him. It was one of Udela's sons, Ormod and his family. He was crying, as was his wife, daughter and son. They clung to one another passionately, consoling each other.

"These four rejected our brands," a wolfskin declared. Ator motioned for them to be separated from the crowd. They were pushed along until they were forced into the caged wagon. Ormod looked at Alaric and his family as they passed. He pleaded to them, "They raped my wife," he sobbed. "They rapped my wife! How can I swear to these people?"

"Any others desire not to accept our protection?" Ator asked sarcastically.

A few men, Udela's sons, ran to their brother's side. "We won't let you rape our family!"

Elisial looked to Alaric. He looked around, taking in the surroundings. He could hope to rush one, disarm him and what, fight the fifty other armed men, fourteen on horseback. "Get in line, just stay toward the back," he said to his wife.

He began to walk toward Grindan with deliberate steps. "Brand me then, Grindan. I will take each of my family's brands on my body."

Grindan laughed mockingly. "This is not a punishment, everyone must be branded. They must bear the Theign's mark."

Ator called from across the gathering, "Still, grant his request. Brand him for each of his family members."

Elisial gasped.

"Come, hero," Gindan replied. "You might want to close your

eyes to this, for once."

Alaric stepped inside the temple, feeling a pulse of sheer repulsion. A collar was thrust on his neck. The priest held him so he could not retreat from the pain. Grindan took a fresh brand from the forge and pressed the searing metal into Alaric's cheek. Black smoke rose up and flames leapt out. Tears blurred Alaric's sight, distorting Grindan's superior expression.

"Well that's one. How many children were there, six right? Seven, with the miscarriage. And one for beautiful Elisial."

"Where's your mark, friend?" Alaric spat back sardonically.

Grindan lifted his shirt revealing a black inked tattoo over his chest. "The chosen of Vylkinus are not marked like beasts, they are adorned with the painted flesh of warriors."

He pulled another brand out of the furnace.

"Wait," Ator said slipping off his horse, approaching the temple. "I will do this," he said seizing the iron. He plunged the brand into Alaric's other cheek. The sadistic youth let the brand linger far longer than the first, until the iron cooled and he needed another.

Alaric refused to yell out. He bit down on his tongue until he tasted blood. He could easily bite through it, like fresh meat. He could bite it off and just end it. He sunk his fingers into his thighs and tore at the flesh. Pain anywhere felt better than the pain surging through his face.

"That's two."

"Papa!" came a boy's voice from the crowd. Edrick, seemingly hidden among the people ran toward Alaric.

"Edrick!" Elisial yelled after him. He shouldn't have come. Wolfskins seized Edrick just as Halig ran to protect his brother. A fight broke out between Halig and the others. Halig pushed two of the warriors off Edrick, sending his younger brother sprawling over the ground. The other boys soon bested Halig, immobilizing him.

The distracting scene did not phase Ator as he took pleasure not in just torturing Alaric, but in full view of his family. The putrid smell of burning hair and flesh bloated the air.

"Bring the eldest here," Ator commanded. The wolfskins dragged Halig, next to his father. Ator seized another brand and seared Halig's face. Halig flinched. The brand slid off the skin catching his hair on fire. The warriors dragged Halig to a nearby trough and drowned his head, extinguishing the flames.

"Stay still," Ator said to him as they brought him back. The brand sizzled with steam against his drenched head. Halig looked at his father, and screamed through clenched teeth. The wolfskins dropped him after it was done.

Halig mumbled, "I hate you. I hate you all."

Alaric's heart broke.

"Go!" Ator yelled. "Bring me the little Woodcutter."

"No, your father said he hangs," the Huntsman said, from aside.

"Still, I will brand him," Ator said in sadistic glee.

But the warriors hauled Edrick to the cart and threw him in the cage. "Once he is branded, he is your father's property, not yours. You desire to destroy the Theign's property?"

"Fine, then," Ator pointed to the crowd. "Bring me that boy. I want to brand a child."

They pulled a boy, a little younger than Edrick into the temple. One wolfskin grabbed his locks and pulled his face against his chest. Ator struck. The boy screamed terribly, then something unexpected occurred. The boy's éardian lit up like a sun. The light washed over the boy, setting his skin alight, but then quickly faded. The men released the boy and stepped back, afraid of the magick displayed before them.

The boy stood crying. His mother called his name. He ran to her and hugged her. She looked at his cheek, but there was no mark, no wound. The boy screamed when his mother touched it. "It hurts," he yelled and pulled away. His light was gone from his head.

"It protected him," one warrior observed. "There is no scar, no blood."

The Huntsman took in the situation quietly then spoke. "Spare the children for now. We will see what the Theign wishes."

"What of the Woodcutter family? They all have theirs," Ator asked.

The Huntsman took a good look at Alaric and Halig whose light still burned above their heads. There was no flash, no display of magick. "They seem different than the others." He snorted as if their difference was that of an inferior quality. "I care not if they lose their light. Brand them all, then send them back home."

They seized Meghan, Elisial and Eadwyn forcing each through the branding. Alaric felt far worse seeing his beloved treated so harsh, listening to their anguished cries and the overwhelming powerlessness he felt as he watched on, than all the punishment dealt to himself.

The Folthnir youth continued applying all nine brands to Alaric swollen face.

Ator spat on every wound, rubbing his thumb over each festering gash, "How come your pretty light won't save you? You would think after nine, it would do something for you."

"I'm done," the youth declared handing the branding back to Grindan. "Finish with the rest of them."

Ator had Alaric dragged away from the temple and dropped in front of the cart. Edrick reached for him through the bars. "Papa! I know where Sunniva is! We can find her. I found the Woodcutter King! He's in a cottage with…he's there with my friends."

A wolfskin struck the cage with his sword. Ormod scrambled to pull Edrick back, covering his hand over his mouth. Edrick fought against him.

Ator walked up to Edrick. "Your father asked to receive your punishment." He looked to the wolfskins. "Beat him."

The warriors fell over Alaric like a pack of beasts. They beat him in front of all. Beat him until the world fell away.

When Alaric opened his eyes, no one remained. He was alone. Time had passed.

Alaric did not want to move. His flesh was on fire long after the brands has been lifted off his skin. He could barely see through his swollen face.

Edrick called to him like a dream.

Alaric closed his eyes. He had trouble remembering where he was, what had taken place that caused him so much pain. He thought of that place he went before, the place of gray where he felt no more pain. He wished to return there again and never come back.

But it did not return.

Instead a blue light surrounded him, blanketing his body along with a cool sensation, as if Ysig breathed over him. His wounds, the pain, it was released. Alaric knew his éardian was finally leaving him. It would not come back until his soul was separated from his body, to guide it into the Hallowed Halls.

He sank into the earth.

He needed to follow Edrick, to save him. But this time, he could not.

"Alaric…..Alaric," a voice called out. Someone shook his head gently as if wakening him from a night's rest.

"I'm alive." He opened one eye. The swelling had gone. He found his eyes opening to Beran.

"What is it?" Alaric asked.

"The Elders sent me to take you home to your family. I will carry you if you can withstand your wounds…." His voice trailed off. "Your wounds…what happened?"

"I was branded and beaten."

"I know, but what happened? How did they change?"

The young man looked on him with wonder.

"Your éardian is gone," he said, as he stood Alaric up.

"I know," he replied, defeated. Such a thing has never happened to his family. Each had their lights until death. First Edrick, then him. Remarkably, the intense pain was not present, instead he felt hot, as if burned by the sun.

"Each brand is different than the other," Beran described to him, "well, there are some similarities among them. There are four pairings, two marks that are similar to another, and an odd one unlike the others."

The young man was obviously curious, nervous even, but Alaric did not care. He needed to get to Edrick. Maybe the young man noticed Alaric's disinterest, for he changed the subject.

"The Folthnir will be searching everyone's home for those that escaped the mark. We all know you have strangers in your cottage. You must lead them away before they are discovered, or they will join your son on the tree."

The youth's words jolted Alaric to his feet. No! It cannot be! By Telanthyan's will, such an evil cannot be true!

Alaric scowled at the young man. "He's not dead. Take me to the yew or go home. I'm taking Edrick back home."

"All right, I will take you to the hill, but I won't risk letting them see me help you."

That did not surprise Alaric at all. A village filled with cowards, and they punish those who sacrifice everything to help them.

Alaric leaned on the young man until they reached the hill. The sun was setting. The yew cast a long shadow before them. Beran let Alaric go and stepped aside.

"I know we have never really accepted you Woodcutters as one of us, and I know it wasn't right to do so. A lot of us know that, but it's easier to reject you than…."

"Than what? Understand us?"

"Yes, something like that. I don't know. If any of us did, maybe things would have been different."

Alaric considered the young man. "Go home. Take care of your family."

Beran lingered, looking Alaric over. It seemed there was something on his mind.

"Go before they see you," Alaric whispered, betraying his irritation.

"When I look at you I see a brave man, I just don't know if it's foolish like the Elders think, or admirable in a way we never known." With that, he turned and ran.

Alaric turned and stepped into the shadow of the yew tree, remaining there until he reached the top.

What he found, brought him to his knees.

A corona of crows perched above, silent and watchful. Nine bodies hung dead from the branches, Udela, hers sons, their wives and children, and Edrick, his youngest son.

17

THE YEW TREE

THERE WAS DARKNESS until a soft voice dismissed it in two words.

"Hello, Edrick."

Light entered Edrick's eyes like dim, faint particles drifting through a sandglass aperture.

"It's you," Edrick said in surprise, the young elf girl, Aslenissia.

"I am sorry, Edrick. I warned you darkness was coming," replied the lyrical voice. Night had fallen, but he could not remember the sun setting. It seemed only moments before daylight loomed and he was carted to the yew tree. There around him hung Udela and her family, their faces partially torn apart from the voracious crows. They did not leave the world peacefully.

"Am I….dead?"

"Mostly dead."

"Mostly dead?" perplexed by her cryptic answer.

"Indeed, mostly dead had I not happened upon you and kept you from wandering. Like them." Pointing at the other eight.

Like them? Poor Udela. "Why did they have to kill them?" He always thought her mean and bitter, but seeing her dead filled his heart with pity. Something he never imagined he would feel for the feisty old lady.

Aslenissia bowed her head in condolence.

This seemed similar to the dream, the one he had the night Father returned home, but stranger, odd, as if he stood where dreams and waking collided.

He scanned the area for his body. It was nowhere to be found. If he was a ghost then where was his corpse? He lifted his hands, felt for his chest and stomach, squished his nose and rubbed his eyes. His body felt reassuringly solid, yet slightly numb, like sleeping on his arm until it lost feeling. His body was that state when feeling starts to return, limp and paralytic.

"Are you dead too?" he finally asked.

She shook her head softly and laughed, as if he made a jest. "No."

"Oh," he looked at her carefully wanting to understand what she was really. She was so beautifully perfect. Flawless. "Are you a goddess then?"

"Oh, Edrick," she laughed and took his hand. "I am just an elf." Life spread through him with her touch, up his arm and into his body. At least it felt like life.

"No, you are more than that."

She smiled at him shyly and looked away letting his hand slip through her perfect fingers. He could not keep his eyes off her. Amongst the dead and cooling night, her presence was a warm light that brought him peace. How could she not be a goddess?

"You have a great many deal of things to learn, Edrick, so you must return to your family and grow to be a man."

Memories of the Folthnir stirred slowly within him. They killed him, same as the others. Hung him from a rope that reached high into the tree. His life was squeezed out of him. They denied him breath. It was violent and cruel. Yet he did not feel their cruelty in the moment. Life was just a detached memory.

"I can wait, for that," he reassured her.

He remembered seeing his father at the bottom of the hill as he hung, his father's face, his expression of immense loss…and something else. Something that did not belong on his father's face, something he could not recognize: defeat. Edrick moved his feet, they were sluggish and seemed heavy, seemed disconnected from him altogether. He needed to tell his father he was fine, that it was all right. He knew his father needed that.

"No, wait Edrick!" The elf cried out, seizing his arm with both her hands. Her grip was tight. She felt as if she were tied to the tree, immovable and immense. He could not budge.

"Was that my father down there? It was, was it not? He looked so.......sad." He pulled against her delicate fingers.

"Edrick you must stay near your body," there was a desperation in her voice that stopped Edrick faster than any hold on him.

"What body?" There was nothing there, in the tree or on the ground.

"You can't see it. You are not allowed. When you are this near Death, you are blind to your own body because It wants you to leave it behind. You must not move or you can't return."

Haunting caws erupted above him in the dark. It felt ugly and wrong, like gleeful laughter at the news of someone's death.

"The crows are near, Edrick. They are searching for you."

He wanted to doubt her, wanted to disbelieve that he was mostly, or any part dead, but he knew she did not lie. She would not lie to him.

"What do I do?"

"Just stay and talk to me. We are waiting for someone to come here. They will get you back into your body and you will help them."

"Who?"

"Your brothers."

"Baldice?"

Her face fell at the mention of his brother's name. "No, not Baldice." She sighed and regained her composure. "Brothers you never met. Brothers that have known you since birth."

"What brothers?"

"They were born before you, but died in the same day. I saved them from Her. I kept them secret. They told me you can send them into the Æthyr."

Edrick didn't understand anything she described. His thoughts turned back to his father. "Where's my father, can you see him down there? Is he still there?"

"No, some of the villagers took him away, back to your house I think. He is being cared for."

"Why don't they just kill him?" he asked with a heavy heart, incomprehensible to the Folthnir's desire to torture any of them. There was no reply. A young child's crying rose up from somewhere in the village. A little boy sobbing, calling for his mother. The cawing crows became excited, mocking the sound of distress. Again, Edrick moved, this time toward the child.

Aslenissia blocked his path, holding out her hand. "Edrick, you cannot help him, yet. You cannot follow that child until you wake."

The unseen crows chanted louder, and faster. They chased after the child's cries of anguish.

He bent sideways to peer past her, into the darkness blanketing the village. The child wailed, lost and alone. It was too much for him, if no one was going to the child, he had to. Then three strange orbs floated up the hill toward them with three distinct colors, gold, silver and amber.

"Faeries?"

"Yes and no. Your brothers have arrived."

"These are my brothers? Why don't they look like me?"

"I'm not entirely sure I can answer that question. These are their éardians and they have held on to their infant souls for quite some time. These faeries are weary and need rest. Protecting their souls from Her and Her minions is difficult and strenuous."

The orbs surrounded her, circling her body, spiraling up to her crown and sat above her brow like a starlet diadem. Each, as wide as his hand, scintillating with life.

"They are beautiful."

"Yes. It is time for you to go back, Edrick. What will you do when you awake?"

Edrick thought about it, fought against the fog that settled over his mind. He wanted to see his father, to see how much he suffered from his injuries. More importantly he wanted to see his face, to see if the unbendable strength he came to know all his life returned to his father's eyes, that what he witnessed at the yew tree was a mistake in his perception.

He shook his head in frustration. There was more. That was not why he was there, back in the village, why he even came to the Elder Hall. He needed to take the children away. He needed to find that crying child and take them all away until the darkness lifted.

"I'm going back into the woods with as many children as I can. And I am going to find Sunniva and bring them all into the Faerie Realm."

"Oh no, Edrick! You must stay out of the woods. There are terrible things in there I fear!"

"I know," the terrible witches flashed through his thoughts, and that tall, horned dæmon, the Erlking. "But I have an ally, a long lost king who knows the way to the Faerie Realm." It felt good boasting of his new ally, his new relationship with this legendary figure no one knew existed. As if he were someone of great importance, doing something that mattered.

"Really?" Aslenissia leaned closer, her eyes wide as if told the best news in the world. "Who is this king? I am sure I must know him."

"Well, I don't know his proper name, but he is the Woodcutter King. The King tricked into a woodcutter's life. "

"Tricked? How?"

Edrick quickly conveyed his tale of the Woodcutter King, without any of the flare of theatrics that usually accompanied his recitals.

"Your tale sounds familiar, I'm not sure how. I forget a great many things when I'm away from home. I....I," she collapsed onto the ground, thoroughly distraught. Her lips pouting like plucked rose petals, her face darkened, hung low. "I just need to find my way home, Edrick, and I might be able to help you."

Edrick knelt down next to her. He wanted to put his arms around her, lift her head and console her, but touching her seemed disrespectful. He, unworthy to share her space.

"Where is your home?"

"In the woods. Somewhere." She gazed out into the darkness, out over the hidden forest.

"How have you lost your way?"

"The woods were not always as they are now. It used to be possessed with its own light, before I was born they say. Now there is no light and I cannot see my way past. I have been wandering for a while now. It wasn't until I found you children playing in the woods that I realized I was not alone."

"Were you there when they attacked us and stole Sunniva?"

She slowly nodded her head.

"I sat at the circle many times, hoping it could lead me home. My people built it, so I hope someone might find me."

"Where are all the elves? I thought they should be protecting the woods."

"They sleep. They sleep and dream, dream of a world that once was, dream of a world that should be."

"Oh. Then we will wake them when we find them."

The little elf girl looked up into the Edrick's face. She placed her hand on his cheek and kissed him, a small gentle peck on his cheek.

"I believe you can, Edrick. Someday I hope you become a Master of the woods like your sires, and expel this darkness, and return the light."

Edrick breathed heavily. A strange sensation as there was no breath from his ghostly form, no air exchanged, just the empty movement of his lungs, but none from his heart.

"I will my goddess. I shall worship you as my own."

"No, Edrick, you cannot." She was upset by what he said, troubled. He meant to honor her but instead he seemed to offend her. "Do not worship me or my people as your sires have done in the past. It will not benefit me, nor you."

Edrick felt he could not worship another, but did not wish to upset her further. He reached for father's torc. It was heavy now, uncomfortable and constraining. He did not want it anymore, it seemed fitting for her to have what was so cherished by his father, by his family for generations. The three orbs floating above her brow were of the same color as the metal flakes, one copper, one silver and one gold.

"Did they have names, my brothers?"

"No, they did not live long enough to bare names. You could ask your mother or father, but these spirits do not know it. But every being has a name at their creation, Edrick. A secret name given to them by Ilpha."

"Ilpha?"

"She is the light of the stars; she is the fragrance of the flowers; she is the warmth of the light; she is source of laughter and the reason we smile." The elf girl spoke with a soft reverence and passion, Edrick was moved by her words.

"Is she your Goddess? Is she your name for Lhodyn?"

"NO, Edrick, you must not say that!" she corrected with harsh whispers. "Ilpha is no goddess. Ilpha is more. Deeper, higher, fuller."

"I am sorry I don't understand."

"It is not your fault. We are forbidden from discussing this with mortals. My father said that mortals easily misunderstand certain things and speaking partially, without full instruction can cause more harm than good. I am sorry, maybe someday we can speak more, but I am afraid I cannot speak now. Anyway, we have indulged our childish desires with this idle talk. I must get you along your way,

Edrick. That is all that is important right now, in this moment. You must leave the dead before Death remains on you too long. Remaining as you are is like standing in the rain, at first you are only partially wet, but stand for a while in the rain and you will be soaked same as plunging into a pool."

"Will I see you again? Will you remain here?"

"I hope we will see each other again. My heart says such a thing will happen. I will try to remain with you, Edrick, at least until you near the forest, even if you do not see me. It is such an evil place now."

"I will look for you in my dreams. And I will find a way to your home. I swear to you." After I find Sunniva, he thought.

"I accept your oath, Woodcutter son. And it is my desire you do so."

She lifted her hands up to her brow, both together, cupped. One of the orbs, golden with light, floated into her palms.

"Edrick, your brother loves you very much and thanks you."

"Thanks me for what?"

"Your journey here has allowed him an escape to the Æthyr. This one will stand in your place tonight."

"And what of the other two?"

"They will endure on as they always have. I will see to that."

The gold light grew, expanding in diameter until all the world was awash with golden brilliance.

It burned into Edrick's mind.

The darkness did not return, but when Edrick opened his eyes, night remained and all the brilliance of the starry skies opened up to him, and in its midst, a golden orb hung glimmering, shining with delight, prominent amongst all the other stars.

And still the lost child cried out in the night, as the crows descended upon the world. Edrick sat up from where he was lying, rope still cinched tightly around his neck like a dead serpent. He pulled at it and managed to open the noose wide enough to slip his head out. The other end of the rope had been severed, cut clean by a blade.

In the dirt he caught the flicker of metal. It was a strange knife of chatoyant steel, plunged into the earth. Edrick pulled it out and tucked it beneath his belt.

He rubbed his wounds, the skin was torn and bled around his

neck. It ached and throbbed, but he took no notice as he deeply inhaled the cool night air, drank in the night until he felt it in his veins. His heart pounded hard against his ribs. He was alive, fully alive.

"Maaamaaa come back!" Droned the little voice. "Come back mama! Maaamaa….maaama!" came the wailing cries of the little boy. "Mama! Mama!" the voice continued, each syllable erupted out like a hiccup, convulsed between sobs, "I want mama, come back!" The boy's voice felt so alone and helpless, lost and hopeless. Edrick stood up, paused as he regained the sensation of his feet, of the solid world beneath him. There was an overwhelming urgency to rescue the boy, to hold him, take him away from the village before he was discovered by the wolfskins and silenced forever.

Edrick ran down the hill until he nearly lost his balance, staggering a few steps as he reached the bottom. I'm coming, he told the child in his thoughts. I will take you from here, where you won't need to cry again.

The boy was easy to find, near the Hall hidden in the shadows of the buildings. It was one of Udela's grandsons, a child but a year younger than Sunniva had been. Edrick scooped him up and bolted through the darkness like a thief, stealing off before he was discovered.

The two of them rushed south, away from the village, until Edrick marked a person in the short distance, with a faerie light lighting his path. Edrick halted and stared into the dark. It was Halig. His brother was jogging closer. Edrick waited until they met.

"Edrick!" his brother nearly shouted. He embraced his youngest brother, until he noticed the boy clinging to Edrick's back. "You are alive! Incredible! How did you escape!"

"Someone cut my rope." He pulled out the knife and handed it to Halig. "I got lucky." He kept his experience with Aslenissia a secret. "Your face, Halig, looks bad." His brother's cheek was a swollen, blistering gash.

"Nothing a Woodcutter can't endure," he said dismissively. "Mother treated it and said the best she could do is leave a beautiful scar. You know how she is."

Halig kneeled down, looking at Edrick and the boy. "Who is this? Is he injured?"

"I think he is one of Udela's grandsons. He has not spoken to me yet. I found him crying for his mother."

"I am glad you found him. Quickly, return home. Mother will be overwhelmed to see you. She will attend to the boy. Edrick, listen now, I can't stay here anymore. Father has lost his strength and cowers same as all these other villagers. He almost had you killed, didn't he? I can't take it anymore. I'm leaving for a while. I am going to do what father should have done, find a way to defeat the barbarians. Tell mother and Meghan I love them. Tell them I had to leave and not to worry."

Edrick was in disbelief. How could he leave? Mother needed him. Should he tell him about the Faerie Realms? He would feel better for sure. "Where are you going? What will you do?"

"I am not sure where, but not far I hope. I have not abandoned you, Edrick," he was quite earnest. "It is madness to live here. Father should have had us leave before today. Now I must find a way for us to leave. Stay with mother! Do as she says. Promise me, Edrick."

"I promise."

"You are growing older, Edrick, and you need to become a man quickly or you will die. Like this boy, you found him and rescued him. You must see to his care. You made it your responsibility. A man honors his responsibilities."

"I understand. I can do it."

"Good. Well, then I will see you again, little brother. I can certainly use someone with your courage by my side. Someday."

"Someday…"

"Goodbye, Edrick."

"Goodbye, Halig."

He watched his brother run off into the dark night until his éardian disappeared from sight. He suddenly remembered the torc. Take the torc Halig! But it was too late.

Edrick thought about his brother's words, to return home, but he already had made a promise to his friends and so ran back to the byrgen where Gaebria and Tredan waited with other children just outside the burial grounds. Relief swept over him seeing most of the village children farther away from harm, closer to a sanctuary that will keep them all safe.

"Edrick!" His two friends called to him and rushed to meet him. "Unbelievable!" Tredan exclaimed seeing his friend come into view. Gaebria held out her arms to relieve him of the child, but Edrick clung to the boy who finally calmed, falling silent for most of their travel.

"Who is he?" asked Gaebria.

"I found him in the dark. He is under my protection now. Wurt is his name."

"You want me to take him," she offered.

"I can carry him farther. He is not heavy."

"I thought you were dead," Tredan interrupted. "I saw you, I mean I saw them take you to the tree. I heard the screams from Udela's family. And a murder of crows rushed out of the woods, flying swiftly to the yew. I thought you died."

"Almost died."

Gaebria stepped a little closer and touched his cheek with the back of her hand. Her face shifted from apprehension to relief as she rubbed her skin over his, as if to make sure he was truly a living thing.

"Oh Edrick, your neck. We should take you to your mother…"

"NO!" Edrick shouted more harshly then he intended. Wurt jumped and started crying. They all waited and said nothing until Edrick had the boy calm again.

"We cannot go back," Edrick whispered now that Wurt had quieted. He clung to Edrick like a frightened bear cub to a tree. "I will be fine enough until we reach the faerie lands."

"We gathered as many as we could," Tredan said. "Since they were all at the Hall mostly, it was not as difficult as we thought."

"Some of them saw you taken away. Tredan and I were discussing if we should see if you were alive and needed help or," her voice dropped off into a near whisper, "should we just leave without you."

Edrick could tell that most of them did not wish to return for him. He did not expect the other children would, but he wondered if Gaebria or Tredan hesitated to come help him. The thought wounded him so much he avoided asking, so as to avoid an answer he wished not to hear.

"Well, there are a lot here," Edrick said hopeful. "It is much too dangerous to attempt to rescue more children. I say we take who we have to the Faerie Realm and try to come for the others in a week or so."

Gaebria looked at Tredan, confusion written on both their faces.

"Are you sure we can do that? We ought to ask the woodsman first, I think."

"Of course, we can and will do that," Edrick said with all confidence. "If he truly cares for us he would make sure we are all safe."

Edrick led them away toward the forest. Many stopped as they drew near, yards from the tree line. None of them had ever stepped a foot inside, nor imagined doing so. It was as if asking them to walk into a nightmare. They all spoke in whispers, voicing their trepidation, questioning Edrick's plan. The night was dark but the light of the children's faeries was as good as any candle. The golden star, Edrick noticed, twinkled above them, as if encouraging him.

They couldn't go back now.

"I know all of you are scared and I hear your concerns about walking into the forest, at night. But you all have seen what horror awaits all of us in daylight outside our very doorsteps. Our parents cannot protect us! My father, who is the strongest man I know, cannot stop this world of evil. So we must escape if we can. It would be no different if out in the wild you and your family encountered a bear. You would hope your father held off the bear while you could run away. That is heroic. Every one of us would wish we could stay and fight the bear, but we would all perish. So too if we remain here."

"Yes," an older girl replied, "but this feels as if we are leaving our parents behind as they sleep, so the bear can fall upon them, while we escape." Many boys and girls nodded in agreement.

"It feels like that. I understand. These are not the best of circumstances. But I will say this because it is the truth. They invited the bear into your home, to allow it to sleep and eat whatever it wished, and now they cannot object if the bear wishes to eat you, to devour your families. That is their fault, not yours. So let them face their decisions without harm falling on us, who rely on them to protect us. And if they fail that consideration, then we deserve better!

"This little boy clinging to me is the same as you and I! He just wants his mother to return to him, but she never will. For she hangs at the end of a rope! He is the last of his family. For his family took a stand against them. Finally! And left him behind in the shadows. Luckily, it was I that found him before the wolfskins. Take a look at Wurt, who had no one until I came for him. How long until we find ourselves in the same situation? You can return home, and stand by your family if your honor calls you to do so, that I understand. Or instead follow me. Together we will be fostered by the faeries and guarded by the elves. There will be no evil among those people who could never abide by such corruption. There is a king of men in this forest that will lead us to the Faerie Realm, lead us away from this evil. We will find peace, and I hope, our family will find us there, someday."

There was no reply at first, not a child stirred in reaction. Edrick surprised them, surprised himself with his own feelings, finding his voice.

"All right, Edrick, we trust you. Lead us," the girl replied.

They moved on into the darkened forest. Behind him, children held back their screams, muffled their cries, but each one was taken by terror. Gaebria did her best to calm them, she retold the story of the cottage and the wondrous food that awaited all of them. She speculated about how the Faerie Realm must be, like the woodsman's cottage, but tenfold better. Then some of the children started to add their idea of it; honey-bread houses, rivers of sweetened wine, fields of ponies and fluffy white sheep, sheep with golden fleeces and other such fanciful notions. Suddenly Edrick felt relaxed, listening to their banter, getting more and more excited; reminding him of his brothers and sisters and all the moments they had in the woods, their private place of fancy.

This felt right, he thought. Finally something felt right.

Before they reached the cottage, faeries of purple and blue lit up around them, descending out of the tree canopy and rising from the shrubs. They escorted the children through the forest, making the children far more at ease, for it was apparent Edrick spoke the truth.

"It's a sign, Edrick," Gaebria shouted, "that they trust us! They are so beautiful! There are so many."

Edrick nodded. Wurt stirred in his arms.

"Faeries!" he said shyly, in his small voice.

"Yes, they are here for you little one." Edrick could feel the boy smile over his shoulder where he rested his head.

The woodland lights delivered the children to the cottage, without harm of beast or monster. "This is it! This is the cottage!" Gaebria proclaimed raising the excitement among the group. The cottage door cracked open. Bron stepped out to greet them, followed by Rodor and Rinan.

"Edrick, you actually did it. The Brownman had his doubts but I told him that you were the most stubborn, relentless child I know." As he drew close he leaned closer. "Traits you inherited from your father."

"Maybe," Edrick replied, more to himself. He once admired his father, yet now, seeing his father falter, he wished not to be compared to that.

"Come inside, we arranged the room to fit everyone inside."

The cottage was not as it was before, the long dinner table was gone as with all the chairs. Bron led them inside and had them all sit on the floor. The Woodcutter King was standing by the hearth, greeting them all with wordless nods and an awkward smile, but did not speak until they were all seated and Bron closed the door.

Edrick passed Wurt, who was now fast asleep, to Gaebria. The four, with Tredan sat at the front with Rodor and Rinan. Total, thirty six children from nine families, out of twenty seven, crowded the small cottage. There was no space for one to cross from the back of the room to the front without someone leaning into another's lap.

The Woodcutter King stroked his beard seemingly calm, taking in his new guests. His eyes roved over each new face, winking reassuringly at the younger ones. "What brave and daring children you are. Hoorah! Many times in the past, people are called to partake a difficult journey and only a minority have the bravado to undertake this calling, as all of you have demonstrated. Well done, children! Well done! I must apologize that I cannot provide the food that you no doubt heard report, but what I do have is sweetbread with butter, from my own personal stock. And rare fruit from foreign markets. Please take as much as you want."

Baskets of bread and fruit were passed around. The bread was warm, as if freshly baked. The fruit sweet and tangy, plump and exquisitely ripe. None of the children were disappointed, though the selection was limited, the flavors were beyond any of their experiences. And even though they ate enough to fill their bellies, the flavors left them desiring more. Many of the children surreptitiously pocketed a fruit or torn loaf when they believed others were not looking.

"Worry not, little ones," the woodcutter began as most of the dining drew to an end, "we will only remain this night and by morning we will be off to the Faerie Realm! There, you shall feast as the faerie king's guest. I have sent word, to expect such a fine company at their court by tomorrow evening. You are greatly anticipated and will be well received. All your worries will be lifted by sunset tomorrow."

The children erupted in excited chatter. This was really going to happen! It was incredible, that they should walk out of their village and into legend and faerie tale. It seemed so magical.

"Thank you, Brownman!" said one girl. "We never knew that you, or any of this could be real."

"Thank you, Edrick," shouted another, followed by all the children shouting their gratitude. The woodcutter walked up to Edrick and lifted him up. "You have done well. Greater than I expected, in fact." Then, the woodcutter's face changed, it fell from glee to concern.

"Something strange about you, Edrick." He said, looking the boy up and down, examining him as if searching for something. "Something has overcome you Edrick, am I right?"

Edrick looked to his friends for help, but they were as stunned as he. "What happened to you, Edrick? You are not the same as you were when you left."

"I don't know, sir? I am…just me."

"No," he corrected and let go of Edrick, taking a step back. He looked out over the children in the room whose gaze were all transfixed on Edrick and him. "You are not the same."

Silence settled over the room. No one stirred. Edrick felt anger rising in him once again, unwelcomed like a bear crashing through the wall. He could not understand the sudden change in the man. He suddenly felt like the outcast once again, like the unwanted child. "If I had changed sir, it is for the better," Edrick offered weakly. He searched for a reason the man suddenly disliked him. "I know I was mistaken about you a day ago, but I know better now."

The woodcutter folded his arms, shaking his head slightly, as if saying, "this will not do." Instead he said dismissively, "find a place on the floor to sleep." He turned to the others. "Sleep now my children, we travel by morning light into the Twilight Kingdoms. It is a short journey but we will have to move fast, for the forest is not entirely without with its dangers."

The atmosphere in the room shifted fully from celebratory to sullen, and it felt as though they blamed Edrick for the sudden change. Edrick lay with his friends, who offered reassuring half-smiles. He kept his back toward them and stared at the fire burning low in the hearth. The woodcutter made his way to the back of the room, toward the door. He grabbed the lantern and wood-ax, then exited. No one knew where he was going or when he would be back. The children whispered amongst themselves until one by one, sleep overtook them.

Edrick stared into the fire, watching it dance and twirl until it failed and only the red coals glowed in the darkening room.

Edrick woke up several times, sleep was not his friend that night. He sat up each time, to look around the room. There was no sign of the Woodcutter King and Edrick was sure he could spot the larger figure if he had lay down amongst them.

All night, Edrick remained still until dawn's light spilled through the cracks of the door and shuttered windows. He thought of the children still in the village. If he were to return, how would he get them to join him? He concluded they must first arrive in the Faerie Realm, then he must bring one of the other children back to corroborate their journey. But who among them, he wondered, would be willing to leave, to risk the woods again to bring back the others. He hoped his friends were such people.

He heard movement outside, so he decided to investigate. He caught sight of other children, stirring, eyes open and marking his path through the room. Edrick stepped outside and found the Woodcutter King attending the long table that was once inside the cottage. It was laden again with fine, curious foods. The aroma drew him until he found himself sitting.

The other children were quick to rise and were out the door, beckoned by the savory food filling the crisp morning air. Strangely, no one spoke, but simply ate, as if they had just walked out of the woods, starved for days. They all ate until their bellies ached with too much food, but still they craved more, to taste more.

Above them in the growing light of dawn, blue and purple lights swirled around the tree canopy, like excited glow bugs.

The Woodcutter King sat at the end of the table through the entire meal, seemingly merry and content. "Eat up, children, for you will certainly need energy today. But we will not march hard, indeed I hope you find the stroll through my woods pleasant. I have made sure our path is secure and will be without disturbance. The faeries will accompany us and see us through."

Edrick caught a peculiar look passing across the man's face as his gaze settled on him for a moment. "Sir, once we arrive in the land of the faeries, when will we be able to get the rest of the children?"

The evasive king rose up, as if not hearing the question. "Gather your things, children, we should be on our way."

The company of children marched out into the forest, led by the woodcutter with his ax upon his shoulder, then Bron, Edrick and the rest. Most marched in pairs, holding each other's hands as they traveled this strange world of the trees. Birds chirped and shrilled, insects buzzed and clicked, animals shook and rustled the shrubs and branches above, alarming the children. The deeper the forest, the more fear set upon them.

The king, ever cheerful, kept reassuring them. "Fear not children, this is my forest. The only way goblyns or worse will get ya is through me, you have my word." His words had little effect on the smaller ones, who began to cry and called a return to home, to their mothers and fathers. The older ones tried to explain that home was not safe anymore, that they were going to a safe place. Wurt cried for Edrick, to hold him.

"It's fine little one. Just shut your eyes. When we are in the Twilight Realms you may open your eyes and behold the wonder. I think all our troubles will be lifted."

As they journeyed farther into the thick of the woods, the feeling of something evil emanated through the trees, even Edrick felt uncomfortable. It was the same feeling he had the night father returned. The children became afraid and started crying. The woodsman laughed with zest. "There is nothing to fear, children," his voice booming and crashing through the trees, "I am master of these woods!" His voice was loud and deep, heavier than it needed to be, certainly it startled many of the children further.

Gaebria too, seemed to have lost her enthusiasm, and grew concerned. "Sir," she said shyly, "the children are upset, maybe we can rest? How much farther is it?"

"Rest?" the man asked, as if the idea were a foreign notion to him. "It would be just down the path there." He said pointing. "We must cross the river, then not too far. Can't you hear it?"

Indeed, the sounds of water filtered through the trees. In moments, they were upon the river where an old, ruined stone bridge spanned the width, seemingly repaired recently. Timber had been used to connect the spans on both sides of the river, lashed together with leather, as if it were hastily made. The timber beams were stripped of bark, smooth and moist.

"We shouldn't cross," Edrick said to Tredan. "My father said the river marks the truly wild part of the woods. We were told to never come to the river."

Tredan looked around, wide eyed and shook his head. "These are the wild woods, Edrick. I can't imagine the other side to be anything different."

"They are. My father said so."

"Edrick, I respect your father," Bron interjected, "but as you said, our parents have let us down, so we must decide for ourselves. We have come this far, we can go all the way." Bron looked out across the river. He was the only one that seemed unafraid, indeed he was curious about the forest.

"Watch your step, children." The Woodcutter King said. "Stay in the middle of the bridge. Take small steps for the wood is slippery, and rounded."

The river spanned some thirty yards. It flowed slow and smooth up river then rushed against boulders directly beneath the span, churning the water further downriver. Edrick looked up river and down. He wondered where it came from and where it flowed. Could it possibly reach the great Lake Ythrodor? Or the even the Sea?

"Do you think this flows into the lake or the Sea?" he asked Bron.

The young man merely shrugged.

"There's no way it could reach the Sea, it must empty into Ythrodor."

"What lake?" Gaebria asked.

"There is a great and huge lake east of this land, the size as any sea, but the water is sweet like spring water, on the other side of the Wudelic. It is the end of civilization. Beyond that, nothing but monsters and devils."

"Really? I can't imagine such an awful place," Gaebria replied. She walked behind Edrick and Bron, stepping exactly as they stepped.

"It's true. Elzera is from beyond Lake Ythrodor. All her people fled their lands ages ago. She says there is nothing for men beyond the lake."

"The Sea, it flows into the Sea," answered the king.

"Really? All the way to the Sea?" Tredan asked in disbelief.

"Yes, it flows far north through the desolated lands of an old kingdom of men then through mountains and then the Sea."

"Have you seen the Sea?"

"No," he said simply.

"Moira!" a girl cried out, followed by a large splash. A girl fell into the river, now thrashing about, desperately keeping her head above water.

"Diera! Someone do something," her sister cried out

"Everyone off the bridge quickly," the king yelled. "Fast, but do not run!"

The children moved swiftly, holding one another's hands tightly. Gaebria squeezed Edrick's hand hard and they both moved off the bridge. The king was the last off, making sure everyone crossed safely.

"Hurry," Edrick said, moving through the crowd of panicking children, stepping toward the king. "We must do something, go after her."

"Can you swim?" he asked calmly.

"Yeah, but, we must…"

"We must what? The silly girl leaned over the edge and fell in. Did I not say the woods were dangerous, and the bridge is the least of what should concern you."

Edrick looked at him, taken aback. "It was an accident. Surely there must be a boat around."

"Feel free to search for one. We must get going, come children."

The king moved along the path away from the river. No one moved.

"Let's go, children." An angry glare flashed over his face. The children hesitated, but relented. They shuffled their feet slowly down the path. Diera's sister remained, pacing at the edge of the river bank. Bron and Edrick approached her.

"We will look for her, too. Maybe there is a boat."

Edrick looked around. The trees here were hewn back, there were wooden stumps all along the river bank surrounding the bridge.

"Hurry!" the woodcutter called impatiently. "Any that stay behind will be on their own."

Bron looked at Edrick, seemingly sharing his growing doubt in the woodcutter's leadership.

"Come on, Moira, we must go. We can't get left behind."

He reached out to her, but she pulled away. "I won't leave."

"Bron, you see all the stumps," Edrick asked.

"What?" he looked up, and glanced around. "Yeah, why you want to make a boat?"

"Bron, the bridge was repaired from this side of the river."

"So?"

"No one lives this side of the river."

"Maybe the woodcutter did it. We have to go, I don't see the children. Moira come. Don't stay here alone."

She shook her head. Bron lifted her gently and held her in both arms, to their surprise, she did not fight back. She leaned into him and cried into his chest.

"Let's go then."

Edrick took one last look at the river, seeing if he could see Diera. He saw nothing but the sparkling surface of the water. He wondered if she would be taken all the way to the sea.

They ran off after the group and found them not very far down the path. This side of the river, the woods grew thick, the forest floor choked with brambles and thorny shrubs, dots of blood red berries dispersed throughout. The forest path grew wider, the packed dirt yielded to an ancient cobbled road like exposed forest bones, bent and twisted, lined with weeds erupting between the stone gaps.

"This is a road," Edrick remarked with surprise. "How did a road get in here?"

"My guess would be the same people who built the bridge."

The map! Edrick shoulders slumped. He lost it. No, it was taken from his dead body. Those bastards stole his map. Of all the things he could lose. He shook the torc around his neck. He would rather they have taken this then his map. He was sure there were secret villages in the forest revealed there. If he only had it, he could ask the Woodcutter King.

"The old bridge, maybe, but who built the new bridge?" Edrick replied.

He gave Bron a knowing look and moved to the head of the procession. Gaebria walked with Tredan. Edrick looked at their hands, to make sure they were not holding one another, to his relief they were not.

"Sir," Edrick asked.

The king did not reply, or really seemed to hear or notice Edrick.

Gaebria looked to Edrick apologetically, "Sir," she repeated for him.

"Hmm, oh. Yes little one?" He glanced at her as if waking from a dream. "What is on your mind?"

"Well it's Edrick. He was trying to get your attention."

The king half turned to see the young Woodcutter standing next to her. "Oh, didn't notice you boy. Letting a girl do your talking for you? Ha! What is it then?" he asked curtly.

What?! She wasn't speaking for me, he thought, you just weren't listening!

"Who repaired the bridge? I mean, who would use it?"

"The bridge? Not sure. I use it."

Edrick wasn't satisfied. "But something must have built it from this side of the forest. No one lives in this forest except goblyns and monsters, you said so."

The children were listening, he knew. He wanted them to hear.

"Yes, but the path is clear today as I said. We will be safe all the way there. See, those lights above us. Beautiful faeries they are. Cast charms over us you know."

This seemed to reassure the children.

"Was it, the goblyns?"

The king stopped suddenly and sharply turn around. "Don't speak of such vile creatures while they are near, boy!"

"Maybe you should let him guide us without more interruptions, Edrick," Gaebria suggested attempting to diffuse the tension.

The woodcutter king stood tall, crossing his arms. "Well boy, shall you waylay us further or do you have more questions. Have them out now."

"I do have more questions like how did this road get here and where exactly is this Faerie Realm, I mean how do we reach it. Is it in the forest, like a city, or is it hidden with magick, because I have seen structures built by the elves in other parts of the forest. And I have spoken to an elf, and she warned me not to take the children into the woods, which I thought would be fine until we crossed the river and now I am thinking she is right. That we ought not be crossing the river. Father says never to cross the river and that there are secrets that are best left alone."

Gaebria, Tredan and Bron were dumbstruck by Edrick's fuming reply. Gaebria motioned for him to calm down, but he ignored her. By this time, the entire group halted and watched the two.

"And when are we going back for the other children?" Edrick demanded. He knew there would be time to discuss this, but he wanted to know what the woodsman would say in that moment. "I think we ought to go back for them as soon as we reach safety. They can't spend another day with those bastards that tortured my father, branded all their parents like livestock, stole and ate our food and call themselves our protectors. We have to go back for them tomorrow."

The woodsman did not react, he remained still, looking down to Edrick. Edrick felt as if he were shrinking beneath the larger, taller man with every second he stared at him, blank faced and annoyingly unperturbed.

"The faeries," little Wurt shouted in dismay. "Where did they go?"

All the children looked overhead. The blue and purple streaking light had dissipated above them, like candles at the end of their wick. The children grew suddenly concerned. Such an unexpected change could not bode good things.

The king simply raised his eyebrow, then shook his head slightly.

"Yes, they are gone," he spoke gently, then his voice raised up, booming over them once again, "but they will be back as soon as we get along." He placed his hand beneath Edrick's chin, lifting his head, his entire hand nearly wrapping ear to ear. "I see now," he didn't seem to be addressing Edrick, rather thinking out loud, "I see what has changed."

"What?" Edrick asked, muffled through a jaw that could not move in the large man's hand.

"I see they nearly killed you, didn't they. Weeeeeeell...." His voice trailed off. There was a change in his voice that caused Edrick to jerk back, but the man's hand squeezed down around his skull with the weight of a boulder. Edrick even tried to shake his head, but couldn't move. His strength seemed to drain away, like falling asleep when you fight to stay awake.

"Bron," the woodsman ordered with authority. "You have been a good lad. I trust you to handle the children for a moment. He released Edrick who slumped to the ground like a caught rodent released from a dog's maw. "You are nearly a man now, so I'm putting you in charge. Lead the children down the path. We will catch up with you shortly after Edrick and I have a discussion."

Bron hesitated. He looked at Gaebria and Tredan, Rinan and Rodor and the rest. The children were frightened. They were scared. Each one were looking to them for safety.

"But Edrick raised some good questions, sir, I think I would like to know the answers myself."

Some of the braver children nodded, and voiced their agreement as well.

"Children," his voice was filled with dire urgency. "We cannot wait here. We have to keep moving. Edrick's anger has driven the faeries away. They will return if we show them they have nothing to fear. They love good children, but boys like these," he pointed an accusing finger at Edrick, "that murder these beautiful creatures and defy their betters with suspicious questions, will drive the faeries away. Then we will have no protection through these woods and no way of getting into the Faerie Realm."

The children clung to one another, trembling, afraid of the woodsman, the forest, and even Edrick. He could see it in their faces, their own doubts about him had swung the other way, in his disfavor.

"All right," Bron agreed, "let's keep moving. Tredan take the rear make sure no one wanders. Everyone stay in pairs. Gaebria, let's go."

The children moved off, just like that. Edrick knew he wouldn't be joining them. He felt that they knew that as well and simply walked away.

He watched them march down the winding road until they were out of sight, and out of hearing.

"Wahahahaha," rolled a deep rumbling laugh, one Edrick heard not too long ago, a laugh that startled him, jolting him out of his skin. The woodsman's hand seized Edrick behind the neck and lifted off the ground and into the air. His feet dangling.

"What are you?" Edrick choked.

"The Woodcutter King, whahahaha," the deep voice mocked. He turned and sprinted into the woods holding Edrick like a rabbit caught by the ears. He crashed through the forest, busting brambles, using Edrick to open the way. He cried out with every tearing slash and barbed thorn gashing his skin.

"Now what to do with you little trouble maker. Throw you to the wolves? Leave you for the goblyns? Or should I skin you myself?"

Edrick scratched and tore at the man's hand around his neck. The woodsmen skin quit its normal hue. It felt like leather now, dried and tough. His features changed, shifted into something he did not recognize as human.

The woodcutter dashed through the woods with unnatural speed and strength, such of which a man could not possess. Was it a witch or something worse? Edrick knew he could not trust Gaebria's dream. NO! The children. He led them into a trap, just like his family, just like Sunniva. All their faces flashed across his mind, Wurt, Moira, Gaebria, Tredan and Bron. What has he done to them?

They stopped abruptly, they might have traveled a hundred yards in thirty heart beats. The mannish thing held Edrick up, his gaze bearing into him. He was silent with a wicked grin. The man's eyes were not human. It looked unsettling familiar.

It was him! That creature in the clearing. It was the ogre, somehow disguised.

Then Edrick's heart stopped as shouts for desperate help, pleas for mercy rang out over the forest. Voices of children.

"Ha! You hear your sweet friends. So delicious they all are. Could not allow you to spoil them, a bad apple you are, would have cost me gold you would. So now I shall finish what those inept men failed to do. They should have buried you. Not hung you."

With that, the ground trembled, as it had that day in the clearing. A torrential vibration shook the very earth apart until a large gaping hole fell away in front of the monster's boots, a crevice as wide as Edrick's cottage.

"Your little sister brought in fifty stones of gold. Her alone! Such a pure, soft little thing. Undervalued amongst you stupid humans. She would have fetched a fraction of that with your kind. And for what? To rut on her all day like a…" it shook its head in disgust. "Like animals. I train my livestock better than how you humans behave around each other. Filth."

"I will kill you," Edrick muttered through his clenched jaw.

"Mwahahahahaha. Feisty until the end. You would have been worth near your sister's price had you not had this taint about you. Have you heard of the Vaults of Lhodyn, boy? When men die, she doesn't allow their souls to pass into the Æthyr, instead she keeps them under these roots, in the earth and she grows stronger. Your human blood feeds her; your souls strengthens her. But now she's an engorged sloth. And she will be slaughtered, just like the rest of you."

He held Edrick out in the center of the pit by elongated arms, the earth itself shaped into teeth like a buried beast widening its maw. Edrick caught a glimpse of the hole leading to unknown depths.

"Down you go," the ogre said with indifference, releasing him. Edrick fell into the deep pit, swallowed by darkness.

18

CONVALESCE

ALARIC HAD SEEN too many deaths.

Hundreds.

Men falling all around him on the Nitherlic Vale, the battlefield in the wars against the Folthnir two decades ago. Warriors gallant and noble, others murderous and cruel, fell to their enemies without reason. Weathered veterans and youth alike. Dear friends. Hated enemies. Death was indiscriminate.

Death once was, and innocently, a natural completion to life, an end to a full cycle of any being that served its purpose. Whether it was a chicken raised for slaughter or a stag hunted in mid-winter to feed his family, death was nothing to fear. Death had as much a place in the world as any animal, as much as the sun belonged to the sky and the water found its way to the ocean.

But in war!

It was the first time he realized Death walked the earth like a predator. Death too, had a kingdom, a place where it was sovereign and everyone who wandered into its realm, made its subject.

Such a place lived in war. Such a place belonged to the yew tree.

Not the kind of death that came for the elderly, not the kind of death that took the sick or the starving. Those were all different kinds of Death, the kind his father spoke of, each one more severe than the other.

This was the kind of Death that stood on the backs of men, shoved their faces into the mud, inspired horror and panic in their hearts until they did Death's bidding. Thralls of Death, soldiers were.

It was a tyrant that seized the many lives for which it had no claim, lives that had more to offer than succumbing to war. It consumed, always. It was a glutton that did not feed, but feasted.

Alaric left the war knowing what life was, seeing what death is: counterintuitive, capricious and inevitable.

Every person's life: a water droplet clinging beneath the branches of a tall pine.

As the droplet falls, life begins, and a person's journey is measured from the height in which they fall. But none can escape the inevitable collision into the ground.

In youth, you cannot perceive the earth rushing up at you, but feel weightless, light, as if the wind can carry you far. As if nothing else exists, not the tree from where your journey began, not the ground where all ends, just the unrestrictive air around you.

In war, as in old age, the ground comes into sharp, crucial focus. Upon its initial revelation, the ground is the prime concern, and the height from which you have fallen through the air, either from a great height or near the tree's roots, you come to one single conclusion. Death is your only purpose.

Death was always your master.

His father told Alaric and his brothers stories of the world, stories of how life was before men, how the gods once lived and how the world will be in the future. Yet all those stories never spoke the truth, that life contained unjust burdens. That impermanence was the constant and men's hearts always sought permanence, thus their spirits were broken long before their bodies through the span of their lives.

He witnessed how his father, his mother, experienced this. It was an unavoidable sorrow. He did not know how to rid himself of the desire to grasp the impermanent.

And there, hanging upon that yew tree, another painful reminder of the truth he discovered. His son, so passionate and relentless, rendered in absolute stillness.

Alaric did not know how he was carried back to his cottage, whose voices offered words of comfort, of profound regret at his lost. He looked into his wife's eyes and she knew instantly. She cried into his chest, but he could not feel sorrow for her or for Edrick. Alaric collapsed on their bed with Elisial, stricken with grief. He did not understand why he could not feel, did not care if his wife was in agony once again or if she were in complete bliss. Nothing moved him in the moments he left the yew. He was numb. No, it was more like he was dead, that something in his heart died, and his body was a cold corpse. His wife's tears burned his chilled flesh. Meghan joined them, sitting at Elisial's feet, Eadwyn sat by himself in the shadowed corners of the room. Bresigia wept in silence out of respect, Sarghan remained ever quiet. A thousand thoughts flooded his mind, questioning the decisions he made over the past year that led them here to this point. It was as if he were on a chess board, the novice up against a master, slowly watching his pieces being removed from the game with impunity. He was beyond frustration and the realization that he was outmatched settled in.

Elisial fell asleep, exhausted from her sorrow, her head on his chest, her acidic tears soaking his shirt, Meghan by her side clinging to her skirt like a babe. His eyes remained open as the images of forty-two years of life thrust themselves into his mind, all his accomplishments, his disappointments and losses. Each thought smoldered like coals of a fire, flickering into darkness.

Morning came and the sun never looked so dull as on that day. Elisial tended to his wounds, bandaging each one carefully, lovingly. He looked at her in wonder, questioning silently why she did not hate him, why she did not blame him for his flaws. Wondering if she too, was breaking inside.

All the world remained in silence. Words were clumsy to dispense on one another, instead his family held each other's hands, embraced one another when the tears came, and this was extended to Bresigia and Sarghan, who wondered if Gaebria was dead as well. And if the birds chirped that day, they kept their distance from the village, and if butterflies danced in the air, they did it elsewhere. The entire community did not stir.

Not until that evening when the Folthnir returned in full battle gear, faces marked with grim determination. For word had reached the Theign, that there were children missing from his village, the same children spared from the branding.

"They are searching each home, counting every brand," Beran shouted through Athelyn. He was sent to warn others of the inevitable visit, running from house to house. "Children are missing from all over the village."

"Whose children?" Elisial asked when he stopped at their home.

It was too much to hear, losing Edrick was a tragedy, losing more children was unbearable to all.

"Many have gone missing. And already they have found those that escaped the branding hidden in their homes. They drag them out and just," he made a swing motion with his hand, as if chopping a tree, "take their heads off right there. They place their heads on spikes on the cart for all to see."

"Horrible! Alaric what are we going to do?" She looked to Bresigia and Sarghan who remained hidden in their cottage during the brandings.

"They should leave now!" Beran offered, his voice was high, in a state of panic, as if the Folthnir would leap out of the ground any moment and seize him for revealing their agenda. "I have to go! Have to tell the others!"

The youth ran swiftly down the Lane and disappeared from view.

"Alaric!" Elisial called to him, shutting the door. He remained in his bed since morning. The numbness lifted, only partially, just enough to allow the sting from the nine branded wounds emerge through all thought of loss, feelings of misery and self-pity. So much that he forgot his family in fleeting moments, and felt relieved to do so. Now Elisial was calling him back.

He looked to her. She was afraid.

"Alaric, we must do something for Bresigia and Sarghan. The Folthnir are coming to the house."

He looked away. She continued talking, but he no longer heard the words.

Night fell as if day never existed.

Bresigia had refused to be branded. The Folthnir already left their mark on her daughter and granddaughter without burning their skin. Shouts and cries could be heard nearby.

They were nearing.

Elisial pleaded with the women to go, but Bresigia refused. She claimed she's too old to be a whore and her daughter too lame. The old woman remained stoic. "No! We fled once and left our lives to chance and this is where we were delivered. If we can't escape these barbarous men, how can we flee evil spirits in the forest? We are ready to join our loved ones," she said. She was resigned to death, resigned to endure nothing more than the last blow.

Their lives were nearing the ground, when their souls would be released.

There was a pounding on the door. Everyone froze.

The earth came into crucial focus.

"Alaric, you old Woodcutter," came a familiar voice, "don't keep an old woman standing out in the night where murderous men wander about."

"Elzera! Elzera!!" Elisial shouted in relief.

She quickly lifted the crossbeam that barricaded the door. There stood Elzera, wrapped in loose scarves. The two women embraced. "Come in Auntie, hurry." Elisial pulled her through the threshold.

Elzera took in the mood of the house, the fresh wounds on their faces, Alaric's prone position on the bed. "I should have never left my dear. I am so sorry."

"How did you escape their detection?" Elisial asked as she replaced the crossbeam.

"The weak minded are easily fooled, aren't they?"

"Auntie, please, leave while you can. If they catch you here they will hang you on the yew tree or worse," Elisial pleaded.

Elzera moved to Alaric's side, concerned at his bed ridden state. She clucked her tongue twice, then felt his skin, placing her hand on his neck. "He is not well. Where are the boys? I just see Eadwyn and Meghan," she asked as she continued to scan the room.

"Much has occurred lately," Meghan replied. Elzera turned and hugged Meghan, kissing her head, stopping to look at the brand. "Those monsters," she said under her breath. She held out an arm for Eadwyn. Tears slid down Meghan's cheeks.

"It will be all right, dear," Elzera said.

"No, it won't," Eadwyn answered. "They killed Edrick and Halig abandoned us."

"What?!" the old woman shrieked. She jumped, startled at the news. "What's this about Edrick?" She asked, turning to Alaric and Elisial.

Alaric did not move.

"It is true, Alaric tried to save him," said Elisial, emotionless.

"Edrick," Meghan replied before the Alvini asked.

She sat down, shaking her head in disbelief. "This…this cannot be."

"I know," Elisial lamented. She sat next to her Auntie and held her.

"This can't be!" she repeated, her voice became defiant. "How?"

"They hung him, with others, from the yew. Yesterday."

A puzzled look came over the old woman's face, her nose twitched and fidgeted. "Yes, I saw eight bodies there, some of them children, but not Edrick! I laid blessings on each of them, made the mark of Zveda so their souls do not wander forever, or worse, wander into these woods."

"But it is true. Our neighbors brought Alaric home last night, he could not walk on his own. They confirmed that Alaric collapsed at the sight of our son," Elisial said.

"I am telling you, child," the Alvini held Elisial by the shoulders, "Edrick was not there as I passed just now on my way here! I made note of each face, not one of them was of sweet Edrick."

Alaric rolled into a sitting position. He looked across the room, at Elzera. She spoke truthfully. He did not understand. "You must leave if you want to live," was all he said. He was harsh, his face unkind.

"I'm not leaving," she replied, obstinate.

"Auntie," Elisial pointed to her burned cheek, "you are not marked like us. They are coming here and will find you, Bresigia, and Sarghan are without these marks. If you came in unnoticed then you might be able to leave unnoticed. Please take them with you."

"My poor, poor family," Elzera said, examining the wound on Elisial's face, ignoring her dire warnings. "I have just the medicine for this. And what about the children?" she asked.

"We were branded." Meghan said. "But they spared the other village children."

"Well, I have enough medicine for you all and more in my wagon. I left it hidden outside the village. Thought it would be more inconspicuous on foot instead of dragging that wagon about. I will fetch it later."

"Father took nine brandings and they beat him horribly!" Meghan blurted out.

"You all have suffered beyond anything decent folks deserve," she lamented. "Well, let me treat the children first then I will tend to your parents."

"No," Meghan refused, "let father have my medicine, and mother." She looked to Eadwyn to get his agreement. He nodded his head, reluctantly though it seemed.

"I don't need it," Alaric said laying back down. "Go, you old hag, and take the women."

The others were stunned at Alaric's rude words.

"I am sorry, Auntie, he has been through much." Meghan offered.

"What do you think could have happened to Edrick? You think the Folthnir stole his body?" Elisial asked.

Just then, a commotion, a stomping of horses and creaking of a wagon approached.

"No. I doubt it." She stood up and walked toward the fire burning in the hearth.

"They are coming," Meghan gasped, turning to her mother and father for help. "Auntie, please," she pleaded, moving toward her mother, holding her tight.

The Alvini tended to the fire, knocking around logs with a poker, extracting a piece of burnt wood that had fallen off to the side, just smoldering.

The creaking wagon stopped in front of the cottage. Horses snorted and jangled their reigns.

Elzera took the burnt stick and approached Bresigia and Sarghan. "Hold still and trust me, same as that day you crossed the road to be with Alaric and I." She cusped each woman's jaw firmly in one hand and drew a symbol with the ashy brand on each cheek.

The others were speechless.

"DO NOT," Elzera threatened, "touch that."

A pounding shook the door. Then slamming. The crossbeam held the door tight. "Open or we will burn your house down, Woodcutter!"

Elisial looked to Alaric who did not stir. She looked to Elzera.

"Well, go on, you need a house, don't you?" Elzera finished blindly drawing another ash symbol over her own cheek.

Elisial lifted the beam and stood back as the door flung open and five armed warriors crashed inside, knocking over chairs and tables. Wooden dishes ricocheted onto the floor, broken and stomped under heavy boots.

Meghan screamed.

And another voice shrilled out loud and piercing. Sarghan hands were to her face. She trembled violently.

"Bare your marks now!" One of them ordered. A sixth man walked in behind them. It was the southerner they saw at the tower. He had a parchment and quill. He scrutinized the people in the room. His mouth fell slack. "An Alvini, here in this village? Let's see her mark first."

The lead wolfskin stepped toward the old woman, seizing her by the arm, tilting her head back.

Elisial gasped. It was plain that nothing more than ash was on her cheek.

"She's fine. Check the rest." The other men walked the room, stopping at Sarghan and Bresigia, who cowered before them. The Folthnir seemed satisfied.

"They are all accounted for."

"He's missing a son, the oldest." The southerner accused.

"Just like the others."

"Shut up! Just search the house," the southerner ordered.

The Folthnir moved about the small house but didn't have far to look as the home did not have many concealing places.

"There's a small barn out there, check that too." Two men left.

"So, you sent your eldest to protect the children of this village? There is no protection but Vylkinus, and if they are found outside this village they will be sent south."

"Other children are missing too?" Elzera asked genuinely curious.

The southerner didn't answer, but her questioning drew his attention sharply. "I want the names of all that live here, starting with this Alvini. She is no relative of yours. Where did she come from?"

He was addressing Alaric, but Alaric made no response. He did not even react when the men charged into his house and threatened his family.

"South, of course. I can speak for myself, Uthræsian," Elzera strode forward beside Elisial. "You are a lettered man, read this then," she reached under her robes and produced a scroll. "Useless on these stupid brutes. I thought I'd never leave this village. I even took a brand to the face so as I can live long enough to get back home."

The southerner took the scroll and read it. "The Imperial Seal," he whispered in surprise. "You are a foreign merchant then, with

Imperial business? So, what interests could you possibly have in this unremarkable village?" he asked disdainfully

"Don't you know? This village holds many secrets. Many valuable commodities. I'm one of the few merchants that do business here. Elisial makes rare and remarkable healing potions and salves. The honey produced here is reputable all over the kingdom. And until recently, the stoutest draft horses were bred in this valley, that is until those stupid northerners hung the breeder."

The southerner raised an eyebrow. "The famed Mithlian honey comes from here?"

"Why yes. Elisial uses the honey in her medicines, part of what makes them so effective. The reason her family settled here. You see the bees are kept at the forest edge and visit the woodland flowers. That is the secret to its rich flavor."

This news seemed to be giving the southerner pause to think.

"So how do I ensure that I keep my business uninterrupted from the new lords? It seems they are unfamiliar with writs and documents."

"I have no answer for you," he handed back her scroll. "You are not my concern but I am always open to new business ventures. I can act as your sponsor with them when the time is appropriate. My business tonight is taking inventory of the lord's holdings and it seems a great deal of his assets are missing, to which I must ascertain the whereabouts. So, until you have his leave, do not depart this village. I would be disheartened to have lost a potential business opportunity." The southerner let the threat linger.

A scuffle could be heard outside, the bleating of a sheep, panicking, crying. Then sudden silence.

The two Folthnir that searched the barn, returned. "Nothing but animals," the one who spoke stood near, as if there were more but hesitant to speak further. Blood spots speckled his chest.

"Were you attacked?" the southerner asked, irritated.

"No. They kept a lame sheep."

The southerner looked perplexed so the Folthnir continued, "It pleases Vylkinus to slay the lame."

The southerner shook his head, looking frustrated. The other seemed to wanting to say more. "Just speak."

"It's just that this home is the closest to the woods, closest to the witches and evil spirits. In our land, witches take children as well." The northerner's eyes settled on the Alvini. The other three Folthnir followed his gaze and became tense, as if they discovered a monster in their midst. A strange old woman suddenly appearing there was very threatening to the northerners. "And I was there at the brandings, I would have noticed this strange…woman."

"At ease, it is not likely she's a witch. I was there at the battle and the witches revealed themselves plainly. In my land, people such as these are unfortunately all too common. Some are slaves, but most of them belong to secretive merchant clans that have also grown rich and powerful. Not a group to cross without good reason."

Elzera stood a little taller crossing her arms defiantly, playing into the fears of the wolfskins and the southerner's concerns.

"We will leave guards at this house. No one is to leave this night. Kill anyone who tries. And if you see any children, send word. And if we see your son…" He glanced at his list. "Halig. We will send you his head."

It seemed they pulled all the air right out of the cottage as the door slammed shut. The last threat about Halig jarred Elisial.

"How was it they did not take notice of the ash on our faces?" Bresigia asked.

"Like I said, weak-minded," was all Elzera offered.

"That southerner is not weak-minded. How was it you fooled him?" Elisial added.

"I didn't. He knew I was Alvini, did he not? There is a grudging respect amongst his people."

"Yes but…"

"Tsk, tsk," she rubbed off her mark which disappeared as fast as she drew it. "There are other things to discuss than all your curiosity at my craft. Where has Halig gone off to, to search for the children?"

Elisial spoke to the Alvini late into the night recounting everything that took place. Elzera's face was unusually concerned and revealed a sense of dread.

"So they are revealing themselves," she finally commented. "Something stirs here, Elisial. I have seen it in the stars and…" she looked Elisial in her eyes and paused, "on Edrick's palm. Something tremendous and significant. Both dark and mighty. Something ancient will reveal itself here. Yet there are only hints and I had to seek star charts to get to the true meaning. Unfortunately most of the significant star charts are scattered across the world. There seems to be time, but I can see I must remain here for a while. We must find Edrick."

"Do you think he is alive, that they were mistaken?" Elisial gasped.

"Yes, I do." Her answer was firm and straightforward.

"And what did you see on Edrick's palm?" Meghan asked.

Elzera became quiet in thought. "I will tell you what I told him," she said after a moment, "and it is the truth, for Chiromancers and all Diviners swear an oath to seek and share the truth. Reading a child's future is difficult to discern unless death is written there." She cut her explanation short.

"And was it written there?" Elisial bravely asked.

The Alvini became stiff, slightly flustered. "I am not sure what I read," she confessed. "It was confusing even to me and raised more questions in my mind. But I have to admit, it did not fully come as a surprise to hear Edrick died because what I saw there written on his hand."

"Why not? What was it?"

"Death was written there, or rather the Mark of Death. I am not sure about what it exactly means, but he carries it far into his life and I don't understand what it portends, but I am sure about carrying it far into his life. So I believe he is not dead, and will not be for a long time."

Elisial hung on her every word, and smiled as the Alvini proclaimed her final revelation. She nodded, and hope returned to her.

"I believe you. My heart, too, says he is not dead, though what you say about the mark is disturbing."

"I saw him. He was dead," Alaric spoke from the shadows in a flat voice.

"I believe what you saw, but something must have intervened. One of your neighbors, someone. He just was not there, Alaric.

"His life will cross evil again," she continued, "and greatness too. It seems he will be at the center of the coming storm. He will survive, but as you can witness with your guests," she indicated Bresigia and Sarghan, "surviving is sometimes no gift, and death can seem preferable. Edrick faces such trials."

Everyone remained quiet contemplating the Alvini's cryptic words.

"What is this Mark of Death, if it does not mean Edrick might die," Eadwyn asked, almost whispering.

The Alvini looked at the children, each one gravely concerned. "The Mark of Death is even ambiguous to me. A riddle was written on his palm, death and long life. What does that mean?" she asked Eadwyn back, genuinely perplexed. "I questioned whether I read correctly what I saw. Questioned what I even saw at all.

"Not to alarm anyone, but the Mark of Death, at least one interpretation means Death himself has singled Edrick out. He will act as his agent or, is the cause of death, something terribly morbid like that."

"That is horrible," Meghan gasped.

"Dear, I am sorry. Do not worry, fate is not written in stone or flesh. A person's character is always in a state of development and the choices one faces decides fate in that very moment you act. I believe that this mark will fade over time, that Edrick's character, such as it is, will overcome Death's schemes."

Meghan nodded, what other conclusion could they wish to make. All their eyes wandered to Alaric, lying motionless in bed.

Elisial leaned closer to Elzera, whispering, "He has fallen so far, so quickly. He is not the Alaric I know."

Elisial fought off the tears, biting her lip. Meghan held her, rubbing her back. The moment passed and Elisial composed herself. She held Elzera's hand, kissing it lightly. "There is no cure for what ails him. He has seen much evil, I am afraid it is turning his heart cold. He has not left that bed at all since last night."

Meghan nodded in agreement.

Elzera stood up, placing her hands on her hips and shouted, "Alaric, son of Accenen! Get up this instance! You are Warden of these Woods and the children of this village have gone missing! UP! UP! And go find your sons!"

Everyone jumped, save Alaric, who remained still. Yet, anger overcame him, a viciousness filled his veins. Thoughts went to his woodcutting ax.

Elzera stomped across the little cottage, heels hitting the floor like a stabled warhorse eager to charge into battle. She shook Alaric's shoulder. "UP!"

Alaric threw off the blankets, bolting to his feet. How dare this old woman mock him!

"Ah, so there is some life to you still."

"Get out of my house!" Alaric barked back.

"Alaric!" Elisial cried.

"You don't order me in my own house! Get out!"

Elzera lifted a hand to keep Elisial quiet. "Well now, since you are up and talking, then let's talk. Yes, this is your house and I will leave, milord," she chided. "But it seems to me there are things a man like you need to tend to and it's not getting done with you lying in bed. I say Edrick's alive and you care not."

"HE'S DEAD!" he yelled into her face. He was a breath's width from her. Tears came unwillingly, staining his eyes red.

"He hung, but he's not dead," she said softly, fearless. "Let's go find him and the children. They need us." She placed her hand on his chest, above his heart. "They need you."

"Me!" Alaric mocked. "What am I that everyone supposes I am?"

"Remember who you are." Elzera said.

"Who am I?"

"This man I see before me I don't know." She brought the ax to him and held it out. "You are a Woodcutter, and the hunter of Wudelic. You are Warden because you made these woods yours from a place of love, not by any station given to you by kings. Your household is yours, Rhitterheort, as any man's house is theirs. And you are nothing if you do not tend to your house."

"I haven't tended to my house?" He shoved the ax back into her hands. "Then show me how it is done, old woman. Because if I haven't tried, then maybe it's time I learn from someone who seems to know better."

Alaric lifted the crossbeam and threw it against the wall and stormed outside. He slammed the door. The calm dark lay across the ground. It felt welcoming, a contrast to the women's babble inside the cottage.

Two wolfskins drew their swords on him. Alaric locked eyes with them. He could kill them. He would not live, but he could kill them with his hands.

The notion felt comforting. It felt like something he had been desiring for years.

He retreated to the barn. Mathilda lay inside, slain in the hay. Edrick's sheep, the one he pleaded to spare. Edrick, always the one filled with compassion and a sense that everything had a right to be. Even if that life were horribly scarred, it was far better to endure than perish.

The barbarians hacked the lamb's head off. It was nowhere to be found. Under different circumstances, Alaric would have butchered it and threw over the fire, cooked it in a stew. But he would not ingest what the barbarians desecrated. He dragged the animal to the forest edge and tossed the carcass over the Wall. It landed with a hollow thump.

"Take it!" he yelled into the night, directing his anger at an absent Lhodyn. "I am broken before you! You have taken everything I care for. Everything!" The forest chirped and hummed with the sounds of night creatures, his shouting did nothing to deter the nocturnal chorus.

"Show yourself! Come and take me! All of us!"

He stared at the bloodied carcass, legs sprawled about. The same sheep he spared from being dragged into the woods was now there at the forest's domain. He spat at it, at the forest, at his fallen goddess.

He shuffled back to the barn, skin afire with fresh wounds from two days before. He welcomed the pain because it tamed his thoughts of family and self-pity. He stepped through the muddy earth, wet with spilt blood, into the barn where he found Edrick's napping nest of padded hay. The place where his son would lay down with Mathilda and Sunniva. He collapsed and slept.

He was buried in straw, like a rat. It kept out the light even when the sun reached high noon. How much would he give for another moment to lay down with his son in the barn, listening to the wind rush through the tree branches. Elisial's mother told him it sounded like the ocean waves, a small echo of it. Edrick would have enjoyed that, Alaric thought. He rarely spoke to any of his children about the stories told to him in his youth. Never seemed important.

He shook off the hay and stepped into the sunlight. Distant horns sounded across the village. The same horns heard at the tower, accompanied by the booming of drums.

The guards were gone. The village was a ghost of itself.

The cottage door was wide open, allowing sun to flood inside. Meghan was sweeping out the dirt, framed by the threshold.

"Good afternoon, papa," she greeted him with an unsure smile. Alaric nodded back. "How are your wounds, we should be changing your bandages."

Alaric went inside and sat at a chair pulled out for him. Meghan set down her broom and went to fetch fresh linens. Elisial attended her apothecary alcove.

She noticed him walk in but did not say a word. She handed Meghan a small jar of salve to soothe his wounds.

"Eadwyn is checking the traps and delivering wood," she spoke.

"Fine," Alaric responded. The other two women were at the table. Bresigia was helping Elisial with her medicines, smashing ingredients in a pedestal, then weighing them out in grains and scruples.

"Elzera went with him. Thought she would look around for Edrick. Marvelous how much energy she possesses."

Alaric said nothing as he let Meghan attend him. "A few are swelling mama," she said, worried.

Elisial walked over and looked at them. "Wash it with the water we boiled. Then apply the cream."

"How long have those war horns sounded?" Alaric asked after a while.

"Since dawn at least," Meghan answered. "Many more Folthnir arrived through the night. The giants. Their mounted warriors. People are saying they seem as if they are preparing to leave, as if for war."

After receiving new bandages, Alaric took his ax and sat at the front porch.

The cottage remained quiet, but not still, as Meghan found another chore to do and the others went on with their work.

Alaric began sharpening the ax blade, listening to the sounds of war.

Elzera and Eadwyn returned after a while.

"You are up!" Elzera greeted him, voice filled with faux surprise.

Alaric said nothing, keeping his attention only on his ax. Eadwyn offered a meek smile.

"The traps are empty," his son said.

"Go tell your mother."

Eadwyn scooted by his father quickly.

Elzera bent over, shielding the sun from her eyes. She hovered near his face as if she were taunting him again. He would not let her get to him, he determined.

"Your brands are not as the others," she reached to his face, wrapping her palm under his chin, moving his head back and forth as if he were child. "Runes that look vaguely familiar." Her voice trailed off. She straightened up, lost in thought. "They no longer hurt?"

"No."

"I see." She continued to stare at him in silence.

"It's good you are sharpening that," Elzera said after a while, "they will be coming for you soon."

"Who?

"The Folthnir."

"For what?" he asked detached and uninterested.

She looked at him steadily. "Alaric. You must wake up. Whatever it is that weighs your heart down, you must cast it aside. I need you, your family needs you, this village needs you."

"Why?" He flipped the ax over and continued sharpening.

"You are their protector, whether they deserve it or not. I know your family does. Do not fail them."

"But I have…so many times." He remained still, staring at the ax blade. He placed his thumb across it. He sensed every nick, every imperfection in the steel.

"So that is it then." She slowly squatted down, a motion that seemed awkward and stiff for her. She looked Alaric in the eyes. "I know something of what you are feeling Alaric. I know the burden of great responsibility. I know the load can bury any man or woman alone, but you are not alone in this, Alaric. Elisial will die for you and her children. She would trade her life, right here, right now, for her triplets, for Baldice, Sunniva and Edrick. She would."

Alaric shook his head. He wanted her to stop and leave him be.

"I know in your heart I have always been a stranger, a foreigner, an outsider to you. But trust me now, Woodcutter. You must fight this! You must! You must fight until you are dead, because Death preys on the weak and stupid and we both know you are neither of those things."

"You are wrong. Nothing is beyond its reach. When we are young, we think we can out run it, outsmart it, just like Edrick. It leads to an early grave, if there is even a body to bury. I cannot protect the lives where Death pulls them out from beneath me, at any point, any time. Just…" he seized her wrist suddenly. Squeezed her thin, frail arm. "…snatches you, and that's it."

"I care not to argue. I care for your family and for you." He still held her arm in a clenched grip. "I made a choice to return last night and might have very well saved two women's lives." She twisted her hand slightly, rotating it until pain shot up his arm, forcing him to let go, and she in turn seized his wrist. "So it was I that snatched life from Death's grip, I believe." She placed both hands on her knee, bracing herself, using all her strength to stand back up. "Life and death are two sides of a pendulum. It swings both ways."

The blaring horns were getting louder, closer.

"They are on the move. I think your ax is sharp enough. You better ready yourself."

"What do you know?"

"I have been around the village this morning. They want revenge, Woodcutter."

"Don't we all," he muttered, continuing his work.

"Yes, that's the spirit Alaric. If you feel you have nothing left, you do have one last thing. Revenge. Let that move you if nothing else will."

The cavalcade of barbarians threw up dust behind them as they made their way down the Lane. War horns blared out intermittently and heavy deep shouts Alaric guessed to be the giants rumbled after.

Elzera looked to Alaric, as if waiting for a reaction. He remained exactly as he was and carried on with his sharpening. "Move woodcutter, let an old woman through." She stepped into the house.

Alaric waited.

The Folthnir arrived with their mounted warriors in front, clad in mail, helms with dragon visages, shields painted and spears raised high into the air.

The giants followed just behind equally equipped, skin painted for war. There were five total, a fist it was called. Just their presence alone spoke to the Theign's power. It was said the giant race lived for war, children of chaos, their history boasted of battles against dragons and gods, halls deep in the hillsides filled with vast war treasures.

Behind them were the Theign's oathmen, The Blooded. Warriors sworn to serve and expected their service well rewarded, accoutered in dragon scale hides, ripped off the carcasses of those deadly creatures when young, when steel blades could still cut into their flesh without breaking.

And last, were the Ulfserkers, defeated warriors and peasant men that chose to join their former enemies, rather than die or become slaves. They had to become killers, instruments of war. Wolf hides replaced the rags and trappings of their former life.

Someday they hoped to be Blooded, Chosen of Vylkinus.

The Theign rode out ahead of the main host toward Alaric's lychgate, accompanied by his guard, including the garish southerner, ostentatiously outfitted in rich urban attire, appropriate in a court setting, but remarkably foppish now. Grindan, too, rode with the vanguard, haughty and distant from the man Alaric once knew.

He stood as they approached, ax in hand.

The Theign dismounted his horse, one of Temen's best, a large black beast filled with spirit. As the others motioned to follow their lord, he held out his hand to stay them.

He approached Alaric alone. "You bear your marks well. You have the substance of a northern warrior, Woodcutter," he said with grudging respect.

"I have a master healer for a wife."

The Theign looked at Alaric with curiosity. "The Northmen never praise their women for the strengths they possess."

"We are not alike. It is no surprise."

The Theign smiled cunningly. "That I am sure. Your people could never match us. But I do need you now. Among my men, they possess not your knowledge of these woods."

"I won't help you. Whatever your needs are."

"It is a command, Woodcutter. And the alternative to what will happen. I would let my giants have your wife and daughter first, so much they desire female company. And I have young warriors eager to wet their blades in your son."

The warlord let the threat sink in. But Alaric said nothing. "I see the kind of look you have, Woodcutter. Desperate. Lost. So I have brought something else to appeal to you."

Thoughts of Edrick flashed through his mind. His heart lunged forward, slamming into his chest as hope surged through him. They have Edrick.

"A Folthnir and his weapon are Blooded. They share the same soul, so to be disarmed is to die."

He turned and raised his hand. Ator pulled something off his back and raised it in the air. It was Nithledan, in the hands of the one that tortured Edrick. His heart sunk into his viscera. Edrick was dead once again.

What he could do to these men with his bow.

"Your heirloom, I believe. Amongst our people, heirlooms are more precious than life. It is the honor of your kin, your sires."

"So what is it then?"

"This forest goddess, this Lhodyn, seems reluctant to relinquish her throne. Same problem we had with Sithric."

"I build a temple to Vylkinus, she responds by hiding all the children. Sounds like a woman to me, only they are not hers to hide. So now I must beat this bitch, like I would any woman."

He stood tall, over Alaric. "We northerners are sons of Vylkinus and we will burn his name across all the lands, the skies and even this forest. Today, Vylkinus rapes this slut."

Alaric was dumbstruck. This warlord was truly mad. "She will destroy all of you," he calmly stated. She will destroy us all, echoed a forbidden thought.

There was a harsh murmur through the gathered warriors. "NO!" Ator yelled. "It is *this* wayward whore that will be thrown upon the forge of the Almighty and struck down by his iron hammer."

"Then go. Why stop here?"

"I need a hound to sniff her out. You. You will take us to her."

"She is not far. She is the forest," Alaric pointed toward the trees behind his house, "step inside and there she will be."

"We will see if that is the outcome. And if she hides, as we know she will, you will take us to where she dwells. My spear longs to plunge inside this goddess."

"Hyuk-ra!" the warriors shouted in unison. The giants brayed a deep booming sound. It sounded ugly and evil to Alaric's ears. Elzera emerged from the house with Elisial, each carrying Alaric's travel gear. Elisial slipped it across his shoulders.

Elzera once again had ash on her cheek.

The group calmed slowly. "Is this the Alvini you mentioned?" the warlord asked his advisor. "How strange to find one here. Are you sure she is not one of those witches? We should remove her head and burn her now."

"I can make no assurances sir, proceed in a course you deem wise."

"I am a healer," Elzera spoke up, "same as Elisial. I taught her mother who in turn taught her. That is my trade and why I travel such extreme distances to reach this little village. If you are going to war with a goddess I suggest you take someone to quickly mend your men's wounds."

"It is glorious to die in the battlefield," shouted out a warrior. The others barked out in agreement.

The warlord's face remained stone solid.

"It was a similar story she related last night," the southerner said.

"These women come too," the Theign declared. "If one of you fail to obey, we will burn down this hovel with your children inside. Bind them together."

The Huntsman slid off his horse and bound Alaric, Elisial and Elzera around their necks with leather lashes.

"Keep my new hound alive, women, for as long as we hunt."

The Huntsman took their leash, leading them on foot. He studied the ground then led them to the byrgen, where he pointed out the children's prints.

The troupe entered the woods in the mid-day sun. It was eerily quiet. It was not long before the men reacted as if seeing movement out of the corner of their eyes. But when they looked, or investigated, nothing could be found.

"We are chasing children, not shadows," the Huntsman rebuked the skittish wolfskins. The men began shouting at the forest, purging any of their fears and demanding to see their foes. The woods though answered with silence.

"How long do you want to keep marching? Until dark? That might be unwise," Elzera asked the Theign.

The Huntsman struck her. "Do not speak, witch."

"Control your hounds," the Theign replied coolly.

They arrived at the forest cottage as the sun began to descend. Alaric did not have to look far to see where the children had went.

"Whose cottage is this?" the warlord asked.

"My grandfather's," Alaric answered.

"They passed through here, but someone was with them. Someone heavy and tall I would guess," the Huntsman said. He studied Alaric's reaction.

It was plain that many children passed through here, heading down an established path through the woods.

"Lead," the Huntsman commanded to Alaric, loosening his sword.

They marched now into the deep forest.

Alaric led them along a familiar trail he hadn't trodden since he was a young and foolish man, one that led to the haunted ruins of the Unnamed King. And written in the dirt path were the prints of creatures other than the children.

Goblyns.

They were heading for a trap. Alaric willingly led them.

19

THE BROWNMAN OF WUDELIC

EDRICK FELL THROUGH endless dark. Tumbling. Tumbling. He expected to hit earth as soon as light of day evaporated around him. The air became cold and moist, laden with the stench of death. His impending death, he thought. Still, he tumbled farther down.

Then after long moments, something seized his ankle, arresting his descent. He hung by a leg in the deep nothingness. Something grasped him tight, a pain wracked crush.

Pain is a better alternative to death, he thought.

A rustling noise erupted around him, so near he could reach out in the dark and touch it. Dirt rained on him from above, as if something crawled and crept near. His position shifted and then something else grabbed his other leg, just as the first grasping thing released its hold, then another, then another. He was descending slowly, passing from grasp to grasp through the dark.

He suddenly stopped.

There was silence.

Edrick summoned the courage to speak.

"Hello," he squeaked, surprised at his own timidity.

Long moments passed and nothing moved or made a noise. The air weighed on him under the silence. Edrick decided to feel the thing that was holding his leg.

He struggled to pull his body up toward his feet. He began to swing, to build momentum. He gave one last effort and bent forward enough to catch his captive leg. He pulled himself up to feel the thing that held him. His fingers slid up his leg onto the phantom hand. It was hard, somewhat rough; skeletal and cold. As if in reaction to his warm touch it released him and he fell only a couple of feet onto a pile of damp, but soft ground. He lay there not wanting to move.

Where was he? And what was it that held him moments before, protecting him from that reckless fall. Was it still there watching him? How was he going to get out? He could try climbing, to escape, but what if those things grabbed him, held him in this pit. The ogre mentioned the Vaults of Lhodyn. Was this where the dead settled?

Perhaps this was the Land Beneath.

Edrick held his breath for as long as he could, for fear of disturbing the motionless air.

He was as still as the darkness.

Yet if there were something morbid, something dangerous around him, would it not have revealed itself by now? Nothing stirred save the thumping of his heart. Heavy, violent pounding beats thrummed into his ears.

Then he felt it, as if he fell into a well and was doused with it.

Fear.

It was on him like the cold, leeching life; a languid poison seeping out of his bones into every muscle, seizing his heart and erupting out of every pore of his skin.

He was afraid. And fear itself scared him.

He was alone, and no one knew where he was.

He cried. Cold tears fell down his face. He was afraid for the first time. He did not know why, but the thought of his helpless friends about to be slaughtered or taken away like his sister, chilled him from inside. And he was responsible! It was his doing and no one else. His father would be ashamed of him, his mother disappointed, the same as the day when he returned without Sunniva and Baldice. He cried until the tears ran dry and his body ached.

This is Death. Unknowing, uncaring and lonely. He hated it with all his heart.

He laid motionless for maybe hours, wondering when Death would seize him.

Then he realized he could feel the ground. It was something other than himself. Something tangible beyond the darkness. He dared to wriggle his fingers along the slimy surface. It felt familiar, likes leaves sitting on the forest floor for too long, decaying in the winter before the first blanket of snow obliterated them from the known world.

Edrick grabbed a handful of the moist foliage and held it to his nose. Reflexively, he recoiled from the stench. This was worse than what was on the forest floor. It was like all the leaves, falling in all the graves of the world, settled here in this one pit.

Edrick threw the muck in disgust and rolled to his knees. He decided to crawl toward the pit's wall, hoping to find an exit. It was not long before he found a tunnel leading out.

He crawled slowly, gliding and slipping on the slimy mat. He hoped no shaft or pit plummeted suddenly in front of him. He stopped, terrified at the thought of plunging farther through the dark depths. Maybe he should stay and wait. Yell for help.

Wait for whom?

Yell for whom?

No, he knew he could only help himself, or he would die – if he was still a living thing at all.

That woodsman from the cottage. He wondered if it truly was the ogre in man's form. It took his friends away. How could he have trusted anything in these woods anymore? The Wudelic had forsaken his father, and nothing seemed safe, not even the faeries. He needed the help of the gods, for that's all he had. But which ones. His father spoke of many hidden gods that no other villagers knew. Dragons, he said. Mighty nature spirits they were.

He couldn't always remember their names. What was the one for the earth? Wohr? Or should he invoke the dragon of the underworld, Baeloth. Or the dragon of the sky, Maey. Ashura was the imperishable dragon of summer. Ysig, winter.

The one Edrick remembered above all others was Aeyah, the woodland spirit. Father said she retreated from Lhodyn, and slept. But one day, the dragons will emerge again and burn the world.

Torch the world of evil.

He remembered the torc his father gave him, buried beneath his clothes. He reached beneath his shirt and pulled it free. A faint light crept forth, a blend of gold, copper and silver. Each metallic leaf glowed in the perfect darkness, something that he never noticed under star lit skies. It gave him hope. He removed the torc from around his neck and held it out. It cast a faint light, enough to see his hand, but nothing farther.

Some light was better than nothing. He placed it back around his neck and began crawling once again. In the faint light, if he bent low, he could see the ground, enough to see if darkness were to open up suddenly beneath him, he might have a chance from falling into a precarious pit. He crawled hand over foot for quite a while without another hole appearing. He was in a tunnel of moist earth, big enough for him to stand, but he dared not. The air remained cold and damp. It stole the heat away from his flesh and it wasn't long before he found himself shivering.

Edrick began thinking of all the animals that lived in the earth, rabbits, mice, badgers, and weasels. If he met one he would follow them to the surface, he thought, hopeful. Then he thought about what else might dwell down here, things that never left their underground confines, and therefore unknown to people. Were there any such creatures that lurked only in the dark, never knowing the sunlight?

This would be a good place to hide, from the Folthnir and the monsters in the forest. He wondered if people could live underground for a while, eat bugs and worms. He knew his sisters would hate it. But then they say the earth is the place of the dead. He wondered what ghosts looked like, if they were more than globes of light like he had seen at the yew tree. He had heard stories, of course, but never caught sight of one.

Fear faded as his curiosity piqued. Maybe it was the light of the torc. It felt like hope. He wished he had his éardian. Maybe that was his shield from fear.

It was not long in those dark tunnels, before they came to him.

Ghostly lights appeared suddenly far off, down the tunnel. Green orbs burning with unnatural flames, floating from the walls like seedlings aloft in the summer air. More and more materialized, rising from the ground to the roof. Others descending and passing through the floor, or traveling listlessly down the tunnel until they seemingly flickered out. Edrick did not know whether to keep still or pass through them. At least in their presence he could make out the tunnel. Rough and wild as it was, as if carved by some large beast or an army of rabbits. He wondered again where he had been dropped. Then from the mass of lights, a form appeared. A child, he thought. A boy with a familiar face but whose features were not distinct, blurred, to his frustration.

He stood and slowly approached, plunging into the green light. The orbs moved around him, away from his passing. The boy spirit faded, diffusing into a multitude of green baubles, moving down the corridor. Edrick continued following them as they floated down the passage, lighting his way. The green orbs led him through tunnels that split and passed numerous side passages that either ascended or descended, but always into darkness. Occasionally there were orbs of varying colors, but these lights brightened then diminished, like spectral eyes winking at his passing. After a while, only the green orbs remained, and Edrick followed, trusting their guidance.

He was led through the underground labyrinth into a long passage that ended with a curtain of animal furs, hanging like a door or barrier. Golden light slipped through the cracks along the ground. Something was on the other side. Edrick did not hesitate to plunge through.

He left his fear in the dark where it belonged.

A lantern lit chamber greeted him, stinging his eyes slightly as he adjusted to the intensity. As he regained his focus, Edrick saw the familiar furnishings any person keeps in their house: a large bed covered in thick animal furs, a few tables, a couple of wardrobes, stools and a few chairs. A fire burned in a large stone hearth at the far corner, filling the chamber with hospitable warmth. There were some chests the like ones Edrick always imagined would contain treasure, filled with jewels and gold. Along the wall were long stretches of shelves with books and scrolls, and hanging in decorative frames were incredible maps. Beautiful, large colorful maps that showed the oceans and mountains, rivers and forests with flowing scripts adorning each image.

Edrick wondered if he had stepped into the chambers of Lhodyn herself!

He then noticed a slight movement from underneath the furs, the rising and falling of restful breaths. Someone slept there.

Edrick waited in silence. He crouched down low against the wall, peering into the chamber wondering what strange creature dwelled beneath the earth but lived as a person. He could hear his heart race once again, sweat beaded across his brow despite the cool air. He thought of the passage he came through; solid darkness now that the green orbs vanished. Maybe they were evil faeries, delivering him to Lhodyn's executioner. He was in the Vaults of the Dead after all.

He tucked the torc away for fear that some small sound might betray him. On the far side of the chamber was another fur curtain, much like the one he stepped through. Perhaps another passage, one that led to the surface. Then again, there were worse things than this cozy room.

Think this through, Edrick said to himself. If this were some creature of darkness, it would not require lanterns and firelight. And if it is a creature of daylight, it would need a way to reach the surface. Edrick always imagined the Vaults were some other world, beyond the living, but perhaps it was nothing but the space where the dead were buried, the place where worms crawled and snakes slept.

He looked around the room carefully. On a long dinner table were wooden dishes, a knife and fork. Bones lay scattered across the chamber.

Well, the thing eats meat. Maybe it would not care for a skinny boy, he thought hopefully.

He decided to peek into the wardrobe. If this thing wore clothes then the type of clothes ought to tell him more about it. Edrick crawled over the dirt floor slow and deliberate, wishing not to disturb the resting creature. An hour might have passed by the time Edrick reached it. He turned the handle and opened the door.

Creeeeeeek.

Edrick winced and looked back. The figure hidden beneath the furs moved and bounced on the bed. Edrick trembled. His stomach shrank, rapidly falling into his colon where all his innards collapsed. He needed to vomit or release his bowls, and the more he thought hard about keeping one side in, it made him want to release the other.

The figure began snoring.

Edrick breathed a sigh of relief, then moved the door open even wider until the dim light illuminated the interior. Long fur trousers and cloaks, along with…long dresses, small like his mother. A few of them, patched together, repaired many times, showed long use.

Whatever was in that bed must have a wife? What if it is one of those witches?

A scratching and shuffling arose in the far passage beyond the chamber, startling Edrick. He wanted to run back out into the tunnel where he arrived. Instead he slipped inside the wardrobe and closed it.

In just five heartbeats, a cete of badgers waddled out of the passage and spread across the room, followed by a large brutish man covered in leathers and heavy furs. He had a long unkempt beard resting upon his chest, mostly gray with a few slivers of jet black streaking down like iron bars.

The badgers were huge in size, as large as the biggest hog Edrick had known. They sniffed and scratched up the ground, some stopped and snuffled the bones, turning them over with their snouts.

The man sat down at the table. Edrick nearly fell out of the wardrobe when the man turned to face him. It was the real Brownman! The one that rescued Edrick and the rest of his family from the monsters. Edrick wanted to shout out, but thought it wiser to exercise a bit more caution.

Quickly, the badgers seemed to all converge around the wardrobe, sniffing the air furiously. One badger barked like a suspicious dog and scratched at the wardrobe's base.

The tall man blinked his eyes then sniffed the air too. "Yes, you are right. I smell it." His posture straightened, he stood, placing his hands on the table, spreading his fingers across the oak surface as he leaned forward. "Come on out..." he sniffed the air again, "boy. You are surrounded and have been caught. Explain what you are doing in my private chambers."

The badgers began snarling and snapping. Edrick recoiled, falling deep into the wardrobe, but not nearly far enough.

"I'm Edrick...the Woodcutter's son." He called out. No use trying to hide at this point. "I am lost in this underground grave."

The badgers lurched forward, snapping at the sound of Edrick's voice. They scratched their shovel like paws against the door. Edrick held the door, tight. "Don't eat me!" was all he could think to say.

"Always hungry, badgers are. You seem harmless enough. Go," he shouted at the cete, "he will never come out of my wardrobe with you scaring him like that."

The badgers turned, then kicked dirt toward the wardrobe and shuffled off, gathering around the Brownman.

"Come on out now, so I can see you," the wild man demanded.

Edrick leaned toward the door, peeking out. "I am not scared of them. Yet I don't want to be their meal either."

The Brownman laughed. "Used to creatures much larger, like ogres, is that more like it?" He sat back down, staring hard toward Edrick. "Yes, I recognize your smell and voice. Go ahead boys, check him out!"

Edrick pushed the door open and stepped out. The cete of badgers rushed forward, sniffing Edrick, shoving their noses in just about every crevice. Edrick stood still, hands raised in case he needed to fight them off, but they soon lost interest after satiating their curiosity.

The Brownman looked Edrick over. Edrick could not read his face.

"You are fearless, that was no boast."

"I only fear for my family and friends," Edrick answered, or so he believed. His thoughts returned to the dark pit. It made him shiver.

"Oh, but you are young," he said. "Plenty to be fearful of in life…and death." The way his voice settled on the word 'death', made Edrick flinch. Death seemed to wander the halls of this labyrinthine grave.

"Yes, sir." He agreed politely.

"Well now, Edrick, son of Alaric, why are you in my home? Did I not warn you the ways of the forest are now closed to the Woodcutters?" he asked sternly. He was clearly irritated by Edrick's presence.

He leaned away, the man's cold demeanor took him by surprise. "I am in need of rescue again, I suppose."

"Well is that it?! Had I not done enough for your family?! I owe you and your father nothing else! GO! Be gone! Run away before my snapping badgers tear you into tiny morsels!"

Edrick took a step back. The wild man's words were unexpected. He had the impulse to dash back into the darkness, but as he stared at the stranger's face, he just wanted to know why. Why would he risk his life to save his family a month ago only to cast him off to his inevitable death now? Edrick's inaction provoked the man. He kicked his chair out beneath him, sending it flying across the room.

Edrick took two steps back as the Brownman rose from his seat, revealing a huge ax from beneath his cloak. He rested the butt of the haft on the table.

"What?" spoke a frail voice from the behind the Brownman. The figure under the furs stirred.

"What is all this yelling?" asked the hidden figure. It was the strained voice of an old man, weak and gravely concerned.

"Vitherian?"

"Yes, father, I am here," the large man said, laying the ax down. He turned and took a knee by the bedside. His voice softened like freshly hewn wood steamed over a fire.

A hand reached out from beneath the furs, reaching toward the Brownman. A ring slipped off a finger and fell to the floor but the Brownman took no notice and took the hand in both of his.

"There is a boy here from above. I was just sending him on his way."

"A boy? Help me, I want to see."

The large man removed the covers from the figure revealing an aged man, hair white and thin. He wore what was once fine linen and silk, now dirty and torn into rags. He must have been severely wounded for he was bandaged across his legs and chest. The color of his aged face was a mix of yellow, brown and faded black. The old man had taken a beating. That, Edrick was sure of.

The Brownman, this Vitherian, helped lift the old injured man into a sitting position.

Edrick crept closer to get a better look. Another person then appeared from behind one of the curtains. A woman carrying a heavily laden basket on her back, froze still, seeing Edrick standing in the middle of the room. She was middle-aged, deep lines etched around her mouth and in the corners of her eyes. Half her hair already fading into a dull silver.

"A boy?" she echoed, mouth falling slack. Edrick was feeling like he was a ghost wandering amongst the living. "A real boy?" she asked in disbelief.

Edrick walked past her until he stood at the bed. He met the gaze of the injured man. He appeared so frail. He could hardly keep his eyes open, half-closed as they were; unfocused and the light long stolen from what seemed like a once robust soul. The man's mouth hung slack, and his breathing was shallow. Edrick recognized a look about him, as one close to death.

"It is a boy. Is he your son Vitherian?" his voice grew stronger. "My heir?"

"No father, he is just a boy. Son of a woodcutter."

The old man groaned, a sound of grave disappointment, mixed with contempt.

"Let me back down, I need to rest," he said curtly.

The Brownman gently laid the elder down and covered him again with the fur until only his face could be seen. The woman was by their side with a steaming bowl of soup.

The old man took the Brownman's large hands in both of his. He looked on him, as if pleading for his life. "Remember, search for it, my son. You are the only one that can now. Take back our kingdom. You must!"

The Brownman nodded. The old man seemed to rest at ease.

"You must take your medicine, milord," the woman spoke, quiet and humbled.

Edrick looked at the floor where the ring lay. It was gold! He picked it up and turned it in his hand. It was heavier than he expected for such a little thing. Edrick had never held gold before and it felt remarkable. Magical. There was a crest on the face, a sun and crescent moon divided by a sword, and words along the border. He looked to the Brownman, then the old man who took no notice of him. Edrick kept the ring in his hand for the moment.

The woman continued spoon feeding the old man, who sipped quite delicately, like a baby learning to eat. Edrick stepped back from the bed, feeling out of place. He sat on a stool and watched. Tears fell from the woman's eyes, her lip trembled slightly as she fed him. The Brownman held his father's hand, looking over his face, the rising and falling of the old man's breath, which slowed with every minute until it stopped all together.

The Brownman laid his father's hands across his chest, crossing his arms.

"And so the last of the Mark-Lords passes," he said somberly.

The woman dropped her bowl and covered her grieving face. She stood and moved into a dark corner of the room where she mourned in solitude.

"The last of us, you were my father. And so I shall follow soon enough."

He stood and threw off the heavy furs covering his father. He cradled the king's body into his arms and lifted him off the bed. Edrick stood too, wanting to help if he could, but he did not know what to do or say.

"Keep an eye on this boy, Wilona. He is not to leave until I return."

Edrick made to speak, but the large man stepped on past him

and disappeared into the tunnel behind the fur curtains, followed by the cete of badgers. Edrick followed but stopped at the curtain. He listened to the heavy footfalls fade farther away until he was gone.

"Please," the woman said meekly, "do not go, but remain as my husband commands."

"Where is he taking him?"

"To a private place where he can lay his father's remains. A place only he knows. As it should be."

"Did you…" Edrick began to ask, but he did not know if he should. The soup, it seemed poisoned.

"He was dying my boy. He was suffering. He came here to see his eldest son one last time."

Edrick wondered at her words. Not only was the Brownman a prince, but he knowingly killed his own father. How did the Brownman come to be in this place? Why did he abandon his family?

"Sit and I will feed you if you are hungry. And do not worry," she was quick to add, "I will not harm you." She said with heartfelt emotion, as if she needed him to believe it. She approached him, but seemed unsure if she should come too close. "I would never harm your family."

"I believe you. I am hungry."

She brought him bread, thick black mushrooms and salted meat. It did not compare to his last meal at the cottage, but it was nothing less than what his mother provided. He had the sudden impulse to return to his home, to see his mother's face and hear her voice. Yet he had an uncompleted task. He was confident there must be a Goblyn Market near, after being deceived and almost killed. He hoped he could not only find Sunniva but was even more determined to rescue Tredan, Gaebria, Bron and the others. All the children. He did not know how, but he had to do it.

Wilona watched him as he ate, eyes still filled with grief. But he also noticed a sense of relief. Something about his presence calmed her greatly.

"You are a handsome one. Same as your father and brothers."

"You know my family? I am not familiar with you."

"Knew them? Yes, before you were born. I was a colleague of your mother's."

She ran the back of her hand down his cheek. Her hands were cold, her skin rough, signs she had labored hard her entire life. She smelled of sage and pine needles. Possessed the penetrating gaze of an owl. "You are quite precious to your mother and father."

"How do you know them?"

She looked away and became quiet. "Do not ask me that," her voice fell into a whisper, obviously pained in some way from the question. "Please. But I am a friend. You must believe that."

He nodded, and quickly changed the subject. "Is this your home?"

"Yes, it is, because it is my husband's home. I am from another place, another village."

Edrick's eyes wandered around the room. "Where did all those books come from? And those maps?" He got up from table to have a closer look. "They are amazing!"

"Those are the prince's things. They have been here a long time. That is all I know. You want to rest? I will make you a place by the fire. The prince will be back, and we should wait for him."

Edrick complied. Wilona laid layers of furs down in front of the fire and invited Edrick to lie down. He did and she covered him with a soft linen, then a heavy mink fur. It felt warm and safe there. Edrick closed his eyes, but told himself not to sleep.

But his body betrayed him.

He was woken by the voices of Wilona and the Brownman talking quietly, only the Brownman's low voice reverberated in the earthen chamber. Edrick couldn't imagine the imposing man could be, or ever sound, quiet. He sat up, drawing their attention. They fell silent.

"Come sit, boy," the man invited.

Wilona moved into the back of the chamber as her husband sat at the table in the center of the room. The bed where the king died had been made, as if no one ever lay there at all. Edrick took a seat directly in front of the Brownman. He held the man's intense gaze.

"So tell me lost boy, how did you come to wander into my home? Speak truthfully."

Edrick recounted his tale from when the Brownman rescued him, to his father being captured by the Folthnir and the battle with the witches to finding the cottage. He told them he thought he found the Woodcutter King, but it turned out to be a trick and he was separated from the group.

The Brownman listened attentively, sitting very still and

occasionally shaking his head disapprovingly at certain parts of the story.

"I was thrown into a pit that opened like a mouth of a huge beast. Yet something caught me when I neared the bottom. I followed my way through the tunnel until I found this room."

"How did you see your way through?" Wilona asked. "You could have been lost until you starved to death."

"There were these green lights. I thought they might be faeries at first. They did not feel like faeries, but sad and lost. Like me."

"Those would be the lost souls caught by Lhodyn."

"Then these are the Vaults of Lhodyn?" Edrick said. "This is where the dead pass on?"

"Yes and no," the Brownman replied cryptically. He paused in reflection then said, "These tunnels were not always here, and neither was Lhodyn. The elves were the first in these woods, and they reluctantly welcomed her into their homes, shared their knowledge and love of the forest with her. But she betrayed them, like all of us!"

He looked into Edrick's eyes, "Like she betrayed your family and mine."

"What do you mean?"

"I have not the time or desire to share all I know. But as for your family is concerned, there is a dark secret among you Woodcutters. The Warden of the Woods you see is a servant of the goddess, like me. No. Thralls and slaves she has made us. We have no choice, thanks to the oaths our forefathers took.

"A long time ago, your sires were a noble people, as Lhodyn once was compassionate and protective. Yet as the centuries passed, she took more pride in her importance, and demanded all creatures worship her as supreme goddess, including your ancestors. The elves would not. They have their own beliefs and they could not forsake it. So Lhodyn tormented them and drove them out. This was a wicked act and darkened her forever. She craved more power and began stealing the souls of the deceased.

"The dead of all those villages and towns surrounding Wudelic would never know rest. Their souls would not pass on into the Æthyr, instead were stolen by Lhodyn. The faeries, who are spirits from the beginning of time, also came under her influence. Faeries are spirits of life and when they fade from this world, not even Lhodyn can stay them. Keeping the spirits of the dead in the forest changed those faeries. They became dark creatures.

"Spirits of life and spirits of death should not be in the same place. It is not natural. I'm afraid these faeries have changed into something that cannot be reversed. Anyway, as long as Lhodyn remains in these woods, they will too, and we will never know if things can be returned to their proper balance."

"Is there a way to free the spirits of the dead?" Edrick thought of Aslenissia. She said she protected his brother's spirits from Lhodyn. She was able to send one to heaven in his place.

"Yes, only if Lhodyn wills it, or she is forced to, or if she leaves, one way or another. So it's not likely. Curse the gods! There is not one worth your time, lad. They are tyrants, even the ones that profess benevolence. Never trust something with that much power if you have no influence over it. What would motivate them to care for your concerns or needs? We are to them as the animals are to us. Serve the same purpose, like farmers keeping pigs and cattle for slaughter and nothing more. So it is with them. You must act as sheep to receive protection from the gods, but your life is always theirs for the taking. Refuse them then you will be hunted for sport."

Edrick reflected over this. He spoke as if the gods were no different than the Folthnir, just barbarians that take what they want, devoid of any compassion, filled only with fury and selfishness. Yet father held a deep respect for his gods, a reverence that surfaced whenever he spoke of them.

"You spoke of the elves. Where are they? Do you know of one named Aslenissia?"

The Brownman lifted an inquisitive eyebrow. "No need asking about them. They are no longer here, nor care for the mortal world. They have all been asleep in their lands, which is like death for them. Their bodies do not perish, but they sleep and their spirits sometimes wander the land like ghosts. As long as Lhodyn reigns, they choose to sleep to escape her."

"How can we rouse them?"

"Rouse them? You know nothing boy. Wake them to do what? Set things right. If they had the power to do that, wouldn't you think they would have done that by now?"

"But I have met one. A little girl. She knows me and my family. There is a power in her that is good. She is lost and maybe if we help her, she and all the elves might help us."

The Brownman scoffed. "Whatever childish fantasies you have, please spare my ears with your nonsense. You know nothing, child! And what you do know is mostly made up stories told by your mother to lull you into sleep. I have studied many years on true lore," he said, waving his arm across his collection of books and scrolls. "I alone know many things that have been forgotten, knowledge that has been abandoned for childish stories with pleasant endings."

He spat on the floor. "To hell with you, child. Look at what your ideas led your family and friends. Death and worse."

Edrick jumped up. "Shut up!"

The Brownman moved to strike Edrick across the face but Edrick deftly moved and stepped back.

"No, please, no!" Wilona pleaded from the side.

"Remain quiet, woman," the Brownman shouted.

"You should respect your wife!" Edrick rebuked.

"Why you little mooncalf!" The large man tossed the oak table aside like it were made of paper. Edrick ran around the room as the Brownman charged behind him.

Wilona moved between them. "Stop milord. I beg you, he is just a boy!"

"Insolent child! I will beat him until he learns respect for his betters."

"Just try it, old man!" Edrick taunted back.

"Out! Out! Get out of my home! Back into the goblyn tunnels with you!"

"No!" Wilona pleaded. "Do not send him away. He will perish in the dark."

"If the goblyns don't find you I will make sure my badgers will!" He growled.

"I don't care! I wasn't planning on staying anyway." He removed his torc from his neck. He was ready to face the dark again. Better than to remain in the light with a man that revealed himself to be more and more like the Folthnir in nature; self-serving and brash.

"I have to find my sister! Remember her? She's barely older than a baby. It's adults like you who abandon children, who choose injustice and selfishness! I don't need you!" He turned and rushed out of the Brownman's lair, tossing aside the heavy fur curtain.

"WE don't need you!" Edrick yelled out into the darkness of the tunnel ahead. His voice reverberated down the hall.

"Wait, Edrick!" the Brownman called after him. His voice changed, deflating, his tone lightened. Seemingly desperate at Edrick's sudden departure. "I have been too hasty!"

Edrick ignored him. What wasteful lives some adults choose to live, he thought. To have great strength and lineage to combat monsters and the Folthnir, but instead, decide to live like hermits deep underground, pretending the ills of the world are someone else's problem. All men like him deserve this existence. All them should be placed deep underground with the dead.

"Wait!" Wilona's voice cried out. Edrick stopped and looked behind. Wilona rushed toward him from behind the curtain, but stumbled and fell into the ensuing dark. Edrick ran to help her up.

"Thank you," she said. She wiped her face with her hands. She stood but she remained hunched over, head hanging low. In the dim light of his torc, he could not see her face.

"He really is a good man," she said. She was apologetic and somber. "Too much has he endured Edrick, a child couldn't imagine. You are a good, courageous boy. Do not change, but be not overly stubborn and prideful."

"Come with me. My mother will care for you, help you if you desire help."

She was quiet. Edrick tried to see her face, to see what she could possibly be feeling.

"Come back. Milord wishes to speak to you, say one final thing, then you are free to leave."

"I will. Only as favor to you, not him."

She nodded. They both returned into the chamber, where the Brownman greeted him with a large smile and arms held out wide. The table had been set back into place.

"That's my boy, have a seat. I lost my temper. I apologize."

Edrick sat down, laying the torc on the table. The flakes of metal gleamed under the lantern light.

"What is that you have there?" the Brownman inquired. Something peculiar came across the Brownman's expression, taking a sudden interest in the torc.

"It is my father's."

"Your father's torc," he whispered to himself, "you have Alaric's torc? How?"

"What a treasure," Wilona gasped, leaning over Edrick's

shoulder for a closer look.

"When he was captured he had me keep it as to prevent the Folthnir from taking it."

"And he is dead now?"

"No, I don't think so," though had not seen his father in a few days.

The Brownman leaned back into his chair and stroked his beard. "You are a foolish child, Edrick, for coming into the forest a second time, after what happened to your brother and your sister," he gently said. Edrick was still wary of any genuine concern, however. "How could you bring more children here? Tell me why you did it?"

"I thought we could save them! I just wanted my sister back..." tears came unbidden. He wiped his eyes. Wilona hugged him. After his guilt passed, his stalwart determination rushed back over him. "I was doing what I knew to be right. I just trusted the wrong person, even when my gut said not to. I was deceived, all of us were. I did what those cowards in the village were afraid to do."

"And what was that?"

"Protect them!"

"Protect who, Edrick?"

"The children! All of us, from them! The Folthnir!" He stood up and glared at the man and woman, as if they had a hand in it. "They tricked him into leaving. If he had not gone, Sunniva would still be here. And then they handed him back over to be tortured when all he wanted was to help them."

"Your father?"

Edrick nodded. "They broke his spirit," he said, in a whisper, as if admitting such a thing were sacrilegious to everything he believed in.

"It is a cruel world, boy. The sooner you see that, the more aware of it, the better you learn to react to it."

"NO!" Edrick lashed back. "It is not the world that is cruel! It is not the sky, the earth or the water. It is people who are cruel! When they choose selfishness over sacrifice, when they choose easy riches over toil. It just takes one person to stand up to those people, like my father, a person that shows strength and resolve. That shows people that it is acceptable to be afraid, but it is not right to allow evil to take root, no matter how small."

"And yet they broke his spirit," the Brownman repeated back to him.

Edrick looked the wild man dead in the eye. "Even a single rock breaks under the waves of the sea. But enough rocks can hold back the tides."

"Well said," Wilona told him.

"My mother told us that. She loves stories of the sea."

The Brownman stood up, and turned. He paced the room, falling into thought. "This is what will happen, Edrick. I will take you to the surface and we will complete what you set out to do. If your sister is still alive, if your friends are still alive, there is only one place they will be."

"The Goblyn Market?" Edrick said.

"Yes! That is where we must go, but be forewarned Edrick if you thought the ogre and witches were terrible, then the Goblyn Market will be filled with such vile creatures. And they will snatch you up at the first chance they get."

"But you wouldn't let that happen would you, milord?" Wilona asked softly.

"I will do my best. Or," turning back to Edirck, "I can take you home now. But you must swear to never enter these woods again, and convince your family to flee far away."

Edrick thought of the choice, return home without Sunniva, without Gaebria, Tredan and Bron? Or face a nightmare of creatures with but one man to protect him.

"Sir? You are surely a great and mighty man. I have seen you thwart that ogre and beast by yourself with your wolves. But could you possibly withstand the monsters you say will be there?"

The Brownman huffed in derision. "You are a child, so I will forgive your ignorance, but I am only matched by one other here in this forest. I am Prince Vitherian, son of King Sithric of the Gheldenmark, thrall of the great lady Lhodyn!"

Edrick fell off his chair. His mouth dropped open. His head spun. Was this the true Woodcutter King? An aura of power and self-determination filled the room.

"I walk through this forest with all the monsters and beasts at my command, save Lhodyn command otherwise. We shall walk into the Goblyn Market and see what we might find. I know for a fact children are there. So if any of your kin or friends are alive, that is where they will be."

A faint smile appeared across Wilona's face.

The Brownman stood over Edrick suddenly and held out his hand. Edrick took it and stood up. The large man knelt down so they were face to face.

"But, for this service you must pay me."

"I do not have anything to offer or I would."

"I will take this," he said, lifting the torc from the table. "This will be my payment."

Edrick did not know how to answer. He would have said yes instantly, but such a loss would infuriate his father. He would let him down, his whole family down. "Is there anything else? This is my family's heirloom! My father would be terribly angry at me."

"Edrick, what I offer is much. Think like a man, Edrick."

"All right," Edrick agreed quickly.

"Excellent!" the Brownman raised the torc, as if proclaiming victory. He smiled for the very first time, wrinkles lined his face from his eyes down along his mouth until it disappeared into a nest of whiskers.

"Very shrewd. Edrick. You will not regret this," he patted him on the back and Edrick nearly fell over. "HA!" The Brownman's mood became merry. "We must move at once. Wilona, ready my things. Food, for the two of us. Just for three days should do."

She went to it without a word, disappearing into the pantry.

Edrick's heart sank as he watched the large man ogle his father's prized possession. Such a precious thing remained in his family since Renweard. Father told few stories, but those of his grand sire, every male Woodcutter knew. Then the ring came to Edrick's mind, the one that slipped off of King Sithric's hand.

"What is it boy? You have something to say?"

Edrick took out the king's ring and held it toward the large man. "Your father dropped this. I was going to mention it before, before our disagreement. It belongs to you. I guess it would be as precious to you as the torc is to my father."

Vitherian gave Edrick a look, a respectful regard. "Yes, I saw you pick it up." He took it between his finger and thumb, holding it to his eyes. In one hand he possessed the torc, the other, the signet of the realm.

"Your father said something, to search for something," Edrick remarked, intent on the man's reaction, and to his surprise, he handed the ring back.

"What?" the Brownman asked. His eyes still rested on the ring as Edrick received it. He then huffed and made a dismissive wave with his empty hand. "The prattling of a delirious old man. Faerie tales and legends. Keep the ring, Edrick. Straight forward exchange then: your father's heirloom for my father's. And I will still take you to the surface and see what business the goblyns have with your sister and loved ones."

He held out his hand to shake on their agreement. Edrick took it and shook. His hand seemed so small by comparison.

"You are giving me the king's ring?" Edrick asked still doubtful he should keep a precious object such as this.

"Yes! Keep it. I have no use for it. It was not destined to be mine, so it might as well be yours." The large man patted Edrick on the back, which launched him a few feet forward. "Perhaps you will be the next king of all Gheldenmark!" he said with a mighty laugh. "You seem to have a knack for leading and don't flinch at danger. Who else better suited for such a lofty station? But this is no mere trinket to be kept in your pants." The large man stroked his beard looking around the chamber.

Wilona appeared with a shoulder pack stuffed full, but waited patiently for her husband to acknowledge her.

"Ah!" the Prince said is sudden realization. He reached around his wife's neck and removed a thin metallic necklace Edrick had not noticed before. The prince removed a pearl pendant from the white gossamer metal, placing the piece on the table, and took Edrick's ring and threaded the chain into the finger hole. The chain's surface danced in rainbow colors.

"If I were you, I would keep this out of sight until you find a very special place to keep it." The prince laid the chain over Edrick's neck, lifted his shirt collar and dropped the ring inside. Its cold surface rested against his chest. The chain felt almost like silk, light and smooth.

Edrick nodded in all solemnity, as if it were his duty to carry on with the kingdom's legacy.

Wilona placed the pack over the prince's shoulders, while her eyes looked to the pearl on the table. "A gracious gift milord has bestowed you, Edrick. Honor him by taking care of it." She rested a hand just below her neck and watched the prince fetch his large ax.

"We must leave now," the prince said. Wilona hurried to the prince and stood on her tip toes while he leaned over to receive a kiss on his cheek.

"Farewell, milord. Do take care of this boy. He must have arrived here for some good reason. To wait all these years and to see him, a Woodcutter, here. There must be something written in the stars," her voice trailed off. She looked to Edrick and opened her arms for a hug. Edrick shyly let her.

"Edrick, listen to milord. He is as noble a man as you will ever meet. He will see you to your kin and make sure you and your sister return home safely. His word is his oath, like all great men." She paused as if she had more on her mind to speak, but remained silent.

"Let's go, boy," the prince said. "And lend him a lantern," he commanded.

Without a farewell to his wife, the two hurried into the tunnel, the large man leading with a bright lantern held aloft, pushing the dark far out. He led Edrick into even smaller tunnels breaking off the main one, through a maze of disorienting passages. They rushed down the barren paths, passing side corridors, turning into others; it was all confusing and bewildering for Edrick to gain his bearings as they rose and dipped in elevation, spiraled, slid and dashed their way through. All the while occasional lamp-like souls floated through the air, in and out of the walls, sometimes clinging to Edrick. They always avoided contact with the prince, parting to allow him passage. He paid no attention to them.

"The entire forest has tunnels beneath its roots," the prince remarked after a time, "carved by all sorts of creatures, and just like the land above, there are creatures of good and creatures of evil and they do battle. These tunnels are now home to a growing number of goblyns and evil things that are starting to claim the forest. And the goblyns are feeding nasty things to the trees roots. The trees are now hateful. And the animals have become hateful. And Lhodyn is hateful and ready to succumb to the will of evil beings."

"How did she get to be so evil? You said she was not always that way."

"How does anyone become evil, Edrick? I thought you already had the answers."

Edrick remained quiet. It would not be prudent to start an argument.

"Come, we have farther to go."

Edrick wondered exactly how far underground they were. If one could, how far could you dig into the earth? He wondered if the prince knew the answer. He would have to remember to ask him later. Then the man stopped and stood still. He held his finger up to Edrick, motioning for silence. He then placed his ear against the wall, listening. He looked behind him, past Edrick, into the dark.

"We have to move faster or we will not make it," he said in a low voice.

"What do…."

"Shhh, don't speak," he said.

They hurried at a brisk pace, running hundreds of yards. Edrick broke into a sweat, his heart racing. He was wondering if he would be able to keep up with the prince's long strides.

Just ahead of them, a badger popped out of the wall, ran around the prince and dove back into its hole, disappearing as quickly as it arrived.

"Damn!"

"What was that?" Edrick asked.

"They are near," he replied ominously. He looked around, then took out his small whistle and blew it. Curious, it emitted no sound. The badger appeared all the same, out of the small burrow.

"Take him. Lead him to the surface. I will have to distract them from his trail."

"No! We had a deal. You can't leave me. Who is near?"

"Goblyns! Vicious, flesh eating, nasty goblyns. And they have smelled you in their tunnels. Do you not know who expanded Lhodyn's Vaults?"

"Goblyns?" Edrick gasped in surprise. It was all unbelievable, even though he expected everything he heard, but when it happened to him in the moment, he could not believe it.

"Oh, yes," the prince said, seizing Edrick by the shoulders, lifting him high off the ground until they were face to face. "Goblyns, Edrick! Like the ones that gathered your friends in the woods. You thought the ogre works alone? They love children and smelling one in their tunnels drives them mad with ecstasy. They will tear you apart, limb from limb, fighting one another over every little morsel that they are incapable of sharing amongst themselves. Fighting for a small taste before the Lady claims your soul."

Edrick shook his head in dismay realizing the true danger he led his friends into. What a fool he had been.

"They are almost here." Vitherian dropped him suddenly. Edrick collapsed to his side, his breath knocked out of him. "Get inside that burrow and go! Follow the badger no matter what. I will meet up with you on the surface. Follow, then wait!"

"I don't believe you," Edrick shouted back. "You just want to be rid of me. You didn't want to help me before, until your wife talked you into it. Now that we are away from her, you are going to feed me to your badgers. You said it yourself."

"Damn, child!" The prince struck Edrick across his face. "Has your father raised you to be so defiant?"

Just then, there was a scuffling and commotion echoing down the walls. A great stomping and clanging of metal approached them.

"They are nearly here!" he said desperately.

Edrick looked at the prince, his face still as stone. It held no deception. Edrick scurried into the burrow.

"Take your lantern!" the prince said passing it into the tunnel. Then, took his ax and collapsed the entrance quickly, sealing off Edrick's retreat. Edrick scurried far into the barrow as yelling and mad screaming seeped from the dirt barrier behind him.

Beyond him, the badger had long disappeared ahead of him. Edrick scrambled desperately to catch it.

20

WUDELIC WOODS

THE FOREST TRAILS changed directions as fluid as a stream, writhing like a wild serpent beneath the war band's feet. A path that held a straight course would suddenly part to lead elsewhere, or narrow and close altogether as branches and vines reached out over the trails to erase all signs of its passage. Alaric encountered this before when he sought out Lhodyn.

"Reveal yourselves, witches!" the Theign shouted into the empty trees. "Your magick will not deter us. We need not follow any path save the one Vylkinus has set before us!" The others followed their leader's bravado, shouting insults toward unseen enemies, calling them whores and lovers of bestiality.

There were no replies at first. No response that first day when the sun was high and the spring air retained its warmth.

"Where dwells this goddess of whores, Woodcutter? We will get at her whether she desires it or not. She will suffer the loins of my Vauldkyn warriors. They have not encountered a suitable female capable of surviving their lust. We will see of what stuff this woodland goddess is made."

Alaric did not answer right away. "She is here. It would surprise me if she did not respond before the night is over. Already she tries to delay us. She is attempting to lead us where she desires us to be."

"We will thwart her plans!" The Theign declared. The wolfskins hooted and grunted in agreement.

"That is to be seen," Alaric said in a low voice, heard only by his wife and Elzera.

They finished the day treading the alternating paths until the sun's light dimmed and faded into a blanket of utter darkness. Frustrated and weary, they stopped to make camp.

Then the laughter started.

A disturbing gleeful chorus surrounded them, haunting, mocking, untraceable. They rushed to make camp expecting an impending battle, scrambled to fall into defensive positions but the creatures never revealed themselves.

Pebbles and pine cones pelted the group every now and then, only to have the barbarians give chase into the darkness in pursuit of the attackers. But they quickly returned to camp without discovering their assailants. Then the haunting laughter would erupt once again, mocking their efforts.

Night deepened. The Folthnir quickly wearied of the childish games. A few times there was a rousing commotion, the sound of fighting erupting around camp, only to discover a warrior attacking a tree or shrub. Each man claimed that it was a goblyn a moment before. The Theign rebuked them for their foolishness. The entire war band became apprehensive, feeling they would be attacked any moment, but it became evident they were being toyed with. Alaric noted the suppressed rage behind the Theign's eyes. For their kind, there was a sacredness to war. This kind of behavior insulted them. Alaric realized the tactical advantage it gave their enemies as well, for the warriors had lost all calm and composure they first carried into the woods.

Alaric recognized an ambush in the making.

The Folthnir set guards around the perimeter as the others ate their evening meal. The southerner found his way over to Alaric and his wife, who had their own fire burning away from the Folthnir. Elisial already prepared a protection circle to keep any harmful faeries from cursing them as soon as they settled in.

"Good evening," greeted the dark man with a forced smile.

"Is this an evening that seems good to you, Uthræsian?" asked Elzera.

"No. I suppose I am a creature of formalities and platitudes. I am a business man that has learned that a positive attitude in all situations precipitates good business. My apologies, it is just I do not usually go traipsing off into dark forests to hunt down begrudged goddesses just to demonstrate to my inferiors just how large my testicles are."

"Oh, so how do they do it in the south? By the number of women they rape and enslave?"

The southerner drew his robe tight, fighting the urge to spit an angry retort. "Cleary none of us here are amongst friends, but that is not to mean we cannot form an alliance should these brutes discover they have bitten more than they can chew, as they say in these lands."

"They have," Elisial promised.

"Which brings the reason for your visit now," Elzera added. "When new allies fall, past enemies will make do, as they say down south."

The southerner stared at the Elisial in contempt. "Yes, something like that."

"You will free all the slaves at the tower and leave these lands or else I promise you will not leave these woods alive," Alaric threatened quietly. "Do this and we will watch your back. I will guide you out from these woods as long as I still breathe. If you can keep up."

The southerner looked squarely at each of the three villagers. He gave a slight nod. "So we have an agreement. Goodni..." he stopped himself. "Until dawn then."

"Despicable coward." Elzera spat as the Uthræsian walked away. "It seems now we must guard his life if we are to see those people freed. He should fetch back those women that he has already sent south."

"You are right," Alaric replied. "I will have him agree to that as well." Alaric stared at the southerner from across camp. He sat miserably by himself, an outcast amongst northern warriors. Even Grindan sat comfortably amongst the Folthnir. How quickly they took to him.

The fires burned low as sleep took some in the camp. Alaric, Elzera and Elisial laid close to one another, resting but not asleep.

In the darkest time of night, blue and violet motes of light seeped down from the dark canopy. Floating like colorful snowflakes. Flickering like ghostly fireflies, same as the first battle at the Ruined Tower. Alert, the warriors were on their feet, swatting them away. Fear could be heard in their shouts as they called to arms.

More wood was added on the campfire to create enough light for battle while others formed a defensive circle around the camp.

Their battle-priests started singing in low, strange voices. Alaric knew not what they said, but their words were powerful and passionate, the music of thunder.

The horses were startled by the ghostly lights. Frightened, they jumped about, kicking to get away as the lights swarmed the air. The horse-master tried to calm them but they would not settle, even as he covered their eyes. They broke free from their tethers and bolted off into the forest. Soon after, their death cries were heard in the distance. A victory cry rang from the distance, from the same voices that taunted them with laughter earlier.

"Goblyns!" the men whispered. They shouted defiant challenges to their enemies. All men despised goblyns, cruel, twisted and demented creatures that preyed on humans of all lands. They were wicked and brutal monsters.

The priests' song rose in volume and tenacity, sheltering the men from the dark faeries curses.

"Stay close, Ulfserkers," the Theign said to all. "These spirits cannot touch warriors of Vylkinus. Cast them back into the dark! Banish these dæmons!" the Theign commanded his priests. As the song rolled out through the woods, the lights slowly dimmed and faded. The night remained still and quiet as death until the break of dawn. This everyone knew, for nobody slept.

They traveled at first light. Alaric followed the children's tracks, even as the trails shifted, their tracks remained constant in the earth. It was not long before they discovered the hanging carcasses of their horses from ash and elder trees, decapitated and bound by the rear hooves. Directly beneath the suspended bodies, the bowels were arranged to look like scary faces, the kind children would draw in the dirt.

There was no response from anyone at first, just stunned silence.

Then the horse-master swore in the words of the Folthnir, yelling, shattering the silence. All twelve horses had been slaughtered.

"Cowards these goblyns are," the Theign roared.

"Your horses, Theign!" the horse-master foamed at the mouth. "Come out monsters, we are equally skilled at decapitating beasts." He pulled a great knife from his belt.

The warriors shouted bloody war cries, clashing their shields with thunderous racket. There was no doubt that these men were as fierce and brutal as the creatures that hung these horses. Alaric's only thoughts were to keep Elisial and Elzera safe, and that bastard trader too, if he must.

"Stay always behind me," he said to Elisial.

"How close are they?" she asked.

"They are here, watching, as they have been since we left the cottage."

Alaric saw the fear behind his wife's eyes, perhaps the same look displayed on his own. Not fear for his own life, but fear of having harm come to Elisial, his beloved and mother to their children. He knew too, her fear was not for herself, but for him and Elzera, and the possibility they would leave their children orphans.

"When will they attack? Is this always how they behave, taunting humans like a cat plays with a mouse?" Elisial asked.

"From what little I know about them, they attack when they have the advantage. And they take pleasure in humiliating and taunting their enemies. They do not think or act like humans. Not even like murderous humans. They are something worse."

"I have had experience with them," Elzera said, "there are different kinds and they act in different ways, but one thing they all have in common is that they take pleasure in cruelty."

Their discussion was soon drowned out by the blaring of warhorns and priestly chanting. The five giant Vauldkyns cut down the horses and began to quarter them, turning their bodies into food for the march. A fire was started and fed until it was a roaring mass of flames reaching the height of a man's head. They were preparing for battle. The Theign shouted in his tongue and that of the Gheldenmark, challenging his enemy to meet him in battle.

"What are they doing? They should be passing through this place," Alaric said to his wife and friend. He urgently walked over to the Theign as he was addressing his warrior host.

"Vylkinus claims these woods!" The Theign shouted. "Now and forever. He demands the bitch goddess submit to His sovereignty and prostate herself before His servants, His Blooded. We are the unending champions of the Hellforge, and everything beneath the sky falls under His hammer, established since the beginning. Every treasure hidden shall be upturned and seized, piled onto His ever expanding domain!"

This was the sort of speech the Folthnir recited during every battle, in every land. Alaric had heard it before. The speakers' face differed but never the words or their fervor.

"We need to leave here," Alaric pressed. "They hung those horses here not because they believe you would flee, but to keep you here. Look around, to our right is a river and to the left a hill. We are vulnerable. We must leave."

Grindan stepped to Alaric, blindsided him with a heavy punch across his jaw, blurring his vision. Alaric stumbled, pulling Elzera and Elisial with him by their tethered necks. He fought to remain conscious. "You speak to your Theign, Woodcutter, not one of your sons," he rebuked.

Elisial cradled him, attempting to help him to his feet, but he shook her off. She recoiled from his rage, her mouth dropped in her confusion.

"You touch me or my wife or any of my family again, Grindan, I will kill you."

Grindan took a step forward to meet the challenge, but the Huntsman moved between them. Grindan, clutched his forge hammer, his body stood rigid.

"Let them fight. The smith will break him!" Ator said to his father.

"Now is not the time!" the Theign yelled to all. "Dog!" he shouted at Alaric, "behave yourself or I will throw your wife to my boys. Grindan. You act only by my word. Forget again, and I will throw a leash over your neck."

"As you command, my Theign."

"What has caused this change in your heart, Grindan?" Alaric asked, rubbing his cheek. "When we were young men and I counted you as my true friend, you were noble in thought and action. Why this darkness upon you?"

The big man laughed heartedly, as if being asked a question from a child that was so obvious to an adult. "What changed me? Alaric you are the biggest fool for refusing to change. The weight of the world will crush an iron will like yours. At first, I thought I needed to protect you from it, but then the wars convinced me that life only survives through desperation and treachery. The valiant always die with flowery words and grand ideas, but it is the wretched that bury them. Just as I will bury you."

"Enough!" the Theign yelled. The Huntsman yanked Alaric's leash, choking all breath from his throat. Alaric pulled at the leather strap with his fingers. Is this what Edrick felt in those final moments, he wondered? Did he hate him for not protecting him? Did Baldice? Did Sunniva?

"I will cut all your tongues out if I hear any more of this quarreling!" the Theign roared.

Alaric eyed Nithledan resting over Ator's shoulder. If he could just get to it, he would spit words of death.

The Theign called the southerner to his side. From a cylindrical case slung around the merchant's back, he pulled out a scroll, and unfurled it. It was the village Writ! He, the southerner and the Huntsman studied it in private.

The southerner then moved from the two and approached Alaric. "Is there some hidden city here? With a wall around it as depicted on the map."

Alaric nodded.

The merchant smiled. "Take us there. How long will it take?"

"It will take us into the night. But it is not a place for mortals. That place is cursed. Not even I range there."

"This whole forest is cursed. You will guide us there. And I will remind you that you will stop and start when you are told. Do this if you wish no harm to these two," he said, nodding to the women.

"We would do better to survive this day if we left these fools to Her. Stand with them and I will leave you here to die," Alaric responded.

The southerner's eyes narrowed. "We have an agreement," he whispered.

"Deliver me my bow. Or I have no better chance than you. I cannot survive without it."

The man nodded and walked back to the Theign.

"Alaric, look!" Elisial said.

There, slipping beneath the shadows, the Greyorn darted. It watched them, followed them.

"A forest spirit?" Elzera asked, curious.

Alaric said nothing. Its presence did not bode well. He tracked it until it disappeared behind the elder tree where they cut down the horse carcasses. Then there was a loud crack, like a mighty splitting of wood, where Alaric lost sight of the Greyorn. In the bushes beyond, he saw evil eyes staring back at him, adorned with cruel smiles that flashed like quick steel daggers out of sight.

More loud cracks exploded from the trees. Then the large ashes and elders fell. Directly beneath them, were the unwitting giants. The trees landed across their backs, pinning them, swallowing them from sight with their bushy foliage.

From above their camp, black arrows streaked into the unaware Folthnir. At once, war horns sounded out, blaring loud, shaking the trees. The wolfskins circled around their Theign, shields held high.

From all around, goblyns stepped out from every tree and bush. Yet all their attention were drawn up the hill where a contingent of goblyn archers trained their drawn bows down on them all. They were easily outnumbered three to one.

And their giants were immobilized in a single blow.

Elzera pulled out a small knife from somewhere hidden in her clothes. "Should have had this out already, I suppose."

The goblyns were an ugly, savage people. Of many sizes and shapes they came, tall and skinny, short and wide, large and powerful. It was as if whatever dark god that created them gave little thought into shaping their forms, instead, took care to craft evil spirits bent on doing its bidding.

These goblyns wrapped themselves in leathers dyed in grays and browns, dull and washed out earth tones that cleverly hid their forms in the forest, behind brush and tree. Pouches and pockets of all kinds were sewn on to their attire, like outlandish craftsmen, from boot to cowl. Many hid themselves in deep hoods and masks so as to never allow sunlight soil their skin. Yet their eyes flashed in their dark disguises, like hardened diamonds.

Upon the hill, a group marched down. A particularly tall and wiry goblyn stood above the rest, commanding their attention. He laughed gleefully, like a drunken fool hours before sunrise.

"Whoa ho," it said, pulling its mask below its pointed chin. "You north boys make me laugh too much, it hurts. Never have we seen men walk other men as pets through our forest. Strange hounds you keep!"

The Theign shouted back, "To monsters, we men may appear alike, but the Folthnir are the Blooded of Vylkinus, Lord of the Hellforge! Bring your whore goddess before me so I may slit her throat and drink her blood! Today, I become a god!"

The goblyn laughed again, as a king would when threatened by a peasant. Others joined their leader in laughter. Then six large muscular goblyns with the heads of their horses attached to sticks like a child's hobbyhorse, began skipping around the circle, make believing they were riding their mounts. "Watch out for the fierce northmen, lads!" one goblyn chided. "They feel tall on their horses. I wonder how they are on their feet!"

Then one of the mounted goblyns threw the horse-head stick to the ground and pushed over one of his fellow goblyns, bent him over and started rutting on him like a beast in heat. It made rude gestures and faces, wagging its tongue and grunting with each thrust.

"We hear your men like to rape pretty little things, well our lads do as well," the tall leader said. "Such pretty beards these northmen have."

"Aye, will give me something to hold onto," another said, thrusting his hips back and forth as it pulled on an imaginary beard at his waist.

Alaric and the women stooped down low. He did not take his eyes off Nithledan. He extended his hand to Elzera. "Give me the knife." He cut his bindings, gave the knife back to her to do the same. No one noticed as all eyes were transfixed elsewhere.

"I will have my bow back, then we will run," Alaric told them.

Elisial and Elzera nodded. "We will get you arrows," Elzera said, "but hopefully not any through the body."

The fallen elder trees shook, then bobbed up and down. The Vauldkyn giants were alive, yet struggled to free themselves. The battle-priests chanted their war songs, casting a protective magick over the Folthnir.

A priest shouted in their northern tongue, something to Vylkinus. In response, the cloudless sky thundered.

The goblyns shuddered, revealing their cowardess.

One giant stood to his great height, holding the fallen elder over his head. With a great effort he hurled it at the archers and goblyn captain.

The archers let loose a black rain of arrows.

And as if in answer, lighting ripped through the sky, striking the skyward tree, exploding into hundreds of flaming pieces, taking the archers out with fiery splinters.

The Ulfserkers charged the goblyns behind them into the trees while the Theign and his Blooded charged the hill. The battle priests continued their chanting, remaining where they stood. Grindan stood with them, guarding, hammer in hand with a crazed look across his face.

Alaric charged after Ator who followed his father. They scrambled up the hill, against arrow volley. Archers were set all around, as high as the crest. One missile narrowly passed by Alaric's head, finding its way into the face of a wolfskin sneaking up behind him.

The charging Folthnir soon found themselves pinned down a quarter way up the hill, crouching behind their shields, until the four other Vauldkyns finally freed themselves. Alaric wondered at their brute strength and imperviousness to harm. They cried out aloud, "Jhyrl vegruut Theign!" and pounded past the men, up the hill, swiping through a handful of goblyns with their large powerful hammers in one mighty swath. Arrows flew without bias, hitting Folthnir and finding giant flesh. The Folthnir waded in behind the giants who seemed more like siege engines, rolling over the goblyn warriors.

Lightning continued to crack through the sky, descending on the hill, setting goblyn flesh afire.

Alaric found Ator, alone, crouched behind a tree.

The youth spotted him rushing toward him. He grinned. "You will be the first to wet my blade today!" and launched himself at Alaric, raising his sword high, with both hands.

Alaric struck quickly, hurling a hefty rock at the youth's face. It struck him in the cheek, smashing the helm beneath his wolfskin hood. The youth's charge faltered, his grip relaxed. Alaric seized his arm in one hand and disarmed him with the other, taking his weapon. In one swift movement, he slit his throat and threw the boy to the ground. He freed Nithledan and ran back to his wife.

The Folthnir had scattered from the camp, took the fighting into the trees and up the hill. They could escape easily.

Or so he thought.

Grindan now stood over Elisial and Elzera, holding his hammer above their heads, waiting for Alaric's return.

"Drop the bow," he demanded.

"Come with us," Alaric said desperately. "These are not your people. We are Gheldenmark!"

"Still trying to save me? Or just saving yourself?" Grindan kicked Elisial in the back of the head. She fell forward and did not move.

Alaric's soul punched out through his heart, through his chest, and sunk next to his wife.

Grindan stood across Elisial. "Lie down, Alaric, or she dies. Then the old woman."

Alaric dropped his bow. He surrendered.

"You dumb, big ox," Elzera said, plunging her knife into the back of his meaty leg. "Sleep!" she commanded him, leaving the knife sheathed in his body. To Alaric's surprise, Grindan fell back, dropping his hammer, and slept.

Elzera rolled Elisial over. With her index finger she drew a symbol over her forehead and whispered some words. Elisial opened her eyes. "Uh, my head," she spoke softly.

"You were kicked by an ox, it ought to hurt."

Alaric leapt to Grindan's body. He picked up his hammer and was about to withdraw Elzera's knife.

"No, leave it!" Elzera shouted. "He will awake as soon as it is removed."

He recoiled his hand as if the knife were a hidden viper. He looked at her with amazement, surprised by her actions and words.

"So I might have a little bit of witch in me. I charm all my knives."

Alaric looked back down at Grindan's prone form, feeling the heft of the smith's hammer in his palms. He made a promise to the traitor, harm Elisial, he would die.

"Don't do it, Alaric. It won't sit right in your heart," Elzera said.

Alaric stared at the blacksmith chest, rising and falling smoothly as if he were sleeping in his own bed. His chest made a wide target. Alaric wonder how many ribs he would break on his first blow.

He was not like Grindan. He would not be like Grindan. Alaric reclaimed his bow, Nithledan, from the ground.

"Can she walk?" he asked Elzera after a few moments. He quickly scanned the battlefield. "Can she run?"

"I can," Elisial said, getting to her feet. "Here," she handed him a quiver of stolen goblyn arrows, hidden beneath her. "Where do we go?"

"The river. Do you have another knife?" he asked. He gave Elisial Grindan's hammer then slung the quiver of arrows across his shoulder.

Elzera fidgeted, patting herself around her bosom. She reached inside her blouse and pulled out an even longer blade than the first. "This should work."

Alaric nodded. They crossed the clearing into the trees where the fighting still raged. Men and goblyns' bodies lay across the ground. Here, the Huntsman took charge, repelling the goblyns back from their encampment.

The lightning ceased, but thunder still shuddered the skies. Rain fell soon after, from the cloudless blue.

"Thinking of leaving me behind," came a voice. It was the southerner walking toward them. He held his staff in front of him, crystal pulsing with light, like a trained soldier. "Lead on."

Alaric realized that taking this stranger was a dangerous deal.

"Alaric, they spotted us," Elisial said. Wolfskins closed around them. The Huntsman took up his bow, readying an arrow at them.

"Kill him!" the Folthnir shouted. Blurring arrows raced through the air.

A bright flash issued from the southerner's staff, momentarily blinding them all, swallowing the arrows in flight, burning each into ash. "Move, Woodcutter!" the merchant said.

Alaric grabbed Elisial's hand and ran through the trees. He didn't stop to see if Elzera could keep up. Somehow he trusted she would.

Light kept flashing off the trees in front of them as they ran. The river neared. Alaric took in his bearings to discern where the old bridge stood.

Elzera came huffing and puffing behind them. "Are you trying to kill me or save me?" asked the elderly woman.

"I can carry you on my back if you prefer," he said bending down.

She slapped the back of his head. "Only when I'm dead."

He stood back up. "Move in that direction. Wait for me at the riverbank."

Elisial started to ask something, then just nodded and ran. Elzera chased after her like a crazed, knife wielding grandmother.

Alaric took up Nithledan. It quivered with fury in his hands, having been handled by so many it hated. He notched an arrow and drew it back. A throng of Ulfserkers chased the southerner through the woods. He now ran fiercely to stay out of their reach.

Shnikt, flew each arrow, followed by the *shnakt* as it bit into flesh. One by one the wolfskins fell.

The merchant caught up with Alaric, stopped, and leaned against a tree catching his breath. "There will be more. They have sent most of the goblyns back into the woods, now they will be after us."

Alaric said nothing, waiting for more wolfskins to show their vile faces. Nothing moved.

Nithledan felt ecstatic, pulsing in his palm.

"Which way did the women go? I will look after them," the dark man said, stumbling past Alaric. "We must stick together now, Woodcutter. I will make you a rich man."

Alaric turned to face the southerner. He pulled another arrow to his cheek. Nithledan hummed with hatred, with vengeance.

"Slaver!" Alaric shouted. The merchant stopped and turned about, staring down a flying arrow. His face contorted with rage.

Shnakt. Shnakt. Shnakt. Shnakt.

The southerner fell dead.

Alaric stepped on the foreigner's chest as he marched toward the river.

21

THE FOREST SPIRIT

AN ENDLESS DRIZZLE of dirt fell over Edrick, irritating his eyes as he crawled, worm-like, through the crumbling tunnel, scrambling to match pace with the badger. He scurried as fast as he could, imagining the goblyns had already tunneled through the collapsed wall and were at his feet. There was no room in the confined space for him to look back, he was shoulder to shoulder against the earth.

"Wait!" he cried out. He shook his head vigorously keeping the dirt out of his face, though it stubbornly clung to his skin and eyes despite all efforts. One hand awkwardly held out the oil lantern as he kept it as upright as possible. His elbows scraped and pinched against stones and compacted earth. The badger seemed to take no notice and was soon lost from sight.

"At least there is but one path to take, or I should lose him," Edrick remarked to himself.

On and on he went, squirming up and down the winding tunnel, sometimes hitting a pocket of open space, wider chambers where he could get to his knees for a few feet only to have to squeeze back into another narrowing tunnel.

"This would be fun, in better times. I'd like to crawl through here when there aren't any goblyns about." He thought Tredan would love to explore these tunnels with him. They could play hide and seek or pretend he was a king's man and Tredan was the goblyn. That would be grand. Then thoughts of Sunniva and Baldice surfaced, how he would try to convince them to follow him into the badger tunnels, teasing Sunniva that it was filled with creepy, wormy things, and she would flee to Baldice for protection. And he would smile, holding her, enjoying his role as protector, the big brother. Thoughts of them sharpened his determination. He had to emerge somewhere on the surface, he just hoped that the prince would keep his word and take him to Sunniva.

He then wondered about the Brownman, and his revelation as prince to Gheldenmark. He did not have the appearance of a prince. The Brownman figure was a story that was older than his great-grandfather, surely the prince could not be that old. When the time was right he would have to ask him his history, if in fact they did meet again. Edrick believed the man to be honorable, after all he risked his life to save him and his brothers and sisters weeks ago. But Edrick began to doubt the intentions of all adults. Everyone seemed to let him down. He would never treat children like that, he promised, when he grew up.

It was not too long and not too far when they emerged above ground. The air was heavy, but fresh; the mere act of breathing above ground seemed so precious to Edrick. He took a few moments and remained still, filling his lungs with the fragrant forest air, with eyes shut. He simply breathed.

It was daytime. The sunlight stung his eyes, even though the heavily filtered forest canopy subdued its brilliance. Sunlight seemed a visitor of diminishing frequency now.

Something then bumped hard into his thigh. It was the badger, urging him to keep moving.

"You are in a hurry aren't you? I do suppose the goblyns haven't forgotten us have they? I hope we meet the Brownman again. Are you going to take me to him?"

As if understanding the speech of men, it was off again, waddling like a startled pig. Edrick grabbed the lantern and followed. He found keeping up with the badger less difficult now that he was back on his feet, not to say it was entirely easy. They were still in a forest filled with trees, bushes, hedges and all kinds of obstacles that a badger could dive through or between, but a larger animal, Edrick in this case, needed to find a path around and therefore break sight with the animal and skillfully predict where they might meet up.

It went on like this for quite a while until the sun sunk low in the sky. Edrick's stomach grumbled and he wondered if he might eat that day. Not an entirely new sensation as winters were usually lean, but unusual for the plenitudes of spring.

Finally they arrived at a small clearing where the badger stopped and waited for Edrick. It remained still, seemingly resting itself.

"I never knew a badger with such robust legs. That must have been a tremendous distance for you in one effort." The badger did not respond, but its chest heaved steadily revealing its exhaustion.

Nearby, an ancient pine with the width of a full grown man lay on its side, fallen decades ago. Its interior was mostly hollowed forming a shallow cave. Usually, such a place would be an attractive home for many a creature, so Edrick cautiously approached, determined to know if it were occupied or not. Under normal circumstances, his father would tell him to avoid it and not invite trouble; under normal circumstances Edrick would still investigate away from his father's sight. Yet this time, he needed to know if he was in danger or if it would be safe to rest.

He held up the lantern, entering slowly and saw indeed it was empty for the moment. On the floor of the hollow was a bed of leaves and grass, the size of which Edrick could lay down comfortably and fall asleep for the night. Some animal claimed this tree as a home, something far larger than Edrick.

Edrick backed away when the badger nearly tripped him, blocking the entrance. Edrick stepped to the side, at first to keep from falling at the sudden appearance of the obnoxious animal, but now he wanted to get around him. But the stubborn badger moved in front of him again and barked.

"What? " Edrick asked as he tried to move away from the wild thing. It snapped at him, lips taut, exposing its many teeth. Edrick jumped back, hitting his head on the roof of the hallowed tree, nearly bitten by the animal.

"Are you mad?" Edrick yelled at it, perturbed that it seemed to forget that they were friends. "What is it?"

It snapped and stomped, gnashed its teeth, growling fiercely, as if it mistook Edrick for the creature that made the nest. Edrick had no other choice than to retreat farther into the tree, until he sat on the nest and watched the smug badger sit down at the entrance, staring blankly at him. Edrick made several attempts to move, but the badger would snap back into an offensive posture and snarl at him.

"You are a nasty beast. I hope your master has better

temperament or I should lose all hope in men and beasts," Edrick remarked. Just as he thought things could not get worse, he heard the rustling of bushes just outside, then the fall of heavy, padded feet. There was a huffing of air leaving large nostrils, just outside the opening. The badger quickly darted off, seemingly afraid of whatever had just wandered near.

"Coward!" Edrick yelled. Then not a moment later, the great blocky head of brown bear poked inside, sniffing and snorting at the unwanted visitor. Edrick suddenly desired the company of the stupid badger as he was sure that a bear would not be as understanding.

"Uh, hello master bear," Edrick said with a feeble voice. He did not blink, or shiver with fear, he did not know how to react at all. It seemed the world had stopped while the bear stared at him, smelling the air saturated with his blood. A wounded animal would be irresistible to a predator. An easy meal conveniently delivered to his doorstep. Edrick had heard stories, told by his father no less, of men unaccustomed to the woods, encountering bears. It never ended well. They were the undisputed kings of the forest, save what his father called unnatural beasts.

The bear suddenly bellowed, causing Edrick to jump in anticipation. But it did not charge, or swipe at him as Edrick. Instead it retreated out of sight.

"Oy boy! You in there?" a heavy voice called with a chuckle, one that Edrick recognized belonged to the Brownman.

"Aye, just a little scratched up," he answered thankfully. The Brownman stooped down and looked inside. He seemed surprise and angry all at once.

"Were there goblyns, boy? Are they close by?" he asked urgently.

"No, you're stupid badger nearly took my hand. He's mad."

"The badger?" he echoed. "Come out here where I can get those wounds set right. We need to put some food in ya and then be off. We must get traveling."

All Edrick heard was food and he was out. There in the clearing, Edrick found not just the Brownman and a bear, but nine bloody bears! A whole herd of them, filling the great empty spaces of the little clearing. There seemed even more concealed in the trees.

"Do not be afraid, we are amongst friends," the Brownman said, seeing Edrick's reaction.

"Friends?! Like that mad badger?!"

"Aye, like the badger but a bit fiercer and deeply loyal to me."

Edrick's wounds became aggravated by his movement. Blood ran down his arms and legs. He told the Brownman of his fight with the badger, not understanding that the badger was commanded to bring Edrick to this meeting place and wait for the Brownman. The prince's apology came as an amused chuckle. He dressed Edrick's wounds properly after applying his own medicine, then offered a drink that tasted sweet, like honey. Edrick's pain quickly subsided.

"I have to say, Edrick, you are an impressive boy to take on a badger. You might be foolish, but you are a fierce fool."

"Well, you could have told me the plan," Edrick said as the man was finishing up dressing his wounds.

"I did! I said follow the badger and wait for me. What could you not understand?"

"You fought off the goblyns?" Edrick asked, forcing the change of subject.

"No, but those nasty goblyns were in a foul mood. There are others here in the woods that has stirred their wrath."

"Who?"

"I am not sure."

Edrick wondered. No doubt the missing children would have been noticed by now. His father came to mind, but he alone would have traveled without notice. There had to be more than his father. He ate quickly, a meal of bread, wild honey and nuts.

"When you have finished eating and have recovered your strength, we will be going."

So many questions filled Edrick's mind that he could hardly concentrate on eating, if that were possible. He blurted them all out at once, overwhelming the wild man.

"Where are we going? How did you escape from the goblyns? How did you find these bears and how are they so tame? How did you come to live in these woods? How old are you?"

"Calm yourself now. I will answer three questions then we must be on our way. I then believe we have time for more conversation as we approached our destination."

"Who are you?" Edrick asked directly. "We have known about the Brownman all our lives and have stories about you sneaking around the woods, scaring woodsmen and hunters, chasing off witches and dæmons, but never did we think you served the goddess."

"Don't you know Edrick? Stories are just lies and truth wrapped up in fine packages, woven together to please the audience."

Edrick was taken aback. No one ever quite claimed that stories were false, he only thought there were people who believed in them for their own reasons and there were those who did not. But to think that there are bits and pieces to a story that are somewhat truthful and altogether false never occurred to Edrick. It was an intriguing idea.

"I can only imagine where the story about the Brownman started, not from me or any other that came before me."

"Came before you? You mean there are more."

"Unfortunately, there are many more. So many more I don't not know where this dark business started. But somehow, my story and that of your family is all spooled together back in time originating with my mistress, Lhodyn. She made all of us what we are."

Now Edrick was deeply intrigued with his cryptic riddles.

"I am the Brownman of the woods, as the villagers around here say, and have been for forty years. Before then, I was a young prince, your age no less when this forest took tribute from the king, my father. Tribute he loathed to render willingly."

Edrick was spellbound and silent. His mind clung to every word uttered by this intriguing figure. It seemed he stepped into one of his mother's stories of princes and kings, and somehow through some turn of fate, his path has crossed into legend. He could not speak and he had stopped eating, as he did not want to do anything but listen.

The Brownman called over a bear with a wide wicker basket hanging of his flanks. "Brutus, is a trusted friend. He has agreed to carry you. Walking, you would slow us down, even if you were not injured." Edrick was lifted by the large man onto the back of the bear. Edrick clung to its thick fur. Its skin was loose and fat, but beneath, the tough thick muscles flexed as it shifted its weight slightly, revealing its magnificent strength.

"Out of all the animals, I love bears the most," the large man said. "They are my spirit kin."

Edrick held on as he began his journey with prince Vitherian and a whole troupe of bears by his side. The man walked with the animals, lumbering and moving swiftly in giant strides, remaining close to Edrick for he had much to say.

"I have not told my story, the curse of our family, fully to any one person. Considering where we are headed, I suppose it's time I do, lest my memory fade from all the world."

And this is how he began.

"It is true my father is…was King Sithric. And I was his eldest, first born son and child, thus subject to a curse placed on our family, but in truth it was an agreement made by our ancestor to Lhodyn, to offer the eldest son in every generation in tribute, not as a sacrifice but as servant. In those days, it was custom to exchange princes between houses of two contentious lords to pursue peace. Thus, each lord could not attack the other without causing harm to their heir. Such an agreement was made so the kings could dwell and make use of the forests and treat with the elves. I cannot understand why such an agreement was ever made. Why such a price was deemed worthy to pay for these woods, but such an agreement was settled and unaltered since.

"My father, whose brother was given to Her years before, was loathe to endure a loss such as he and his father suffered. He was close to my uncle at an early age and resented his father for not resisting the goddess. Father hid me for the first nine years of my life, but to no avail, for her servant, the child-snatcher called the Erlking, stole me away one night, and I never saw my parents' faces ever again, nor any human for many years. It was difficult and lonely, and I desired to succumb to my grief and perish. But the Lady did not allow it and sent me to labor for her immediately.

"She taught me the secrets of the woods and I gained power through her that I would not otherwise obtain. My new family became the wild animals and I came to know their intelligence and compassion, their strengths and vulnerabilities. They adopted me as one of them, and I in turn could advocate on their behalf to the Lady who became ever more distant. Such has been my role in recent times, times of desperation."

"I am sorry, lord. That is a harsh fate," Edrick offered, pondering. What if his own family had to endure something as dreadful, if Halig had been stolen away before his own birth? Just then Edrick realized something, "If you are the eldest, then you are heir to Gheldenmark! You are now our king!"

The prince shook his head, his features remained blank and calm. "My father had other sons. My brothers were groomed to be rulers just as my own father. Not I. Of their fate, I would like to know."

Edrick wished he could offer any news of the royal family. It was assumed, by many, that all of King Sithric's lords and family perished in Athéalgian. Of course, there were always rumors of the king's men held up in some remote stronghold, but it was beyond Edrick's knowledge.

"So your wife, Wilona, is your only family?"

"Aye, she is."

"How did you come to meet her then? How does she know me?"

"She cared for your mother once when she was pregnant, before your birth. All did not end well and your mother nearly died. The babies did not make it.

"The villagers chased her into the woods, accused her of being a witch. They would have killed her. I found her lost and in despair. She would have died..." his voice trailed off.

The prince fell silent for a while. Darkness crept over them and soon night ran thick in the lightless woods. Edrick could not see his way in the murk, but the prince and accompanying bears easily managed.

He then told Edrick how once he went into the badger's tunnel, he collapsed it and sprinted through the corridors. "The goblyns caught me soon enough and confronted me, asked of my knowledge of any wandering children. I laughed at them and said they were chasing ghosts, which would be true on any other occasion. But they smelled you on me and knew I was being evasive. Their threats did not scare me, but they dare not meet me in battle for they know I would skin each one of them, regardless of whose orders they were following. So instead, the majority of the group left, presumably to chase after you while a handful were left to follow me.

"But when I reached the surface they became less inclined to follow, for the sun was still high. Even in the forest, they avoid the light of day unless forced to do so. So I was down to just three goblyn escorts until I led them to my friends here, who made short work of them. The sensible ones scattered, but the slowest of them was not so fortunate. After that, I gathered my brothers together to set out to see where you had made to."

"So, you know the goblyns? They are not your enemies?"

"My enemies, yes! My mistress's enemies, no. Not anymore. That means we must tolerate the other."

"Until they come across your bears."

"Yes," he chuckled wickedly in the dark, "we have our secrets ways of dealing with each other indirectly. Their ways are nefariously cunning, so I have to remain vigilant."

A distant howl of a wolf broke the surrounding silence, then another and another in reply; behind them, to their left and right. The bears became alert, twitching their ears and snorting derisively. One stopped and stood on its hind legs, raising its nose into the air, taking in large puffs of air into its massive chest.

"What is it?" Edrick asked, feeling the mood shift from vigilant calm to growing alertness. "Wolves are friends of yours, right? Like in the clearing when you saved us."

"No, not my wolves! All my wolves were killed as we pursued that dæmon pig. Lhodyn does not tolerate disobedience." He paused, then added with a hint of melancholy. "I raised each one from pups. They were my sons, in a manner."

"Did you raise these bears too?"

"No. They raised me," he said proudly.

How could bears raise a man? But that would explain why he acted so...blunt. The more Edrick thought about it, the more fascinated he became.

"Not all wolves are the same, in this forest, or in the rest of the world. Those wolves you hear now were bred for wickedness and crave man flesh. Kept in goblyn stables for hunting. They will soon find our trail, then we will have little time."

"What will we do then? Will the bears be enough to keep us safe?"

A chorus of owls droned over the tree tops. Others answered from a great distance. Their voices drew nearer and nearer.

"There is an elder spirit here that even Lhodyn avoids, a creature she could never conquer, like the elves. It is as ancient as they are, possibly even older than Lhodyn herself."

"So then it is another god?" Edrick concluded.

"I don't know, but I would say not. It seems to be as a beast, not desiring any kind of worship or seeking power, unlike Lhodyn or other gods. We call it the Forest Spirit as it enjoys the woods and loves the animals as a parent. It is Ancient, and therefore mysterious to us mortals. The spirit seems mad at times, capricious. The way it speaks is strange, even to me.

"But I do know it hates goblyns and things of a dark nature, any being that will destroy and kill for pleasure. It can't stand such things and will stamp them out of existence. The Forest Spirit primarily feeds on plants and only eats flesh of defeated enemies. It is their souls that it really desires. Its enemies named it the Soul-Eater and gains strength through this act. This is how Lhodyn came to learn of this power and therefore traps human souls in her Vaults... so I have concluded. Only for some reason, she and all the gods seem to be inebriated with this power, where this creature is not. Maybe this is why it seems mad. I do not know."

"If it is so powerful and strong, why does it not take care of Lhodyn, chase Her away? Destroy Her?"

"I cannot say for certain. I have wondered that for many years. All I can conclude is that it thinks like an animal in many ways, not like men or other gods. The Forest Spirit will only destroy the evil that is at hand, I do not think it perceives evil as a force or understands the intelligence behind choice. It has a nature of a beast, what exists outside its senses does not exist at all. I believe Lhodyn is all too aware of its blind spot and dwells there. I think centuries ago she did not have to hide in the shadows and met with this creature many times to learn from it. She envied the Forest Spirit. She might have thought she could control and dominate it, but she learned that such a thing was impossible. That is, until someone showed her how."

"Who? Someone more powerful than her?"

"Yes. She has been influenced by potent witches. They feed her pride and tell her she must slay the Forest Spirit and consume its power. If such a thing happened, the forest will be blighted with darkness."

More howls drew near, rising from all directions, even in front of them. Edrick instinctively lowered himself until he was nearly laying on the bear, clutching his fur tight in case it lurched suddenly in an attack.

"They are closing, are they not? So are we!" the prince announced, breaking into a jog. The bears all charged through the forest, running over bushes and crashing through tree limbs like boulders falling down mountains.

Just then, flanking Edrick, he heard wolves snarling and biting at the bears in the night, then the unmistakable whimper of wolves dying in the night.

"We have been found!" the prince declared. "We have not far to go, but they will be on us soon!" he said, huffing and puffing as he sprinted to keep up with the galloping bears.

Then a braying chorus of howls, short piercing wails surrounded the mighty band. The shrilling cries were nothing like Edrick heard before. Too disturbing to endure, he covered his ears in hopes to fight the dreadful sound from reaching his senses. It was a sound that would ring in his thoughts in times of darkness, when he found himself alone and the bleakness overbearing. A feeling of dread that only could be born in night.

Then just ahead, as the bears continued to crash and surmount all obstacles of the forest, an area of light appeared through the trees. Not a brilliant or shining light, but an area of the forest where starlight filtered through and clung to the leaves like dew, flowing over the ground like a glowing mist filling the air. It was the part of night that Edrick loved, the kind of darkness that belonged above ground and not the kind that issues forth from deep holes or lurked behind crypts.

It was in this lit area that the bears made to and the wolves fell suddenly silent. And the air changed significantly, a new fragrance rose to meet Edrick, calming him instantly. It was as if they entered into an Ancient part of the woods where the air had not stirred since the very first sunrise, when Time formed from celestial movement. It was a kind of smell that Edrick only detected when he was deep in the forest during autumn, like the period after it had rained for days; when the rain first relents, giving the forest a fresh chance to breath. Earthy and green, heavy and saturated with forest life.

The bears slowed and Edrick realized he could see many more of them. Their numbers had swelled into two dozen or so as they traveled. Some bears so huge, Edrick thought it some strange monster. Brutus could easily sit upon those bears' shoulders as Edrick sat upon Brutus.

An even larger creature moving in the distance commanded his attention, something he could barely make out through the screening trees. So large, it was bending and shaking the high canopy branches.

"Come," the prince whispered urgently. He lifted Edrick off the

Brutus's back and the two made their way through the trees as the bears remained behind without a word. They seemed to give the creature ahead plenty of room, though they did not seem afraid, if bears were able to be afraid of anything.

The prince remained crouched low and stopped a short distance from this creature, this Forest Spirit. There, they found the divine beast wading through the tree grove, eating canopy leaves like a farm cow, with the same vacant, thoughtless look in its eyes. Its appearance was strange, it was large, like something the size of a dragon Edrick always imagined. It had a total of six limbs, four thick legs like large tree stumps supporting the massive animal like body. The other two limbs were attached to the upper torso that was more like a man. It was covered completely in a coat of shaggy brown fur.

It continued to bend tree limbs and strip branches away, munching on wood and leaf alike. Edrick could not make out its face in the dim light. He wondered if it was like a man or that of a beast.

"It does not have a single defined shape," the Brownman whispered. "It can be tremendously gigantic, larger than this, or very small like a mouse. Yet, it never looks like a common beast, but something from another world, or ancient past. Like something that passed from the gates of this world long ago, before there were men to remember such things."

The howling erupted once again, fierce and angry. Edrick covered his ears, though he could not fend off the haunting quality of the dissonance.

"They have gathered in force and will attack! Let's move quickly," the prince said. The two left their place of concealment and approached the creature. It did not seem to notice them at all. The prince walked over to a fallen log, slipped off his ax and swung it into the wood where it stuck fast. He then sat down and waited.

"You are not going to talk to it?" Edrick asked looking somewhat confused.

"Would not do any good, like talking to a rock and expecting a reply. It's a force of nature, even though it seems like a beast. It just moves through the forest and reacts. You can't appeal to it, reason or intimidate it. It just is."

They waited in the darkness until the wolves closed around them. They were horribly loud, their excited baying rung through the trees until they were very close, then fell silent. The Forest Spirit stopped its chewing. Its ears twitched. Its relaxed body shifted into an alert stance.

"Here it comes, just stay out of the way, and watch out for any wolves that might get by."

A canine whining pierced the silence to Edrick's surprise, then the shouts of goblyn voices, followed by cruel cracks of the harsh whips. Wolves poured out of the forest, the largest pack of wolves Edrick had ever seen assembled, rushing forth like a tide of shadows. Before Edrick could leap behind the still sitting man, the Forest Spirit launched itself with the grace and speed of a startled doe, yet when it landed, it made sure a wolf was beneath each paw. Edrick recoiled from the loud crunch and popping made by the squashed beasts. It then grabbed, lifted and hurled wolves into the air in a wild furry, swallowing each one whole. Wolves whimpered and whined as they scrambled away from the crazed forest guardian. Goblyns too, wandered into the fray, meeting the same deadly result. The Forest Spirit ate wolf after goblyn, until all were dead or wisely retreated.

The battle was quick and decisive. The bears wandered over to where Edrick and the prince waited. The forest guardian departed, as if it could not stand the stench of the tainted forest left by its enemies. It ambled away as if a cow looking for greener grass.

"That was incredible! I have never seen of such a thing. Has anyone in the village seen it? Has father?" Edrick asked, thinking he just encountered something that not even his father knew.

"Of course your father knows. He does not speak of it because it is the forest in a way Lhodyn is not, but wishes she could be. To speak of the forest, is to speak of this thing. To speak of this thing, is to speak of the forest. They are one in the same."

"But what about Lhodyn? You said that She does not challenge it. How come?"

"I don't possess the answers to all the questions in the world, Edrick. But if you meet Her, then you can ask Her yourself. Until then, sleep. Morning will come all too soon and we will be off once again."

Edrick laid down and sleep overcame him like a spell.

Morning fell upon the forest as the troupe continued their journey toward the Goblyn Market. There was no path, just the Brownman's meandering way through the trees. After mid-morning, thunder erupted in the cloudless sky. The prince sniffed the air, along with the bears. Then it rained out of the blue.

Not soon after, they came across a trail that cut through the trees, paved with cobblestones. It was some kind of road in the middle of the forest, lost to the outside world. Edrick wondered where it led.

"What is this?"

"It was the road of a king, as all roads are. But now it is my road, and your road."

"Where does it lead?"

"To more goblyns, and worse," he answered gruffly.

"This is the way to the Goblyn Market?"

"It is for now, but the market moves often. It is never in the same location."

Wooden sculptures stood along the roadside, some hidden, some proudly greeting them. Their features were blurred by the weathering effects of time, but their forms looked to be like people, beasts and even long murals depicting scenes of some great, but forgotten event. Edrick could have spent the entire day looking at all of them, guessing and discerning their original appearance and meanings. He realized he was on one of the hidden roads depicted in the old village map, heading toward the hidden city.

"We are close now so you must gather your courage. You will not be facing badgers, but much worse."

"If my sister is there, I care not what stands in our way."

"Well, wisdom teaches one the difference between blind foolishness and calculating courage. I hope you live to know the latter. So I have a ruse in mind." He called Brutus over. The bear still wore the wicker baskets across his back. "I am putting you inside the basket. Stay low and out of sight. I will warn you, we are visiting an area where they are most unkind to children. I will get us close enough to locate your sister and the other village children. The bears will stay in the forest, but not far from us. Then I will set loose a distraction that will frighten all of them. They will not know what to do with themselves."

"What kind of distraction?"

"Something the forest has not encountered in centuries. It is better you not know for now. But once the creatures flee, my bears will swoop in and kill or chase off any of those near the children. I will lead them back home. From there, we go our separate ways."

Edrick's heart dropped upon hearing this. He was such a powerful ally and friend, Edrick didn't understand why he would just abandon them to the same situation that caused the children to flee from the Folthnir in the first place.

"I truly appreciate all that you have done and are doing, but you can't just leave us with the wolfskins. They will enslave us, or slowly starve us by stealing our food and animals."

The Brownman straightened his back, appearing very uncomfortable at Edrick's conclusions.

"We made a fair pact Edrick, in my den, now there is no time for amending that agreement."

"But you are the king now! You have the means to save us. I will give you anything," Edrick thought quickly, "my father's bow! It is a mighty weapon, as old as the torc. You can have it. I will convince my father..."

"NO!" the Brownman shouted. Edrick shrank back. The bears all snapped their head toward the two, alert. "There is no discussing my affairs with you, child!" He lifted Edrick up and dropped him into the basket and covered the top. "Hold your tongue! Or I will not be responsible for what happens if you fail to heed me again."

Edrick shook his head as tears welled up in his eyes. This could not be. How could a king act so cruelly? He should be protecting them, all of them, not just from monsters but from all harm. Despair welled up in Edrick's heart, distracting him from the world outside the basket. He failed to notice anything beyond. He did not mark when they entered the Goblyn Market, or that the bears had already dispersed except loyal Brutus alone with the Brownman.

He heard a clamor of strange sounds, ugly voices and sorrowful cries. Offensive odors enveloped the pair. Yet, he did not look up from his feet, or try to peek through the wicker wall into the foreign market where they just arrived. A horrible and powerful emotion crept over his heart, a feeling of hate and anger at a world that was hopelessly broken and he fought alone to keep it from falling to pieces. That madness was the realization that he alone could not do it, but if everyone made the effort, it could be done.

Adults seemed to care so very little.

22

HAUNTED PATHS

ELISIAL AND ELZERA waited for Alaric below an embankment, by the rushing forest river. They seemed relieved as he emerged from the woods seemingly unhurt and well.

The wide river flowed swiftly, angrily behind them, darkened with silt. Alaric never knew its name. He guessed it was written on the Elder Hall map. Someone named it and built a bridge across it leading to a hidden city. Those builders died a long time ago and kept their secrets.

"Where is the Uthræsian?" Elzera asked, yet her expression told Alaric she already guessed.

"Dead. We must go at once to the bridge. We must put some distance between us." He replied, stiffly, avoiding his wife's eyes.

They followed a rough trail that hugged the river bank, below sight of any who might pursue them. Alaric knew at once where they were and what direction he would find the bridge, an old decrepit structure, much like the Ruined Tower, built of ancient stone and iron.

It was not far from them. Alaric was surprised by its appearance. Not how he remembered the bridge from his youth. More sections of the stone span had collapsed into the river. The rocky rubble had turned the water below into a craggy rapid. Only the foundations remained rooted in the earth, connected by newly laid, rough timbers lashed together hastily, providing access to the other side.

"How far are we going Alaric? The forest is still a menace to us, would it not be wiser to return home?" Elisial asked.

He stopped and looked at them. He desired more than anything to lead them home. To gather their things, with Meghan, Eadwyn and the two women and leave the village behind. Yet, he could not. He could not be that man as long as Elisial stood by him.

"We should find them, the children, first."

Elzera smiled with a sense of satisfaction. "Yes, we will get the children."

They crossed the bridge taking care over the wet footing. On the other side, the path widened significantly and smoothed out. They soon found themselves treading a cobblestone road, paved like a city street, leading deeper into the forest. The rain stopped, leaving them drenched and shivering.

"What a strange thing to find here in the middle of the woods," Elzera commented.

"Where does this road lead, Alaric?" Elisial asked. She placed her hands out toward him. The light from her éardian flashed with bright intensity and he was no longer wet. She did the same with Elzera and herself, her hair once again became thick and bouncy as it always been.

"It leads to the dead city." He said evenly. "A cursed part of the forest that my family has avoided always."

"We should not go there then," Elisial said.

Alaric halted.

"If the children are there, if Sunniva still lives, would you still leave or would you look for her?" Alaric needed to hear her answer. If she allowed him, he would leave. They would leave this all behind and face the uncertainty of the road than this menace he hates. No easy choice is this. There have been no easy choices since childhood.

Just say it my love and we will go home, make a new life far away, have more kids, keep them safe, allow their fire to burn bright.

"If they are here, and I think they are, we are the only ones, Alaric, that can bring them home. We have to try," she said, almost instantly.

Alaric nodded. He turned and led them at a quick pace without another word. He could not abide his wife to witness one more tear.

They tore through the woods as fast as Alaric could drive them. All the woodland animals seemed to stop and take notice. The gray squirrels flinched and fidgeted their bushy tails, stamping up and down oaks, chirping in distress. Tawny magpies darted in and out of their arboreal cover. Then a red stag startled Elisial as it bounded out onto the road. It paused for a moment, scrutinizing the woodland intruders. It scraped the stone with its mighty hoof, snorted derisively then shook its massive woodland crown. It reared up, kicking its front legs out wildly before crashing through the brush, sprinting quickly out of sight.

"Something spooks the animals," Elzera said.

"They are warning us. We are on our way toward peril," Alaric replied.

"Why hasn't Lhodyn hindered our path as she did before?" Elisial asked.

"Perhaps she wants to draw us in as well."

"It will be all right, dear," Elzera said, "we have Warden of the Woods by our side, there are still those loyal to him here. Not all the animals love Lhodyn, I think."

Midday came and went, but time seemed strange even if the sun told them the day wore on. They twice came upon crossroads that diverged north and south. Each time Alaric kept their course due east until they came upon an imposing stone structure spanning the road.

Before them rose a great monolithic arch, set over the road like a mighty gatehouse that seemed more at place protruding from a king's castle than an empty woodland road. Curtains of ivy and carpets of bright verdant moss hid most of its dying features, outlining its bare form against the woodland scene. A tunnel framed by soaring lancet arches swallowed the road like a gaping maw. Water dripped from fissures within, breathing a chill air over the visitors. The ruined structure seemed eager to swallow the three, where travelers rarely tread.

"What a strange thing to find in the wilderness," Elzera said, breathless. She and Elisial craned their necks to take in the structure's great height. They walked up to the entrance and peered behind the ivy to glimpse at the dark stone beneath. What were once ornate carvings had been worn smooth into near featureless bumps and pits.

Elisial ran her hand over the smoothed stone. "What is this?"

"Just a remnant of the past. Beyond, the ruins. We are close now."

"This is magnificent, Alaric," Elzera said pulling the ivy aside. "I have been searching for this all my life."

Alaric looked at his old friend, a light smile adorned her face, shedding years from her aged features. She smiled as a young girl, catching the eye of a lover for the first time. Her eyes never left the ruin, as her hands roved the ivy, pulling the leaves to side like pulling back a drape, allowing light into a long darkened room.

As they stopped to admire the ruin, there rose a clopping of hooves rising off the paved road not far off, echoing through the archway, directly ahead.

"Hide," Alaric said with dire urgency.

They scrambled behind a grove of stalwart oaks and waited until the woodland travelers passed. A bull like creature with long scythe shaped horns and shaggy brown coat emerged out from the tunnel, pulling a lone wagon. Tall and unusual, it resembled a small cabin with windows, an iron chimney stack rising from the roof and a door fixed in the rear wall. A hunched over goblyn draped in a dark ragged cloak concealing most of his ugly features, drove the cart. Trailing behind, two children, no, young adults, a girl and boy, hurried after, tethered to the wagon by black iron chains fixed to collars around their necks. They wore no shoes and looked as if they traveled hundreds of miles. Their éardians, drifted above their heads like shredded flags caught in a storm.

Elisial was about to speak, but both Elzera and Alaric placed their finger to their lips, keeping her quiet. The wagon rocked and swayed as it passed, jingling with chains, creaking like an old house.

They waited, motionless, by the side of the road until it was out of sight and hearing. They dared not blink or even breathe, until it passed. They sensed it would have been disastrous had their presence been detected.

"Witches," Elisial said, her voice a mix of fear, wonder and dread. "Poor children."

"Very powerful, old witches," Elzera replied. But there was no fear in her words, but a kind of malice. "Edrick was right."

"Right about what?" Elisial asked.

"There is a Goblyn Market here, and they have been capitalizing on the Folthnir's invasion," she proclaimed, putting it all together in her head. "We must go, Alaric, while there is a chance to rescue the Athelyn children."

But Alaric could not move. He realized how harsh he had treated Edrick; how brave the boy had been holding to a belief his sister lived. He never gave up on finding her.

"He was right."

His hand found Elisial's hand, entwined his thick fingers between hers, so thin, but held more strength than he. "I had been harsh to our sweet boy. He said there was a Goblyn Market and I ignored him thinking it was just another of his fanciful stories. I was blinded by rage because of the villager's betrayal, my friend's betrayal, all of it. I summoned all the courage and concentration I could to endure the Folthnir's abuse. Worrying about the concerns of a boy, even our boy, seemed a small matter. I am sorry, Elisial, for letting you down, for letting Sunniva, Baldice….Halig and Edrick down."

"Husband, you are strong by any measure. You have always endured more burdens than your share in this life. If this world breaks you, you do not break alone, we break with you. We share pain with you and we will heal with you. The hardest times were when you were away, and now that you are back, despite the evil that has befallen us, we are happier for it. You are here now. The worst has past."

"I don't feel it has."

"That is because darkness is at hand," Elzera added, laying her hand on his shoulder, "and light seems a foreign thing. But it will not always be so."

"These woods," Alaric continued, "have been changing for ill, for a while, and I had turned a blind eye to what I wished not to see. The ogre, the witches, the goblyns…they had been the final overwhelming signs that Lhodyn grew an evil heart. But I would not accept it, for it would mean the end of my heritage, my purpose, the last thing in this world that made us more than sodding Woodcutters.

"So easily do children see truth in the world. So easily do they find hope in emptiness. Always I thought Edrick too easily taken by false hope, I failed to see the strength that it is. But you always saw," he said looking into Elisial's eyes.

"Children are born to hope until cruelty smothers it," she replied. "We must foster their faith while we can, so it can endure through their life. Edrick clung to my stories because it was the only hope that he heard, the only hope that he could imagine, and he fought to make it so. He challenged us all to make it so."

"Then we must make it so. Let's free those poor children." He kissed her, lightly, yet the feeling was so strong, it radiated down his spine and into his boots. It felt like raining sunshine. He smiled with warm tears, like the ones caught in her eyes.

"You two talk as if Edrick has passed. Well, he has not!" Elzera asseverated.

They crept around the arch and found the path on the other side. Elzera's interest in the arch lingered as they walked passed. As soon as they rejoined the road, Alaric prepared an arrow on Nithledan's string. Elzera walked just behind him, Elisial staying near her side.

"What cruel creatures to prey upon children. I thought there could be no crueler people than the Folthnir," Elisial said.

"Such tragedies have been known to happen in other lands," Elzera said. "It is a sad matter of routine, like wolves snatching sheep, or foxes stealing hens.

"There are companies of fighting men and women that are hired to protect roads, search for lost children and even drive away or slay monsters from entire realms. It was more common in the elder days when there were old bloodlines of kings and queens who had the wealth to hire such people. Now, these guilds are mostly removed from the lands where they are needed and operate in cities as hustlers and criminals, often letting loose beasts in a population so they could get paid for removing it. I have had the misfortune of witnessing these crimes. Children die for profit and families suffer for nothing but to scare people into handing over what little they have."

"How awful this world is," Elisial declared.

"And that is why hope is a most treasured possession," Elzera reflected.

"Tell me, Alaric, what are these ruins," Elzera asked after a while. He could tell she had been wanting more answers since their arrival at the ruined Gate.

"Where we are headed is haunted and my father and uncles always warned us...my brothers and I...to avoid hunting there. They said there was a part of the forest that is cursed, that even the animals avoid. Trees do not grow straight, water flows uphill. When asked what this place was, all father ever said was that it is a cursed land. He said nothing more of it.

"Over the years, I wondered in my foolish youth what this place was, so I searched for it and found it. Actually, as soon as I made up my mind to find it, a path opened up to me, that led to an ancient road, right in the middle of the woods. It was paved with stone, like the kind of roads that lead to the king's palaces and grand cities. This is the very road I found. I followed it until the ruins were revealed.

He paused, taking in a deep breath, "And in the ruins I found a dæmon.

"Fortunately for me, my brothers were close at hand. They followed me and marked my direction. This dæmon descended quickly as I entered. They saved my life, confronting the thing like the noble men they were, and allowed me to escape injury.

"I ran into the woods and did not look back until after reaching a great distance, for fear of what harm could have come to my brothers, for fear that evil thing gave chase. Their bodies were already laying in pools of blood and the fiend was gone. I sprinted for what seemed like a dozen miles, until I was so far into the forest, I thought I might have come close to the other side. I couldn't face my father that day, so I left and decided to find what lay on the other side of these woods."

"I had no idea, Alaric," Elisial lamented.

"So ashamed was I, it was years until I returned home. My father was not there and never did I see him again. My mother soon died and I was all that was left. He left me his bow and torc, as if he knew he would not return. I asked my mother where he went. 'To search for you' was all she said, but I knew it for a lie, perhaps the only one she told to me."

They walked in silence for a while. Elzera finally asked, "What then did you do after, knowing all your family were dead?"

"I was in despair. I swore to my father, as he swore to his father, to uphold the family duty. I was the youngest of seven boys, so most of the responsibilities laid with my other brothers, but they became unworthy of it. And I felt I did not deserve it, until I met Elisial. She restored me, healed me. She was my saving grace, as she seems to be again and again."

"And what happened to your other brothers?"

"He does not speak of it," Elisial replied in almost a whisper.

Alaric paused and motioned the two women to stoop down. He led them off the road and back into the cover of the woods. He noticed the forest had gone quiet. It had been nearly thirty years but he recognized the feeling this place gave him. An unfamiliar and awful stench wafted through the trees. Alaric raised a hand indicating them to stay as he crept forward. It was a mix of acrid smoke and roasted meat with strange spices. The smell disgusted him. Alaric crept quietly, until the trees thinned and opened into a great clearing. There, amongst the ruins of an ancient walled city was a gathering of monsters of all kinds, selling their strange wares like common folk. Yet the items they sold were not common at all.

They were children.

23

THE GOBLYN MARKET

IT ROAMRED FROM LAND to land, from desert bazaar to mountain cave, sometimes boldly venturing into the civilized cities, beneath crowded streets in the buried and avoided sewers. Next to the thieves dens they set their wares, peddling strange fruit begotten from exotic plants that once bit, drove mortals mad with desire. A glut of stolen goods acquired from innumerable realms could be found here, trading hands a dozen times, yielding more and more profit. Forbidden wares, such as exquisite poisons, sold like common vegetables. Powders that burned a lethal smoke. Liquids that dissolved without scent or taste. Salves that smelled candy sweet, preserving a corpse long after death as not to provoke suspicion. Such were the kind of things traded at the Goblyn Market, but it was the flesh that made everyone rich.

Flesh that induced pleasure, the most rare and highly sought variety of females gathered in one location. Auctioned off to the most lascivious purse. Flesh of labor, of the strongest and most docile creatures who endured the harshest treatment, but obeyed better than any beaten dog. From giants of the snow lands to those of the dunes, along with men of all kinds and the occasional dwarf could be had. Yet, it was the flesh of youth that lured the most evil and vile of creatures. Man flesh of the child had many, many, diabolical applications, the worse, arguably, kept these monsters well fed.

Under the Blood Moon they convened.

The Witch's Moon.

The Devil's Night.

This celestial orb that no goodly creature could see, for it appeared only to those of pure wickedness. The Blood Moon had irregular phases, as it was governed by Chaos and moved against the tide of stars, from west to east it sailed, always. When this dark moon appeared full, a new location was selected to convene the Goblyn Markets. Often they chose remote locations, for these loathsome creatures were always hunted by those who called themselves good and righteous.

Edrick did not view this nightmare unfolding as he and the prince crossed into the Goblyn Market outside the ruins of an abandoned woodland city. Children crammed into barbed pens were haggled over by boisterous and monstrous merchants. There were more children here than all those that lived in his village or those that neighbored Athelyn. Children stolen from lands afar, still wearing their strange garb of foreign nations.

A child was seized from his pen and dragged to the goblyn butcher as the Brownman guided Brutus through the maze of merchant stalls. The boy's screams chilled the air like the voice of winter, snapping Edrick from his inner turmoil. He stood up, hitting his head against the basket lid, finding it secured and immovable. It did not budge as Edrick shoved and pounded against the barrier.

The screams!

What horrid sounds ripped from the boy's lips. Edrick could not escape its haunting pleas or come to the boy's aid. Other children cried out around him, some woeful, others with desperate alarm that longed to flee their captors.

Edrick shook the basket, his own cell that seemingly held him prisoner.

"What are you playing at Brownman!" Edrick yelled through the woven wicker. "You coward! I should never have trusted you! You are just like all the others. Children are nothing to you!"

Edrick's face burned, he found it suddenly wet with salty tears, but he did not cry, he raged. Following the silenced boy's cries were the laughing and cheering of uncaring things, the kind of mirth found in any city tavern when the roasted mutton had finally been tabled.

Edrick found himself immersed amongst anguished children, crying out all around him. There were so many voices, Edrick strained to recognize just one.

"Tredan! Gaebria!" he shouted. A girl's shrilling scream sounded out not too far away. Could that have been Gaebria, he wondered.

Finally the lid flung open and a large hand snatched him up as if he were but a caged rabbit. The Brownman held him aloft with a single arm, held him out before an audience of monsters.

All eyes suddenly shifted to the newcomer, assessing his value, or perhaps how he tasted.

There before him was a vision of nightmares manifested. Figures clad in tattered rags the color of ash and rotted wood, milled about the compact space. A forest of tents and booths spread out before him, with garish colors, signs and sigils, it hurt the eyes with all the muddling forms and shacks set so close to each other nothing could be discerned, except that which drew Edrick's attention even when screened from behind the wicker basket. Large pens held children together, no different than what Edrick saw at the Ruined Tower, save infinitely more menacing as monsters poked and prodded the captives with sticks and claws.

Vitherian now approached such a pen and held out his hand to the guard. It was no man. It stood bent over, torso unnaturally long, head slender like a goat or sheep, but the entirety of its features were concealed in a deep hood and mask across its face. It extended its lanky arm and dropped a coin into the large man's open palm.

"I found this little one wandering in the forest," the Brownman said.

"Put it in," the guard said, taking keys to a lock and opening a door on the top of the cage. The Brownman gave Edrick a stone still look and tossed him in.

"Where is Lord Devouebrol?" he asked.

"Feasting down in the Cook's Lane. He is in a merry mood."

The Brownman left Edrick without a second glance.

Just when he thought all was lost, hope drifted in his ears, uttered with one sweet word.

"Edrick..." asked a soft little voice.

There, surrounded by a mass of children Edrick recognized as the villagers he led into the forest, lay little Sunniva, curled up on her side in the corner of the rusted iron cage. She was covered in mud and muck, her golden hair now dung colored and matted. Edrick rushed to her immediately, shoving every child out of his way. He did not care if he was rude or brutish. It was Sunniva! He knew he was right. He knew she lived. He knew she waited for him.

"My sweet Sunniva!" he said, diving to hold her. He pulled her close, so tight. She did not move, a doll in his arms. Limbs loose and unresisting. He looked into her face.

"Are you all right? Are you hurt?" Her eyes looked to him, but not at him. As if she saw past him or she dreamed awake.

"Edrick?" she asked again, unsure, scared, exhausted.

"It is me, Sunniva! You must know. Your brother! I am here with you now." He pulled her into another embrace. She tensed, as if life were budding anew, as she shook off the memories of the nightmares clinging to her sight.

Edrick was then yanked back as an arm coiled around his neck, pulling him tight into someone's chest. Sunniva fell out of his arms as he was pulled away.

"You dirty little woodpecker!" a harsh voice whispered so close to his ear it burned. "I was hoping they would bring you to me. I will make sure they rip you apart first before they seize another one of us." It was Rodor. The other children that now surrounded him looked frightened, but a few looked satisfied, even wicked, with promise of pain.

"Tried to escape and leave us behind?" Rodor asked, squeezing into Edrick's throat.

"No, the monster nearly killed me…" Edrick tried to explain, coughing out the words.

"I will make sure he does this time. They will take you before they take another one of us. Your mother brought this on us. We all knew she was a witch. She summoned those things at the tower. We all saw it!"

"No, she protected us," Edrick fought, but the larger boy held him tight. Two other boys seized his kicking legs.

"Really?!" Rodor cinched his arm into his neck. The world flashed black for a moment. "How stupid do you think we can be? She sold us to these monsters. Look! These witches are all around."

"Where's Rinan…and Tredan and…?"

"You don't get to ask that," he shook Edrick violently.

"We haven't seen her since we arrived," said one child.

"Let them have his sister first. Let him see what they do to children," suggested another boy.

"No, they keep her for *him*. He owns her."

"If we scratch out her face, maybe we can fool them. He won't recognize her."

"We can try."

"Help, Edrick!" Sunniva squeaked. The children seized her. Yet, they hesitated as if no one wanted to act first.

"Do it!" Rodor ordered.

"Hey, you worms!" the goblyn guard yelled. He shoved the butt of his spear into the cage, smashing the face of the boy holding Sunniva. The guard bashed his face twice, first, breaking his teeth, the second knocked him unconscious. Rodor released his grip swiftly as soon as the guard spoke, fleeing to the far side of the cage.

"I will have none of that. First to scratch her face will be the first on the butcher's block!"

Once free, Sunniva dove into Edrick's arms. The two embraced for long moments, feeling the rhythm of each other's heartbeat, realizing it beat in one rapid pace, in unison. Edrick loved her little fingers, how they clung to him, her little nose pressed up against his chest, the way she tucked her head beneath his chin. She was so perfect, and finally she was back in his arms. Back with family.

"I will take you home, little one."

Sunniva nodded, so slight.

"Father has returned." She squeezed him. He wanted to tell her Father will protect them, that he will save them. But he could not tell her lies. She deserved so much better. "He searched for you. We all have. I will protect you now. I won't leave your side, Sunniva, I promise."

"Say it again," she whispered.

"I promise, Sunniva, on grandfather's grave and all the Woodcutters."

She nodded, and squeezed him over and over.

"I hate this place, Edrick. They scared the faeries away."

"We will find them once we escape."

"But you can't hurt them, Edrick. Never again."

"I promise. No more traps."

Edrick looked at all the children. Their hate seemed to have retreated as fast as it surged. It was as if the entire evil market infected them like poison. None of them meant to harm him. They were just scared and desperate.

"We will escape, all of us. We won't die here," he declared.

The Brownman, that coward! Edrick thought of the Forest Spirit. He didn't think that the forest god would suffer the presence of an evil man. Maybe he was only half evil, partial evil. Perhaps just a selfish, lonely old man. Just then, he saw a commotion across the crowded lanes. A group of monsters gathered closer, approaching the pens.

Led by the massive ogre, the Brownman, the fat mannish pig dæmon and a host of goblyns sauntered down the lane until they stood before them. All the children around Edrick, including Sunniva fled to the center of the cage, keeping away from the perimeter where the goblyns reached in and hurt them.

"You want the whole lot of them!" The ogre's voice boomed. "What would Lhodyn desire with them?" In the ogre's hand was the half eaten leg of what Edrick guessed belonged to a child, as if it were a piece of chicken.

"Lord D!" Master Wergedswyn, the pig dæmon, interrupted, "it's the boy you disposed of." He pointed his chubby finger toward Edrick.

"The man brought him in, just now," the goblyn guard offered.

The ogre looked at the Brownman with suspicion. "What is this?"

"I found him in the woods. If Lhodyn wanted him dead she would have killed him by now. And it is fortunate she did not," he gave Edrick a long, earnest look. Whatever the Brownman meant speaking to the ogre, Edrick could only guess, but his words felt true to him. The Brownman seemed indebted to meeting Edrick and conveyed his sincerity now.

"You cannot have them. I do not forget your misstep in the forest," the ogre said, rubbing the wound where the spear lodged in him. "Besides, half of them already have bids and you know the rules. I cannot take late bids once bidding begins. Now as for this one," the ogre pointed toward Edrick. "I will give him to Master Wergedswyn. And his sister I have already given…"

"To me!" shouted a stern reply behind them. The crowd parted as a group of women, young and old, walked to stand beside the ogre.

The witches were not what Edrick imagined for they were varied in appearance and dress. Most had pale skin, as if they walked with Death, yet around their eyes were splashes of brilliant colors, reds, oranges and violets. And painted around their temples were pictures of feathers, gossamer insect wings, fanned out droplets of water or scrolling flames. Some who did not bear these adorned eyes, instead had circles of gems pressed directly on their foreheads.

There was a mix of ages from young women to the old and ancient. The young ones were practically nude, wearing dresses or skirts short and long, but did not cover their bare chests. They wore talismans of beads, feathers, stones and bones. Some had black markings on their bodies, some their arms. It looked like letters to Edrick, but ones he had never seen before. The elder ones seemed more modest wearing blouses and shawls wrapped around their shoulders. Their hair was silver to white, some thick and course, others mangy to entirely bald. Beauty was vulgarly flaunted amongst the youth, accentuated like no other women Edrick encountered, but the older ones wore their age with great pride, without regret.

"This precious little one is mine. This is her brother?" a particularly ancient witch asked, curiously. She stepped to the caged to inspect Edrick. "Very curious this little boy. Come look, sisters!" Two more elderly ladies stepped to each side of the first.

"A black halo?" asked the other. "What do you make of that?"

"It would be worth investigating this more. Buy him," the other said impulsively.

The first one rolled her eyes, as if bothering with a boy was beneath her. "All right, let's have this one."

"He is not for sale!" the ogre repeated.

"In fact," said Master Wergedswyn, stepping forward, "he is mine and I will be taking him now." He looked to the guard who snapped to action immediately. He fumbled with the keys and opened the caged as another goblyn crawled up and over, dropping inside.

It stood, facing Edrick, and lurched forward to seize him. Edrick jumped back and ran around the children. The goblyn gave chase, but another goblyn immediately was crawling over the cage toward the door. As Edrick looked at the new threat, a foot stuck out of the crowd of children, sending Edrick rolling to the ground. The two goblyns snatched him up and extracted him. Edrick looked back for Sunniva, but she hid herself behind the others. He did see Rodor's smiling, vengeful face looking back.

Edrick was bound by rope around his neck, the other end

handed to the corpulent pig-man. It jerked the rope a few times, playing with Edrick as he struggled to stay on his feet. "Oh how I wanted to taste this one's blood. I am sure he will be as sweet as his brother."

"I will take the girl now!" demanded the witch. Within the cage the children pushed Sunniva to the front where a goblyn snatched her up. She didn't struggle or cry out. She wept only, in silence.

"And this is what we will offer for the boy!" the other witch said. She threw a small pouch at the ogre's feet. Jewels spilled out as it plopped down on the cobblestone. The creatures that now crowded around the scene swelled at the sight of the small pile of wealth lying exposed on the ground.

The ogre's eyes opened wide, a flash of greed spilled out of his gaze. Even Master Wergedswyn seemed more interested in the wealth than the promise of a meal.

"Oh, Esthrima, please!" said the first witch. "Why waste our money on a boy."

"It's my money, but I will still share him with you sister. I must know how he came to have this halo. Only read about this kind of thing. This is our chance to study it."

The Brownman, impatient, unable to contain his anger, kicked the bag away, scattering the jewels into the anticipating crowd. Creatures of all kinds dove down to snatch the wealth, then ran off like the thieves they were. "I have a counter offer," he said.

The witches' jaws dropped at his complete impertinence.

From beneath his furs, he pulled out a silver dragon scale and held it up. "I will buy all these children back with this." Everyone looked up at the big man as the light gleamed off bauble at his fingertips. Their eyes shifted from greed to horror and they recoiled in fear, parting quickly from the man.

Edrick recognized the silver arrowhead, as it was the same that once hung from his father's torc.

A commotion erupted around the perimeter of the market. As if watching the entire seen unfold from afar, Vitherian's bears surged into the gathering from their hidden positions.

"Who is this man that challenges your authority, Lord Devouebrol?" asked a witch, but they all recoiled, involuntary it seemed, at the sight of the silver token. "How does it possess such a thing?!" they hissed. "Lhodyn!" They cried out in unison.

"Slave! What insolence you have brought to my home, insulting me before our guests!" came the instant reply. Out of the shadows of the trees stepped a towering woman of exotic beauty. Her hair was leafy green of varying shades, from deep pine to glowing moss. Her skin was a flawless clay brown, even golden like varnished wood. From her head grew elegant tines of a stag, a natural crown befitting a woodland queen. Where clothes would be worn, she was adorned with a variety of leaves and flowers, though most consisted of a lush violet and golden yellows.

To Edrick, she appeared everything he thought an elf would look like, walking majestically toward the crowd, in a way he had never seen a woman walk. She was accompanied by ferocious beasts the size of horses, brandishing quills over their backs. On the largest beast rode the Erlking, her champion and prime servant.

Edrick felt the prince hesitate in his resolve as he looked to him. "You promised me," Edrick uttered. Even if the prince did not hear the words, he straightened his back and faced the wrathful goddess. Edrick thought he caught a glimpse of a deep sorrow buried behind his eyes.

"Slave, your goddess asked you a question," one of the witches said. "Lhodyn, allow me to teach this slave his place." The witch then pulled a concealed dagger and hissed, "all men should feel the prick of my dagger deep inside them." The other one snarled with laughter.

Edrick turned, to look for Sunniva. She was gone, as was the witch holding her. "O prince, my sister!" Edrick shouted. "SUNNIVA!"

No answer came.

The Brownman ignored him, engaged with Lhodyn now. "I am no longer your slave, nor shall my family ever be enslaved again. My father is dead and there is no more of my line. I care not of my life for it has been wasted. But I will not allow these children to come to anymore harm."

The bears were among them now, tearing down tents, destroying booths and scattering the attendants.

With a gesture of her arm, Lhodyn sent the massive quilled beast after Edrick and the Brownman. The crowd of monsters rushed to get out of the way, knocking one another over, pulling on each other to get ahead of the fleeing mass. The witches flew up into the air. The ogre sank into the ground as if the water opened beneath its feet.

The fat mannish thing transformed himself into a beastly boar.

The prince lifted Edrick up into his arm protectively and called out, "Ærathyr! Spirit of Oaths. Champion of Ilpha's Warriors! I beg for aid. Break my bonds from this false goddess! I summon you to free these children, purge this land of evil, and smother the darkness with your light!"

The beasts descended on him.

Edrick was ripped out of his arms by deft maws, snatching him by his clothes. The beast leapt passed the crowd and out of the fray. Then as the beast made great strides around the market seeking its mistress with Edrick in its bite, two arrows came streaking out of the forest, *shnakt, shnakt*. Each one sank feather deep into the eyes of the beast's head. Edrick fell and rolled across the dirt. He had only one thought: Sunniva. He ran to find her as hell erupted around him.

24

OLD GODS

"SUNNIVA!"

All the world shattered. Like falling shards of glass, Alaric was eviscerated from head to toe has he heard his dead son yell out his dead daughter's name, with such pain and terror.

He could not believe it. The truth cut him, bled him.

"Edrick!" both women said in unison. They looked at one another then Alaric. It was written all over their faces, Elisial especially. She was ready to bolt into the crowd of monsters to reunite with their children.

"My baby," Elisial whispered, color drained from her face. All those moments of stoicism washed over her as grief pulled her down. Her strength finally gave. She leaned into Elzera.

"GO!" Elzera commanded. "We will stay hidden. Send the children this way if you can and we will keep watch for them."

He could not move.

"Save our children," Elisial pleaded. "We must bring them home, Alaric. I will create a circle of protection. Bring them all."

It was a plea, a command. Like a spell from her lips, he moved. Against his will, he moved.

As Alaric left the tree line, blaring war horns sounded out through the forest. What was left of the Folthnir stumbled and crashed through the woods, having discovered the same cobbled road Alaric took there. Only two giants survived and a handful of men including the Theign, and even Grindan.

Alaric dashed toward the market, sprinting toward the

monstrous crowd. In the middle of gathering stood Aweirgan. Directly in front of him, the great towering ogre of his children's story. Alaric didn't hesitate to pull an arrow from his quiver and pull Nithledan's string back to his cheek.

Then events shifted and changed quickly.

Nithledan's will enveloped Alaric, frenzied, like a hound begging to be let off his leash. Alaric used all his strength to master the bow so as not to begin striking down everything there as the bow wished.

Two of the witches by Aweirgan's side invoked the goddess's name. "Lhodyn!" they shouted.

To Alaric's left the goddess appeared with her entourage of creatures. Nithledan forced Alaric to fire.

Lhodyn must die! It screamed to Alaric.

The arrow raced toward the goddess. Instantly, her eyes went from the crowd to Alaric as she snatched the arrow out of the air. Five beasts charged Alaric with nothing more than a thought from the woodland deity. Nithledan raged and set loose another arrow, then four more, each hitting their mark in the eyes of each beast. Two more streaked toward the ogre.

Lighting tore through the marbled blue sky. A flash of silver drew everyone's attention, and through the din, a distinct name was heard with crisp clarity, "Ærathyr!"

It seemed as if the name itself discharged the mob of creatures, as they scrambled away from Aweirgan. The ogre vanished as two of Alaric's arrows sailed through the space it stood a moment before. The witches flew into the air, above the crowd, avoiding the circle of lightning raining down from the near cloudless sky, striking dozens of creatures dead. Lhodyn leapt high, backwards in a graceful bound into the shelter of the trees as the lightening tore up the earth. Lightning unaccompanied by damning thunder.

Lhodyn's beasts dipped and dodged their way through the mass of panicking bodies and struck Aweirgan sending him to the ground. And there too was Edrick, snatched by one of the beasts, his son dangling from its filthy maw.

Alaric forgot all else, focusing on his son. He moved again as the Folthnir came crashing into the market place. He heard the warlord shouting, invoking the name of Vylkinus, cursing the gathered beasts and goblyn people.

Another terrible battle began.

The beast that held Edrick dashed about, running the circumference of the market. Alaric fired two arrows at a full run as the beast turned toward him. Each arrow sunk into the animal's eyes, trapping the spirit of the beast so it could neither pass beyond the gates of the world, nor be one of Lhodyn's slaves.

The spirits were consumed by Nithledan only.

Released, Edrick rolled through the dirt, but was on his feet quickly running again.

"Dammit," why can't he just stay still, he thought. He realized his boy was chasing after Sunniva. Alaric took a few steps toward his son when a great thunderous boom shook the ground, causing Alaric to stumble. All the creatures were sent reeling, falling down or seeking something to hold as the earth rumbled.

The lightning storm formed a ring of dancing strikes across the earth. Mist rose from the center, billowing high above the trees. From this ring emerged a massive shape, a beast so feared and full of dread everyone and everything stopped in disbelief as a dragon of silver emerged from the obscuring cloud. It roared and extended its enormous wings, casting shadows over the entire market. Lightning continued its dance, illuminating the metallic scales, bathing it in arcing light.

"Ærathyr," Alaric whispered to himself, filled with awe at the sight. He fell to his knees.

His torc! Aweirgan called him down? He looked for him through the chaos. The beasts that had pummeled Aweirgan fled the area. The cursed man stood, mud clinging, mixed with his own blood, yet he was smiling.

"Come Lhodyn!" The smug prince taunted. "Come claim your slave now."

"I am summoned by an Unfeyn to a place of evil," the dragon intoned. It flapped its massive wings, shutting out all the sky. Thunder boomed forth with each flap, stunning everyone around, paralyzing all. Lightning danced about the earth where it sank its claws. Alaric knew in his heart, this was a true god. It exuded unfathomable power. It was imperishable.

"Speak, Unfeyn, your reason to call me here, or die with them."

The prince stood up. "I called you, yes. To free these children. To redress the evil afflicted on my sires and break my bonds, as well as those that will come after me. I called you for vengeance, to destroy Her, as She has destroyed so many."

At the mention of the goddess the dragon roared and turned its head toward Lhodyn who remained in the trees. She was furious, her beauty burned away revealing a dæmonic visage.

Lighting rained down, striking the open ground from the dragon toward Lhodyn and her entourage. As the bolts fell over her, a barrier of dark and opaque magick absorbed the electrical energy. Witches began appearing at her side, as tumbling leaves blew across the ground, spun and twirled into the forms of women. They surrounded their goddess, guarding her.

With a single claw, Ærathyr ripped open the iron cages, allowing the children escape, though they dared not move. "Lead them away then, prince of men. I release you from bondage as well. But from this moment on, I watch you. You will be judged when you pass me in death and I will measure your soul's worth."

Aweirgan coaxed the frightened children out of the cages but their way to freedom was not clear. The baying of horns approached them, though now they sounded more like the mewing of sheep in the presence of Ærathyr.

"Vylkinus!" The Folthnir shouted, hurling their spears at the dragon. The weapons struck the silver scales, tips bending and shattering, falling impotently to the earth. The two giants charged the god-spirit. In legends, giants and dragons hated one another, and here legends were flesh and walked the earth.

"More Unfeyn!" the dragon boomed. "Call not to your fallen Dominion in my presence. He will not hear you, for I have quelled his power."

The giants swung their mighty hammers, striking the dragon's stout legs, but on impact they dropped their weapons, for it was as if they struck hard iron and the blow injured their hands. With a blurring whip of the tail, the giants' torsos were severed in half. They bled out, dead.

The Folthnir stopped. They recoiled from the dragon. They were like children before a timber-lion.

"Your god is greatly despised and will be hunted down with all other Fallen. He stole my image and remade it to strike fear and inspire worship in mortals. The Nine will come again, to hunt them down, to break their bodies and send their spirits back to Ilpha. The First is here among you, and will wield the Master Sword. Vitherian, you cursed man, you think you have summoned me? I was sent here by Ilpha to speak prophecy. The Nine Immortals that perished long ago will rise again and take up the Nine Swords. They will cleanse the world for the Anointed One. He will come and remake this broken world."

The dragon lifted into the sky, its shadow falling on everyone gathered. "Lhodyn, it is not my obligation to remove you. That is for the Nine. It would be useless to drive you away, for you desire to rule wherever you find residence. I will destroy your body and allow these mortals a period of rest."

Lhodyn stood tall, amongst her followers, the witches and woodland creatures. "I have matured, spirit, we all have. We discovered how to feed and gain power. We know Ilpha's secrets now. We will attain Her stature and break our imprisonment. Even if you break me now, there are others far more stronger than I. Together, we will return, or the very least cast Her from this world. It is ours now. She gave it to us, we will keep it from Her."

Alaric heard beneath Lhodyn's voice, the chanting of witches. A great darkness arose in their midst, billowing high like the darkest of smoke. The ground trembled again, issuing from where Lhodyn stood.

Ærathyr roared, inhaled deeply, and then screamed horror! Silver blue lightning streaked from its wide maw striking the area Lhodyn stood. Alaric was blinded. He threw his hand up to shield his eyes.

"I have strong allies spirit," he heard Lhodyn say, her voice fading. "Tell me truthfully, are not the Telru mightier than the Eshenar? Come meet your better!"

The earth vibrated, then stone and soil exploded from the dark shadow, raining across the field. Out stepped a gargantuan dragon of ash gray and burnt brown, so much larger than Ærathyr. As it walked, the ground trembled. Dread fell over Alaric's heart, as he forgot about Edrick, Sunniva, Elisial; everything. He was compelled to run, to flee far and never return.

Ærathyr roared, renting the whole sky in half. The brown dragon, Alaric knew as Baeloth, Dragon of the Deep, roared in reply. In a mighty bound it crashed against the silver dragon. The two fell into the forest, like plummeting stars, swallowed by the trees, shaking the ground on impact. The entire forest was filled with their deathly battle as trees snapped and crashed nearby. The dragons roared and howled, sending shivers across Alaric's skin. His courage slowly returned as he regained his wits. It was as if his heart had been momentarily stolen from his body, leaving him with only fear and despair. It passed as soon as Baeloth withdrew.

Just as if everyone stopped to watch a passing eclipse, the chaos resumed as goblyns rushed to gather their merchant wares and flee. The children screamed out as goblyns ran by, snatching them under arm, carrying them off into the woods, away from the battling dragons. Aweirgan fought them off, but children now fled in fear, freed with no destination in mind.

Lhodyn, too, was gone, either fled or having been destroyed by the dragon breath.

The bears returned, gathering around Aweirgan in his need. He sent them away to create a safe area for the children to gather. He climbed the torn cage to gain elevation and shouted out, "Children to me, children! I will bring you home!"

Alaric ran up to him. "Go exactly in that direction!" Alaric said to the children. "My wife is there. She will lead you back home. Have you seen Edrick or Sunniva?" They did not answer at first. Then Tredan stepped forward from the crowd of gathering children, "they were taken," was all he said.

Alaric knelt down. "Where is Gaebria and Bron? Are they with you?"

Tredan did not answer at first. "They separated some of us. I think they were," his voice became near silent, and then whispered, "eaten."

"I am here," Bron said leading a large group of frightened children behind him. He held a long sword in his capable hands. Directly following him was Gaebria, trembling as if the ground still shook.

"Bron! Take these children to the clearing's edge. I need to find Edrick and Sunniva. Gather as many children as you can, but do not wait long. Leave the woods now!"

"He ran that way, Alaric," Aweirgan said. Alaric regarded the wildman. How came he to own his family's heirloom? "Go now Woodcutter, if you wish to save them. But I would advise you to care for these children instead. I can use your help gathering them and keeping them safe."

"I will, when I have found my own children," Alaric replied

starkly.

Alaric ran through the littered lanes of destroyed stalls and scattered market wares. He found children there, tied like beasts, to posts and behind fenced pens. And near them, little bodies hung from butcher hooks, like pigs back in his village. Flies swarmed over piles of discarded viscera. What horrors these children must have bore witness to.

Alaric freed any living child he could, but there were an unfortunate few still remaining in the chaos.

The goblyns soon fled, leaving the market deserted, except for the dead bodies left behind. Alaric called out, "Edrick! Sunniva!" He rushed through the lanes searching for them, under collapsed tents and refuse. Frequently he came across a hidden child and sent them toward the others, toward Aweirgan and Elisial. Then he caught the sight of witches gliding over the earth as if sliding on ice. They followed something.

Edrick appeared, darting through the broken stalls, keeping just out of their reach. He threw rocks and whatever he could find at the hags. One witch in particular watched on from high, atop the ruined stone wall where the market ended. Beyond the wall, there dwelled a devil that slayed his brothers thirty years ago.

"Edrick!" a little girl's voice screamed out. A flying witch landed next to the first on the ruined wall, Sunniva next to her side. A collar and tether was fastened around her neck, held by the witch. This witch looked particularly ancient and nasty. She projected an aura of strength Alaric could feel from the distance between them.

The witches laughed and seemed to be making sport of chasing Edrick. Even when he managed to send rocks flying into their faces, they remained unharmed and laughed at the sheer audacity of the child. In return, they sent barrels and entire carts flying back toward him, simply by pointing their finger. They seemed to be at a stalemate at the moment unable to reach Edrick, and he unable to flee.

"Matron, may we have the girl, we will see if she can draw him out."

The old woman allowed the request and lowered Sunniva by her neck down the wall. Sunniva kicked and squirmed as she was momentarily strangled. Nithledan screamed at Alaric to send arrows toward them, yet he doubted that his attack might work. He scrambled to think of something that would have both children out of harm.

Then a series of deafening roars and screeches took the witches attention from both children. "Baeloth is overpowering it." The ancient witch stated calmly.

"He will repel Ærathyr. It cannot stand the two of them," one witch said.

"And She will be stronger for its death. Gods' blood flowing into Her Vaults, She will become unquestionably strong," the ancient one replied.

"Which means you chose well, Matron." The witches turned and bowed to her, "always do you guide us well. She will serve us well in the coming years."

"This region will soon know the light and darkness of Zarya, Zorya, and Zveda. Their light guided us to this forest and we have come to know why. There is something here in Wudelic and these events have shown us that we are in the right place."

"The gods are clashing and even they don't know why," one witch said and they snickered. "No more than these foolish men."

They took Sunniva, pulling her by the leash around her neck to the rubble where Edrick hid. One witch pinched Sunniva's soft cheeks until she cried out. Another ripped out pieces from her golden locks, flesh still attached. "You hear the sweet cries of your sister, boy?" They laughed cruelly

"Go to hell!" Edrick's hidden voice called back. They laughed again, shoving Sunniva to the ground.

"Wait!" the Matron cried out. "There's a man there."

"Ha!" one witch said. She flung her cape around her form and dissolved into a swarm of gray moths, fluttering toward him in an undulating mass.

Alaric spit arrows at the witches standing over his daughter. They were struck and stumbled. Alaric ran, charging toward Sunniva as the swarm of moths pursued him.

"I am coming, Sunniva!"

Nithledan flew from his grasp, ripped from his hand by some dark force. Alaric drew his Crossroad knife and confronted the two wounded witches.

"Run, Sunniva!" Edrick called. Sunniva stood up. She didn't run, but stood crying. She recognized her father. "Papa," she cried. She held out her arms to him, wanting to be held. "Paaapaa," she moaned.

Alaric's heart broke.

He lunged at the women, stabbing at them but he seemed to misjudge their distance. Their images moved and shifted strangely, like spearing fish in a stream. He could not judge their location accurately. Nithledan rested on the ground. He thought his only chance was to get his bow.

"Edrick, get your sister and run!"

"Pa?" Edrick peeked from behind his cover and dashed toward Sunniva. He lifted her in a great hug and began to run.

Alaric lunged toward his bow but a witch appeared over it. Alaric slashed at the woman's throat, slicing a gash in her neck to his surprise. The woman stumbled back. Alaric took up Nithledan. He turned and fired at the other witch behind him who disappeared. Alaric looked back at his children running. They ran toward the gate that led into the ruins.

"No, Edrick, stop!"

He ran after them in desperation.

Then the Greyorn darted out from debris ahead of him, making its way toward Edrick and Sunniva.

The swarm of moths overtook Alaric, obscuring his view, swirling around him for a moment then flew after Edrick.

"Edrick, stop!" Alaric pleaded. They neared the gate. The Greyorn lurched forward, nabbing Edrick's calf. Edrick tripped and dropped Sunniva. She rolled into the gatehouse's shadow.

"Sunniva!" Alaric called. He wanted to tell her to run to him, to get away from the ruins, yet the moths nearly caught them. The swarm stopped and spun like a cyclone when out of the blurring gray stepped the witch.

Alaric notched an arrow.

The Greyorn dragged Edrick away, away from Sunniva, away from the ruins.

"Run, Sunniva!" Edrick yelled. "Don't let them take you!"

Sunniva gave a short scream and ran beyond the wall.

"STOP!" Alaric yelled. He shot at the Greyorn, the witch pursuing Sunniva, until all his arrows were spent.

The witch on the wall dropped to the other side.

"Sunniva, run back!" Alaric yelled, breathless. His heart sunk.

He reached Edrick, struggling against the Greyorn as the

creature dragged him farther from the gates as if he weighed no more than a rabbit. "Release him! You will not have my son!" Alaric stabbed at it.

The Greyorn jumped back and seemingly smiled. It then dashed through the gatehouse into the ruins. Edrick jumped up and took two steps toward Sunniva, but Alaric seized his arm and jerked him back.

"Father, Sunniva! I promised her, Father! I would not leave her!"

Then a scream ripped from Sunniva's lips rose up from behind the walls. The old witch appeared atop the wall again, her back toward them. She looked onto whatever took place below, then collapsed into a pile of dead leaves and blew away.

Alaric remained still, clutching Edrick as he hit and kicked against his father, yelling out for his sister.

She was dead. Alaric knew it.

Alaric picked up his son in both his arms, pinning him tight and ran before the dæmon came for them.

"NO! Papa go back! Why are you leaving her?"

"She's dead, Edrick," he said evenly.

He ran across the empty market. Ran from the ruins.

"You killed her! I could have saved her! You killed her!"

Alaric had enough. It was all too much. Edrick had to know how much he suffered, how much he bled to preserve what little he could. To hold on to just any of his family, to keep going when he was alone and in pain. He threw Edrick to the ground. His son was too stunned to move. "Look around Edrick! Children torn apart, sliced open and feasted on like animals. You led them here. Not me! They believed in your stories, your faerie tales, your belief that there is a place evil can't touch. Well, it doesn't exist. What did these children ever do that they deserved this? Nothing! They died innocent, just like Sunniva and there was nothing I could do against these monsters. I have been fighting all my life. I am sorry it has not been enough for you, boy. I am sorry it was not enough for Sunniva…"

"Liar! You let them burn us! Hang us and do what they wished. Halig could not stand your cowardice and left. Only I had the courage to do what was right to protect the children, like Sunniva. But I was tricked, because none of them would listen to me."

"They would not listen to me, Edrick." Alaric fell to his knees, his rage evaporated. He was too exhausted to yell anymore. "They gave up. They tricked me too, or I would have stopped this before it started. There are no right choices sometimes, Edrick. Just like now, I could only choose you or Sunniva. In my heart, I wanted you to live more than Sunniva. I know that sounds evil, but maybe I need you more than I need her. I could not lose you again."

They were both quiet. Edrick stood, arms crossed, unforgiving.

"You are right," Alaric whispered, "I did allow this to happen."

"You made the wrong choice! You should have saved her!"

"You heard the screams, what could I do?"

"You should have ran to her! You should have never have left us!"

Alaric threw his bow at Edrick's feet. "Take it. Tell your mother I love her so much. I am sorry I failed you, Edrick. I failed all of you." He thought of his brothers who died for him. The truth was he chose Edrick out of fear. Inside, he remained a child, afraid. He could not make the sacrifice his brothers made. He always feared he could not.

"You were supposed to take care of us! You were supposed to be better than them! You were something! Our Warden, our protector....You should never have left us...look what happened!"

"I will go get her. I will bring her home. Now go to your mother. Don't wait for me."

Edrick kicked Nithledan away. "I don't want it. You should be passing it to Halig. He still deserves it." Edrick turned his back on his father and walked away.

Alaric watched, heartbroken, as Edrick left his view. He stood. He did not retrieve Nithledan. He left it for his sons, should they return for it. Instead, he turned and walked to the ruins.

"Sunniva, forgive me my daughter. I am coming."

He entered the ruins. All was silent and still. Perched above the stone archway a murder of crows gathered, watching the entrance. A single bird caw three times at Alaric's approach. Their heads turned, the bodies leaned down, scrutinizing his movement.

A crumbling manor crowned a small hill in the center, hidden behind browned ivy leaves that clung all the way to the roof. Ancient gardens surrounded the structure, overran by nettles and wild brambles. Strange plants unwanted by the forest preyed on the unprotected flowers and shrubs that once adorned the estate. And somewhere within, the devil dwelled. It might have been the one that sowed the weeds to keep it company, alone and secluded in these woods. He suspected it could not pass the walls.

Alaric found a path where Sunniva had pushed the tall weeds aside, crossing over small retaining walls, passing broken statues and dried fountains. It led closer and closer to the manor. Closer to her death.

Sunniva took the path least overgrown, and that is where Alaric followed. He did not venture far before her path ended abruptly. Alaric found a bloody pool of blood and flesh, torn to repulsive pieces. Scattered about over a few yards, he could not tell whose body he looked upon, the witch, Sunniva's or both.

It mattered little. The dæmon had done its dark business again, took his family away, again.

He expected to cry, but he did not.

He stood, helpless.

"I am Alaric, Hero of Athelyn! Son of Accenen the All Hunter, son of Aldred the Hidden! I have come to stand by my brothers. I have come to be with my daughter!" he shouted with all his strength, toward the manor ruins. His knees gave out beneath him.

He gave up. No more pain. No more struggle. He awaited release.

Blue and violet lights began rising from the surrounding plants. Dark faeries swirled around Alaric. Then a rustling of something moving, far off drifted from the estate house, rushing toward him.

The rustling became louder, drawing nearer to him. He felt it watching him, excited and filled with dread. A deep shadow rolled toward him, sucking in the surrounding light like a hole in space. Alaric remained still, though he trembled. He could taste it, the death in the air as he breathed heavily. Then he noticed it, a solitary tree, some two hundred yards away, stunted, misshaped, yet green with life.

"A mathelian," he uttered. It was a sign. A reminder that all things perish and are forgotten. Great things and small things. He wondered which would be remembered of him.

The dæmon was nearly on him. The air cooled, like the winter he killed the timber-lion. A wretched cold that stole the souls of little girls.

"Get out you stupid, Woodcutter!" The Greyorn growled abruptly, crawling out from beneath the weeds and brambles. The shadow swallowed them, yet a silver light radiated from the fox, pushing the darkness away, within arm's reach. "It is not your time to be a spirit. Now go! I can't hold it back forever."

Alaric faltered. "I want to be with Sunniva and Baldice. I want to see my father and mother....my brothers," he answered weakly.

"You won't. So rejoin your family in this world." The shadow swelled in size. The Greyorn was shoved backward as the dark force lunged at Alaric.

"There is more for you to do, Alaric. Protect Edrick! If you die here now, your whole family dies."

Alaric thought only of Elisial. She willed him to act, without her, there was only despair.

He looked once again to the mathelian. He wondered how long it lived here, how long it struggled to endure, alone, in hope one day someone would return to the garden, revive this place of evil and restore the beauty that once existed.

"This had not be a trick, spirit."

Alaric ran.

He felt the shadow break free and pursue him. It leapt and bounded close. Alaric sprinted with all his might, pumping his legs as fast as he could, as fast as when he fled there thirty years before. He reached the gatehouse threshold when his legs gave out. He stumbled then rolled into market grounds.

Yet nothing lurched past that archway. The crows had fled as well. There was nothing around.

With death at his back, he faced a life he no longer knew how to live.

25

THE WOODCUTTER KING

FATHER STUMBLED his way through the market debris as if he were a lost child. Edrick looked on him as a stranger, a man he did not recognize, a coward, the incompetent Woodcutter the villagers despised. This was the man Edrick now beheld. The Warden of the Woods left them a year ago and never returned.

His eyes were glass like, a man who saw nothing, as if he wandered through a fog filled land not noticing anyone until he nearly walked through them. Upon his brow, a silver light glowed with brilliance. Edrick thought his éardian returned, yet to all their amazement the light radiated from the lines of his scar, from the brand above his eyes. Everyone remained quiet as he passed. He was like a ghost emerging from the grave, distant and out of place. In his hand he carried Nithledan.

Mother wept, seeing how he appeared, alone, without Sunniva. Auntie held her, consoled her. Father walked by as if she were a stranger. He simply held Nithledan out for her to take. She did not stir, but stared at him through thick tears. Auntie received the bow instead. He continued by, walking past all the children and their fearful looks until he came upon prince Vitherian. He held that man's eyes for a moment before he staggered away. He did not look back, as if he did not care if they followed or remained behind.

Beastly howls and thunderous roars still sounded from deeper and deeper inside the forest, with diminishing frequency. The prince kept the gathered children all focused, kept them all together. The bears now surrounded them, and despite their wild ferocity, no one seemed afraid of these woodland sentinels, for the prince commanded them. They felt very safe for the first time since they entered the woods.

Grindan too, found them, barging his way out from the market, tossing tents and tables aside. He wore the scarlet dragon scale hauberk of the Folthnir Blooded with a sword in hand. The bears sniffed him suspiciously but allowed him to pass and join the rest of them. He walked up to this son, Bron, and said, "It is all over. They are dead." He spoke without passion or regret. It was a simple statement. Bron later told Edrick that his father claimed to have murdered the Theign, struck him down in the chaos and stole his sword and armor which seemed precious to the blacksmith. Bron said this with shame on his brow.

They did not dwell long there. Prince Vitherian made a sweep of the area, looking for straggling children before he urged them to leave.

"We must get you children back to your parents. Let them know this nightmare has passed." Edrick knew for the first time, nightmares don't pass. They linger always in the dark.

The Forest Spirit emerged from the woods as Prince Vitherian led them back to Athelyn. It stalked the woods, walking alongside them, as if guarding them. As if it suddenly became acutely aware of people and took a protective interest.

In the passing months, villagers spoke of seeing it at the forest edge, or upon the crest of the western foothills across the fields, or stalking south beyond the pastures. The village animals would flock to it, followed it like ducklings chasing their mother, especially the Wultherons. Those horses came to roam the fields north of the Ruined Tower, enjoying their freedom without masters.

Wherever the Forest Spirit passed, crops would flourish in its wake, beyond even the Elder's experience. The villagers started leaving fair portions of their harvest by the forest edge saying they ought to share their bounty with the faeries and elves who finally seemed to grace them as spoken in old stories. They named the Forest Spirit, the Wudelic Beast, and believed the elves sent it to them to protect them from the witches and dæmons of the woods. Edrick knew it was another lie the villagers told themselves, to feel comfort instead of fear. And for a period, there was peace and a feeling the Wudelic was a safer place.

Still, no villager dared enter the Wudelic to confirm these attributes. After all, some risks were never worth taking.

And thanks to Auntie, word spread of the Folthnir defeat and the villagers were able to sell their surplus grain and keep all the profits without sending tribute to a king. There were no rumor of the barbarians anywhere along the Merchant Road. The Elders managed Athelyn's affairs, purging the Elder Hall of the foreign god's presence, repainting it, furnishing it, transforming the hall into a true seat of power with all their newly acquired profits. It became a proper place to conduct business for the Athelyn masters.

One day, Grindan remounted the village Writ, now in a new frame, onto the wall above the hearth. He did this without a word or look to anyone. Villagers considered the blacksmith with great suspicion now, but dared not speak a word against him, for his disposition became grimmer, his eyes smoldered like forge coals waiting for the plunge of cold iron.

Bron came to live with Edrick and his family, helping out and taking on many of Halig's responsibilities. Edrick came to like the older boy, pestering him often with questions of sword making and armoring.

"I wish to make a sword of my own. Would you show me?"

"A bow seems more your instrument, why would you take up a sword?"

"I have always wanted a sword, a shield and armor like in the stories of Emperor Abellious and his warriors."

Bron gave him a thoughtful look. "Those things are the tools of men, Edrick, not for playing. And they are used to deal death, like the Folthnir. That I will never forget."

"Or to defend against them."

Bron gave a half smile. "Perhaps. But death just the same."

"Sometimes it is better to die than live," Edrick paused. His father walked by, his heavy wood-ax across his shoulder. His father said little to anyone in the days after they all returned from Wudelic. "Live like that. Like all of them. I'm not going to grow up to be like one of them. Afraid. Hopeful only when hope is assured by someone or something stronger than yourself."

Edrick touched King Sithric's ring still hanging secretly around his neck, beneath his shirt. The prince never returned to Athelyn after delivering the children safely home. He wandered west away from them, turning his back on his kingdom, his people, on the responsibilities that a prince should be willing to shoulder.

"I suppose hope is always a choice," Bron said after consideration.

Edrick looked at his friend fiercely. "It is not. Hope is a gift from your parents, something they must blanket you in as a babe. It is a birthright, once taken from you, you have to fight to take it back. Athelyn never had hope."

"It seems different now, with the Wudelic Beast."

Edrick remembered his first encounter with the Forest Spirit. It seemed like hope and strength incarnate, but blissfully sheltered and unaware of the darkness in its own home. Prince Vitherian said Lhodyn desired to slay it, and steal its strength. "That's what I mean. Athelyn has no hope. That beast won't always be around. Then what?"

Bron left the question unanswered, shrugging his shoulders.

Edrick picked up his ax, Bron did the same and followed him toward the woods. He no longer tended to mother's faerie traps, keeping his promise to Sunniva. Mother understood and gave those responsibilities to Eadwyn. Edrick harvested wood now. His mind and heart remained in the Wudelic. Remained with Sunniva and the others that failed to return.

Father was tearing down the small barn that Mathilda once slept in. No one asked him why or if he would rebuild it. Mother seemed content that he was doing something other than lying in bed. Edrick locked eyes with his father. He saw dozens of things in his father's eyes in that moment.

Hope was not one of them.

Edrick hated him, for the words he put into his heart three years ago, that day the timber-lion showed Edrick the face of death, the rumor of fear, the first unkindness Edrick felt in his heart.

His father once removed all those unpleasant things with his actions, with his words, with the way he lived his life. He once taught his family how they can live with silent strength and self-possessed nobility derived from doing the right thing, always.

This was no longer the man before Edrick. It was as if his father's heart, a place Edrick regarded as much a sanctuary as their home, where mother whispered stories of wondrous things by candle light, was suddenly removed into darkness by a cold northern wind.

Blackness fell on them and nothing could be seen. They awaited to hear father's reassuring words in the dark, to tell them that everything would be fine, to remain where they were at and he would fetch a lantern. That he would cast out the darkness.

But he said not a word.

The memory of what his father spoke to him three years ago stung Edrick's heart, for he longed to hear those words repeated to him now, and always.

But he said not a word.

***

"Father, what if another timber-lion comes for us?" Edrick asked, warming himself by the hearth.

"There might be another, this winter or another. They fight only to survive, as we do."

"What will you do with the skin?"

"I will give it to Grindan. They are about the same in size and disposition."

"I want to see the girl's grave."

"Her name is Wylla. She is from Wuldenor. We can go."

"Wylla of Wuldenor," Edrick repeated. "I will never forget her. She should not have died. It was not right."

"Death seldom feels right. Often life can feel this way too. But those moments pass soon enough. Life is always a struggle, Edrick, but things worth keeping are worth a fight, always, with all your strength, like the timber-lion. Like us. Then death will have no hold over you."

"Life always feels right. Death scares me. Not my death, but just Death itself. That something can remove what you spent your life loving, protecting. I hate it."

Alaric put his arm around Edrick. "Do not worry your young heart about such matters. Your mother and I, we protect and provide. Let us worry about those matters and you just keep loving life."

"I hate being a Woodcutter. I want to be a king! A warrior and keep people safe, always."

"Remember this, Edrick, a man must be like a bow staff. When relaxed, he stands straight. When at work, supple with stored strength. When provoked, strike like a shooting star."

"That is the life of a Woodcutter," Father said, looking deep into Edrick's eyes. "That is the spirit of a king."

ACKNOWLEDGEMENTS

There are so many that have supported me, I wanted you all to know it was always, always, needed and appreciated…

First, I would like to thank Prof. Tolkien for being the visionary of epic myth and lore. Also, Gygax and Arneson for inspiring a kid who hated books and all things reading.

My family, for always being there to support my passion. Dad, Mom, and Jeremy. Thanks so much for enthusiastically reading and re-reading and then re-re reading all the drafts. You all have always been there for me!

Chuck, for all the discussions about writing, when there was no one else at work who understood this dream.

Vicki, for being a great cheerleader and always encouraging.

Mike, for asking me every week, for four years, how the book is coming along. It's done man, it's done.

Thanks to Amber, for inspiring this writer and guiding me with your knowledge. *Au large!*

To my precious and dear children, Isabel and Azaél. This story would not exist without the gift you gave me, fatherhood.

Last, I would like to thank my wife for sheltering me when all was broken, for just about everything you do and have done. If it weren't for you, this would only be a half started tale.

ABOUT THE AUTHOR

Ærick Graham lives in the Pacific Northwest with his wife, Aleja, and two children. He loves nothing more to sip on coffee while reading a good book, especially in front of a warm fire during Oregon winters. THE WOODCUTTER KING is his first novel.

www.ingramcontent.com/pod-product-compliance
Lightning Source LLC
Chambersburg PA
CBHW030545260626
47157CB00006B/2191